The third book in the Marquess of Templeston's
Heirs trilogy

Always a Lady

When Kit Ramsey arrives in Inismorn, Ireland, to lay claim
to his inheritance, he realizes the townspeople of this tiny,
impoverished village are convinced that he is the miracle
they've been praying for. But Kit—the natural son of George
Ramsey, the fifteenth marquess of Templeston—isn't interested in being anybody's hero. All he wants is the chance to
become his own man. But inheritances come with responsibility, and Kit quickly learns that his new title of earl of Kilgannon comes with plenty of strings attached—including
the guardianship of Mariah Shaughnessy, the beautiful baker
of Inismorn . . . the beautiful baker whom he must teach how
to be a proper lady . . .

Fresh out of a convent, Mariah knows that, with Lord Ramsey's deep pockets, he is Inismorn's last hope for survival.
She accepts Kit's lessons in social graces—not because she
wants to become the perfect gentleman's wife—but because
she dreams of becoming the love of Kit Ramsey's life . . .

A Hint of Heather

"Rebecca Hagan Lee captures the allure of Scotland through the eyes of her memorable characters. Her gift for describing a time and place enables her to enchant readers."
—*Romantic Times*

"*A Hint of Heather* gets stronger and more exciting as the pages turn. The sensuality . . . is steamy, the wit and humor bring smiles, the romance has you sighing, and the ending has you cheering."
—*Under the Covers*

"A seductive Scottish historical . . . *A Hint of Heather* is going to be a big hit."
—*The Romance Reader*

"For those who love Scottish romances . . . *A Hint of Heather* is likely to please. [It] features the sort of well-defined characters that enrich the world of the romance novel. A real treat."
—*All About Romance*

"An entertaining Scottish romance . . . filled with action and intrigue."
—*Painted Rock Reviews*

Gossamer

Always a Lady

Rebecca Hagan Lee

JOVE BOOKS, NEW YORK

ALWAYS A LADY

A Jove Book / published by arrangement with
the author

PRINTING HISTORY
Jove edition / October 2002

Copyright © 2002 by Rebecca Hagan Lee
Cover design by George Long
Cover art by Leslie Peck

Visit our website at
www.penguinputnam.com

ISBN: 0-515-13347-7

A JOVE BOOK®
Jove Books are published by The Berkley Publishing Group, a division of Penguin Putnam Inc., 375 Hudson Street, New York, New York 10014. JOVE and the "J" design are trademarks belonging to Penguin Putnam Inc.

PRINTED IN THE UNITED STATES OF AMERICA

10 9 8 7 6 5 4 3 2 1

Codicil to the Last Will and Testament
of George Ramsey,
fifteenth Marquess of Templeston

My fondest wish is that I shall die a very old man beloved
of my family and surrounded by children and grandchildren,
but because one cannot always choose the time of one's
Departure from the Living, I charge my legitimate son and
heir, Andrew Ramsey, twenty-eighth earl of Ramsey, Viscount Birmingham, and Baron Selby on this the 3rd day of
August in the Year of Our Lord 1818 with the support and
responsibility for my beloved mistresses and any living children born of their bodies in the nine months immediately
following my death.

As discretion is the mark of a true gentleman, I shall not
give name to the extraordinary ladies who have provided me
with abiding care and comfort since the death of my beloved
wife, but shall charge my legitimate son and heir with the
duty of awarding to any lady who should present to him, his
legitimate heir, or representative, a gold and diamond locket
engraved with my seal, containing my likeness, stamped by
my jeweler, and matching in every way the locket enclosed
with this document, an annual sum not to exceed twenty
thousand pounds to ensure the bed and board of the lady
and any living children born of her body in the nine months
immediately following my Departure from the Living.

The ladies who present such a locket have received it as
a promise from me that they shall not suffer ill for having
offered me abiding care and comfort. Any offspring who presents such a locket shall have done so at their mother's bequest

and shall be recognized as children of the fifteenth Marquess of Templeston and shall be entitled to his or her mother's portion of my estate for themselves and their legitimate heirs in perpetuity according to my wishes as set forth in this, my Last Will and Testament.

George Ramsey,

Fifteenth Marquess of Templeston

Prologue

Continuous as the stars that shine
And twinkle on the Milky Way.

—WILLIAM WORDSWORTH, 1770–1850

INISMORN, IRELAND
Summer 1824

The stars sparkled like finely cut diamonds spread out on a background of black velvet. A solitary figure huddled against the wall of the crumbling tower of Telamor Castle. She sat with her back pressed to the rough, moss-covered stone and her neck tilted at the optimum angle for stargazing through the battered crenellations. Below the tower lay the beach. She could hear the low roar of the ocean and the occasional sounds of voices, but she ignored them. Her attention was focused on the heavens as she studied the array of constellations visible in the northern sky, reciting the fanciful names her mother had taught her. She stared at the brightest star, then breathed a reverent sigh as one of its lesser companions streaked across the heavens.

"I wish that when I grow up I can marry a rich, handsome prince and live in this fine castle," Mariah Shaughnessy prayed with all the fire and fervor a six-year-old could muster. "That I can have dogs and cats to love and ponies to ride, and that I can sit in the tower and eat cakes and biscuits and look up at the stars every night until I die." She took a deep breath before continuing her litany of wishes. Falling stars were rare. They didn't happen every night, and Mariah had learned to make the most of their magical powers. "And . . ."

"You'll get fat if you eat cake every night."

Mariah sat up straight and stared into the night. A boy stood holding a lantern on the top step of the spiral stairs that led to the tower.

"No, I won't." Mariah stuck out her bottom lip and dared the intruder to contradict her.

"Of course you will." He left the top step and walked over to her. He leaned his back against the stone wall and slowly slid down it until he was sitting beside her. He trimmed the wick on the lantern so the light wouldn't interfere with her stargazing, but he kept the light burning low. "And if you get fat eating cake, no prince will marry you."

Tears welled up in her eyes. "But I like cake," she replied.

He gave her a disgusted look. "Everyone likes cake."

She sighed again. "It was good."

"That's why they call it cake," he told her. "If it tasted awful, they would have called it turnips."

"Will I get fat if I just *wish* for cake and biscuits every night?"

He shook his head. "No," he promised. "Wishing for cake won't make you fat. Only eating it."

She shrugged her shoulders. "Can you get fat from eating it once?"

"No."

"Then I guess I'll never get fat."

"You've only had cake one time?" He was genuinely surprised. "In your whole life?"

"I think I had it when I was little," she said. "But only once since I came here."

"How come?" he asked.

"The sisters don't believe in spoiling us."

"How many sisters have you?" he asked.

She giggled. "I don't have any sisters."

"But you said—"

"The sisters in Christ. The ones at St. Agnes's Sacred Heart Convent where I live."

The boy shuddered, recalling the rambling old stone building a mile or so down the cart path from the castle. He didn't have to be Catholic to know what convents were. But he had always thought they were reserved for nuns and older ladies. He had never heard of little girls living in them. "You live in a convent?"

"Yes," she answered. "Down the hill and beyond the wall. I come here after evening vespers so I can look at the stars. See there!" She pointed through the hole in the ancient stonework. "That's Draco, the Dragon."

He looked to the heavens as she pointed out the cluster of stars that formed the shape of a dragon. "You come all the way up here just to look at the stars? Why don't you just look out your window?"

She shook her head. "My room doesn't have windows."

"Oh." He was thoughtful once again, almost unable to comprehend the idea of a room with no windows to look out. "How do you sneak out?"

"It has a door, silly," she replied in a tone tinged with superiority. "It just doesn't have windows." She lifted her chin a notch. "I'm very good, you know. And very quiet. When you live in a convent, no one pays much attention to you as long as you're quiet. I sneak out after everyone else goes to bed."

He eyed the little girl with new respect. To sneak out of a convent and come all this way without a lantern was an enormous feat of bravery.

"Where are your mother and father?"

"I don't remember my da," she told him. "He died when I was little, and now my mummy's gone to heaven, too. She's a star. See that one up there? The shiniest one?"

He nodded.

"I think that one must be my mummy 'cause she used to wear lots of sparkly things." Tears welled up in her eyes once again, and her voice quavered with emotion.

He reached over and covered her small hand with his own, stunned by the magnitude of her loss. Life without his mother and father was unthinkable. "I'm sorry."

She sniffled, then wiped her nose with the back of her other hand.

"Here, take this." He reached into his pocket and pulled out a clean handkerchief.

"Thank you," she answered politely as she accepted his handkerchief and began to blow her nose. When she finished, she crumpled the handkerchief in her hand and held it out to him.

He shook his head and shifted uncomfortably against the wall. "You keep it."

Mariah gifted him with a brilliant smile and hugged the handkerchief close. "If you're sure it's all right."

"It's just a handkerchief," he told her. "You may need it again, and I have plenty more at home."

"Thank you ever so much."

"Did you ever come here with your mother?"

She nodded once again. "All the time. My mummy said that if you wish on the stars, God listens to your wishes, and if you wish on a shooting star, God makes the wish come true."

"Do you always wish to marry a handsome prince and live in this castle eating cake and biscuits every day?"

"No," she answered truthfully. "Most of the time I wish for my mummy to come back down from heaven and get me. But sometimes I wish that I'll grow up and marry a handsome prince and live in this castle and have cake to eat whenever I want it." Her voice broke and she quickly covered her mouth with her hand.

"A handsome prince might marry you," he said, offering what comfort he could. "And give you cake to eat. As long as you don't eat it every day."

She shrugged her shoulders. "It doesn't matter. My wishes won't come true now anyway."

"Why not?"

"Because I told you about them."

"So?"

"So, wishes don't come true if you say them out loud or share them with anybody else. They only come true if you keep them all to yourself."

"Kit!" A loud masculine shout echoed through the ruins from the ground below. "Your mother's finished. Time to go."

The boy shot Mariah an apologetic glance. "Papa's calling me," he told her. "I have to leave now. My mama and papa were collecting sea creatures from the beach for my mama to draw. Papa only let me come to the ruins because the groundskeeper swore they were safe. We're going home tomorrow, and I wanted to see the old tower."

"Oh."

She sounded so bereft that his heart went out to her. "Will an earl do?" he asked.

"Huh?"

"I'm not a prince," he explained. "I'm an earl. But my mama says I'm handsome, and one day when I'm all grown up, I'll come back and marry you if you like."

"Truly?" she breathed. "You would come back and marry me someday?"

"Why not?" he answered with a nonchalant shrug of his shoulders. "I have to marry someone. It might as well be you."

"Will we live here at Telamor?"

He shook his head. "I don't own Telamor. But we have a very nice house in England. It's not a castle, but it's as big as one, and the attic stairs go all the way to the roof. My papa and I go up there and look over the estate, and I'll bet it's a grand place for looking at the stars."

"All right, then." She smiled up at him. "I wanted to live at Telamor, but your house sounds very nice and I like you."

"Then it's settled." He pulled her close and planted a clumsy kiss on her lips the way he'd seen his papa do to his mama.

"Kit!" His father's voice sounded louder, closer. "Where are you?"

"Coming, Papa," Kit called down the stairs, before turning back to look at the girl. "I have to go."

"You won't tell anyone about this?" She glanced around. "About my being here? If the nuns find out . . ."

"I won't tell." He turned and started down the stairs.

"Wait!" The urgency of her whisper halted him in his tracks. "You forgot your lantern." She picked it up and held it out to him.

"You keep it," he said. "And use it to find your way to and from the tower in the dark." He smiled at her once again. "Now that we're betrothed, you have to take care of yourself."

"You won't forget?"

"I won't forget," he promised.

He waved once more, and then he was gone.

Chapter 1

A mother's pride, a father's joy.

—Sir Walter Scott, 1771–1821

Swanslea Park
Northamptonshire, England 1838

"*Talk him out of it, Drew. He's too young.*"

Andrew Ramsey, the sixteenth marquess of Templeston, stared down at his wife. Tears shimmered in her beautiful eyes, and her voice held a barely discernible note of panic. Kathryn was on the verge of bursting into tears at any moment, and Drew felt powerless to prevent it.

He had been her husband for nineteen years, and he ached to see the pain in her eyes. There were streaks of silver in Kathryn's hair now, but she was every bit as beautiful to him today as she had been the first time he'd seen her. And he loved her more than he had ever thought possible, but he loved Kit, too, and Drew would not—could not—forbid Kit to pursue his destiny. He didn't have that right. Not even for Kathryn.

"He's old enough to know his own mind, Kathryn. Older than you were when I first proposed to you."

She shivered. After nineteen years of marriage, Drew still had the power to take her breath away and to reduce her to a mindless, quivering mass of anticipation without so much as a touch. All he had to do was speak her name in that special way of his. *Kathryn*. Only Drew called her

Kathryn. The rest of the world knew her as Wren. "That's beside the point," she insisted.

Drew shook his head. "It is the point, my love. Kit is two and twenty years old. He's not a child anymore. He's a grown man and he wants and needs a place of his own."

"He can have a place of his own here," she said. "He needn't go all the way to Ireland for that."

Drew laughed. "Are you suggesting I give him Swanslea Park just to keep him at home?"

"I would if I thought it would do any good," Kathryn admitted.

Swanslea Park, the countryseat of the current marquess, had been handed down to Drew from his father, the fifteenth marquess of Templeston, who had gained possession of it through his marriage to Drew's mother. The Ramsey family estate lay farther north, too far from London for convenience, so the fifteenth marquess and his wife had chosen to live and raise their son at Swanslea Park. Drew and Kathryn had continued the tradition.

"Well, forget it." Drew laughed again. "Because I'm not ready to turn over the keys to Swanslea just yet." The title of marquess of Templeston and the keys to Swanslea went hand in hand, and although Drew had already given Kit his lesser titles of earl of Ramsey, Viscount Birmingham, and Baron Selby, he intended to keep Swanslea Park awhile longer.

"But, Drew, Swanslea Park is Kit's home, too. And it's large enough to accommodate his desire for privacy." Kathryn looked at her husband. "He can have the whole east wing to himself and come and go as he pleases. It has a private entrance."

"Yes, it does," Drew agreed. "And a household staff who will note his private comings and goings as they go about their daily activities, and those remarks will reach the ears of Newberry, who will report them to me even though I've no desire to infringe upon Kit's privacy." Drew reached out and enfolded his wife into his arms, hugging her close. "I'm the marquess, Kathryn. Everyone answers to me"—he pressed a tender kiss against her brow—"except you. And nothing goes on at Swanslea Park without my knowing about it. Kit wants to go to Ireland, my love. He delayed his departure for a year because he didn't want to upset you, but he's eager to take possession of his inheritance, and I see no reason to detain him any longer. Kit needs to be his own man and the lord of his own domain in a place where the staff answers to him instead of to me."

Kathryn pulled out of his arms, looked up, and sighed. "I wish Martin had never delivered that letter to Kit."

Drew frowned at her. "You don't mean that."

"Yes, I do," she replied. "If Martin hadn't delivered that letter, we all would have remained in blissful ignorance, and Kit wouldn't be moving to Ireland."

The letter their solicitor, Martin Bell, had delivered to Kit on his twenty-first birthday was one of two letters that George Ramsey, the fifteenth marquess of Templeston, had asked Martin to hold in trust until Kit reached the age of majority. Martin had kept the packet of letters for over twenty years, until finally delivering it on Kit's birthday.

When Kit opened the first letter, he'd been surprised to learn that the Irish earl of Kilgannon had died after naming Christopher George "Kit" Ramsey his heir. Father Francis O'Meara, the late earl's representative, and Martin Bell were the only men alive who knew the two letters existed, and both men were bound to secrecy.

Kit had inherited the title, the ownership of Telamor Castle, and the surrounding estate in the village of Inismorn in County Clare.

And neither Drew nor Kathryn had known anything about it.

What was even more surprising, to Drew's way of thinking, was that Kit had accepted the news and his inheritance without asking whence it came. If he was curious as to how he had come to inherit an Irish castle and a title to go along with it, he had never asked his parents about it. In fact, Kit never asked them why he had no grandparents or aunts or uncles or cousins. Nor had it ever seemed to bother him. Kit simply accepted the fact that his family was Drew and Kathryn, his sisters, Iris and Kate, his former governess, Ally, their solicitor, Martin, and the staff of family retainers at Swanslea Park and the town house in London. And he accepted the notion that it was quite right and proper that Telamor Castle should belong to him.

Kit had been quite enthralled with the castle as a child—the summer the family had visited Ireland. Kathryn had been working to document the flora and fauna of Ireland when Martin suggested they reside at Telamor Castle while she completed her work. They hadn't realized it was Kit's inheritance. But Martin had known.

In retrospect, it all made sense. Martin had known that the estate and the castle belonged to Kit, and it was only right that his family make use of it. But at the time Martin's ability to secure a castle and an estate for their use just when they needed it had seemed quite miraculous. A miracle none of them had thought to question. Kit, least of all.

When Martin presented the packet to Kit a year ago, the deed to the castle and the estate had been enclosed with the letter from the earl of Kilgannon's priest. The other letter had been addressed to Kit from George Ramsey. Drew knew there was another letter because Martin had told him it existed, but its contents remained a mystery. If Kit had read it, he had kept the information to himself and had never mentioned the letter to either of his parents.

Kathryn was the only mother Kit had ever known, and he had grown up accepting Drew as his father, but Kit was actually Drew's half brother and was eight and twenty years Drew's junior.

Drew hadn't known he had a brother until after the death of their father when he journeyed to Swanslea Park and discovered Kathryn and Kit living quietly on the family estate. Drew had fallen in love with and married Kath-

ryn and adopted Kit as his son. Kathryn had become the
marchioness, and Drew had privately petitioned the Crown
to amend the original letters patent that created the marquess of Templeston and the earl of Ramsey to allow Kit
to become his legal heir.

Drew sighed. He didn't like the idea of Kit leaving
Swanslea Park any more than Kathryn did, but it was time
for Kit to be on his own. He'd seemed without purpose
since completing his university studies. And he'd spent
entirely too much time gaming and wenching with his
friends in London. The Irish property would give him
something to occupy his time. And Kit needed a challenge.

"Swanslea Park came to us through *my* mother," Drew
reminded his wife. "You are Kit's mother. There is no
question about that. You are the woman who has loved
and nursed him and molded him into the wonderful man
he is today. Nothing will ever change the way Kit feels
about you, but he carries the blood of the woman who
gave birth to him in his veins. And this inheritance has
come to him through her." Drew paused, carefully con-
sidering his words. "He wasn't granted the opportunity to
know and love that woman, but he has a chance to know
the place she called home. Shouldn't we, the parents who
love him the most in the world, give him the wings he
needs to fly out of the cozy nest we've built for him? Isn't
it our duty to encourage him to use them?"

Kathryn choked back a sob and nodded her head in
agreement. "But I don't want him to go. A lot of things
can happen in a year. And I'll miss him so much."

"I know you will," Drew soothed. "So will I. But, my
darling, we always knew this day would come some day."

"It's come too soon, Drew," she whispered. "I thought
I would be ready, but it's come much too soon."

"He won't be gone forever, and we'll still have each
other and the girls. The time will pass faster than you
think." He planted a kiss against Kathryn's forehead. "Remember that Iris has her London season coming up."

Drew took the opportunity to remind his wife that they had two other children—daughters, seventeen-year-old Iris, and twelve-year-old Kate—to think about. "And you have paintings to complete for the new exhibit at the museum. There will be lots of things to keep you busy. Before you know it, Kit will be back to visit."

"What if he doesn't come back?" she asked, giving voice to her deepest fear. "We know your father had a mistress in Ireland. She must have had family other than her father and friends. . . ."

"Martin said she was an only child. . . ."

"*Martin,*" Kathryn growled his name. "I'm so angry at Martin. He's known the truth all these years, and he didn't see fit to tell us."

"He *couldn't* tell us," Drew said. "He was bound by his oath. You know that. He didn't tell me about you, either," he reminded her. "But he did what he could. He sent us to Ireland, and when I asked if he knew how Father could write me and speak of Kit's illegitimacy in one breath and ask that I make him my heir when he knew adopted children could not inherit, Martin told me to seek an amendment to the letters patent and provided the Crown with the documentation proving Kit's claim."

"And now we know that his other mother was connected with the earl of Kilgannon. What happens if he decides to remain in Ireland?"

"Ah, my darling . . ." Drew leaned down to kiss Kathryn soundly and to chase away her tears. "If Kit decides to stay in Ireland, then we'll visit as often as he will allow."

"Allow?" Kathryn wrinkled her brow and narrowed her gaze at the suggestion that Kit might not welcome them with open arms every time she felt the need to pay him a visit. "Why wouldn't he allow his parents to visit?"

Drew wanted to bite his tongue, but it was too late. Kathryn had latched on to his promise to visit with all the tenacity of a terrier on a rat. He had expected that. But he hadn't expected her to balk at the idea that Kit might not appreciate long visits at regularly scheduled intervals. "What's the point of setting up housekeeping and becoming lord of your own castle if you have to answer to your mother and father while doing it?" He reached out and tilted Kathryn's chin up with the tip of his index finger so that she was forced to meet his gaze. "We have to let him go, Kathryn. We must let him become the man he's meant to become. *We* need it and, more important, *Kit* needs it."

"*You* didn't move to Ireland to escape your father's realm of influence in order to become the man you were meant to become," she said.

"That's true." Drew's voice took on a harder tone. "But only because *I* went to war. I joined Wellington and went to Belgium to fight Napoleon." He caressed Kathryn's cheek. "My character was refined by heartbreak, betrayal, and war. I became the man I am today because I survived the horrors of war. I would rather Kit build and refine his character in the relative safety of the Irish countryside as lord of Telamor Castle. Wouldn't you?"

"Of course I would!"

"Then do your best to pretend to be excited and happy for him." Drew grinned. "For heaven's sake, Kathryn, the boy inherited a castle!"

"A crumbling castle," she retorted.

"The tower may be crumbling, but the new castle, as you well know, is quite modern and comfortable. But Kit wouldn't care if it weren't. He wouldn't care if the new castle were as tumbledown as the old one," Drew said. "Because it's his. Just as Lancelot was his pony. Remember?"

Wren smiled in spite of herself. Lancelot was Kit's first pony. A shaggy old Shetland with a white blaze on his face and black coat mottled with flecks of white and gray. Lancelot had been destined for the rendering pot when Drew bought him. Kit had loved him instantly, and the two had become constant companions. Even now, Kit refused to part with Lancelot. The ancient pony still held the place of honor among the thoroughbreds in Drew's magnificent stables. "What should I do?"

"Help him pack, wish him Godspeed, and don't let him see you cry."

Kathryn lifted herself up on tiptoe and pressed her lips against Drew's. "How did you get to be so wise?"

He smiled. "My father was an excellent judge of character. I inherited the gift from him."

"Is that so?" she teased.

"Yes, indeed," he answered. "You see, I once fell in love with a woman thought to be the most notorious mistress in Northamptonshire."

"Was she?"

Drew laughed. "Of course she was. That's why I married her."

Chapter 2

Good fellowship and friendship are lasting, rational, and manly pleasures.

—WILLIAM WYCHERLEY, 1640–1716

"*I'm going to Ireland!*" Kit Ramsey shouted above the racket of the ball rattling around the pockets of the roulette wheel and the noise of the crowd of gamblers placing bets. Kit and his two closest friends, the Honorable Dalton Mirrant and Ashford, the eighth marquess of Everleigh, were engaged in a night of gambling and drinking in their favorite gaming hell.

Dalton Mirrant placed his bet with the keeper, then looked over at Kit and shouted back, "You're going where?"

"Ireland!" Kit repeated.

"What?"

"He said he's going to Ireland!" Ash told him.

"That's what I thought he said." Dalton shook his head, then took a step back, and shuddered in mock horror. "No one goes to Ireland these days except for the hunting, and you don't hunt."

"Maybe not. But I'm going to Ireland," Kit replied with a grin.

"Whatever for?"

"To find my destiny."

"Your destiny?" Dalton laughed. "You think you're going to find your destiny in Ireland?"

"If not my destiny, at least my inheritance."

"I've heard it reported that there are instances of blight in some of the potato crops there. Such talk makes the farmers and the tenants uneasy. And there's always political unrest. The Irish hate the English, and the Catholics hate the Protestants. The poor hate the wealthy. Need I remind you that you're a rich, Protestant, English lord and that you might do better to either forget about your Irish inheritance for a while or leave it alone entirely?" Ash asked.

"Unless, of course, it's a large inheritance," Dalton added. "And if that's the case, you'd do best to send someone to claim it for you." Dalton's wry tone of voice made it sound as if, political unrest or no political unrest, he was the man for the job.

"Someone like you," Kit suggested, tongue-in-cheek.

"Why not?" Dalton asked. "I can go to Ireland, pick up whatever it is that you've inherited, and bring it back to London."

"My inheritance is a castle." Kit couldn't help but grin as Dalton's blasé expression turned to one of surprise. "And a title."

"Another one?" Dalton grumbled, fighting to keep the pang of envy out of his voice. "You already have a title. You're the earl of Ramsey."

"Yes, but my title, unlike Ash's, is only borrowed. My father granted me the use of his lesser title of earl of Ramsey as a courtesy," Kit explained. "But the title of the earl of Kilgannon is mine."

"From whom did you inherit an Irish title?" Ash's voice held a note of undisguised curiosity.

"The late earl of Kilgannon," Kit replied. "It appears that I'm his closest male relation."

Ash was thoughtful. "You? Not your father?"

Kit shook his head. "I'm the late earl's relation through my mother's side of the family."

"I see." Ash studied Kit's expression and decided not to shake the family tree any further. Everyone knew that Kit had been adopted by the sixteenth marquess of Tem-

pleston when Lord Templeston married Kit's mother and
that Lord Templeston had moved heaven and earth to
have Kit recognized as his legal heir. But the debate still
raged in some society drawing rooms as to whether Kit's
natural father had been the fifteenth marquess of Templeston or the sixteenth. Kit knew, of course, that George,
the fifteenth marquess, had been his father. He didn't discuss it except to say that his much older half brother had
adopted him and raised him as his son, and he paid no
heed to the gossip that still swirled about him. None of
the gossip about his paternal family tree seemed to bother
him. The current Lord and Lady Templeston were the
only parents Kit had ever known, and he loved them un-
conditionally, but he was completely reticent when anyone, even his closest friends, began probing his maternal
family tree. "So you've added an Irish title to your name."

"Yes," Kit acknowledged. "An Irish title and property
complete with a castle and a tidy fortune."

Dalton smiled. "I like the sound of that."

"You would," Ash retorted.

"And why not?" Dalton shot back. "Not all of us come
equipped with titles and tidy fortunes. Some of us have
the misfortune to be born younger sons, to have the breeding and the education necessary to move in aristocratic
circles, but to lack the fortune needed to sustain the life
we were born to."

"So it would seem," Kit agreed, good-naturedly ignoring Dalton's sarcasm. "But you are fortunate to have generous friends with titles and tidy fortunes." Kit shoved a
rack of gaming counters in Dalton's direction.

"And heaven forbid that they should ever call in all of
my chits, for I would never be able to repay my debts to
my generous friends." Dalton elbowed Ash in the ribs to
get his attention and to remind him that it was customary
for the marquess of Everleigh to match the earl of Ramsey's monetary gift to their always-pressed-for-cash
friend. "Much less my tailor and gentleman's gentleman.
Still"—Dalton placed his bet and reached for his snifter

of his brandy—"I admit that I would willingly give my eyeteeth for a title—even an Irish one." He frowned at Kit. "We've been mates since we were in short trousers. Why haven't we heard about this before?"

"Because I only learned of it when I reached my majority."

"You reached your majority last year," Ash reminded him.

"And you neglected to mention your Irish inheritance to your two closest friends," Dalton said. "You've never done that before."

He was absolutely correct. Dalton Mirrant and Ashford Everleigh were Kit's closest friends. They'd met during their first term at Eton, and even though the three of them were as different in temperament as three boys could be, they'd instantly forged bonds of friendship that outlasted their years at Eton and had gone on to flourish during their university days and beyond. The three of them remained boon companions to this day.

Dalton Mirrant was the youngest son of the fourth Viscount Mirrant. Although his father was only a viscount, the family was an old and distinguished one with a country home a day's ride from Swanslea Park and a Mayfair town house two blocks from the marquess of Templeston's London house. The Mirrant family fortune wasn't quite as large as the Templestons, nor the holdings quite as diverse, but Dalton, like Kit, had grown up in the lap of luxury. But Dalton was not the Mirrant heir. Dalton had two older brothers, the eldest of whom would inherit the title and the fortune. His second brother, a graduate of Sandhurst, was expected to make his fortune in Her Majesty's army. And although he had never exhibited a calling for it, Dalton, following family tradition, was destined for the clergy.

Kit's other schoolmate, Ashford Everleigh, had inherited the marquessate of Everleigh two years ago. The family surname of the earls of Lawrence and the marquesses of Everleigh was Ashford. Ash had been christened Edward Ashford, but because he held his father's lesser title of earl of Lawrence until he had inherited the marquessate, he'd been known at school as Ashford Lawrence and always called Ash to distinguish him from the other Edwards and Lawrences.

Most of his schoolmates would be surprised to learn that Ash had another name. His father had even taken to calling him Ash. Only his mother called him Edward. And Ash often joked that he was the only peer in England, other than the sovereign, who had given up his Christian name for the sake of a title.

"Why Ireland?"

"Because the earl who died and left me the title was Irish."

"Of course he was," Dalton said. "But you can be the Irish earl of Kilgannon and the English earl of Ramsey in London. Why go there?"

"Because it's mine," Kit told him. "And I want to see it."

"So, Kit, why did you wait an entire year to tell us?" Ash looked Kit in the eye.

Kit held up his hand, waiting until the keeper spun the roulette wheel to a halt and announced the winning number.

Dalton gave a little whoop of triumph and collected his winnings. Kit shook his head in wonder and motioned for his friends to follow him from the noisy gaming room to the relative peace and quiet of one of the private salons. Kit paid the attendant who stood guard at the door, then motioned his friends inside the room.

Ash glanced around the opulent room, complete with silk-covered divan and modesty screen and commented wryly, "This is a first for me."

"You've frequented private salons on numerous occasions," Dalton corrected.

"I escorted women on those occasions," Ash said. "This is the first time I've ever been escorted by rogues like you."

Kit laughed. "Your reputation can stand it." He closed the door behind them, then crossed over to the drinks table. He offered drinks to his friends, waiting until they'd settled comfortably in their chairs before he helped himself to a brandy. He took a sip of his brandy. "I asked you in here because I owe you an explanation and an apology. We have been friends since we were in short trousers, and I've never kept secrets from either of you. Until this one." He glanced at Dalton. "But there is a reason I didn't tell you, and while I want to explain, I didn't want to shout it over the noise of the roulette wheel."

"You're the one who chose to announce his journey to Ireland in the middle of a gaming hell," Dalton replied.

Ash shot Dalton a warning look. "Give the man a chance to explain."

"All right." Dalton folded his arms across his chest. "Explain."

Kit relaxed, exhaling the breath he hadn't realized he'd been holding. Dalton had never been as forgiving as Ash. He took everything to heart, whereas Ash always tried to see both sides of every situation. "I didn't tell you about my Irish inheritance because I gave my father my word that I wouldn't say another word about it until my mother had time to become accustomed to the idea."

Dalton frowned. "I don't understand."

Kit took a deep breath and slowly expelled it.

"Is there a problem with the title?" Dalton asked. "Or the castle? Is there a reason you would choose not to claim it?"

"Other than the fact that it's in Ireland?" Kit shook his head. "Not that I am aware of."

"Then what?" Dalton demanded.

"The idea of my leaving England for Ireland has upset my mother. And you know how my father feels about upsetting my mother."

"So, your mother prefers England to Ireland." Dalton shrugged his shoulders. "I can't say as I blame her. But that's no reason to make a fuss about your deciding to go."

"She's afraid I won't come back."

"That's ridiculous," Dalton scoffed. "Of course you'll come back. England is your home. And no one in his right mind would choose a castle in Ireland over Swanslea Park. Especially the marquess of Templeston's heir."

Kit kept his own counsel.

Ash got to his feet and walked across the salon. He placed a hand on Kit's shoulder. "Your mother is afraid that if you go to Ireland, everything will change. She isn't trying to hold you back," he said. "But she's a mother, and mothers generally want to hold on to their children as long as possible."

Kit smiled. His father had said almost the same thing. "I know."

"How does your father feel about it?" Ash asked.

"He sees it as an opportunity for me to become my own man."

"But he doesn't relish being caught between your opportunity and your mother's objection to it." Ash immediately grasped the situation.

"No, he doesn't," Kit said.

"And you don't want to hurt your mother."

"No." Kit gave Ash a grateful glance. "I gave her a year to get accustomed to the idea. But property needs attention, and it's time I laid claim to mine."

"Is Lady Templeston still opposed to the idea?" Ash asked.

Kit hesitated before answering. "She still doesn't like the idea of my going, but she's no longer voicing opposition."

Dalton grinned. "Then she's gotten used to the idea."

"I hope so," Kit replied. "Because I don't relish the idea of waiting another year any more than I enjoyed keeping secrets from my best friends."

"You gave your word to your father." Dalton uncrossed his arms and smiled at Kit. "And you were honor bound to keep it. We understand that. We're your mates. As long as it doesn't happen again, we won't hold your keeping secrets from us against you."

Kit nodded. "I can't promise that it won't happen again," he said, "because a gentleman's word is his bond. But I promise to be as forthcoming with my two closest friends as possible whenever possible."

"Fair enough," Dalton pronounced.

"Agreed." Ash responded. "And since Kit"—he glanced at Dalton—"invited us to accompany him in the search for his destiny, I only have one question to ask."

"And that is . . ." Kit prompted.

"When do we embark on this adventure?"

"I had planned to leave tomorrow."

Dalton laughed. "Then, we might as well make the most of tonight."

Chapter 3

The Angels were all singing out of tune,
And hoarse with having little else to do,
Excepting to wind up the sun and moon
Or curb a runaway young star or two.

—GEORGE GORDON NOEL BYRON, LORD BYRON,

1788–1824

INISMORN, IRELAND
One week later

"**W**e've a problem," the Mother Superior announced.

Father Francis O'Meara sighed. As the spiritual leader of its parish, St. Agnes's Sacred Heart Church, and the convent three-quarters of a mile away from the church rectory fell well within his providence. "Mariah?"

The abbess matched the priest's sigh with a long-suffering one of her own.

"Is she still sneaking out at night?"

"You knew about it?"

He nodded. "I hear her confession. Do you know where she goes?"

"She won't say," the Reverend Mother admitted. "And punishment seems to have no effect. I try to impress upon her the dangers of a young woman wandering around alone at night, but Mariah refuses to give up her secretive escapades. She simply accepts whatever punishment I mete out to her and continues to sneak out at night." She looked at the priest. "I'm afraid she may be meeting a young man."

Father Francis was thoughtful. "Have you seen a young man or heard Mariah speak to any of the sisters or any of the other children about one?"

"No. But what else could it be? Why else would she sneak out at night?"

The priest shrugged. It was possible that Mariah had succumbed to the lure of sin and lust and fallen from grace, but he didn't believe it. "She's been sneaking out of the orphanage since she was a child," he reminded the Reverend Mother.

"That's true," the Reverend Mother agreed, "but she's a young woman now. It's time for her to put aside her headstrong and childish ways."

"She's a young woman with a good head on her shoulders. Aside from sneaking away from the convent at night, Mariah's most vexing sins have always been her determined nature and a healthy measure of pride."

"That may be true, Father, but I don't know what to do with her anymore." The Reverend Mother made the sign of the cross. "She refuses to tell me where she goes, and her defiance is a bad influence on the other girls."

Father Francis frowned. He had watched Mariah Shaughnessy grow up and was quite fond of her, despite her penchant for sneaking out of the convent. Or perhaps because of it. He and the Reverend Mother had chosen the religious life, but the orphans who had grown up at St. Agnes's had not. And a cloistered environment was no substitute for life within a family. Although he worried about her and often deplored that particular facet of her personality, Father Francis secretly admired Mariah's individuality and her strength of character.

"I know you're fond of her, Father. I'm fond of her, too, but her birthday is fast approaching. She'll soon be one and twenty. She cannot remain at St. Agnes's after that age without becoming one of us."

"Have you approached Mariah with that intent?" Father Francis asked.

"Of course," the abbess replied. "We approach all our young charges to determine if they have the calling. But Mariah insists that she doesn't want to become a novitiate and join the order, so I accepted a proposal of marriage on her behalf."

"You did what?"

"I accepted a proposal of marriage from a local gentleman on her behalf."

"What man?" Father Francis was instantly on guard. "When?"

"Some months ago Squire Bellamy approached me and asked if I would accept his suit of Mariah Shaughnessy with a purpose toward marriage."

"Squire Bellamy offered for her?" Father Francis was stunned by the news that the middle-aged squire had asked the Reverend Mother for Mariah's hand in marriage. "What's wrong with the young men of Inismorn? Haven't you had any young suitors asking for Mariah's hand?"

The Reverend Mother gave the priest a wry look. "Many of them. Single and married. Convent-reared girls are in great demand in a village the size of Inismorn. I must confess to being taken aback by the married men who approached me and offered to make a place for Mariah in their households, but I don't suppose you can look the way Mariah looks and not have young men asking for her hand or anything else she might wish to share with them, but the young men of Inismorn are common men. There isn't a gentleman in the lot."

"But Squire Bellamy?" Father Francis frowned once again. "He's a nice enough fellow and appears to be quite well-to-do, but as a husband for Mariah . . . Well, I'm not certain I can fathom that. How could you welcome his suit?"

"How could I have Mariah's best interest at heart and not welcome the squire's suit?" the Reverend Mother responded. "Mariah's mother charged us with the responsibility of ensuring that her daughter would be the wife of a gentleman, and Squire Bellamy is the only gentleman in Inismorn who has come to call." The abbess of St. Agnes's Sacred Heart Convent sounded more than a little apologetic. "He has been diligently seeking to press his suit, and he appears to have a genuine desire to marry Mariah."

Father Francis sucked in a breath. "Of course he wants to marry Mariah. What man wouldn't? She's as lovely as she can be, and she's the finest baker St. Agnes's has ever produced, but we promised her mother we would see that Mariah had a London season." He met the Reverend Mother's withering gaze.

"Squire Bellamy would be much better for her than a London season."

"That may be true in your eyes," the priest reminded the Reverend Mother, "but not necessarily true in Lady Siobhan's or Mariah's eyes. I'm told that most young ladies dream of a London season and the opportunity to choose a husband from among the cream of society, rather than settle for one of someone else's choosing. I'm sure Mariah is no different. Besides, it was Lady Siobhan's dying request."

The abbess shuddered. "Lady Siobhan met her husband during her London season, and I would not wish her fate on anyone. Certainly not her only child."

"We made a promise," Father Francis repeated. "I gave Mariah into your care because you assured me that we could fulfill that promise and provide the child with a proper education and the opportunity to take her rightful place in society."

"I was mistaken," the Reverend Mother admitted. "At the time I thought we could fulfill that promise, but I was wrong."

Father Francis shook his head. "Simply admitting you were wrong is not enough, Reverend Mother. You must find a way to rectify the error."

"We've provided Mariah with a superior education and the skills necessary to make her way in the world."

"You taught her to read and write and speak Latin and French," he said, "as well as how to cook and clean and sew."

The Reverend Mother nodded. "We have educated Mariah to the best of our ability."

"Exactly," Father Francis agreed. "You have taught Mariah how to succeed in our world—at St. Agnes's or in Inismorn. But what about *her* world?" He fixed his gaze on the nun.

The splotches of angry red color staining the Reverend Mother's face stood in stark contrast to the snowy white wimple framing it. "Father, you cannot expect us to teach Mariah how to be a society lady."

"That is precisely what I expected," Father Francis replied. "I promised Mariah's mother I would fulfill her dying request. I did not promise her that I would allow her daughter to be betrothed to Squire Bellamy because he happens to be the only unmarried gentleman in the county."

"He is, at least, a gentleman," the Reverend Mother defended.

"That he is," the priest agreed. "A gentleman who happens to be twice Mariah's age. I'm not questioning his veracity or doubting that he's a good man, but he'll not be taking Mariah to London for the season. He'll not be wanting the competition he knows he's sure to find there."

"*We* can't take her." The Reverend Mother gasped as if Father Francis had blasphemed. "You're a priest and I'm a nun," she reminded him, her voice shaking with frustration and anger. "We were wrong to make that promise to Mariah's mother. If we had been born into gentle families, we might have succeeded, but you and I were born to poor, hardworking Irish farmers. We can play the fiddle and dance a jig, but we know nothing about London society or its seasons or how to go about providing one." She shot the priest an unforgiving look. "The truth is that Mariah became our responsibility because we made promises to ease the passing of a dying mother—promises we knew we could not keep."

"Don't be so certain," Father Francis said. "The good Lord always provides."

"That he does," the Reverend Mother answered in an echo of Father Francis's earlier words. "He provided Squire Bellamy."

"He provided better than that."

"What? A London season?"

"A way out of this predicament." Father Francis wiped his brow with the back of his forearm, then ran his index finger around the neck of his collar loosening it a bit. "I hope. Because, you see, Reverend Mother, we no longer share sole responsibility for Mariah's education or for her future well-being. Neither you nor I have the authority to betroth Mariah to anyone."

"I don't understand . . ." the Reverend Mother began.

Father Francis held up his hand. "We've done our utmost to act in Mariah's best interest these last few years, but Mariah isn't a ward of the church. She never was."

"What?"

"She's the earl of Kilgannon's ward," the priest answered. "Just as her mother was before her. He is Mariah's legal guardian."

"The earl of Kilgannon is dead," the Reverend Mother reminded him.

"The one you knew is dead," Father Francis said. "But his heir, the new earl of Kilgannon, has recently reached the age of majority and is on his way to Inismorn to claim his inheritance."

The Reverend Mother was clearly surprised. "You are certain of this?"

"Quite certain," Father Francis replied. "I sent a copy of the old earl's will and a note informing the family of his passing to the young earl's father, who placed it in trust with his solicitor until the young earl reached his majority. The solicitor informed me that he had turned the letters over to the young earl on the occasion of his twenty-first birthday. I've been waiting over a year for word from Lord Kilgannon, and I received a letter from him in last week's post."

"What are you going to do about Mariah?"

Father Francis grinned. "I'm going to keep my promise to Mariah's mother by making certain that the young earl is made aware of that promise and of his duty to see that it's fulfilled."

"Does he know? Has he been told that he has a ward?"

The priest hedged. "Not that I am aware of."

"When do you intend to tell him? And what do we do with Mariah until the promise is fulfilled?"

"I don't know," Father Francis admitted, "but I'll think of something."

"Think of something soon. I live in fear that she's allowed herself to be seduced by sweet talk and moonlight." She turned to the priest. "I don't know what will happen to her or to us if she turns out to be with child. . . ." The Reverend Mother allowed her words to trail off. Father Francis understood the consequences as well as she did. Not only would Mariah and her child's future be at stake, but also the future of St. Agnes's and all of the nuns who lived there. If the bishop learned of a scandal, he could have St. Agnes's closed and all the nuns removed to other orders. He could also have Father Francis removed to another church in another parish. It was one of the ironies of religious life that fallen women could seek food, shelter, and sanctuary within the confines of a convent wall, but it was quite common for the nuns, novices, and orphans living within those walls to be expelled for that same failing. The Reverend Mother didn't agree with the practice, but she accepted that it was her job to uphold St. Agnes's standards. During St. Agnes's long history, there had been occasions when nuns and novices had fallen from grace, but those mistakes had taken place long before the present Reverend Mother's tenure. If Mariah were to give birth to an illegitimate child, that child might be permitted to live at St. Agnes's, but Mariah would have no place at the convent. And unless he turned out to be the father, there would be no alliance with Squire Bellamy or any way for the Reverend Mother or Father Francis to fulfill the promise they made to Mariah's mother. Another suitor would have to be found. And neither Mariah, nor her guardian, nor Father Francis, nor the Reverend Mother would have the luxury of first choice.

"She can't marry anyone before she reaches the age of one and twenty without losing her inheritance," Father Francis said. "And she can't marry after she reaches the age of one and twenty without her guardian's permission."

"She can as long as her guardian remains unaware that Mariah is his ward."

"Reverend Mother! I am ashamed of you."

"Well, we can't send her to live in a gentleman's household without a chaperone—unless he has a wife." The Reverend Mother sounded hopeful.

"He doesn't."

She sighed, her disappointment palpable. "Then Mariah must remain at the convent until her guardian decides what to do with her. Unless she decides to marry the squire."

Father Francis shook his head. "It doesn't matter if Mariah decides to accept the squire or not. Now that her guardian has come of age, he has the say in who she marries. The young earl will have to accept Squire Bellamy's suit."

"But, Father, he doesn't even know he has a ward."

"We know," the priest reproached. "That's enough."

"But I gave my word to the squire."

"Then we'll just have to explain the situation to the young earl and hope he agrees with your choice."

"Is that likely?" she asked.

Father Francis shrugged. "Without having met the young earl, it's hard to say."

The Reverend Mother straightened herself to her full height, accentuating her already rigid posture. "Well, there's nothing more to be done about it except to accept the fact that I've more long nights ahead of me, praying for Mariah, worrying about Mariah, wondering where she goes when she sneaks out of the convent at night and who she goes to meet."

"Not necessarily," Father Francis reminded her.

The nun looked up at him.

"I thought we might send Mariah over to the castle with a few dozen or so of those luscious strawberry tarts she makes. You know the ones I'm so fond of. The ones she bakes when I come to supper . . ."

The Reverend Mother was skeptical. "By herself? Suppose he mistakes her for the cook instead of his ward? What then? Do we wait until he's settled in and the household is running smoothly, then go to Lord Kilgannon and explain that his ward is baking his pastries?"

"I wasn't suggesting that she go alone," Father Francis corrected. "Only that she be there to welcome him when he arrives."

She frowned at the priest. "I don't know much about the nobility, but in my experience, an excess of pride goes part and parcel with inherited titles. I don't imagine the new earl of Kilgannon would find the prospect of his ward slaving over a hot oven amusing."

Father Francis's eyes twinkled with merriment. "I don't know about that," he teased. "I've heard it said that the way to a man's heart is through his stomach. Mariah may not be able to dance or to tell a duke from a baron, but she can cook and that might prove useful."

"What gentleman is going to care if she can cook as long as he gains access to her fortune?"

"You've a point there," Father Francis admitted. "There is a question, not only of what to do with Mariah, but what to do with her fortune."

"If she joins the order, her fortune will go to the Holy Church in Rome," the Mother Superior said. "We take a vow of poverty."

The priest shook his head. "Her money is held in trust.

She cannot claim it until she's married, and she cannot marry until she reaches the age of one and twenty. If she marries before the age of one and twenty, the bulk of her fortune reverts to the Crown. She'll have a small stipend to live on, but . . ." He shuddered. "Into the queen's coffers it goes. If she chooses not to marry, her guardian retains control over her fortune until such time as he sees fit to turn it over to her, and if she joins a holy order, similar terms apply. Hers isn't a great fortune, and Mariah could live modestly on the stipend. Of course, if she marries, her husband will gain control of her money and over her, but that's better than losing it entirely. That's why Lady Siobhan insisted her daughter be educated as a lady and to have at least one London season before the age of one and twenty. It was her way of making certain that Mariah would have the opportunity to make an advantageous marriage." Father Francis paused, then turned to look at the Mother Superior. "Allowing the earl of Kilgannon to assume responsibility for Mariah may be the answer to your prayers. As long as we find someone willing to accompany her to the castle."

"*You* are going to accompany her," the Reverend Mother said. "I wouldn't trust anyone else."

"That goes without saying, of course," Father Francis replied. "But I meant someone to accompany her permanently. Someone willing to reside at Telamor Castle with her. I don't like the idea of sending Mariah into the household of a man of whom we know nothing." Father Francis stared at the abbess. "Yet you advocate marrying her off to a man of whom we know nothing."

"Squire Bellamy has lived here for as long as I've been abbess."

"And we know almost nothing about him. He professes to be Catholic, yet he attends church rarely and has made no attempt to become a part of Inismorn society." He paused long enough to give the Reverend Mother time to digest his words. "When it comes down to it, we know a great deal more about the new earl. He is the natural son of the fifteenth marquess of Templeston and the adopted son of the sixteenth marquess. And I've heard that the marquess of Templeston is a true gentleman."

The Reverend Mother gasped. "The marquess of Templeston is English."

"And so is his son," Father Francis said. "Lord Christopher George Ramsey is the earl of Ramsey and the earl of Kilgannon."

The abbess shuddered. While her contact with the outside world was limited to Inismorn and its surroundings, her awareness of the behavior of many of the English lords who invaded the countryside during hunting season was extensive. She was Irish and English lords tended to ride roughshod over everything Irish with little or no regard for the destruction left in their wake. The abbess had seen hunters and hounds ride through potato fields and barnyards, through the village of Inismorn, and onto the post road, forcing farm carts and carriages out of the way as they leaped the stone wall surrounding St. Agnes's in order to reach the downs behind it—all in pursuit of a fox with no consideration for the welfare of the villagers or the laborers in the fields, or the sisters working within St. Agnes's walls. They were, after all, only Irish. And papists. Held in contempt by superior English noblemen. "Let's hope that the old adage 'Like father, like son' holds true," the abbess whispered. "I may have erred in accepting a proposal on Mariah's behalf, but I did so in the earnest desire to see her safely wed to a gentleman. An Irish gentleman. And I've yet to meet an English equivalent. The young earl will have to meet my approval."

"Agreed," the priest answered. "Do you have a suitable chaperone in mind?"

"Sister Mary Beatrix is quite fond of Mariah, and because she is of an advanced age, I think she would be willing to retire from the hardship of life in the convent into a softer life at Telamor Castle."

"And if the old adage 'Like mother, like daughter' holds true, the young earl should have no trouble teaching

Mariah how to become a lady, for her mother, Lady Siobhan, was every inch a lady."

It was the Reverend Mother's turn to frown. "I just wish the girl wasn't so tempting."

"If the young earl of Kilgannon is a gentleman, he'll certainly be able to resist temptation."

"And if he isn't?"

"There will be all the more reason for Mariah to become a lady and for the young earl to stay."

"Father Francis!"

The priest shrugged. "So, we are both guilty of matchmaking on Mariah's behalf. You for the squire and me for young Kilgannon. But I'm also thinking about the good of my parish. Inismorn is in dire need of a savior. I haven't seen Squire Bellamy rushing to the rescue, and Inismorn has waited far longer for a noble savior than anyone ever expected. I propose we be as forthcoming about her future as possible and leave the choice up to Mariah."

"Do you think a girl as sheltered and as inexperienced as Mariah can know what's best for her?"

The priest laughed. "Mariah knows her own heart. She'll make the right decision."

"What if she doesn't?"

"Then she will learn from the experience. It *is* her future. Don't you think it's time we allow her to have a say in it?"

Chapter 4

I like the dreams of the future better than the history of the past.

—Thomas Jefferson, 1743–1826

"*Mariah?*"

Mariah Shaughnessy dropped the rake she was using to weed the kitchen herb garden. She stretched her back, brushed the dirt from her skirt, and looked up to find Sister Mary Zechariah standing over her.

"The Reverend Mother wants to see you in her study right away."

Mariah picked up her garden rake and placed it in the chore basket beside the metal trowel, then pushed herself to her feet. "She knows?"

The novitiate nodded. "Everyone knows." She gave Mariah an encouraging smile. "One of the other sisters saw you climbing back over the north wall before matins. Of course, she felt duty bound to report your absence to the Reverend Mother."

That, of course, would be Sister Mary Damascus. Although she relished her role as the convent dragoon, Sister Mary Damascus had been forced to give up her attempts to follow Mariah. Sister Mary Damascus was too stout to climb over St. Agnes's stone walls or to make the two-mile trek up the hilly path to the ruins of the ancient tower.

"If the Reverend Mother and the sister were the only two people who knew about my absence, how did everyone else find out?" Mariah asked.

"The Reverend Mother was at her morning prayers and could not be disturbed at the time the sister saw you." Sister Mary Zechariah's cheeks reddened, and she gave Mariah an embarrassed look. "But she was bursting to tell someone, so she told Sister Mary Stephen who told Sister Mary Lazarus who told—"

"Everyone else," Mariah finished for her. Sister Mary Lazarus was an inveterate gossip who couldn't keep a secret if her life depended upon it.

Sister Mary Zechariah nodded. "Reverend Mother was the last to know."

Mariah grimaced. The Reverend Mother wouldn't be happy about that. It was one thing for Mariah to sneak out of the convent on a regular basis when she and the Reverend Mother were the only residents of St. Agnes's who were aware of her evening excursions. It was quite another for everyone in the convent to know.

"Has she decided on my punishment?"

"Not yet," Sister Mary Zechariah answered. "But I wouldn't fret too much about it if I were you. You're already assigned to weeding the garden and scrubbing the floors. What more could the Reverend Mother do to punish you?"

A great deal more, Mariah thought. The Reverend Mother could restrict her to her cell and take away her kitchen privileges. And she would, if Mariah didn't tell her where she went at night.

Mariah swiped the perspiration from her forehead with the back of her hand, then glanced down at the dusty hem of her skirt. "Should I change my dress?"

Sister Mary Zechariah nodded. "You should. Your dress is stained and there's a smear of dirt on your face. But you don't have time to change. The Reverend Mother said she didn't want to be kept waiting."

Mariah made one last attempt to wipe the dirt from her face and clothes, then followed Sister Mary Zechariah into the convent.

Mariah was tucking stray wisps of hair that had come

loose from the twisted bun at the nape of her neck back
into place when Sister Mary Zechariah came to an abrupt
halt outside the door to the Reverend Mother's office.

"Good luck!" Sister Mary Zechariah whispered, reaching out to give Mariah's hand a squeeze of encouragement. "I'll light a candle for you. And pray for leniency."

"Thank you." Mariah closed her eyes and murmured
her own prayer for leniency, then lifted her hand and
knocked on the door.

The abbess looked up at the sound of Mariah's knock.
"Enter."

"You wanted to see me, Reverend Mother?"

"Yes, Mariah, I did. We have important matters to discuss. Come in and close the door behind you."

Mariah frowned. When the Reverend Mother asked her
to close the door behind her, it usually boded ill for the
interview. Her reprimand always began with a lashing
across both palms with a thick wooden ruler and ended
with a list of chores. Her last punishment for sneaking out
of the convent had been fifty lashes with the ruler and the
chores of scrubbing and polishing the refectory floor and
the windows and weeding the kitchen garden for a month
in addition to her normal job as St. Agnes's head baker.
Mariah wondered how many more days, weeks, or months
and how many additional floors the abbess intended to
add to her punishment.

The Reverend Mother took a deep breath and slowly
expelled it. "I understand you left the safety of St. Agnes's
again last night."

Mariah bowed her head and lowered her gaze, studying
the dusty toes of her boots as she did her best to appear
contrite. "Yes, Reverend Mother."

"Would you care to explain why?" The question was
familiar. It was part of the ritual that took place every
time the Reverend Mother summoned her into the office.

"No, Reverend Mother."

"Very well." The abbess straightened her spine.

Mariah did the same; preparing herself for the penance

she knew would follow. She closed her eyes as the Reverend Mother stood up and came around the desk, then slowly opened them. Taking a deep breath, Mariah held out her hands. She opened her fists and presented her palms, awaiting the sting of the ruler.

"Not this time," the Reverend Mother spoke softly. "You've become a young woman, Mariah. I won't be striping your palms any longer."

Mariah winced. She had been a young woman last month, and the Reverend Mother had given her fifty smacks across the palms. What had happened between last month and this one to make her change her mind? And what would she do instead? Mariah almost wished for stinging palms.

"Put your hands down, child."

Mariah did as she was told.

"Such a face you make at the news that I'm not going to cane you," the abbess said. "I thought you'd be happy to hear that."

Mariah met the abbess's gaze. "I would be happy to hear it, Reverend Mother, if I knew what you intend to do instead."

The abbess couldn't help but smile. One of Mariah's most endearing qualities had always been her childlike honesty. It was also one of her most frustrating qualities. If she could not tell the truth, she would not say anything at all. And her stubborn insistence on remaining silent is what most often caused her trouble. "Better the devil you know than the devil you don't."

Mariah lowered her gaze once again.

"Well, perhaps you're right." The Reverend Mother appeared to be in a philosophical mood. "I don't suppose any of us are comfortable with a change in routine or ritual. And these meetings have become a ritual of sorts. But everything changes, Mariah. And so has this. I won't be punishing you for leaving the convent grounds or for any of your other transgressions because I'm not going to be acting as your guardian any longer."

The surprise of that announcement made Mariah look up and take careful note of the Reverend Mother's expression. Fighting to keep the note of panic out of her voice, Mariah asked, "You're not leaving St. Agnes's, are you, Reverend Mother?"

The look of pity that crossed the abbess's face told Mariah she hadn't been as successful as she'd hoped. "No, my child, I'm not leaving St. Agnes's. You are."

"You're sending me away?"

"I have no choice but to abide by St. Agnes's charter," the abbess told her. "And that charter states that our charges must choose between the cloistered life here at St. Agnes's and the secular life elsewhere before they reach the advanced age of one and twenty, and in a few short weeks you, will . . ."

"Turn one and twenty," Mariah murmured softly.

"I've asked repeatedly if you want to remain at St. Agnes's as one of us, the way Sister Mary Benedict, Sister Mary Lazarus, and Sister Mary Zechariah chose to do, but you have said that our life is not of your choosing." She studied Mariah. "Is there a chance you've changed your mind?"

Mariah shook her head. "No, Reverend Mother."

"Very well." The Mother Superior took a moment to consider Mariah's answer, then asked the question she had to ask. "I have asked you many times, over the years, where you go when you leave the safety of St. Agnes's at night, and you have always kept your own counsel and accepted your punishment without complaint. But now I must ask, not where you go, but if you go alone or if you share your evenings with someone—a young man or a lover?"

Mariah was taken aback. "No, Reverend Mother," she answered more sharply than she had intended. "I go alone. I go to be alone. I remain alone."

The Mother Superior nodded once. "I am relieved to hear it."

"I'm sure Father Francis will be relieved to hear it as well," Mariah retorted.

The Reverend Mother smiled. "You do Father Francis an injustice, Mariah. He won't be at all surprised. He had complete faith in you. I was the doubting Thomas."

"I am sorry that after knowing me my whole life, you should find my character in doubt."

The Reverend Mother's mouth thinned into a firm, uncompromising line. "Then, perhaps, I should tell you that you'll be leaving St. Agnes's very soon."

"How soon?"

"That depends upon you, Mariah. Upon the choice you make."

"I've already chosen to leave the place that has been my home for the past sixteen years. What other choices are there, Reverend Mother?" Mariah swallowed the lump in her throat and did her best to ignore the stinging behind her eyelids. The Reverend Mother frowned upon displays of excessive emotion. While none of the orphans who had grown up there doubted that the sisters of St. Agnes's cared for them, shows of affection were rare. Mariah cherished her memories of her mother's hugs and kisses. St. Agnes's was the only home she remembered, but she would rather leave the convent than stay as a nun. She didn't want to be a nun. She had grown up in a convent. But she felt no religious calling.

As far as Mariah was concerned, there was only one reason for her to remain at St. Agnes's, and that reason had nothing to do with becoming a nun.

He knew she lived here. And as long as she remained at St. Agnes's, he knew where to find her. It didn't matter that she had waited fifteen years without a word from him. He had said he would come back and marry her someday. He had kissed her to seal the bargain, and Mariah knew, without a doubt, that he was as good as his word.

She took a deep breath. She had lost her mother when she was five years of age and her father before that. And she had survived the loss. She knew that she could survive the loss of St. Agnes's, the Reverend Mother, and the other sisters. If keeping the sisters in her life meant that she must join the order, then Mariah was willing to leave St. Agnes's behind and venture into the outside world alone. To wait for him.

"Since you've chosen not to join the order, you are to marry." The sound of the Mother Superior's voice penetrated Mariah's thoughts. "If your betrothed meets with your guardian's approval."

"Someone has asked to marry me?" Mariah's whole body seemed to light up at the thought.

And her excitement proved contagious. "Yes, indeed," the Mother Superior acknowledged. "A gentleman."

"A young and handsome gentleman?" Mariah asked.

The Mother Superior wrinkled her brow. "Not young, I'm afraid. But a fine-looking man of middle years."

"Are you certain that a young, handsome man hasn't asked for me?"

"I'm quite certain," the Reverend Mother said. "Why? Do you know such a gentleman?"

"No, Reverend Mother. I just hoped . . ."

The look in the Mother Superior's eyes softened. "Every young girl hopes for a suitor that is young and handsome, my child. But I'm afraid that life doesn't always work out that way. The gentleman who asked for your hand in marriage is a local squire. Squire Bellamy." She looked at Mariah kindly. "He's a very respectable man and quite well-to-do. Perhaps you have heard of him?"

"No, ma'am."

"Well, it may be that that is just as well. Squire Bellamy is a most satisfactory suitor. He has passed the first glow of youth, but he is not so advanced in age that he's seeking a nursemaid. Although I'm told there are advantages to both. A young man is more apt to sow wild oats and to break your heart, while an older gentleman knows what he wants. He is settled and content and once you produce an heir, an older husband is not as apt to bother you overmuch with the more carnal aspects of the marriage bed. You could do much worse than Squire Bellamy. He may not possess a title, but he is a gentleman enamored of you."

"How could he be?" Mariah asked. "He has never met me. Nor I him."

"He must have seen you. He knew you by name. I thought that . . ." She let her words trail off.

"Thought what?" Mariah asked.

"I thought that perhaps he was the reason you sneaked out of the convent several times a month."

Mariah bit her bottom lip. The reason she sneaked out of the convent several times a month was to look at the stars from her secret vantage point in the ruins of the tower. If she also hoped that her betrothed would find her there, that was her secret. She had never breathed a word of her betrothal to anyone. "I have no interest in meeting Squire Bellamy at night or at any other time of day."

"I wouldn't be so quick to refuse his offer if I were you," the Reverend Mother said. "He appears to be genuinely interested in you."

Mariah sniffed. "In me or in my fortune?"

"In you. The squire showed no interest at all in your fortune, and I made certain he was aware of the rather unusual terms of your trust. He seemed perfectly willing to marry you right away. There would be no reason to wait until your birthday."

"What are the rather unusual terms, Reverend Mother?" Mariah asked. "No one has ever explained them to me or what my day of birth has to do with them?"

The Mother Superior was taken aback for a moment. "I don't suppose anyone has ever explained the terms of your parents' will or your mother's last request. You were so young when she died and such a brokenhearted little thing, crying for her mama. I don't suppose you remember much about her."

Mariah bristled at that suggestion. "I have no memory of our life in London when my da was alive. But I remember coming to Ireland with my mother. I remember living in a big house, and I remember the way my mama looked and smelled and the sound of her voice when she told me stories as we walked along the shore and when she tucked me into bed at night." Mariah paused. She hadn't thought about it in years, but suddenly she remembered the warm, comforting smell of her mother's favorite fragrance surrounding her as her mother tucked the bed linens around her before she went to sleep each night— it was one of the things Mariah missed most. No one tucked you into bed at the convent. "I've tried to remember everything she told me. But she didn't talk about our fortune—except to say that even though my da had died unexpectedly, he had left us well provided and that if anything happened to her, Father Francis would see that I was well taken care of." Mariah looked at the Mother Superior. "I don't know how my mother died or the terms of my trust."

"Your mother died from injuries she suffered in a fall. She was found on the rocks below the ruins of the old tower at Telamor Castle. We brought her to the convent in order to make her as comfortable as possible until . . ." The Reverend Mother struggled to find the right words. "You were five and already attending day classes here at St. Agnes's. Your mother asked that you be permitted to stay. When she died, we granted that request. You remained with us. According to the terms of your trust, and your mother's last wishes, if you marry before you reach the age of one and twenty, you shall forfeit all but a very modest stipend of your inheritance."

"Why would the squire be willing to forfeit my fortune?"

"It's only money. That's what the squire said to me when I explained that St. Agnes's charter would not permit young women to remain past the age of one and twenty unless they agreed to join the order. Squire Bellamy assured me that he would be honored to make you his wife and to provide a good home for you—with or without your fortune." She reached out and placed her palm on Mariah's cheek. "That is what convinced me that he would make you a good husband. You and I have had our differences over the years. But, believe it or not, Mariah, I do want what is best for you, and I am not convinced that going to live with a guardian of whom we know nothing is best for you—even if Father Francis assures me that he will make certain that your guardian understands that part of his duty is to prepare you for a London season and to find a suitable sponsor for you."

Mariah frowned. "I don't understand."

"Neither did I until I spoke with Father Francis about you this morning. I knew that you had a trust and that your expenses were paid from that trust, but I assumed you were a ward of the church, like our other orphans, and that Father Francis was your guardian. But it turns out that, in the case of their deaths, your parents gave you into the care of the earl of Kilgannon."

"Why?"

"He was your mother's guardian when she became an orphan. But the old earl died before your mother's unfortunate accident. Father Francis acted as your guardian until the new earl of Kilgannon assumed responsibility for Telamor Castle and for you."

"My mother lived at Telamor Castle?" Mariah asked, amazed.

The Mother Superior nodded. "So did you until your mother's accident."

Mariah was stunned. Why hadn't she known about her mother's manner of death before now? Why hadn't she remembered living at Telamor Castle or heard about her guardian before now?

The Reverend Mother must have read the questions on her face because she answered them before Mariah could form the words. "Lord Kilgannon has only recently come into his inheritance, and the reason you have never heard of him is because I only learned of him when I spoke to Father Francis about you this morning."

"Oh."

"Father Francis will take you to meet Lord Kilgannon and if he meets our approval, you will leave St. Agnes's and become your guardian's responsibility."

"And if Lord Kilgannon doesn't meet with your approval?" Mariah asked.

"You will still be his ward, of course, but Father Francis and I will see that you remain here until you come of age. If your betrothal to Squire Bellamy meets with your guardian's approval, you will marry him. If your guardian disapproves of Squire Bellamy, then he will see that you go to London for the season."

"I don't want to marry Squire Bellamy or have a season in London."

"Your mother wanted it for you," the Reverend Mother said. "She made Father Francis and me promise to provide you with that opportunity. It was her dying wish, and we cannot refuse it."

"She wanted me to marry Squire Bellamy sight unseen?" Was she being too hasty? Was it possible that her mother had betrothed her to the squire before Mariah had accepted Kit's proposal? Would the first proposal nullify the second?

The Reverend Mother shook her head. "No, she wanted you to have a London season."

"Then how did I come to be betrothed to Squire Bellamy?"

"That, I'm afraid, was my doing. You see, I accepted Squire Bellamy's proposal on your behalf before I knew you had another legal guardian."

"Can't you *un*accept it?" Mariah asked.

"It isn't that simple. Other people are involved now—Father Francis, the Church, Lord Kilgannon, even Lord Kilgannon's solicitor. I can inform the squire that I accepted his proposal in error, that I did not know you had another guardian, but that doesn't change the fact that he made an offer of good faith for you or that I accepted his troth."

"Then I suppose you'll have to marry him." Mariah meant it as a joke, but the Mother Superior didn't find any humor in the flippant remark.

"Mariah!" The Reverend Mother was truly shocked by the girl's irreverent insolence. "I couldn't marry the squire even if I desired it. I'm married to the church."

"And did you accept the church's proposal, Reverend Mother, or did someone else accept it on your behalf?"

"You made your point, Mariah. There's no need for further blasphemy. I suggest you pack your things and say your good-byes. I never expected you to be so ungrateful. From this moment on, you are Lord Kilgannon's problem. I wash my hands of you. Be ready to leave for Telamor right after matins."

Mariah swallowed the lump in her throat. "Why don't I leave right after vespers? I was going there later tonight anyway."

Chapter 5

Every departure has an arrival.

—Turkish Proverb

"*Bless me, Father, for I have sinned. It's* been eight hours since my last confession."

Father Francis recognized the voice on the opposite side of the partition and bit the inside of his cheek to keep from chuckling. "What terrible sin have you committed in the eight hours since your last confession, my child?"

"I forgot to keep the fourth commandment, Father."

"Tell me what you have done, my child?"

"I was insolent to the Reverend Mother," she answered. "I didn't mean to make her angry, Father, or to seem ungrateful."

"The Reverend Mother suggested that you were ungrateful?"

"Yes, Father." Mariah nodded her head even though she knew he wouldn't see it through the partition. "I know I shouldn't have said it, but I truly never meant to blaspheme."

"The Reverend Mother believes you blasphemed?" Father Francis sucked in a breath. Blasphemy was a serious offense and he knew the Mother Superior would never level such an accusation without extreme provocation. "What did you say to the Mother Superior that offended her so?"

"I suggested that since Reverend Mother had accepted

Squire Bellamy's proposal without my knowledge, she should be the one to marry him."

"That would do it." Father Francis was seized by a paroxysm of coughing.

"Are you all right, Father?" Mariah pressed her nose against the partition separating the compartments of the confessional. "Should I fetch you a pint of stout? A cup of tea? A glass of water? Or call Mrs. Flynn?"

Struggling to regain control, Father Francis finally managed to breathe without coughing. "There's no need to alarm Mrs. Flynn. She has enough to do as housekeeper here without worrying about me. Besides, I'm quite recovered."

"Thank goodness." Mariah whispered a prayer of thanks. "Forgive me for rushing you, Father, so soon after your fit of coughing, but if you don't mind, I'd like my penance now. I'm in a bit of a hurry."

"What's the rush?"

"I have a journey to make tonight, and I'd like to get started before dark." She gently nudged the little brass lantern sitting on the floor beside her valise with the toe of her black boot. She had never been afraid of traveling in the dark and even less so since *he* had given her his lantern. Next to her mother's jewelry, which had been kept in the safe in the Mother Superior's office in the convent until the Reverend Mother had released it and sent Sister Mary Beatrix to present it to her this afternoon, and a small white linen handkerchief monogrammed with the letter K, the little brass lantern was Mariah's most precious possession.

Father Francis leaned close to the partition and whispered. "You aren't planning to sneak away from St. Agnes's again tonight, are you, my dear?"

Although the partition between the compartments in the confessional was meant to protect the privacy of the penitent, Father Francis served as confessor to nearly everyone in Inismorn and knew his parishioners by the sound of their voices. Although he would die before he would ever reveal her secrets, he decided it was time to let Mariah know he recognized her voice.

"No, Father. Not tonight. Or ever again," Mariah confessed. "It won't be necessary any longer. I'm going to live with my guardian."

"Tonight?" The priest's voice rose in alarm.

"Reverend Mother ordered me to be ready to leave after matins tomorrow, but I told her that since I was no longer a ward of the church, there was no need for me to delay my departure from church property. I decided to leave after vespers. Unfortunately, Sister Mary Beatrix wasn't ready. She refused to leave St. Agnes's until tomorrow morning."

"Your guardian isn't in residence yet, and at any rate, you cannot go to Telamor Castle by yourself."

"Why not?"

"You're a young woman. You cannot live in an unmarried gentleman's house without a chaperone. You must wait for Sister Mary Beatrix."

"Oh." Her voice quivered. "I can't go back to the convent, Father. Reverend Mother is very angry with me. She washed her hands of me because I don't want to accept the squire's offer of marriage."

"What *do* you want?" Father Francis heard the note of panic in her voice and asked the question no one else had bothered to ask.

"I want what my mother wanted for me."

"Your mother wanted you to have a season in London, and I promised her that I would see that it was arranged," Father Francis told her.

"Can it be arranged? Will my guardian agree to it?" she asked.

"Yes," Father Francis promised. "I'll make certain of it."

Mariah took a shaky breath. "Then I suppose I'll go to Telamor first thing in the morning." It wouldn't be the first time she'd spend the night waiting in the ruined tower.

Father Francis nodded. "You shall spend tonight as our guest at the rectory. Come with me. We'll go find Mrs. Flynn. You can help her prepare the guest room and perhaps lend a hand in the kitchen."

"I could bake some of those strawberry pastries you like," Mariah said. "If Mrs. Flynn doesn't mind."

Father Francis chuckled. "I was hoping you'd say that." He stood up and opened the door to the confessional. "Come, my child, let's get you settled in tonight, and I'll go to St. Agnes's and collect Sister Mary Beatrix first thing in the morning, then take you both to the castle."

She remained seated. "Father?"

He paused. "Yes, my child?"

"You forgot my penance."

The priest smiled. "My dear, you confessed your sin and expressed true remorse. That's penance enough for me. Go in God and sin no more."

❧

"Didn't I tell you it was beautiful?" Kit shouted to Dalton and Ash as they topped the rise in the road that led to the tiny village of Inismorn and gazed out over the land surrounding it.

"There's no doubt about that," Dalton agreed. "I think it's as pretty as anything I've ever seen."

"Prettier than Swanslea Park?" Kit teased his friend, knowing that Dalton thought Swanslea Park was the loveliest spot in all of England.

"I wouldn't go that far," Dalton retorted. "But I will say it's the prettiest Irish estate I've ever seen."

"Based on your vast experience . . ." Ash interjected.

"It may not be vast," Dalton admitted, "but I have been to Ireland before, and I have been a guest at other Irish country estates."

"So have I." Kit stood in the irons and surveyed his inheritance. "But this one is the one I remember most. And I had no idea that it was mine."

Everything, except the village and the convent, belonged to him. All of the land as far as the eye could see—twenty-six thousand acres of it—including the castle rising above the mist in the distance, was his. His land. His castle. His place. And by Jove, but it was beautiful!

Kit grinned. He owned a castle. Two castles. And he was eager to inspect his Irish castle and set up house-keeping on the property. To the right of the new castle stood the crumbling ruin of the tower of the original Telamor Castle. The tower, perched on the cliffs, was all that remained of an ancient Norman fortress built to defend the shoreline from marauding Vikings. The "new" castle, built during the reign of Henry VIII, had been constructed farther inland, but the tower remained to mark the spot of the original castle.

Kit had fallen in love with Telamor the summer his parents brought him here. He had been eight at the time and enthralled with the stories of chivalry and the Knights of the Round Table. He had been drawn to the ruins of the original tower the way a honeybee was drawn to blossoms. At the time neither they nor he had known it belonged to him. His mother had been working on her massive volumes of *Flora and Fauna Native to Britain* and was sketching the wildlife of Ireland. Their family solicitor had suggested Telamor Castle as a base from which to work.

It had been the most memorable summer of Kit's life. Even now, staring out over the landscape, Kit found it hard to believe that he owned it. But their family solicitor had known. Martin had been the one to deliver the letters—one from the priest of the late earl of Kilgannon telling of the earl's death and enclosing the deeds to the estate and the earl's will. The other letter was from George Ramsey, the fifteenth marquess of Templeston, and although Kit carried it with him, he had never opened and read it. He wasn't stupid. Kit knew the rumors and he had grown up in the house with his mother and Drew. He knew Drew wasn't his real father, but he liked to pretend that he was. Kit didn't remember George Ramsey, and he wasn't yet ready to read words that would bring the truth home. He wasn't a coward; he simply preferred to keep the status quo.

Kit had always known that he had been born to privilege. He had grown up at Swanslea Park and knew that one day it would be his responsibility to oversee and to protect it. It was the home of the marquess of Templeston and he was the Templeston heir. But Swanslea Park would never belong only to him. In his heart, Kit knew that Swanslea Park would never be his. It would always belong to Drew and Wren. It would always belong as much to his sisters as it did to him. Kit loved Swanslea Park with all his heart. But it held no mystery.

Growing up, he had explored every nook and cranny of Swanslea Park. Until he'd left for school, he'd never lived anywhere else. Or imagined that he might want to. As the only son of the sitting marquess of Templeston, he had held the courtesy title of earl of Ramsey for nineteen years. And although he hadn't been made aware of it until he reached his majority, he had, in fact, inherited the title and been the sitting Irish earl of Kilgannon for even longer. Telamor Castle had been waiting patiently for him to come claim it. And there was a great deal to claim and plenty of exciting new places to explore.

Kit turned his attention to the tower. There was a clear view of the beach below the tower and of the miles of ocean stretching beyond it. And although it was currently shrouded in clouds and mist, Kit knew that it was possible to look through the holes in the massive moss-covered crenellations and see the stars sparkling in the night sky like finely cut diamonds spread out on an infinite background of black velvet.

"See that tower over there!" He pointed to the ruins barely visible through the mists. "That was the tower of the original Telamor Castle. The old castle perched on the cliffs overlooking the beach. But the sea began to penetrate the rock face of the cliffs. The lower part of the old castle flooded and the upper part became unstable. The new castle was built during the Tudor reign. It's farther inland."

"What's that?" Dalton pointed to a group of slate-roofed gables and spires farther east, past the tower ruins.

"St. Agnes's Sacred Heart Convent," Kit answered.

"Well, what do you know?" Dalton grinned. "A convent." He looked from Kit to Ash and back again. "You don't suppose there are any young ladies there?"

"Most likely," Ash drawled. "That's why it's called a convent, rather than a monastery. And it's most likely that any ladies you find there will be nuns."

"I though old King Henry did away with all the convents and monasteries," Dalton objected.

"He did. In *England*. We're in Ireland, where the church in Rome still flourishes." History had never been Dalton's long suit and religious history even less so. Kit found it amazing that he expected to receive a living as a rector as soon as one became available. Even more amazing that Dalton was holding out his hopes that the rector at Swanslea Park would retire soon and that Kit's father would offer Dalton the living.

Dalton frowned. "Don't tell me that we're going to be rusticating on a luxurious estate in Ireland where the closest neighbors are nuns."

"You should be thrilled," Ash retorted. "After all, you've chosen a career in the clergy."

"Isn't there anyone else close by?" Dalton asked.

"Look around," Kit told him. "Do you see anything else besides the village and the convent?"

"You don't foxhunt, you don't allow foxhunting on your property, and you have nuns for neighbors. What the devil are we going to do for fun?"

Stargaze. From the tower ruins. The answer popped into Kit's brain, and he was amazed by the nostalgia he felt at the memory of the last time he stargazed from the tower ruins when once, long ago, one of the residents of St. Agnes's crept out of her room after vespers, climbed over the stone wall surrounding the convent grounds, and made her way up the hill along the coast to the crumbling tower of Telamor Castle in order to wish upon the stars. And how once, long ago, an eight-year-old boy had accidentally discovered her hiding place and impulsively offered to marry her. Kit smiled at the memory, then gazed off into the distance, staring at the slate-roofed gables and spires of St. Agnes's Sacred Heart Convent.

He wondered if she still lived there, then shuddered at the thought of her spending her childhood in a convent. He remembered her the way she had been the last time he'd seen her, but Kit knew the little girl was grown. Grown and probably married and living outside St. Agnes's walls with a sturdy Irish husband and a couple of dark-haired children.

"Kit? Are you in there?"

Kit snapped to attention to find Dalton snapping his fingers and waving a hand in front of his face. "What?"

"He asked what the devil we are going to do for fun," Ash explained.

Kit looked from Dalton to Ash and back again. "We'll think of something. We always do."

"How soon before we reach the new castle and begin this experiment in Irish country life?" Ashford asked.

"Another hour or so."

Ash groaned. Although he was an excellent rider, it had been quite awhile since he'd spent so many hours in the saddle.

"What's the matter?" Kit teased. "Life as a London dandy softening you?"

"That depends on how you look at it," Ash retorted. "My ability to sit a saddle for more than an hour or two appears to have suffered from city life, but my ability to carouse for days on end with little sleep and dubious company has improved."

Dalton turned to Kit with a knowing look on his face. "Life as an Irish earl has already affected you. You should know better than to exchange barbs with Ash. He's a diplomatist. He always has the last word."

"For now," Kit agreed, good-naturedly. "But I live and hope." He pressed his leg against his horse and turned him onto the path that led back down the hill to the post road and the village of Inismorn.

"It's all well and good for you to live and hope. But where the bloody hell are you going?" Dalton asked. "Because your castle is that way." He pointed in the opposite direction.

Kit grinned. "I'm going to church."

"To *church*?" Dalton turned to Ash. "And it isn't even Sunday. This place has ruined him already."

"I've an appointment to meet Father Francis."

"Who's he?" Ash asked.

"He's the priest with whom I've corresponded. The priest the late earl charged with overseeing the estate."

"What does he want to do? Turn over the keys?"

Kit shook his head. "No. The doors should be unlocked. The castle is staffed." He paused. "At least, Father Francis assured me that would be the case."

"Why don't Ash and I ride on ahead to the castle and make certain that's the case?" Dalton suggested. "You don't mind, do you?"

As a matter of fact, he did mind. He wanted to be the first person inside his castle's doors. But there was no point in objecting and being inhospitable to his best friends. "No."

"Good," Dalton announced. "Because I would just as soon skip the meeting with the good father in the church."

"Fine," Kit answered, a bit more sharply than he intended. "You two ride on ahead to the castle. I'm sure this meeting is nothing more than a chance for Father Francis to meet me and to welcome me to Ireland and to Inismorn."

Chapter 6

Welcoming him to Inismorn had been a ruse. While Father Francis had welcomed him to Inismorn and to Ireland, he had also taken the opportunity to present him with a list of duties and responsibilities that traditionally belonged to the earl of Kilgannon, up to and including the guardianship of a minor who had been left in the earl of Kilgannon's keeping.

"So you see, Lord Kilgannon, there is only so much a humble Irish priest can do. I promised Mariah's mother that . . ."

Kit's attention began to wander as he listened to the priest drone on, explaining how the guardianship had come about. How it came about no longer mattered. What mattered was that it had come about. That was enough. Kit clamped his jaw shut to keep from laughing at the irony that he, a gentleman newly matriculated from university, whose sole responsibility in life so far had been the care and feeding of his horseflesh, had become the financial and legal guardian of a child. He was only two and twenty years old. It had been only a year since he had assumed legal and financial accountability for himself. Kit wanted to shout at the quirk of fate that freed him from familial dependence by bestowing a title of his own and land and funds upon him, only to thrust him into the role of surrogate parent—of a girl.

". . . I would see that Mariah was properly educated and given all the advantages—"

"Of course, Father. Anything."

"—her station in life merited—including a London season." Father Francis shrugged his shoulders. "The Mother Superior and I made our promise to her mother in good faith, but I'm a humble priest and she is a nun. We are without the wherewithal to accomplish such a social feat. I'm afraid the responsibility for sponsoring her into society and for readying her for her entrance into it rests upon your able young shoulders. . . ."

Kit groaned. He should have known better than to speak too soon. As it was, he had just agreed to provide all the advantages a young lady was supposed to enjoy. Including the one advantage he abhorred.

If there was anything Kit hated more than the eternal rounds of teas and galas, social calls and balls that accompanied the introduction of the latest crop of young ladies into society, it was the endless preparation for it. One of the reasons he'd been so eager to escape Swanslea Park and London for Ireland had been to avoid the months of preparation surrounding his sister Iris's debut. And once Iris made her introduction into society, it would be time to begin preparing for his youngest sister Kate's debut. It was all the womenfolk in his family had talked about since he returned from university. Evening conversation had centered on the latest in Parisian fashions, the most fashionable dressmakers, and included the discussion of the suitability of a dizzying array of silks and satins.

The whole household had been set on its ear in order to prepare for Iris's debut. Everyone had a role to play in the preparations—whether they liked it or not. And Kit had been no exception. Because his father had detested the local dance master on sight, Kit had been pressed into service as a replacement. He hadn't suffered alone. His father had spent a fair amount of time in the music room himself, but the marquess had other equally important duties to attend to and Kit had become Iris's primary dance partner. In the past few months he'd spent hour after hour whirling his sister around the music room, suffering the pain of trodden toes and bruised and blistered feet so Iris could master the steps to a dozen intricate dances.

Kate's debut was still more than five years away, and Kit heartily despised the notion of participating in it at any level. He hated the fuss and the household chaos, but most of all, he hated the change. He hated the idea that Iris had become a young lady and the fact that Kate would soon follow. He wanted everything at Swanslea Park to remain the same as they had always been, and Kit realized that the reason he resisted the idea of inheriting it was that it meant that his father would no longer be the marquess of Templeston. That his father would no longer be alive.

He wasn't ready for Iris to be making her debut. He wasn't ready for her to be contemplating marriage and motherhood, and Kit resented the fact that nobody at Swanslea Park seemed to notice. Even Ally, his old governess, had gotten caught up in the excitement. And except for his role as dance partner, Kit admitted to feeling more than a bit left out. There had been a time when he and his former governess had been constant companions. Even after he went away to school and Miss Harriet Allerton had become Iris's and then, Kate's, governess, she had remained Kit's special friend and companion. They had shared the same interests: politics and mathematics and horses—especially horses. There wasn't a better female rider in all of England, nor one who could recognize prize horseflesh any better than Ally. She delighted in the study of the breeding of thoroughbreds, poring over the stable studbooks, traveling with Kit and the marquess to the Haymarket sales, and helping to select the latest additions to the marquess's stables. They had ridden together nearly every morning since Kit had begun to sit a horse, and their conversations had run the gamut—philosophy, mathematics, science, history, literature and poetry and languages. Kit had recited Greek and Latin while racing across the moors with Ally at his side.

He supposed he couldn't help feeling a bit betrayed. After all, Ally had been his boon companion for as long as he could remember. She had always been a part of his life. Nothing had ever changed that—not his closeness with his mother and father, not his friendship with Ash and Dalton—until Iris's impending coming out had turned Ally from the best horsewoman in England into a girl. Kit sighed. After weeks of partnering Iris in every dance known to modern man, Kit had decided that he would be perfectly happy to live out the rest of his life without ever dancing another step.

He had left England to escape all talk of a London season, and now some Irish priest was yammering on about providing his personal idea of Purgatory for some poor unsuspecting orphan who thought it was something she wanted, something for which to look forward.

Kit held up his hand, pushing at the air in an effort to discourage the good father from talking. "You say that the child's parents left her in the care of the earl of Kilgannon, not the *eleventh* earl, Allan John Patrick Francis Kilgannon?"

"That is correct." Father Francis heaved a sigh of relief, then lifted a sheaf of papers from the top of his desk and handed them to Kit. "There are the papers."

Kit skimmed the legal documents, making mental note of the girl's name, Mariah Shaughnessy, and the names of her deceased parents, Lady Siobhan and Mr. Declan Shaughnessy, and the fact that in the event of their deaths, they had, in fact, given their daughter into the care of the earl of Kilgannon. Whoever that might be. Kit frowned. His family's longtime solicitor, Martin Bell, would never have allowed such an omission. He would have recorded the earl's number in the legal line of succession. Numbering was the means by which the members of the nobility distinguished one earl Kilgannon from another. And in this case, it was the means by which he had become the girl's guardian. Although he hadn't known it, Kit had been the earl the year this document was written. He peered at the date. The ink was smudged and the letters hard to distinguish, but there was no mistaking the fact that by the time this document was written, he had already inherited the title which meant that . . . Kit stared at the priest. "Where is she?"

"What?" Father Francis was startled by the cold look in the young earl's eyes and his frosty tone of voice.

"Where is she? Where is my ward? I would like to get a look at her."

"I took her to Telamor Castle this morning. She's waiting for you there."

"You took a poor little orphaned *girl* out of a convent and left her alone on a stranger's doorstep?"

Lord Kilgannon's sarcasm stung, and Father Francis replied more sharply than he intended. "She isn't alone. Her chaperone, Sister Mary Beatrix, is with her."

"Her chaperone?" Kit retorted. "How is it that a *child* in desperate need of a guardian comes equipped with a chaperone? A nanny or a governess, perhaps, but a chaperone?"

"I never said she was a child," Father Francis hedged. "You assumed . . ."

"And you let me assume," Kit countered, "that my ward was still young enough to need a guardian."

"She does need a guardian," Father Francis replied.

"For how long?" Kit demanded.

"Until she marries . . ."

"Because according to this"—he waved the parchment beneath the priest's nose before tossing it back on Father Francis's desk—"the *child*, *Mariah*, should be approaching her age of majority very soon."

"Of course she is," the priest said. "That's what I've been trying to explain to you. Time is running out for Mariah. She cannot remain at the convent after the age of one and twenty unless she agrees to take the veil and join the order."

"Find her a husband," Kit suggested. "Before the next anniversary of her birth."

"Would that we could," Father Francis said. "But according to the terms of her trust, Mariah cannot marry until she reaches the age of one and twenty without forfeiting her fortune. And although the Reverend Mother recently accepted a proposal of marriage on Mariah's behalf, she did not have the authority to do so. Only you have that authority. Mariah is currently betrothed to the squire, but she cannot marry him without your permission."

"She'll have it."

"The Reverend Mother will be pleased to hear it. Mariah will not," the priest replied.

"Why not?"

"Mariah doesn't want to marry him. She wants what her mother wanted her to have."

"And that is?"

"A London season."

Kit muttered a curse beneath his breath. "Sorry, Father," he apologized immediately after catching sight of the priest's white face.

"I promised Mariah's mother . . ." Father Francis stared at the young man, focusing his gaze on the earl's eyes, attempting to appeal to his sense of justice and chivalry. "On her deathbed that I would arrange it. All she asked was one season before Mariah turned one and twenty. One season before she married, and as Mariah's guardian, you just—"

"Agreed to provide it." Kit shook his head. "I came to Ireland to escape the chaotic preparations for my sister's London season. I came to Ireland to find my destiny. Apparently, I am destined to endure the hell only a season of coming-out engagements can inflict." He turned his back on the priest, crossed the room, and retrieved his hat and gloves from the wooden chair beside the office door.

"You won't regret it, my son," Father Francis said softly.

"I already regret it." Kit reached for the doorknob. "Because if there is anything I hate, it's the fuss and bother that goes with a London season.'"

"Mariah is worth a bit of fuss and bother," the priest told him. "She deserves it."

"In your estimation, Father," Kit said. "I'm reserving mine—at least until I meet the girl."

Father Francis smiled. "If you say so."

"You took her to my house this morning," Kit said. "How did you know I would agree to fulfill her mother's last request?"

"How could you not?" Father Francis asked. "Once you learned that she is a damsel in distress."

"Chivalry is dead, Father." Kit winked. "Or haven't you heard?"

"Not for you it isn't." Father Francis shook his head. "You've a double dose of it."

"How's that?"

"There's no denying that you are your father's son."

"You know the marquess?"

"I don't know the current marquess," Father Francis said. "But I knew the former one quite well, and if there was one thing George Ramsey could never refuse, it was a damsel in distress."

Chapter 7

Accept the things to which fate binds you, and love the people with whom fates brings you together, but do so with all your heart.

—MARCUS AURELIUS, 121–180

Kit opened his mouth to give voice to the myr-iad questions he had, but Father Francis forestalled them with a wave of his hand.

Kit ignored it. "You cannot make a statement like that without divulging some of your knowledge of the subject. Without answering my questions."

"I do not know the answers to your questions. For me, the past is past and there is no reason for you to contend with its legacy. Not here. Not now."

"Then when? Where?"

"When the time is right." Father Francis shrugged his shoulders. "Life is a circle, my son. The longer I live the more certain I am of it. Claim your future and you will reclaim your past." He smiled at Kit. "Now, go."

"But, Father . . ."

"Your future and your past awaits you at Telamor."

The priest refused to answer any more questions. He hustled Kit out the door of the rectory. Before he quite knew what had happened, Kit mounted his horse and headed toward the castle.

Still reeling from Father Francis's revelations, Kit suddenly found himself in the courtyard of the castle. The door opened promptly at Kit's arrival. He dismounted and

handed the reins over to the boy waiting on the front
steps.

"Welcome to Telamor, my lord." The butler, who iden-
tified himself as Ford, nodded toward the stable boy, who
had appeared to take the reins of Kit's horse. "Sean will
see that your horse is well taken care of. I've assembled
the staff for your arrival. They're waiting to be introduced."

"That will be fine. And then I'd like to speak to my
ward, and then her chaperone in private. In my study. If
I have a private study."

The butler bit back a smile. "You do, indeed. There are
several, in fact. Follow me, sir."

"Thank you, Ford." Kit stepped over the threshold, into
a massive vestibule.

A screw staircase dominated the entryway, curving
around a huge gilt-and-crystal chandelier suspended from
the frescoed ceiling where plump cherubs and cherubim
peeked from behind fluffy white clouds floating across a
sky of blue.

The effect was breathtaking. The painted heavens surrounded him, covering the vestibule walls, reaching from
ceiling to the dark green marble floor. Ascending the staircase was like ascending the stairs of heaven and the sym-
bolism didn't end there. In the center of the marble floor
formed by rays of sunlight streaming through the stained-
glass window above the heavy oak doors was an Irish
cross.

"Impressive, ain't it?"

Kit glanced over to find Dalton, a delicate pastry in
hand, lounging against an arch framing the way to the
interior of the castle.

Kit grinned. "It's a castle, Dalton. It's supposed to be
impressive."

Ash appeared in the doorway beside Dalton. He focused his gaze on the image the rays of sunlight cast on
the floor and casually remarked, "This one was apparently
built to impress Irishmen who might be tempted to follow

England's wicked King Henry and stray from the Church in Rome."

"It appears to have worked," Kit retorted. "The only Anglican clergyman I've seen around here is Dalton."

A gasp sounded from behind the butler, and Ford stepped aside as the line of household staff looked over at Dalton and crossed themselves in unison.

"Thank you, *Lord Ramsey*." Thick sarcasm rolled off Dalton's tongue. He popped the remains of the pastry in his mouth and swallowed.

"Lord Kilgannon, if you please," Kit replied in a smooth Irish lilt. "When we're in Ireland." He turned to the butler. "No doubt they have already made themselves known to you, but allow me to present Ashford, the eighth marquess of Everleigh, and Mr. Dalton Mirrant."

"Lord Everleigh. Mr. Mirrant," Ford acknowledged Kit's companions.

"Lord Everleigh and Mr. Mirrant are my closest friends, and I would have them accorded the same courtesies you accord me." Kit smiled at the butler and the staff queued up behind him.

"Of course, sir."

"Thank you, Ford. And thank you, *Your Lordship*." Dalton bowed to Kit. "Please apologize to your staff for my ancestor's heresy, and do explain that I may be Anglican, but I don't bite and I'm house-trained."

Kit laughed. "Consider it done." Turning his attention back to the butler, he said, "Now, please introduce me to the staff that have been waiting so patiently."

The staff of Telamor Castle, made up of the housekeeper, four housemaids, two footmen, two underfootmen, the cook, and the kitchen maid, stood dressed in their Sunday best—the men in livery and the women dressed in black day dresses and crisply starched white aprons and caps.

"We are thinly staffed at the moment, my lord, as we have been confined to care-taking duties since the passing of the late earl of Kilgannon except upon the rare occasions when your solicitor, Mr. Bell, and Father Francis invited the bishop or other visiting dignitaries to make use of the castle. As such, may I present the current staff of Telamor Castle?" Ford asked.

Kit nodded. Father Francis had explained his role in the caretaking of Telamor Castle shortly before he explained Kit's responsibilities as the earl of Kilgannon and the existence of his ward.

"The housekeeper at Telamor, Mrs. Kearney."

"Mrs. Kearney." Kit acknowledged the housekeeper's status as the highest-ranking female on staff, answerable only to Ford or to himself.

"My lord." The housekeeper curtsied.

The butler nodded his approval, then continued down the line of servants. "Upstairs maids, Bridget and Polly," the butler continued. "Downstairs maids, Josey and Lana."

The housemaids bobbed polite curtsies. "Your Lordship," they replied in unison.

"Footmen, Searcy and O'Riley, and underfootmen, Cohan and Slaney."

"Sir." Each of the men tugged at their forelocks and gave Kit a deferential nod.

Kit acknowledged each of them by repeating their names. "Searcy. O'Riley. Cohan. Slaney."

"And then there is Cook," Ford continued. "Mrs. Dowd and her assistant, Rory."

"A pleasure," Kit told her. "I'm looking forward to a proper Irish supper."

"I'll be doing my best to please you, sir." Her brogue was thick and almost unintelligible to Kit, but her smile was universal. It was a wide, gap-toothed grin. "Do you like Irish stew or skewered rabbit with potato cakes? I can make it for your supper tonight. Or if you prefer something else, just tell Mrs. K. what you want on the menu, and I'll be doing my best to prepare it for you."

"Thank you," Kit replied.

"Lord Ram . . . Kilgannon is very easy to please, Mrs. Dowd. His tastes are quite plebeian." Dalton pushed away from the arch in a movement that was too graceful to be practiced and walked over to stand beside Kit.

The housekeeper frowned at him.

"He means that Lord Kilgannon's tastes are those of the common man," Ash translated as he crossed the floor to join Kit and Dalton.

Mrs. Dowd glared at Ash. "Then why make sport of me? Why not say what he means?" she demanded.

"He didn't mean to make sport of you," Kit soothed the cook's ruffled feathers. "That's simply Mr. Mirrant's manner of speaking."

"It's true," Dalton promised. "I only meant that you needn't worry about preparing a great number of fancy dishes for the earl as he prefers common foods. No of-fense intended."

The cook looked from Kit to Ash to Dalton and back again. "None taken."

"Thank goodness," Dalton murmured to Kit, "because if her meals are half as good as the pastries she bakes, we're all going to be enjoying them. Here. Try this."

"Dalton, please. You know I don't . . ." Kit held up his hand to ward him off, but Dalton popped the last bite of a light, flaky pastry into Kit's mouth.

"Eat cake," Dalton finished his sentence for him. "I know. But this isn't cake. It's a pastry and it's . . ."

"Heavenly." Unlike Dalton, who had a notorious sweet tooth, Kit didn't eat pastries or cakes. He had never ex-plained his reasons for his sudden change of heart, but he had voluntarily decided to do without dessert the summer he turned eight years old. It had been fifteen years since he had tasted a pastry, but Kit was quite certain that he'd never tasted anything as delicious. The strawberry and the pastry seemed to melt in his mouth. He had forgotten how good it could taste.

He smiled at Cook. "My compliments, Mrs. Dowd. Your pastry is extraordinary."

"Well, now, my lord, I wish that I could take credit for the baking of the pastries you're enjoying, but that wouldn't be right, seeing as how the young lady baked them."

Kit looked at the cook's assistant.

Cook shook her head. "No, not that one. The young lady from the convent. Miss Mariah."

Kit turned to Ford.

The butler walked over to Searcy. "Find Miss Shaughnessy. Ask her to join His Lordship in the second-floor study. Show her the way."

"Where . . ." Searcy began.

"When last I saw her, she was in the kitchens putting the finishing touches on another batch of tarts," Ford answered.

Kit stared openmouthed at the exchange.

"Who the devil is Miss Shaughnessy?" Dalton demanded of Kit.

"My ward."

"Your what?!" Ash asked the question as if he had never heard the term before.

Ignoring him, Kit turned to the assembled staff. "Thank you all for your warm welcome. I thank you for your hard work and your devotion to the castle in my absence. You may return to your duties." He waited until the staff had quietly filed out of the vestibule before he turned to Ash and repeated his earlier explanation. "My ward. I'll explain everything later, Ash. At the moment I need to meet Miss Shaughnessy and her chaperone."

"If you'll follow me, sir," Ford said.

Kit followed the butler to the door.

"Her chaperone?" Dalton called after him.

"Yes, Dalton," Kit paused in the doorway and looked back over his shoulder at his friend. "Her chaperone. Sister Mary Beatrix. From the convent."

Dalton groaned. "A nun? You said they were our neighbors. You didn't say anything about them living in the same house!"

"Just imagine what she's going to say about sharing a roof with you," Kit retorted as he lengthened his stride to catch up with the butler.

Chapter 8

Charms strike the Sight, but Merit wins the Soul.

—ALEXANDER POPE, 1688–1744

The second-floor study was every bit as impressive as the rest of the house with four full-length Palladian windows that opened onto a balcony outfitted with deck chairs and a telescope so one could sit and read or stare out over the ocean. A large door at one end of the study connected it to the library. Both rooms contained massive bookcases filled with leather-bound volumes and the same frescoed ceiling of soft clouds against a brilliant blue sky. There were even a few cherubs tucked here and there, lounging among the clouds—reading. Kit focused on the painted titles on the books and found they matched the titles on the shelves. The Bible. Shakespeare. Aristotle. Plato. Socrates. And strangely enough, John Milton's *Paradise Lost*.

Apparently one of his Irish ancestors had found an artist with a sense of humor and one that was willing to lie on his back and paint the castle's massive ceilings as Michelangelo had done on the ceiling of the Sistine Chapel. Kit rolled off his vantage point on the leather reclining sofa and moved to sit behind the huge Hepplewhite desk to await Miss Shaughnessy's arrival.

He didn't have to wait long. He'd barely settled onto the chair behind the desk when the knock sounded on the door.

"Enter."

"Miss Shaughnessy, sir." The footman, Searcy, opened the study door and announced the visitor, then stepped out of the way, allowing her to enter.

Kit felt as if he'd been struck by lightning as he looked up from behind the desk and saw the woman standing in the door. He wasn't quite certain what he'd been expecting—someone younger, someone older, someone plainer, someone plumper. Anything except the vision framed in the doorway.

"Miss Shaughnessy?"

"Lord Kilgannon?"

They spoke in unison.

She stepped out of the doorway and into the room. Searcy backed into the hall and closed the door behind her. Suddenly, remembering his manners, Kit stood up, banged his knee against the desk in his haste, and muttered a profane curse.

She gasped.

"I beg your pardon," he managed as he grabbed his knee and gritted his teeth until the sharp pain subsided.

Mariah winced in empathy. "That's sure to leave a nasty bruise," she said. "Shall I prepare a warm comfrey poultice to help make it better?"

Her voice was a low, well-modulated Irish brogue, completely natural and free of artifice. The sound of it surrounded his senses in warmth even as it sent a jolt of awareness through him. Kit's heart pounded when he met her gaze.

She was, without a doubt, one of the most breathtakingly beautiful women he had ever seen. She had thick black hair confined in a braid that reached her waist, classically elegant cheekbones, a small nose, plump rosy lips, and a delicately sculpted chin and jaw, but it was her eyes that held him spellbound. Her eyes were an intense shade of sapphire blue, accented by rows of dark eyelashes and the slightly winged arches of her eyebrows. Hers was the face poets described when they talked of unrivaled beauty, and the smear of white flour marring her forehead and the thin line of cinnamon dusted across her cheek only added to her beauty and her appeal.

He thought there might be a dozen or so very creative ways she might help to make the pain in his knee go away. But none of his suggestions would ever be considered appropriate for a guardian to suggest to his ward.

"There's no need to go to all that bother," Kit assured her. "It will be fine."

Mariah looked skeptical. "It's no bother. Although I don't normally prepare healing poultices, your kitchens are well stocked with the necessary herbs and ingredients. It would be a simple matter to boil the comfrey leaves and soak the wrapping cloths used to draw out the swelling, then apply a leech or two . . ."

"We keep leeches in the kitchens?"

She stared at him. "Well, no. But we can borrow from St. Agnes's supply if you change your mind. . . ."

"I'll let you know." Kit bit back a smile.

Mariah turned and started toward the door. "If there's nothing I can do for you . . ."

"Wait!" Kit called. "I wanted to see you."

She glanced back over her shoulder as she reached for the doorknob. "I know," she answered. "Searcy made that quite clear when he came to get me. But I've got two more batches of tarts in the oven and . . ."

Kit limped across the room and placed his hand against the door to keep her from opening it. "The tarts can wait."

"No, they *cannot*," she corrected. "Unless you want them to burn, and I am not in the habit of burning my baked goods."

"That begs the question: Why are you doing the baking rather than Cook or her assistant?" Kit asked, placing his hand around Mariah's elbow, skillfully moving her away from the door so that he could open it.

Searcy stood guard outside it.

"Miss Shaughnessy's strawberry tarts are in danger of burning," Kit said. "Please see that they're removed from the ovens before they're ruined."

"You want me to remove them, sir?" Searcy's voice came out in a high-pitched squeak.

"I would suggest you ask Mrs. Dowd or her assistant to remove them, but if the cook or her assistant isn't available, you will have to do it." Kit bit the inside of his cheek to keep from smiling at the expression of horror on the footman's face.

"But I—"

"There's nothing to it, man," Kit said. "Take a cloth and pull the cooking sheets from the oven, then place them on the wooden cooling racks on the worktable. Go. Do it now before it's too late."

"Yes, Your Lordship." Searcy backed away from the door, then turned and ran down the passageway toward the kitchens.

Kit closed the door and turned to Mariah.

"How?" she asked, stunned at his knowledge.

"Our cook used to invite my younger sisters and me into the kitchen to help make holiday tarts and gingerbread biscuits."

He was full of surprises. Mariah straightened her spine and attempted to look him in the eye. But she miscalculated. He hadn't seemed so formidable sitting behind the desk, but he was bigger and taller up close than she first thought. Her gaze struck him at chest level—somewhere between the bottom of his silk cravat and the top button of his waistcoat. She took a couple of steps back and lifted her chin.

She couldn't stop staring at him. She told herself it was only natural given the fact that he was the youngest man she had ever been around. And the handsomest. His eyes were brown, she realized. The color of chocolate. Warm, delicious melted chocolate.

Reverend Mother was fond of saying that eyes were the mirror to the soul. In Mariah's experience, eyes like his were reserved for the paintings of saints and for the faces of innocent children. She smiled at the thought. She knew almost nothing about men, but she knew enough to realize that there was nothing saintly or innocent about Lord Kilgannon.

"Miss Shaughnessy?" He snapped his fingers in front of her face.

Mariah blinked twice before responding. "What?"

He reached over and rubbed the pad of his thumb across her forehead and then again, across her cheek. "You were explaining why you are baking tarts in the Telamor kitchens instead of the cook."

Mariah inhaled the scent of him—limes and a musky exotic fragrance she couldn't name. The scent was as mesmerizing as the soft swipe of his thumb across her face and the warm look in his chocolate-colored eyes. "Because I'm better at it."

Kit lifted his eyebrow in query. "Is that so?"

She nodded. "Ask anyone in Inismorn. They'll tell you that St. Agnes's Sacred Heart Convent's goods are the best in the parish, and I'm the baker at St. Agnes's." She paused. No good ever came of boasting. After confession, Father Francis would scold her and tell her to pray three rosaries. But it was worth it. "Father Francis always asks me to bake strawberry tarts when he comes to supper at St. Agnes's and when the bishop comes from Dublin to visit and on special occasions. Father Francis says that I'm an artist—a pastry chef extraordinaire. But there's nothing extraordinary about what I do."

"I disagree," Kit said. "I rarely indulge in cakes or pastries, but I tasted one of your tarts and found it to be quite extraordinary. Almost as extraordinary as the fact that you baked it."

"I'm a baker."

"You're the legal ward of the earl of Kilgannon and a lady."

Mariah frowned. "What has that to do with anything?"

"Ladies rarely consort with those in trade, and they certainly do not take it upon themselves to enter one."

"English ladies," she sniffed.

"Or Irish ones," he added.

"They would if they grew up in a Dominican order."

He lifted his brow once again. "Why is that?"

"Because, in a convent everyone from the Mother Superior to the youngest student works. No task is beneath them, and every effort is made to utilize individual talents. I bake because that's what I do best. Sister Mary Beatrix supervises the cleaning and dusting and makes the candles because that's what she does best. Sister Mary Zechariah organizes the washing and ironing, and Sister Mary Simon tends the garden because that is where her talent lies. We do what needs to be done because there is no one else to do it. You may consider baking a trade. I consider it a necessity."

"Pastries?" Kit inquired, blandly casting himself in the role of devil's advocate, not because he disagreed with her, but because he found the lively discussion refreshing.

"Bread." Mariah caught herself before she stamped her foot in disgust. "I'm sure you've heard of it." She hadn't known she was capable of sarcasm until a few moments ago. "The staff of life? The food that prevents most of us from starving?"

"My mistake," he replied. "I thought that in Ireland, the staff of life was the potato."

"Starvation is nothing to sneer at."

"Indeed it is not," Kit agreed. He eyed her figure. She was slender, but not dangerously so. Her figure rounded in all the right places. Kit inhaled. She was correct. Starvation wasn't anything to sneer about. Fortunately, no one he had seen so far appeared to be starving.

Father Francis had assured him that although the potato blight had been discovered in the parish, Telamor's tenants and the residents of Inismorn and the convent had not suffered famine or hunger. "Nor are you in danger of starving."

"Not *me!*" Mariah gritted her teeth to keep from screaming. The earl of Kilgannon might be frustratingly dense, but he was also her guardian, and she owed him a measure of consideration for that if for no other reason.

"The poor in the parish. I bake bread for the convent's use and to sell to the households that don't want to bake their own. The money we earn and the leftover bread is distributed to the needy families in the parish. It's one of the ways St. Agnes's contributes. I only bake pastries and cakes on special occasions."

"Such as the first meeting of a guardian and his ward."

"Yes," she said. "I thought the occasion merited strawberry pastries, but perhaps I was mistaken."

Kit pretended disbelief. "You, mistaken?"

"Well, I was expecting a different sort of guardian."

He was intrigued in spite of himself. "What sort of guardian?"

Mariah pursed her lips in thought. "Oh, the Father Francis sort. Older, wiser, plainer, plumper. Politer."

"So you spent the morning baking tarts to tempt your guardian—an old man with a sweet tooth."

"It was the least I could do." She gave him her most charming smile. "After all my guardian had done for me."

"Touché," Kit answered, leaning closer. "The truth, Miss Shaughnessy, is that until I met with Father Francis earlier this morning, I didn't know I was a guardian. And when I learned that I was your guardian, I expected something—someone very different as well."

"Someone younger?" Mariah suggested. "Someone with strawberry jam smeared on her face? Someone who might sit upon your knee, lean her head against your chest, and fall asleep listening to the sound of your voice relating favorite fairy stories?"

The appeal of the picture Mariah Shaughnessy painted in his mind was instant and visceral. Kit stared at her, then through her, into the future, where a little girl with dark blue eyes and long, black ringlets—her mother in miniature—sat upon his lap. Her plump little hands and pouty red lips smearing the remnants of a bedtime snack of toast and strawberry jam on his shirt. He could almost feel her warm little body cuddling against him and hear her breathe the word *papa* as she drifted off to sleep. The vision was real enough to fill him with a sense of longing. And the idea that it could was enough to scare Kit to death.

He was only two and twenty years old. He wasn't ready to be anyone's papa. "Someone young enough to have a governess," he told her. "Not someone old enough to come equipped with a chaperone and a fiancé."

Mariah's eyes widened in surprise. "Father Francis told you I was betrothed?"

Kit nodded. "He also told me that you would prefer a season in London rather than marry the gentleman the Mother Superior chose for you."

"That's true." She studied the tips of her boots peeking out from beneath her skirts.

"Do you have a particular reason for not wanting to marry him or are you against marriage in general?"

She looked up then, right into his chocolate-colored eyes. "I have nothing against *marriage*," she breathed the word in a reverent tone. "I want very much to be married—one day. But I would like the opportunity to choose my own husband and not have the choice made for me."

"Choosing a spouse for oneself is generally a privilege reserved for the lower classes," Kit replied. "Our positions almost always prevent us from having that luxury."

"Has your position prevented you from making your own choice?" she asked.

"No," he said. "As heir to the title, I will be required to marry and produce another heir, of course, but my mother and father would prefer that I marry someone of my own choosing. They've no wish to interfere." He met Mariah's gaze. "However, my family is the exception, rather than the rule."

"I don't want to marry a man I've never met," Mariah said.

"Who does?" Kit asked the rhetorical question. "Everyone would like to marry someone they know and trust, but that isn't always possible. Sometimes you have to marry for the good of the family or the title or the estate.

The reason most young women don't get to choose their husbands is because it is too easy to mistake seduction for romance. And marriage and the propagation of the family name are too important to be based on unreliable judgment."

"That may be true," Mariah conceded. "But if I'm not allowed to choose for myself, I prefer that my guardian have a variety from which to choose. Besides," she added, "my mother wanted me to have a London season."

"What about you?" he asked. "What do you want?"

"I grew up in a convent," she said. "I've never known anything but convent life. Is it too much to ask to want to experience something of the world before I'm forced to retire from it once again in order to fulfill my wifely duty and raise children and cook and clean and sew?"

Kit frowned at her. "Is that what you expect from marriage? A life of drudgery?"

Mariah shrugged. "The only marriages I've seen are the ones in Inismorn, and I've only seen those from a distance. But from what I've seen, the husbands have much better lives than their wives. Husbands frequent pubs and associate with friends. Wives never do."

"Marriage to a gentlemen would offer a woman many more opportunities."

"Would marriage to a country squire offer me many more opportunities?" Mariah asked.

"It should," Kit hedged.

"Can you promise that it will?"

"Of course not," he said. "I've never met the squire. I don't know what he expects of his wife."

"That makes two of us." Mariah stared at her guardian, silently willing him to understand. "And I really don't care to learn firsthand."

Kit sighed. "Despite what you may have heard, London seasons aren't all they're cracked up to be. They can jolly well be a nuisance and more expensive than a stable of racing thoroughbreds. There are endless rounds of morning calls, musicales where you'll be expected to participate, and balls." He frowned. "Do you dance?"

She shook her head.

"Play the pianoforte? The flute? The harp? Any musical instrument?"

She shook her head.

"Can you sing?"

"I don't know. We don't sing in the convent. It isn't allowed."

"What do you do?"

"I bake."

He gazed up at the frescoed ceiling and prayed for patience. "Besides bake?"

"I pull weeds in the garden and scrub floors and . . ." Her face brightened as she thought of something else.

"And . . ." he prompted.

"I read. And in my spare time I practice my calligraphy by copying Biblical text. My penmanship is excellent." Mariah winced at that last boast. Father Francis would be adding another three rosaries to her penance for that.

"The penmanship will come in quite handy when you're writing thank-yous," Kit agreed. "But reading and penmanship aren't exactly what I had in mind." He paused for a moment, then thought of something else. It was a long shot to be sure, but it was worth a try. . . . "What about riding? Can you sit a horse?"

Mariah bit her bottom lip. "I've never tried, but I'm sure I'll be quite good at it. I love horses."

Kit groaned. "In addition to dancing and music and riding lessons, you'll have to memorize the peerage and etiquette. Our meals generally consist of six to ten courses. Do you have any idea how many knives and forks and spoons and glasses you will have to learn to juggle? And then, there are the clothes. You'll be required to change clothes dozens of times a day—" He broke off abruptly as Mariah's face lit up at the prospect. "That means standing for hours while a group of seamstresses and their assistants fit and measure and poke pins in you, not to mention the hours spent poring over fabric swatches and pattern books. I left London, in part, to get away from all that madness, so if I hear one word of complaint from you while we're preparing you for any of this, I swear I'll discharge my duty as your guardian and marry you off to the squire without a backward glance."

Chapter 9

If you must play, decide on three things at the start: the rules of the game, the stakes, and the quitting time.

—CHINESE PROVERB

"*Oh, thank you! Thank you!*" *With those words,* Mariah flung herself into Kit's arms.

"Until I have an opportunity to speak with the squire, you must consider yourself betrothed to him." He caught her in self-defense and held her close as she wrapped her arms around his neck. "But I won't force you to marry him."

"Thank you, Lord Kilgannon! I promise you won't regret it."

He nearly spoke the truth and repeated his earlier pronouncement to Father Francis: "*I already regret it. Because if there is anything I hate, it's the fuss and bother that goes with a London season.*" But Kit couldn't bring himself to disappoint her. When it came down to it, Mariah Shaughnessy wanted the same thing he wanted—the opportunity to make her own decisions and to chart her own course. And when it came down to it, Kit found it impossible to regret agreeing to anything that made her happy enough to fling herself in his arms.

He breathed in the scent of her, an enticing mix of strawberries, cinnamon, and woman, and was within a hair's breadth of kissing her when Mariah shifted in his arms.

Kit released her immediately, but not before he saw the

awakening of an answering desire in her eyes.

Mariah backed away from him, putting space between them. "Forgive me, Lord Kilgannon," she murmured self-consciously. "I don't know what came over me. I've never been alone with a man—other than Father Francis, of course, and then only during confession and I've certainly never . . . Oh—" She broke off, horribly embarrassed by her loss of control and by the fact that she had wrinkled the front of his coat and knocked his cravat askew. "I've crushed your neck cloth." She abruptly reached out to straighten his silk cravat.

Her fingers brushed the underside of his jaw, and Kit reached up and caught her hands, imprisoning them between his own. "No matter," he said. "I'll be exchanging it for a fresh one in time for tea." He could still feel the press of her breasts against his chest and the brush of her fingers against the sensitive line of his jaw and his neck as she attempted to adjust his clothing became torture.

"I could iron it for you," Mariah offered.

"Absolutely not!" Kit answered.

The expression on his ward's face changed from hopeful to horrified in seconds, and Kit hurriedly softened his tone of voice and offered an explanation. "Unmarried ladies do not iron a gentleman's articles of clothing. That's a valet's job, and Ford will see to the chore until I can secure the services of a gentleman's gentleman. Besides . . ." He let go of one of Mariah's hands, then impulsively brought the other work-roughened and callused hand to his lips and pressed a kiss on her knuckles. "I thought ironing was Sister Mary Zechariah's responsibility."

Mariah's heart began a rapid tattoo at the touch of his lips on her hand. She felt the color rush to her face and a spark of awareness rush through her body. An unknown emotion flickered in his eyes, and Mariah was inordinately pleased by it. She held his gaze for what seemed like an eternity, reluctant to let it go. "I-it is."

Kit released her hand. "Then we'll hear no more about

ironing my neck cloths or anything else. Your duty, from now on, is to prepare yourself for your coming out. Forget about the hardships of life at St. Agnes's and concentrate on becoming a lady." His voice was husky and soft when he spoke to her and his eyes sparkled.

"What about my baking?" she asked.

"Someone else will have to take over."

Mariah winced. "The villagers of Inismorn aren't going to like losing the best baker they've had in years," she predicted.

"They'll get used to it," Kit said. He looked at her. "You can be a lady and make your London debut, or you can be a baker in Inismorn in Ireland."

"Why can't I be both?"

Kit thought of his mother's unconventional role as a working botanical and zoological illustrator of note and as the mother of three and wife of the marquess of Templeston and felt a pang of guilt. His mother was an artist married to one of the wealthiest and most powerful men in England, and whether Mariah Shaughnessy knew it or not, whether she liked it or not, there was a world of difference in being a married lady artist and being an unmarried lady baker. "Because that's not the way things are done. You must choose."

Mariah exhaled a deep breath. "My mother was a great lady," she said softly. "And I want to be just like her."

"All right, then," Kit said with a nod. "We'll begin tomorrow morning. Your last official act as the baker of Inismorn is to salvage your batch of strawberry tarts. Father Francis invited himself to supper tonight, and I believe he's expecting them for dessert." He looked at her plain black dress and white apron. "I don't suppose you have anything else to wear?"

"I have two other dresses."

"Like that one?"

"I have a nicer one and one that is less so."

"Then we'll forego dressing for dinner until you have a suitable wardrobe, and we'll see to hiring a seamstress tomorrow to create your wardrobe and a lady's maid to see that you're properly outfitted in it."

Mariah turned to leave.

"Miss Shaughnessy?"

"Yes?"

"When you're in the company of people with a rank greater than your own, it's customary to wait until you're dismissed before you turn your back on them. And you never turn your back on the sovereign or a member of the royal family."

"I thought my lessons were to begin tomorrow morning."

Kit lifted an eyebrow. "Can it be that I hear a complaint already?" He knew it was wrong, but he enjoyed pushing her, testing the limits of her patience.

"No."

"My lord," he added.

"Pardon?"

"I'm an earl," he said. "You address me as Lord Kilgannon, sir, or my lord," he instructed.

"No, *my lord,*" she repeated.

"Good. Now you may go."

"Thank you, *Lord Kilgannon.*" She turned back toward the door.

"Miss Shaughnessy?" He called out in a singsong voice.

"What *now?*" She let out an exasperated sigh, then caught herself. "What now, *sir?* Because if you don't let me out of this room, there may not be any tarts to salvage."

Kit could tell by the look on her face that Mariah was dangerously low on patience, but he prodded her anyway. The next few weeks and months were going to be hell for both of them, and he might as well find out where her breaking point was *before* they began her formal training. "You forgot to curtsy. A lady always acknowledges a person of higher rank by curtsying."

"You mean kneel?"

"Not completely. It's more like genuflecting."

Mariah shook her head. "I genuflect before God and the Blessed Virgin. No one else."

Kit grinned. "Think of me as God."

His blasphemy took her breath away, and before she could recover from the shock of hearing him compare himself to God, he murmured, "And I'll do my best to think of you as the Blessed Virgin."

"Have you lost your mind?" Ash demanded as he and Kit and Dalton sat sipping brandy in the second-floor study three-quarters of an hour before Father Francis was scheduled to arrive for supper.

"Quite possibly," Kit murmured.

Dalton shook his head in disgust. "I thought you came to Ireland to escape that sort of fuss and bother."

"I did," Kit answered.

"Then, why the devil are you agreeing to launch a girl who isn't even related to you into society?" Dalton shuddered in mock horror. "Training her to be some other man's wife. And he, a country squire. Why do that to yourself? It's bad enough when it's your sister."

"How would you know?" Kit demanded. "You don't have any sisters."

"Well, hell," Dalton replied. "We ran away from London to escape the chaos Iris's coming out has created."

"That's not the only reason I chose to come to Ireland," Kit reminded him. "I also came to claim my inheritance and—"

"To find his destiny," Ash added.

Kit glared at Ash, warning him that now was not the time to mock.

Ash raised his hands in a sign of surrender. "I'm only quoting you. A sennight ago you threw down the die at Black Hazard's and announced that you were going to Ireland to find your destiny. Unlike you, Dalton and I aren't seeking our destiny, we simply came along for the adventure."

Dalton drained his glass of brandy, then walked over to the drinks cabinet and helped himself to another. "Here, here!" He lifted his glass in salute to Ash's unflinching appraisal of Kit's situation.

"It's bad form to insult a man when you're helping yourself to his liquor, Mirrant," Kit pointed out.

"Quite the contrary," Dalton retorted. "It's the very best time to insult him."

Ash threw back his head and laughed. "What lucky fellows we've turned out to be!" He looked at Dalton. "This should teach us to be more careful what we ask for. Kit wanted to claim his inheritance and seek his destiny. We wanted something to relieve the boredom of constant drinking and carousing, and we all got what we wanted."

"If he wanted to launch a girl into society, he could have stayed home and helped his mother launch Iris," Dalton grumbled. "Lady Templeston is one of the calmest, most levelheaded women I know, and Iris's debut has her in a frazzle."

Kit and Ash exchanged knowing glances. Although he had refrained from doing so until now, it came as no surprise to Kit or to Ash that Dalton would reprimand Kit for leaving his mother to handle Iris's debut on her own. Dalton had wanted adventure, and he had encouraged Kit to seek his, but he also knew that Kit's mother had wanted Kit to stay home in England, and they knew that eventually, that would prove reason enough for Dalton to take Kit to task. Dalton had been enamored of Kit's mother since he was in short trousers.

"You owe me ten pounds," Ash told Kit.

"You're right." Kit reached into his wallet. "Do you prefer sovereigns or notes?"

"Notes will do," Ash answered with a grin. "Gold sovereigns get heavy."

Kit removed a ten-pound note and handed it to Ash. "I guessed he would do it sooner."

Ash pocketed the money. "No. He was too keen to come along."

"Remember to record the payment date and strike through the wager next time you go to White's," Kit said. "I don't want people to think I don't pay my debts."

"What about White's?" Dalton demanded. "Stop talking around me. What wager?"

"Before we left London, Ash and I recorded a wager in the betting book at White's. I wagered ten pounds that we wouldn't be on the road twenty-four hours before you'd tell me that my mother needed me to stay behind and help with Iris's debut."

Dalton frowned at Ash.

"I knew it would take a bit longer." Ash grinned. "Because you consider Swanslea Park as much a refuge as Kit and you were eager to escape the chaos, too."

"All I'm saying is that if we're going to have to put up with a great deal of feminine folderol, we might as well have done so at Swanslea Park," Dalton defended himself. "Who is Mariah Shaughnessy and what is she to Kit?"

"She's my ward," Kit answered.

"Since when?"

"Since I became the earl of Kilgannon and inherited Telamor Castle and all its environs."

"You inherited the title a year ago, and you're just telling us that you have a ward?" Dalton stalked over to the fireplace, then picked up the poker and jabbed at the bed of glowing peat. "You're packed full of secrets lately."

"It appears to come with the title." Kit set his empty snifter on a side table, then leaned forward in his chair, propped his elbows on his knees, and rested his forehead on his hands. "I actually inherited the title when the old earl died. But I didn't learn about it until a year ago. And when I left you on the crossroads of the path to meet the priest at the church this morning, I had no idea I had inherited a guardianship to go along with my title and my castle." He looked over at Dalton. "I had no idea I had a ward until I spoke with Father Francis. And even then, I expected someone with a governess and plaits. Not some-one about to make her debut."

"Well, expect it or not, wish for it or not, you are her guardian," Ash said. "You are the earl of Kilgannon, and your obligations to the girl are clear. I'm in." He turned to Kit and smiled. "Now, we need to come up with a plan to prepare her for her entrance into society."

He shouldn't have been surprised by his friend's loyalty, but Ash's willingness to put himself through weeks or months of torture in order to help him discharge his obligation to his ward filled Kit with gratitude. "I don't know what to say," Kit began.

"I do," Dalton announced. "She's already betrothed. Marry her off as soon as possible. You don't owe her anything, and you're addlepated to think you do. Especially a London season . . . Because unless she happens to be one's mother, one's sister, or one's mistress, having a female about the house is a damned nuisance. This girl grew up in a convent, for pity's sake. . . ."

"Exactly!" Ash snapped his fingers. "For pity's sake. She grew up orphaned and in a convent, Dalton. Perhaps Kit thinks she deserves a chance to be what she might have been if fate hadn't treated her so cruelly. What do you say, Mirrant? Are you in or out?"

"He knows nothing about her. . . ."

"I know she baked the strawberry tarts you devoured at teatime," Kit said. *And I know she looks like every man's dream come to life.*

That got Dalton's attention. "What?"

"She was trained to be a baker."

"They taught a lady to bake those *heavenly* tarts?"

"She did grow up in a convent, Dalton. Would you have her baking *hellish* tarts?" Kit drawled.

Dalton paused to mull it over. "I've never heard of a lady of our acquaintance baking anything. Most are hard-pressed to locate the kitchens, much less cook."

"Exactly," Kit said.

Dalton nodded. "All right. I'll do whatever I can to help

you get the poor lamb ready for the slaughter."

Kit raised an eyebrow in surprise. "What makes you think I'm sending a poor lamb to slaughter?"

Dalton shrugged his shoulders. "I don't know. It's just the image that came to mind. I mean a lady who spends her time baking pastries most likely samples as many pastries as she bakes. I imagine your ward probably resembles Lady Ann Willingham—plain, plump, and short-sighted, with bad teeth and a rather doughy complexion.

"Am I right?" Dalton grinned at Kit. "I'm right, aren't I?"

"You'll have the chance to evaluate her and her suit-ability for presentation to society for yourself," Kit told him, working to keep his expression bland. "She's joining us for supper tonight. And since I suspect her wardrobe is severely limited at the moment, I told her we would refrain from dressing."

Ash nodded in understanding. A girl from a convent probably owned only one or two dresses and none that would be suitable evening attire.

Dalton agreed. "It would be much simpler if your ward had been a boy, but . . ." Dalton clucked his tongue in sympathy. "We're mates and we're in this together."

Kit's voice held a note of sincerity that was the very soul of gratitude. "I don't know how to thank you. . . ."

"Don't worry about it," Ash told him. "Dalton will think of something."

"He already has," Kit said. "He's come up with the perfect answer."

"Which is?"

"I'll send her to Swanslea Park. She can receive her instruction along with Iris." Kit grinned, proud of himself for realizing the solution to the problem was there all along.

Dalton shook his head. "I'll wager you ten that Lord Templeston says no."

"I'll take that bet," Ash said.

"Kit?" Dalton asked.

"You're on."

Chapter 10

Manners are of more importance than laws.... Manners are what vex or soothe, corrupt or purify, exalt or debase, barbarize or refine us, by a constant, steady, uniform, insensible operation, like that of the air we breathe in.

—EDMUND BURKE, 1729–97

Mariah paused in the doorway of the vast dining hall. The massive oak table was covered in white damask linen, four large, silver candelabra, and three floral centerpieces. Built to comfortably seat one hundred and fifty guests, the table was set for six and held more knives, forks, spoons, crystal, and china than Mariah had ever seen.

How would she ever learn what went with what? She took a step backward and seriously considered retreating to her room when Lord Kilgannon looked up and beckoned her forward. "Miss Shaughnessy."

He was standing on the far side of the dining room near the fireplace. Three other gentlemen stood beside him. Mariah heard enough of the conversation to know that she appeared to have interrupted a lively political debate. They turned to look at her as Lord Kilgannon spoke her name, and Mariah was relieved to discover that Father Francis was among them.

Lord Kilgannon crossed the room in a half dozen long strides. He bowed politely as he stood before her, paused for a moment or two, then offered Mariah his elbow.

Unsure what to do next, Mariah hesitated.

"May I?" Lord Kilgannon asked as he reached for her hand.

She nodded her agreement, and Kit gently tucked her ice-cold hand into the curve of his arm. Once again a jolt of awareness shot through him. He had been correct in his assumption that her wardrobe was limited. She was without gloves, and she wore the same black dress she had worn earlier. The white bib apron was gone, and she had washed the smear of flour and cinnamon from her face, and repinned her hair, but those were the only changes. "Did you come down to supper alone? Where's Sister Mary Beatrix? Isn't she joining us?"

Mariah shook her head. "Sister sends her regrets, but thought that her presence was unnecessary. She said that she is"—Mariah paused, searching for the right phrase— "*unaccustomed* to male company and prefers to dine in the solitude of her room." Sister Mary B. had actually said that, except for Father Francis, she could not *abide* male company while she ate, but there was no need for Lord Kilgannon to know that.

Kit stared at Mariah. "Your tact is admirable, but there's no need for you to soften the sting for me." He smiled down at her. "I met with Sister Mary Beatrix shortly after my meeting with you and she left no doubt of her opinion of men in general and Englishmen like myself in particular." Kit frowned at the memory of his brief meeting with Sister Mary Beatrix. He had expected a gentle, matronly woman, and he'd been presented with something else entirely. He had no doubt that the nun could be gentle and matronly with Mariah or the other residents of the convent, but she clearly did not approve of men—*particularly young, idle men bereft of Godliness or a sense of purpose.* Sister Mary Beatrix hadn't wasted a moment on niceties. She had looked him right in the eye and gotten right to the point in letting Kit know where he stood. The nun had delivered a message of eternal damnation of his soul if he so much as looked at Mariah in an improper manner.

Kit had barely gotten a word in before Sister Mary Beatrix had turned her back on him and walked away. After threatening him with the same fate that had befallen Peter Abelard, she had, Kit supposed, considered her duty as a chaperone completed.

"I'm sure Sister meant no disrespect," Mariah replied.

"On the contrary." He gave Mariah a crooked smile. "She treated me like the idle rich heretic ne'er-do-well she considers me to be. But however much she disapproves of my religion, my gender, or me personally, she is here as your chaperone, and as long as she performs her duty, she will be a welcome member of my household and accorded the respect her position affords her. Tomorrow morning I will make certain Sister Mary Beatrix understands that unmarried ladies of good families are not sent downstairs to dine with a roomful of unmarried gentlemen because, except for Father Francis, the chaperone can't *abide male company at the supper table*."

"How did you know?" Mariah looked at him as if she thought he could read her mind.

"I happened to pass by your room while Sister Mary Beatrix was expressing her opinion. Rather loudly," Kit explained. "I overheard it quite clearly through the door."

Mariah smiled. "She speaks loudly because she's hard of hearing."

Kit suspected Sister Mary Beatrix spoke loudly because she wanted to be overheard and because her advanced age allowed her to express uncensored opinions that she had once been unable to voice. But he wisely kept his opinion to himself.

"Here we are," he announced suddenly, and Mariah realized Lord Kilgannon had led her to his supper companions. He released her hand, then turned to her and asked, "Miss Shaughnessy, may I present Lord Everleigh? Lord Everleigh, Miss Shaughnessy."

"Miss Shaughnessy." Ash bowed.

"L-Lord Everleigh."

"May I say that your presence at Telamor Castle is a pleasant surprise?"

Kit noted the twinkle of devilment in Ash's eyes and frowned.

Ash ignored him.

"Th-thank you, Lord Everleigh, sir," Mariah stammered.

Turning toward Dalton, Kit continued the introductions. "And now, Miss Shaughnessy, may I present the Honorable Mr. Mirrant?"

Mariah managed a polite reply. "A pleasure to meet you, Mr. Mirrant."

Dalton bowed at the waist and would have taken Mariah's hand in his, but she did not offer it. "The pleasure is all mine, Miss Shaughnessy," he answered as he straightened and looked into her eyes.

"And I believe you are already well acquainted with Father Francis," Kit intruded, drawing Mariah's attention away from Dalton's subtle, but unsuccessful flirtation.

"Yes, of course." She smiled at the priest. "We are very well acquainted. Good evening, Father. I'm glad to see you."

"I promised I would come back and see that you were properly settled in and comfortable with the arrangement," Father Francis reminded her. "And I always keep my promises." He reached out and caressed her cheek with his palm. "What about you?" he teased. "Did you keep the promise you made to me?"

"Yes, Father," Mariah replied. "I baked strawberry tarts." She glanced at Lord Kilgannon. "I baked a great many strawberry tarts today. Six batches."

"Six?" Kit was surprised. It was a wonder she'd found the time to wash her face and repin her hair if she'd spent all afternoon baking.

"Two batches for teatime and two batches for supper," she answered.

"That's only four batches," Kit said.

"There weren't any left over from tea, so I baked another batch so Father Francis would have some to take back to the rectory." She looked at Kit. "I hope you don't mind. You see, the sisters don't allow the children to eat sweets at the convent, but . . ."

"We conspire to spoil them occasionally," Father Francis said. "Mariah and my housekeeper take turns baking sweets for the rectory, and I do my part by inviting all the children to the rectory on all the major Saints Days."

"How many children are there?" Kit asked.

"Eleven who live in the convent," Mariah answered.

"And thirty-seven more in the village," Father Francis added.

"So far, you've accounted for five of the six batches of tarts you baked today," Kit said. "What happened to the sixth one?"

Mariah glanced down at her feet, reluctant to disclose the reason for the sixth batch of tarts. "I baked the last batch to replace the batch that burned when you sent for me to meet you in your study."

"I sent Searcy to remove them from the oven."

"He was too late," Mariah pronounced. "They were too brown on the top and nearly burnt on the bottom."

Father Francis was mildly alarmed. "I've never known you to burn a batch of tarts before. The ingredients are too dear for that."

Her reputation as the best baker in Inismorn at stake, Mariah gave Lord Kilgannon a sweet, I-told-you-so smile. "I wouldn't have burned them had I been allowed to leave my guardian's august presence in time to save them."

"I'm sure Lord Kilgannon had his reasons for keeping you from your tarts."

"Of course he did, Father," Mariah agreed. "He doesn't like sweets."

Father Francis looked at Kit as if he'd blasphemed.

"I didn't say I didn't like sweets," Kit corrected, placing his hand against the small of Mariah's back, guiding her to her chair and politely seating her at the table on his left.

Kit waited for the others to sit before taking his place at the head of the table. Dalton was seated on Father Francis's right and Ash was seated on Mariah's. "I said I rarely eat them."

Father Francis took the chair on Kit's right. "Then the two of you have something in common."

"Pardon?" Kit wasn't sure he'd heard the priest correctly.

"You and Mariah." The priest chuckled. "I won't have to worry about either one of you confessing to the sin of gluttony." He shot a glance at Mr. Mirrant before turning his attention back to his host. "Our Mariah bakes like an angel, but she never eats what she bakes."

Kit glanced down at his ward. "If I hadn't tasted your strawberry confection for myself, I'd take that as a bad sign," he teased, nodding to the footman to remove Sister Mary Beatrix's place setting and to begin serving the first course. "A cook who won't eat what she cooks. Let us hope the same doesn't apply to Mrs. Dowd's cooking." He meant it as a joke, but Mariah did not see it that way.

"I cannot afford to enjoy my cooking," she replied. "Mrs. Dowd is a widow, but I'm unmarried. If I eat too many sweets I'll get fat, and it's doubtful that even the squire would want to marry me then."

A glimmer of a half-forgotten memory stirred in Kit's brain. *You'll get fat if you eat cake every night, and if you get fat eating cake, no prince will marry you.* He brushed the memory aside. It was too absurd to consider. And yet . . .

"It should not make any difference," Kit said.

"It should not, but it does."

"You're a lady of considerable means." Kit met her gaze. "That alone would guarantee you suitors. Even if your face and form did not."

"So Englishmen care more about fortunes than they do about faces and figures?"

"Some do," Kit admitted. "Not all. But you've no cause to worry, Miss Shaughnessy, because you have face, figure, and fortune and a guardian to help you select the proper suitor."

Mariah inhaled sharply, unable to determine whether she should feel complimented or insulted. Did he think that being Irish and a lady made her stupid? Or that having a pleasing face and form made her so? "And here I thought the Irish had a reputation for being mercenary," she retorted, covertly watching Ash as he reached for his soupspoon.

Kit recognized an insult when he heard one. "Why don't we ask your Irish squire and find out?"

Her spoon slipped out of Mariah's fingers and clattered against the edge of her soup bowl.

"That's no teasing matter, my son." Father Francis's tone of voice turned serious. "The squire is a mild-mannered sort of fellow, but I should think he'll be very unhappy at the prospect of losing Mariah. He's sure to pay you a visit and offer for her once again."

Kit reached over and retrieved Mariah's spoon and handed it back to her. "If that day comes, then I am sure Miss Shaughnessy and I will both have the opportunity to discover what the squire covets most—her or her fortune."

Chapter 11

The guests are met; the feast is set:
May'st hear the merry din.

—SAMUEL TAYLOR COLERIDGE,

1772–1834

Mariah hadn't thought supper could get worse, but in that she was proved wrong. She watched the gentlemen closely and followed their lead, but still encountered mishaps and accidents every time she reached for a piece of cutlery or a goblet or a cup.

Supper that evening consisted of six courses, served in the Russian style, all with their own special dishes and cutlery. Mariah had never seen so many dishes or such a variety of food. Nor was she certain that she ever wanted to again. She felt inadequate and out of place and terribly embarrassed.

And Lord Kilgannon hadn't made the ordeal any easier. He had watched her all evening and his gaze was far from soothing. Mariah had been as nervous as a mouse in a roomful of cats. She had begun the meal by dropping her soupspoon, and the disasters had continued. She had selected the incorrect fork twice, picked up the wrong goblet once, and spilled sauce on the tablecloth—all before the meat course was served.

At the convent she'd been taught that education and religion separated the working classes from the aristocracy, but tonight Mariah decided that supper parties were the true divining rod between the aristocracy and the poor.

The poor considered themselves fortunate to have food on the table. The wealthy took it for granted that food would miraculously appear. The poor didn't care how the meal reached the table. The rich cared more about the method of delivery than the food. How else did one explain the fact that there was barely enough time to taste a course before the footman removed that one and replaced it with another?

As if the selection of spoons and knives wasn't difficult enough, she was expected to make polite conversation on a variety of subjects. For a girl who had grown up in a convent where meals were eaten in strict silence, the art of polite dinner conversation was harder to grasp than the choice of cutlery.

"Dessert, Miss Shaughnessy?" Kit asked when the tablecloth had been removed and the selection of sweet wines and desserts had been set upon the table. "We've strawberry tarts, and the baker assures me that they're the best in the parish."

"I don't doubt that your baker is correct, my lord," Mariah replied, "but I've had my fill of strawberries today."

Kit nodded toward the footman. "Miss Shaughnessy will take her refreshments in the yellow salon across the passageway."

"Yes, my lord." The footman moved to stand behind Mariah's chair. "Miss?"

The gentlemen rose from their seats.

Mariah remained seated and realized immediately that she had made another mistake.

Lord Kilgannon leaned toward her and whispered, "It's customary for the ladies to retire from the table and gather in another room so the gentlemen can enjoy port and cigars without fear of giving offense."

"Oh."

Mariah looked up at him, and Kit read the panic in her eyes. "My mother always stands up and says: Gentlemen, I thank you for the pleasure of your company, but it is time I leave you to enjoy your cigars and port."

The look she gave him was dubious.

Kit smiled. "Yes, Miss Shaughnessy, I have a mother. A rather extraordinary one. A true lady."

Mariah rose from the table, met each pair of expectant eyes, and replied, "Gentlemen, I've been honored to share your company, but now, it's time for me to withdraw and leave you to enjoy your cigars and port."

"Well done," Lord Kilgannon whispered as she walked by and Mariah found herself warming to the look in his eyes and his praise. "Good evening, Miss Shaughnessy."

Father Francis glanced at Lord Kilgannon. "Thank you for supper, Lord Kilgannon, but I'm afraid I'll have to forego the cigars and port. Mass comes early in the morning. If you've no objection, I'll escort Mariah to the yellow salon and take my leave."

"I'll see you out," Kit offered.

"No need," Father Francis replied. "I know the way. Enjoy your refreshments with your friends. I'll collect my tarts and join Mariah in a cup of coffee before I go."

"Very well, Father." Kit nodded to the footman. "Please see that Father Francis's batch of strawberry tarts is waiting for him when he's ready to leave."

"Thank you, Your Lordship, for a pleasant evening and for the strawberry tarts," Father Francis said. "I'll say good night to you now. And I expect to see you at morning mass."

"Morning mass?" Lord Kilgannon coughed. "Father, you do understand that I was brought up in the Church of England?"

Father Francis's eyes twinkled in merriment. "An unfortunate occurrence to be sure," he teased. "But one I'm hoping we can rectify." He looked at Kit. "Relax, my son, the services are very much alike, and as earl of Kilgannon, your presence is expected."

"Why didn't you explain this earlier, Father?" Kit asked.

"You had enough to digest for one morning," Father

Francis replied. "I decided to leave the rest for a better time."

Kit eyed the priest. "Am I to expect more of the same?"

Father Francis bestowed his most innocent, priestly look on the young earl.

"Surprises, Father," Kit elaborated. "Am I to expect more surprises like the ones you've given me today?"

Father Francis shook his head. "I cannot say what the future will hold, my son."

Kit groaned.

Mariah smothered a giggle.

Father Francis looked from one to the other. "I'll see you *both* at morning mass. Good night, my lord." He bowed to the earl, then offered his arm to Mariah. "Come, my dear, coffee and dessert await us."

"What do you think of your guardian?" The priest asked as soon as the footman arranged the dessert tray and closed the doors of the yellow salon behind him.

"He's . . ." Mariah murmured, staring down at the coffee in her cup.

"A gentleman," the priest offered helpfully, "a young, healthy, intelligent and *responsible* gentleman. And I suppose there are young women who would find him handsome."

"Very handsome." Mariah looked up and met Father Francis's gaze.

Father Francis drank his coffee, then stood up. "I hate the thought of losing you to some man far away in London, my child, but I know your debut will be a success."

"Yes, Father." Her eyes stung and her voice quavered, but she remained steadfast before her confessor.

"No fretting about it, then, eh?" He chucked Mariah under the chin, the way he'd done when she was a child.

"No, Father."

"Good. Lord Kilgannon is your guardian, he'll do what's best for you."

Mariah tried to hold her tongue, but the words tumbled out anyway. "What is best for me? Marrying me off to an English stranger as opposed to an Irish one?"

"I don't know," Father Francis said. "Only you can decide the answer to that. You decide what you want, and Lord Kilgannon will arrange for you to have it."

"If it's up to me, why is Lord Kilgannon my guardian?"

"Because you are a woman, and in this time and in this place, women have few rights or protections. In the eyes of the law you must have a legal guardian to act for you. You don't have to have him think for you as you are quite capable of thinking for yourself." Father Francis took Mariah's hand in his. "I know this is all strange to you, but you've grown up, Mariah, and things cannot stay the way they were. You have been denied so much, lost so much, that I wanted you to have a chance for a different sort of life. This is your opportunity. Make the most of it." He smiled at her. "Think about it. And follow your heart. It will tell you what to do." He reached out and patted her on the hand. "Sleep well. I'll see you in the morning."

"All right, Father." She waited until she heard the sound of Father Francis's footsteps disappearing down the corridor toward the entryway, waited until she heard the low exchange of conversation as the butler opened the door and bid the priest farewell before she walked over to the velvet-covered settee and slowly sank to her knees in front of it.

Burying her face in the soft fabric, Mariah allowed the tears that were burning her eyes to fall, not in a polite ladylike trickle, but in huge torrents. Shoulders heaving from the force of her anguish, Mariah sucked in great, gasping breaths of air and expended them in equal force, kneeling on the cold floor before the velvet-covered settee, crying hot, wet tears into the fabric.

Chapter 12

Whatever tears one may shed, in the end one always blows one's nose.

—HEINRICH HEINE, 1797–1856

"*Sir?*"

Kit looked up as Ford entered the study and walked over to him. The butler leaned over Kit's right shoulder and spoke in a tone of voice too low for Dalton and Ash to hear.

"Are you certain?" Kit asked.

"Completely, sir." Ford assured him.

"All right," Kit said. "I'll be right there." He set his glass of port on the table beside his chair, pushed himself to his feet, and followed Ford to the door.

"Leaving so soon?" Dalton asked, moving a black knight across the chessboard he and Ash had spent the past quarter hour contemplating.

"Check." Ash took Dalton's queen.

"Damn!" Dalton swore.

"I've something I must do," Kit said. "I'll return shortly. Make yourself comfortable."

"We intend to," Dalton called after him. "Do hurry back. Ash and I were going to try out your billiard table, and we'd like the opportunity to relieve you of a portion of your inheritance."

Kit followed Ford out the door and across the hall to the yellow salon.

"I came in to remove the coffee tray and to ask if she required anything else of me. I thought at once that something was amiss," Ford explained in a low voice.

Kit eased the salon door open. There was no doubt about it. Something was most assuredly amiss with Miss Shaughnessy. Kit was surprised they hadn't heard her across the hall for she was crying as if her heart would break or as if it had already broken. "Thank you for alerting me, Ford," he said. "I will take care of it. I will ring if I require your services. That will be all."

"Very good, sir." Ford bowed politely and withdrew.

Kit stepped inside the room and pulled the pocket doors closed behind him. Miss Shaughnessy never noticed. Nor did she hear him cross the floor and kneel beside her. Kit exhaled. "Miss Shaughnessy?"

"Go away." She sobbed harder.

He placed an arm around her shoulder and turned her to him.

She clung to him, burrowing into the warmth of his chest as she cried against his shirtfront. "There, there, Miss Shaughnessy." He patted her shoulder, then began the slow, soothing, circular motion his mother and Ally always used to soothe away his childhood hurts. "What is it? What's wrong?"

"H-how c-can y-you a-ask th-that?" Mariah pushed away from his chest and stared up at him. "Y-you w-were th-there." Her face crumpled before his very eyes, and her shoulders began to shake once again. "Y-you s-saw m-me a-at s-supper. F-Father F-Francis th-thinks I-I'm g-going t-to m-make a-a s-successful d-debut." Her words came out as a series of sobs and hiccups. "B-but y-you s-saw m-me. I-I d-didn't e-even k-know w-what k-knife or s-spoon t-to u-use."

"How could you know?" he asked, his voice as calm and soothing as his hand on back. "When you've probably spent most of your life in a convent?" Kit pulled her back into his embrace and pressed his lips against her forehead. "How old were you when you went to live at St. Agnes's?"

"F-five."

"There. You see?" Kit whispered. "You went from the nursery to St. Agnes's. No one has ever taught you. You aren't to blame for that. They don't serve six course dinners in the nursery nor at St. Agnes's, I suspect."

She shook her head. "N-no."

"I thought you did quite well," he continued in his low, soothing baritone. "Very well. Extraordinarily well." He lifted her chin with the tip of his index finger and looked her in the eye. "You should have seen me the first time I was allowed to attend a dinner party. It was a disaster." He wrinkled his nose at her, then made a funny face. "I was all elbows and thumbs. No goblet was safe. My mother and my governess and later, my tutors, despaired that I would ever learn which knife and spoon went with which dish. But I eventually figured it out, although I do still forget to use my shrimp fork upon occasion."

"Y-you?"

"Me." He grinned at her. "And I have had the benefit of *years* of instruction, plus years spent peeking through the banisters, spying on my parents' dinner parties and country balls. You had no instruction whatsoever." He gently tapped the tip of her nose with his finger. "One slip of a soupspoon is nothing compared to my years of mealtime mayhem."

"I-I c-can't b-believe i-it."

"Believe it." Kit removed his handkerchief from his pocket and handed it to her. "The point is that I eventually learned everything I needed to know in order to be considered presentable in society. And while my mother and my governess and the tutors who followed my governess despaired that my table manners would ever improve, my father never doubted that I would become the sophisticated gentleman you see before you. He believed that I would live up to my potential, just as I believe you will live up to yours. A few lessons and you'll be ready to take London society by storm."

"I-I w-will?" She hiccupped.

"Of course, you will." Kit stared at her. Her eyes and

nose were red and swollen from crying and her flawless complexion was blotchy, but Kit was struck by the fact that she was incredibly lovely in spite of it. And that vulnerable look in her dark blue eyes made him want to protect her and keep her safe from harm. "Come on, now. Dry your eyes and blow your nose and tell me what has you in such a state." He leaned close. "Because I know that it would take more than a dropped soupspoon to upset the best baker and the loveliest woman in the parish."

"You think I'm pretty?" Mariah was clearly surprised.

Kit was as surprised as she was. Was it possible? Could a girl as lovely as Mariah Shaughnessy not know how beautiful she was? He stared into her eyes, and the words that tumbled out of his mouth were sudden, unguarded, and completely honest. "No," he whispered, leaning close, giving into the urge, touching his lips to hers. "I think you're beautiful."

His kiss was soft. A mere brush of his lips against hers. An exchange of breath, like the brush of a fairy's wing against her mouth. It was a light, reassuring kiss—one meant to assure her of her attractiveness, but it was in danger of blossoming into something more. Kit knew he should pull away and put distance between them, but he didn't. Instead of pulling away, Kit closed his eyes and allowed himself to luxuriate in kissing her.

Mariah's heart pounded in her chest. She gasped at the heat and the pleasure his kiss gave her. It wasn't her first kiss. Her first kiss had come from a boy named Kit when she was six. Lord Kilgannon's kiss wasn't her first one, but it was, without a doubt, her best. The pleasure was greater.

Mariah hesitated only a moment before she placed her arms around his neck. He kissed her again. Once. Twice. Nibbling at her lips, seeking permission to explore further. She granted it, parting her lips as he slipped his tongue through and began to taste the warm recesses of her mouth.

Heat surged through his body as Mariah moved closer.

Suddenly Kit was stretched out on the floor beside her, surrounding Mariah with his arms and his firm masculine body. She molded herself against him, enjoying the taste of his mouth, and the slight abrasion of his chin against the sensitive skin of her face, and the warm, citrus scent of oranges and male.

Kit groaned aloud. Mariah pulled away from him, gasping for breath. She was light-headed, giddy, and completely immersed in the sensations his kisses created. She opened her eyes and found herself staring up into Kit's brown ones. Mariah smiled at him, and Kit leaned down to plant a line of kisses from her forehead to her lips. "Mariah," he breathed. "Sweet, beautiful Mariah."

She closed her eyes once again and whispered his name. "Lord Kilgannon."

She called him by his title instead of his name, and her words acted like a splash of cold water in his face, instantly cooling his ardor. Kit was dismayed by his behavior. He'd meant to comfort her, not to seduce her and yet . . . In the few hours he'd known Mariah Shaughnessy, he'd conveniently managed to disregard a lifetime of gentlemanly manners and ethics. Kit broke off his kiss and reached up and gently unwrapped her arms from around his neck. He pushed himself to his feet before helping Mariah off the floor and onto the settee. "All better now?" he asked.

Mariah stared up at him, and Kit read the confusion in her eyes.

"Yes, of course." She pulled herself to her full height, straightening her back and stiffening her shoulders, draping herself in all the dignity she could muster. "Your kiss proved to be hugely medicinal, Lord Kilgannon. I've quite recovered now."

Kit tightened his jaw. "My apologies," he said. "My question was thoughtless and stupid, but I meant no offense by it."

"I was not offended by your question." She lifted her chin a notch higher.

Kit raised his brow in query. "You can't mean to tell me that you found my kiss offensive?"

She didn't answer.

"I know better." Kit snorted in disbelief at her stubbornness. "The exchange we just shared wasn't *my* first kiss."

"Nor mine," she retorted.

His eyebrow inched a bit higher. "Indeed?"

"Indeed." She dared him to challenge her.

"Forgive my ignorance," he said. "But I was under the impression that placing a girl in a convent generally prevents her from gaining the sort of carnal knowledge you claim to have." Kit smirked. "But I forget that you're betrothed. . . ."

"I've never even met the squire," Mariah protested. "Much less kissed him."

"If not the squire, with whom did you experiment?"

She wasn't going to tell Lord Kilgannon about Kit. She would simply make up a name and do penance later. "With a young man named—"

"Kit?" Dalton opened the door of the salon. "What the devil is keeping you? You said you were coming right back."

Lord Kilgannon turned to his friend. "I'll be right there."

"You said that three-quarters of an hour ago," Dalton complained.

"And three-quarters of an hour ago you and Ash were going to try out the billiard table," Kit said.

"We have tried it out," Dalton informed him. "I owe Ash a considerable amount already." He stepped inside the salon, then pulled up short when he saw Miss Shaughnessy. "Oh, I say, I do apologize for interrupting. I thought Miss Shaughnessy had already retired."

"It's all right." Kit waved Dalton away. "Miss Shaughnessy was just saying good night. Weren't you, Miss Shaughnessy?" He turned to look at his ward as Dalton withdrew from the salon and pulled the doors closed behind him.

Mariah's heart had leapt at the sound of his name. She could barely hear his question over the roaring in her head. He wasn't a figment of her imagination or a memory from long ago. He was real. A living, breathing, grown-up version of the boy who had given her her first kiss. And his kisses had improved with age. "Your name is Kit?"

Kit chuckled. "It's a pet name. My given name is Christopher. Christopher George, twenty-ninth earl of Ramsey and the twelfth earl of Kilgannon. Only my family and close friends call me Kit. Everyone else calls me by my title."

"What does your betrothed call you?" Mariah asked.

"I don't have a betrothed."

Her long-held hopes died a horrible death, and her heart seemed to shatter into a thousand pieces in the space of a sentence. "What about me?"

Mariah hadn't realized she'd spoken the words aloud until Kit replied, "As you are an unmarried woman and my ward, you should address me by my title."

"Even while you're kissing me?"

Kit had the grace to blush. "No. But I won't be kissing you again."

"Why not?" Mariah demanded. "Didn't you enjoy it?"

"Of course I enjoyed it," Kit answered. "But that is beside the point."

"It is exactly the point," Mariah told him.

"No," he said. "The point is that I am your guardian and you are my ward and you're betrothed to another man, at least for the moment." He cleared his throat and tried again. "The point is that I refuse to become the sort of low-minded gentleman who would take advantage of our current circumstances."

"What are our current circumstances?" she asked, in a low, throaty whisper raw with tears. "Because I was all of those things when you kissed me. The only thing that has changed is that I've learned your given name." Mariah stared into his eyes. "And the way you taste when you kiss."

Her words stabbed at him like a knife to the gut. She had accused him of being the hypocrite he was fast becoming, and Kit didn't want to be reminded of it. "I suggest you forget about that," Kit said firmly. "I intend to."

"You can try, *Kit*." With those last words Mariah turned and walked away.

Once again she managed to contain her tears. This time she made it as far as her bedchamber before she began to cry. Mariah threw herself upon the bed, buried her face in the pale green satin coverlet, and cried until she could cry no longer. But this time her tears were born of anger rather than anxiety and embarrassment.

She had lived on hope for nearly fifteen years. She had lived on the dream that one day Kit would come riding up to the gates of St. Agnes's and rescue her. In her dreams he had swept her up in his arms, placed her on his horse, and taken her to Telamor Castle, where they lived happily ever after. That dream and the memory of his promise had sustained her through the years of loneliness and hardship. Kit had been her savior. Her knight in shining armor. Her wonderful, magnificent dream.

But the truth was that the reality of Kit grown into manhood was so much better than her dreams. Nature had done what her imagination could not. It had formed sinew and muscles, lengthened and strengthened his body, deepened his voice, refined the lines of his face, and dusted his jaw with the shadow of a beard. He was taller, stronger, and more handsome than she had ever imagined he could be. And the way he made her feel when he kissed her had been the stuff of fairy tales for hundreds of years.

Mariah sat up and wiped the remnants of her tears away with the back of her hand. She jerked the feather pillow from beneath the satin spread, folded it in half, and punched it with her fist as hard as she could.

All those years at St. Agnes's, she had believed in his

impetuous promise to come back and marry her. For all those years she suffered Reverend Mother's punishments— the birchings with rod and ruler, scrubbing walls and floors, washing mounds of clothes and dishes, cooking, cleaning, ironing, weeding the garden—she had never doubted that the promise of discovering Kit waiting for her at the tower ruins was worth the pain and hard work. And she had never faltered, never revealed their secret. Because believing in Kit had been her only purpose in life.

Everything had been for Kit, for the promise he had made. She had become a baker of sweets—of cakes and biscuits, pastries and confections because she dared not eat them. All the years she was growing up, she still heard Kit's voice saying: *You'll get fat if you eat cake every night, and if you get fat eating cake, no prince will marry you.* She had repeated the sentiment at supper, but Kit hadn't recognized it as his own.

She had remembered and believed in him. He had been her secret. The only person in the world who belonged solely to her, and the only person in the world to whom she belonged. She had loved him with all the love she had to give. But Kit didn't love her. He didn't belong to her. And he didn't remember.

But he would, she promised herself. He would.

Chapter 13

Think in the morning. Act in the noon. Eat in the evening.
Sleep in the night.

—WILLIAM BLAKE, 1757–1827

Mariah entered the kitchen at half past four the following morning.

Ford looked up from his tea and toast. "You should not be here, miss."

"Why not?"

"Lord Kilgannon instructed that we were not to allow you access to the ovens." His answer was firm and unequivocal.

Mariah inhaled, lifted her chin a notch, and looked the butler in the eye. If she was going to learn to be a lady, she might as well get started. "Then whom, may I ask, is going to bake His Lordship's bread?"

Ford glanced at Cook.

Cook shook her had. "Oh, no, Mr. Ford. I know how to bake, of course, but Rory and I don't have the time now that we've guests in the house."

"We have bread every day," the butler pointed out.

"Of course we do, sir," Cook agreed. "But that is because we've been buying it from the convent for the past two years."

Cook's pronouncement was news to Mr. Ford. "Who authorized that?" he demanded.

"I did." The housekeeper, Mrs. Kearney, entered the kitchens, her ring of household keys jingling from the belt at her waist. "I am authorized to purchase household goods, and it was cheaper to buy the bread than to hire additional staff to help bake it."

"Has Sister Mary Lazarus delivered your order this morning?" Mariah asked.

Mrs. Kearney looked at Cook.

Cook shook her head. "She delivered a half dozen loaves and a letter from the Reverend Mother explaining that the convent had lost its chief baker and that they would be unable to provide bread for the castle until further notice." She took a folded slip of paper out of her apron pocket and handed it to the housekeeper, who in turn, handed it to Mr. Ford.

"I thought as much." Mariah made a clucking sound. "I wasn't the only baker at St. Agnes's. Sister Mary Joseph taught the three of us—Sister Mary Benedict, Sister Mary Lazarus and me—how to bake bread. But I showed the most talent for it. I assisted Sister Mary Joseph until I became proficient, then I took over the baking, and Sister Mary Benedict and Sister Mary Lazarus assisted me. My departure from the convent was rather abrupt, and Sister Mary Joseph is getting older, so I suppose it will take the sisters a day or two to get back on schedule."

Mrs. Kearney nodded. "That is exactly what the Reverend Mother said in her note." She turned to Ford. "I was just coming to consult with Cook about a change in the breakfast menu for this morning and to ask you if you think Lord Kilgannon's instructions regarding Miss Shaughnessy might be overlooked for one morning? We use a half a dozen loaves of bread for tea and toast for the staff each morning. That number won't begin to cover breakfast for His Lordship and his guests."

Ford debated, clearly divided between his loyalty to his new master and the efficient operation of the castle. He glanced at Mariah and hesitated. "I should go to the master with this. . . ."

"At this time of morning?" the housekeeper asked.

Ford frowned. Lord Kilgannon and his friends had still been engaged in conversation when His Lordship dismissed him at half past midnight. "He gave explicit instructions."

"That's true," Mariah said. "But at the time His Lordship did not realize his daily bread would not be forthcoming." She appealed to the butler. "I am an exceptional baker."

"You are a lady, miss," Ford protested. "His Lordship did not bring you here to work."

Mariah frowned. "I baked tarts the whole of yesterday."

"Without Lord Kilgannon's knowledge or permission. And when the master learned that you had labored in the kitchens all day in order to prepare the tarts served at supper last evening, he instructed that you not be allowed to do so in the future. He expressly stated that from now on, you should only engage in ladylike recreations such as painting, needlework, musical studies, charitable work, and the like."

"And there you have it, Mr. Ford." Mariah brightened. "My baking is charitable work."

Ford looked down his nose at her. "Lord Kilgannon is not a charity case."

"No, he's not," Mariah agreed. "But the castle does contribute baskets of food for the poor on Saints Days."

"Yes, indeed."

Mariah glanced up at the wooden perpetual calendar hanging on the side of the cupboard and struggled for the name of some obscure saint or a holiday. "Today is Saint Elizabeth's Day. I'm certain that it is celebrated somewhere, and since that is the case, I shall be baking bread for food hampers for the poor and for Lord Kilgannon's table."

Ford hesitated for a moment longer before asking, "If he asks, which Elizabeth are we remembering?"

Mariah took a deep breath. "Saint Elizabeth of Bohemia. Someplace exotic and far away from Ireland, Mr. Ford. I understand that Lord Kilgannon is Church of England. I doubt that he is intimately acquainted with all the Catholic Saints."

"Lord Kilgannon appears to be a most unusual and well-educated young man. He may be Church of England, but he may also be acquainted with the teachings of a variety of religions. He may question the veracity of our claim."

Mariah smiled at the butler. "We shall hope it doesn't come to that, but if it should come to pass, I suggest you invent a traditional celebration day for Telamor Castle."

"I beg your pardon, miss?" Ford was astounded.

"He can't know everything there is to know about Telamor Castle or its traditions. Lord Kilgannon surely won't be acquainted with every celebration day." She paused to tie on the apron Rory handed her. "I'm not suggesting that we necessarily deceive Lord Kilgannon. All I'm suggesting it that we find a credible reason to give hampers of food to the poor."

Ford thought for a moment. "I seem to recall hearing that years ago Telamor Castle celebrated the change of the guard from one earl to another with tithes and gifts of food baskets for the poor. We shall take it upon ourselves to reinstate the tradition to honor the new Lord Kilgannon."

"Truly?" Mariah was surprised.

"Yes, miss." Ford, Mrs. Kearney, Cook, and Rory all nodded their heads.

"Very well, then," Mariah pronounced. "I've a lot of charitable work to do before seven o'clock mass." She rolled up her sleeves, washed her hands, and began assembling the ingredients she would need to bake two dozen loaves of yeast bread and a double batch of soda bread.

"Very good, miss," Ford capitulated. "Mrs. Kearney and I shall see that the food hampers are made ready with gift of preserves, butter, clotted cream, soup, and sausages."

"Thank you, Mr. Ford," Mariah said.

"Not Mr. Ford, miss," he corrected. "Just Ford. And you needn't worry about meeting His Lordship for seven o'clock mass. No one in the peerage goes to early mass."

She lifted the large wooden bread bowl from the shelf, then turned and favored the butler with a warm smile. "What time shall I be ready Mr.—I mean—Ford? When do the lords and ladies go to mass?"

"No earlier than nine, miss. And most don't bother to go before eleven. But Lord Kilgannon instructed me to see that you were awakened in time to prepare for nine o'clock mass."

"But that means they must lie abed until seven or eight o'clock in the morning."

Ford fought to keep from smiling. "Or later, miss."

"Really?" Mariah was astounded. "I've never heard of such indulgence."

"Members of the peerage keep late hours, miss."

"How late?" She kept late hours herself, compared to the other residents of St. Agnes's, most of whom went to bed with the chickens, but keeping later hours was essential when one sneaked out in order to gaze at the stars from the ruins of the tower.

"His Lordship and his friends were wide awake when I retired at half past midnight this morning." Ford told her. "In London, supper parties generally begin at nine in the evening so supper can be served at midnight. So it's quite common for those of the peerage to sleep until noon."

"No one at St. Agnes's misses seven o'clock mass," she said. "Unless one is ill. And even then, Reverend Mother always insists that it is best to get up and move about because the Lord frowns upon the lazy."

"I'm not so sure about that, miss," Mrs. Kearney said. "I don't doubt that the Reverend Mother believes what she says, but it does seem strange to me that the poor and those of us in service and in trade get up early and work hard, while the wealthy lie abed. If the Lord is frowning upon them, I wish that he would frown upon me."

Mariah laughed. "It does seem to be quite turned around, doesn't it? But I don't mind as long as it gives me more time to attend to my charity work." She turned to the butler. "And if it is just the same to you, Ford, I see no reason why His Lordship has to know anything about this—unless he asks directly."

"Quite so, miss." With that, Ford bowed slightly and left the kitchen in order to procure the food hampers.

"Thank you for helping out, miss," the housekeeper said when Ford left the room.

"It's my pleasure, Mrs. Kearney," Mariah replied. "In truth, I dread giving it up." She looked at the housekeeper. "For I truly enjoy baking."

"It's a good thing, too," Mrs. Kearney said. "For you'll be doing plenty of it today."

"Please stop me in time to meet Lord Kilgannon for mass."

"Not to worry, miss, we'll have you out of here in plenty of time."

Chapter 14

Nothing is good or bad but by Comparison.

—THOMAS FULLER, 1654–1734

Mrs. Kearney was as good as her word.

Mariah was dressed in her best black dress and seated at the breakfast room table sipping a cup of tea when Kit came downstairs at a quarter past eight for breakfast.

"You're prompt," Kit said. "I appreciate that quality in a lady."

"I have many qualities for you to appreciate, Lord Kilgannon." The look and the smile she gave him was every bit as mysterious as the one on da Vinci's *Mona Lisa.*

Kit was a bit taken aback. "I trust you've recovered from your bout of nerves."

"Quite recovered. Thank you."

She spoke the truth. He studied her closely looking for the telltale traces of a night spent crying, but other than a slight redness around the rim of her eyes, there was no sign of any tears. He tried again. "And I trust you slept well."

"The clear of conscience always sleep well," she answered. "And you?"

Kit frowned. She had an edge to her this morning that he wasn't certain he deserved after the way he had tried to comfort her last night. But Kit had a mother and two sisters, and he recognized the fact that, despite her protest to the contrary, she was not over her bout of nerves at all. "Quite well. Thank you for asking."

Mariah took a sip of tea and watched as he poured himself a cup from the urn on the sideboard, then sat down at the table. Ford appeared at his elbow almost instantly, and Mariah found herself awed by the fact that the butler could move so quickly and so quietly.

"Breakfast, sir?"

Kit shook his head. "It's too early for me. Toast and tea will do."

"As you wish, my lord." Ford walked to the sideboard and returned with a rack of freshly toasted bread and a condiment tray containing a selection of preserves, jams, and marmalades.

"Will your friends be joining you this morning, sir?" he asked.

"No." Kit lifted his cup of tea and drank from it. "Lord Everleigh and Mr. Mirrant have elected to remain in bed this morning. I'll join them for a full breakfast after church."

Mariah studied him covertly, noting the red streaks in his eyes, the shadows beneath his eyes, the tiny cut on his chin, and the raw scrape along his jaw. "Late night?" she asked sweetly. Too sweetly.

Refusing to be baited, Kit looked over at her and answered, "Very late." He unfolded the freshly ironed *Dubliner* Ford handed him, then remembered his manners and glanced at Mariah. "I generally read the newspaper at breakfast. Have you any objection?"

"I am your ward, Your Lordship, not your wife. It is not my place to object to any of your habits."

Kit looked over the top of the newspaper at her. "Or to comment on them, I hope."

Mariah bit her cheek to keep from smiling at his wit. Reaching for the small pot of tea sitting on the table, she lifted it from the warmer and refilled her cup. "More tea?"

He extended a delicate Wedgwood cup and saucer.

Mariah poured tea into the cup.

Kit sniffed at it. "What kind of tea is this?"

"Herb," she answered.

"You drink first," he ordered. "I want to make certain it isn't hemlock."

Mariah sipped her tea. "You think I would poison you, my lord?"

"Maybe." Kit gave the liquid in his cup another suspicious sniff. "Otherwise, why drink this stuff when there's good tea in the house?"

"Because this one soothes away the headache. Regular tea does not."

He drank the herb tea, shuddering at the taste, before offering his cup to her to refill. "In that case, I need a gallon of the stuff before we go to church."

"Don't you like church?" she asked.

"Certainly," he answered. "I have no quibbles with church. It's the sermons I find so tiresome." He laid the newspaper aside and gave her his complete attention. "And I would think that after growing up in a convent, you would find them even more so."

"I enjoy the pageantry of mass," she answered honestly. "The words and language, the incense, and the music. I even enjoy Father Francis's sermons."

"You must be joking."

She shook her head. "It's the Reverend Mother's sermons that I find tiresome. There isn't a single one I haven't heard at least twice. It seemed that I was always in trouble."

"That sharp tongue of yours, no doubt."

"Sometimes," she admitted. "But mostly I was punished for having a strong will. You can't imagine how many rosaries I've prayed over the years or how many floors I've scrubbed and windows I've washed or how many masses I had to attend in order to atone for my transgressions."

Kit leaned toward her. "You don't have to worry about that any longer. No one is going to force you to attend church if you don't want to go."

"I've gone to church all my life," she said. "I don't think I would feel right about not going. I admit there are times when I'd like to be lazy and lie abed in the mornings, but the teachings and habits of a lifetime aren't as easy to forget as one might expect."

Kit thought about the night before. He'd forgotten a lifetime of gentlemanly behavior in a matter of seconds. He'd willingly discarded his ethics for the opportunity to kiss his ward. And, despite his promise to the contrary, he knew that if he didn't keep a safe distance, it would happen again. Thousands of battles of good against evil were fought each day in men's consciences. And he shuddered to think how many surrendered as easily as he had. "It's not as difficult as you think," he told her. "People give in to temptation every day. Take your baking . . ."

Mariah steeled herself for what was to come.

"Many people find the sweets you bake a temptation too great to resist. But I'm not one of them. I am more tempted by—" He had almost admitted that he was more tempted by the baker than the baked goods, but he caught himself in time. "Other things."

"What things?" Mariah whispered.

Kit stared at her mouth. Her lips were a rosy color, soft and as sweet as . . . "Cherries."

"Cherries, my lord?"

"Cherries, pears, apples, oranges. Fruit," he answered, feeling very foolish for allowing his thoughts to escape his lips. "I find fruit infinitely more tempting than pastries."

"Adam was tempted by fruit," Mariah reminded him.

Kit inhaled. "And he paid dearly for it."

"Then I suppose the question is not whether a man is tempted," Mariah said. "But whether or not he is willing to pay the price for surrendering to that temptation."

"It depends upon the temptation." He couldn't stop staring at her. "And the man."

"A man may choose to resist the temptation of pastries because he's not willing to pay the price of a double chin." Mariah fixed her gaze on Kit's strong chin and firm jaw. "But he may willingly succumb to the temptation of drink and the aching head that follows it."

"If his weakness for strong drink exceeds his weakness for strawberry tarts," Kit finished the thought. "But either weakness will tell on him in the end. And every man is tempted by something. The only way to keep from succumbing to temptation is to avoid it."

"Are you good at it?"

Kit blinked.

"Are you good at avoiding temptation, Lord Kilgannon?"

"Not as good as I would like to be."

Mariah gave him a knowing smile. "Neither am I."

"Then we mustn't be late for church." Kit picked up the silver bell on the table and rang for Ford. "Have the carriage sent around straightaway."

"Very good, sir." Ford bowed. "It will be waiting at the front door as soon as we finish loading the hampers."

"What hampers?" Kit asked.

"Food hampers for the poor," Ford elaborated. "It's tradition for the new master of Telamor Castle to present his annual tithe and food hampers for the poor on his first day at church."

"I thought that was Easter," Kit said.

"I believe you're correct, sir," Ford agreed. "In England. Here at Telamor, we observe the tradition at Easter and Saint Elizabeth's Day."

"I'm to pay annual tithes twice?"

"You do hold two titles, sir," Ford took a deep breath. "But it is perfectly acceptable for you to make one offering and pay half at Easter and half on Saint Elizabeth's Day."

"Since I wasn't in residence at Easter, I'll pay them today." He stood up. "Thank you, Ford, for reminding me of my duty and for preparing the food hampers."

"You are quite welcome, sir, but I cannot take credit for the reminder or the food hampers. It has been so long since we had a master in residence that I had forgotten all about the Saint Elizabeth's Day observance until I heard Miss Mariah remark upon the date."

Kit turned to Mariah. "How did you know of the tradition at Telamor?"

Mariah started to form a reply when Ford leaped to her rescue. "Most likely from her mother. You see, sir, Miss Shaughnessy's mother grew up here."

"In Inismorn?" Kit asked.

"At Telamor, my lord."

Kit gripped the back of his chair for support. "I was under the impression that my relative, the late earl, lived here with his only child."

"Oh, no, sir," Ford answered. "There were two."

"Two?" Kit repeated.

"Two young ladies, sir. Lady Siobhan grew up with your mother. They were inseparable."

The hair at the back of Kit's neck stood on end. He had never heard his mother mention Lady Siobhan. Never recalled hearing her name spoken, but his mother didn't talk much about her past. Kit knew that she had been married before she met his father and that both her father and first husband had been renowned naturalists. But her father had died while Kit was an infant, and she had never made mention of the fact that her father held an Irish title—that he had been the earl of Kilgannon. And neither did she say that Telamor Castle had been her childhood home, even when he learned he had inherited it. As far as Kit knew, the trip to Telamor eight years prior had been his mother's first and only visit—and it had only come at Martin Bell's suggestion.

He also knew about the rumors. Ugly rumors, and Kit had heard them all. His parents had tried to protect him, but there was no way they could keep him from hearing what was said about them or the speculation surrounding his birth. He had heard that he had been fathered by the fifteenth marquess, and then there were the rumors that his mother wasn't really his mother and that he hadn't been born a Ramsey at all. Kit knew that his father had been the fifteenth marquess, but he didn't care which marquess had fathered him, because Drew Ramsey, the sixteenth marquess of Templeston, was the only father he remembered.

But the other rumor was a different matter. The other rumor was unthinkable. To suggest that neither of his parents were really his parents meant that his whole life had been a lie. . . .

Kit refused to believe it. His mother had simply never mentioned her close friend. But then, he had never heard his mother mention friends or relatives in Ireland, and except for a few weeks the summer of his eighth year, they had never visited Telamor Castle again.

Kit looked from the butler to Mariah. "My mother doesn't speak of her past very often, so I was unaware of her close relationship to your mother or the traditional observance of Saint Elizabeth's Day. Thank you for remembering and seeing that the food hampers were prepared."

"I was happy to attend to it, sir." Mariah gave him a breathtaking smile. "I have yet to gain the necessary training to become a lady, but I am familiar with some of their responsibilities, and I believe charity work is one of them."

He released his grip on the chair. "I'll need to get some money from the safe before we leave." He started toward the door. "And since I assume your chaperone is breaking her fast in her bedchamber, you'll need to collect her for church."

"Sister Mary Beatrix has already been to church."

Kit frowned. "When?"

"At seven this morning," Mariah answered, "with the rest of the residents of St. Agnes's."

"But she will be driving into the village with us." He had meant it as a statement, but Mariah shook her head.

"What the devil is the use of having a chaperone if she never attends to her duty?" Kit demanded.

Ford cleared his throat. "Strictly speaking, sir, it wouldn't be proper for Miss Mariah to ride in a carriage with a man, but as you are going to church and since you are her legal guardian, it is permissible."

"Are you in mourning for someone, Miss Shaughnessy?" Kit asked.

"No, sir. Why do you ask?"

"You're wearing black again this morning. I thought, perhaps, you were in mourning. You told me when I asked last evening that you owned two other dresses. I expected something other than black for church."

She glanced down at her skirts. "All the girls at St. Agnes's wear black."

"You're not at St. Agnes's any longer," Kit stated.

"Nor am I able to fashion a new dress overnight," was Mariah's waspish response. "Black or any other color."

"Then the seamstress will be the first order of business."

Ford cleared his throat again. "May I say, sir, that I've already taken the liberty of sending for the seamstress? She will be here when you and Miss Mariah return from services."

"My prayers have been answered already." Kit breathed a sigh of thanks.

"I've also taken the liberty of posting discreet notices for a music teacher and a dance master so that Miss Mariah's lessons might begin tomorrow as scheduled."

"Thank you," Kit reached for his teacup and grimaced as he took a swallow. He glanced at Mariah and saw that she was frowning. "What's the matter?"

Mariah sighed. "I was looking forward to a trip to the dressmaker's shop."

"I wasn't."

"Yes, well, you've probably been to one before." She paused momentarily. "With your *mistress*."

Kit would have had to be a fool or a slow-witted dunce to miss such an obvious ploy. "I don't have a *mistress*—at the moment. And if I did, it would be most ungentlemanly of me to discuss her with you over breakfast." He would also have to be a fool or a slow-witted dunce to miss

Mariah's sigh of relief. He was neither. "But it has been my excruciating duty to escort my mother and my sisters to their dressmaker's on occasion where I was required to sit for long periods of time sipping tea and offering opinions and advice on colors and styles while assistants paraded bolt after bolt of cloth and trim and trinkets."

"It sounds wonderful!"

"Believe me," Kit said dryly, "it isn't."

"That's your opinion," Mariah retorted. "And you're a man. I'd like to see it all for myself, and now I won't get to."

"Don't be disappointed, miss. I'll see that Madame Thierry brings her assistants and everything she needs to the castle." He turned to Kit. "If there's no objection, she can set up shop here at the castle until Miss Mariah completes her wardrobe selections. It will be much more comfortable for the master to view the proceedings at home rather than in the close confines of a shop filled with feminine frills. And," Ford added, "it's much more impressive to send for the woman rather than have to wait for service."

Kit nodded his consent. "Very good, Ford. Make the arrangements and have the carriage waiting at the front door when I return. And have someone saddle my mount and tie him to the back of the vehicle. I may be delayed in town, but there's no reason for Miss Shaughnessy to miss her appointment with the seamstress. I won't be a minute," Kit promised as he left the room on his way to his study.

"Good," Mariah announced, almost bouncing up and down on her chair with excitement, willing to take her penance with a smile. For the seamstress would come afterward. "Because I don't want to wait a minute longer."

Chapter 15

'Tis a sad but true fact of life that oftentimes the most stirring of sermons pales in comparison to the excitement brought about by the purchase of a new frock.

—FATHER FRANCIS O'MEARA, 1778–1861

"*Bless me, Father, for I have sinned.*"

"Again?" The question was out before Father Francis could stop it.

"It's been one day since my last confession. . . ."

Father Francis didn't even pretend not to know who was on the other side of the confessional. "My child, what horrible sins have you committed since yesterday?" The moment he asked the question, the priest held his breath, remembering that Mariah no longer lived in the sheltered safety of the convent, but was a young woman living in a household headed by a very virile young man. An honorable young man. But a young man nonetheless with two equally virile young friends in residence.

"I impersonated the Holy Father in Rome."

Father Francis smothered a chuckle and began to cough. If the truth were told, he always looked forward to Mariah's visits to the confessional. Her transgressions were always minor and her confessions so entertaining. "I beg your pardon?"

"I did what only the Holy Father and the cardinals in Rome are allowed to do." She paused. "I created a saint and a saint's day, and I talked the household staff into going along with the lie, and worse yet, I encouraged them to lie to His Lordship, to tell him that it was tradition for the lady of the manor, along with the housekeeper and cook, to prepare food hampers for the poor."

Unable to contain his curiosity, Father Francis asked, "What saint have you created?"

"Saint Elizabeth of Bohemia."

Father Francis nodded. "And your reason for canonizing this new Saint Elizabeth?"

"It all started with the strawberry tarts. You see, Father, my guardian objected to my laboring in the kitchens all day." She paused. "Did you know that ladies aren't supposed to cook?"

"Yes, I've heard that," the priest murmured.

She sighed. "Well, nobody has ever said anything to me about baking not being ladylike." Warming to her subject, Mariah continued, "Ladies don't cook—even if they know how—because they have cooks and kitchen staffs to do it for them, but what happens if a family should suffer a reversal of fortune and can no longer afford a kitchen staff? Who cooks the food the family eats? I'm not complaining, Father. I realize that my guardian is charged with the responsibility of schooling me in the ways of society so that I may take my place among the ladies there. But, honestly, Father, I see no harm in baking."

"But your guardian does."

"Yes," she said. "He told the staff that I was not allowed to cook. But, you see, Father, I knew that unless I was allowed to bake, His Lordship, his guests, and the staff would be denied their daily bread."

"How did you know?"

"Because Telamor Castle buys bread from the convent, and until I left the convent two nights ago, I was the head baker at the convent. And I thought it unlikely that the convent would be able to fill all of its bread orders until Sister Mary Benedict or Sister Mary Lazarus were able to take my place."

"Ah," Father Francis said. "So you found yourself on

the horns of a moral dilemma. To go against your guardian's wishes and bake or to honor your guardian's wishes and allow the household to do without bread."

"Exactly. So I created Saint Elizabeth of Bohemia and made today Saint Elizabeth's Day. Because, you see, Father, as it turns out, charity work is one of a lady's duties. I could bake bread to go into the food hampers for the poor and still be a lady, and if I were baking bread for charity food hampers, I might as well bake extra loaves for Lord Kilgannon's table. For when it comes to baking bread, it's just as easy to bake two or three dozen loaves as it is to bake one. Then I talked the staff into supporting me in the lie so His Lordship wouldn't be angry at me for baking or at them for allowing me to."

"So you did the wrong thing for the right reason," Father Francis summed up the situation in one sentence.

"I'm afraid so," Mariah admitted.

"You have been busy," Father Francis said at last.

"Very busy," she echoed. "And the worst of it was that not only did the staff support me in the creation of Saint Elizabeth's Day, but they chose to add a few details to the story."

"What kind of details?" the priest asked.

"One of the staff members, and I'll not be saying who, suggested that it's tradition for the master of Telamor Castle to pay annual tithes on Saint Elizabeth's Day, and Lord Kilgannon has come to church today prepared to pay annual tithes for two titles and to distribute food hampers to the poor."

"That's the problem with lies," Father Francis said in his sternest tone of voice. "Lying, even for the best reasons, is a serious offense. I'm afraid I can't be as lenient with this list of transgressions as I was with the last one. You lied and you induced the servants to lie. And for that you must do penance."

Mariah bowed her head. "Yes, Father. Three Hail Marys and three Our Fathers?"

Father Francis shook his head. "Since the currency of

your transgression is in loaves of bread, I think it only right and just that you pray a baker's dozen Hail Marys and a baker's dozen Our Fathers."

Mariah groaned, but did not complain aloud. "Yes, Father."

"Have you any more sins to confess?"

"No, Father, but please, don't tell Lord Kilgannon that there is no Saint Elizabeth's Day. I don't want him to feel as if he's been duped."

"But, my child, he has been duped. The master of Telamor Castle only pays half his tithes on Saint Elizabeth of Bohemia's Day. The rest are paid on All Saints' Day."

"Thank you, Father!"

"You're welcome, my child. Now, go and sin no more."

"*Father Francis, might I have a few words* with you?" Kit waited until the priest said good-bye to his last parishioner—a short, rather rotund woman in a blue dress that had obviously been sewn when the woman was several stones lighter.

"Of course." Father Francis lifted the hem of his cassock and hurried across the churchyard to where Lord Kilgannon waited on a stone bench near the walled entrance to the cemetery. He greeted the young lord with a smile, then glanced around for Mariah. "Are you alone?"

Kit nodded. "I sent Miss Shaughnessy on ahead to the castle. She has an appointment with the seamstress this afternoon, and she was so excited by the prospect of a new wardrobe that she could barely sit still during mass." Kit looked over at the priest. "No offense, Father."

"None taken." Father Francis smiled. " 'Tis a sad but true fact of life that oftentimes the most stirring of sermons pales in comparison to the excitement brought about by the purchase of a new frock."

Kit chuckled.

"And Mariah deserves a few new dresses." He looked over at Kit. "It will do my heart good to see her in something besides black. Buy her something in blue. There are enough of us going about dressed as ravens without forcing the innocent in our care to do the same."

"Miss Shaughnessy and I delivered food hampers for the poor to the rectory. Your housekeeper, Mrs. Flynn, was surprised by the hampers and even more surprised to learn it was Saint Elizabeth of Bohemia's Day."

The priest blushed. "Yes, well, Saint Elizabeth of Bohemia is one of our lesser-known saints."

"I'd venture to guess that she isn't known at all, but that would only be my opinion." He smiled at the priest. "Your housekeeper suggested I pay the tithe money I owe directly to you." Kit pulled out a bag of heavy coins. "My father always pays in gentleman's coin. I did likewise. I hope you don't mind the guineas."

"Not at all." Father Francis pretended to be surprised. "There have been so many Saint Elizabeth's Days since we had a master at Telamor Castle, I'd forgotten about the tradition."

"I'm not surprised," Kit said. "The tradition must be at least as obscure as the saint who inspired it. But all that matters is that Miss Shaughnessy remembered and reminded the staff about the food hampers. And we were fortunate that she was willing to spend the morning baking fresh loaves of bread." He gave Father Francis a knowing look. "The tithes were Ford's idea." Kit offered the priest the bag of money and a place beside him on the stone bench.

"Under the circumstances, I don't believe I can accept so large a donation."

"Under the circumstances, I don't believe you should refuse it." Kit shrugged. "I have to pay my tithes, and Saint Elizabeth of Bohemia's Day is as good a day as any. Take it. I can afford it and it's for a good cause."

"For the poor." Father Francis accepted the tithes, but refused the seat on the bench. He slipped the heavy bag of coins in the pocket of his cassock.

"Yes, well, that, too." Kit grinned. "But I was thinking

more in terms of it giving Miss Shaughnessy a reason to disobey my instructions and bake."

Father Francis raised an eyebrow in query.

"The scent of freshly baked bread lingers in her hair."

"You noticed?"

"I never knew the smell of freshly baked bread could be so enticing."

Father Francis gave Kit a mighty frown. "I don't sell indulgences for past, present, or future sins." He patted his pocket, making the heavy coins clink together.

"That's good to know," Kit answered. "Because I'm not in the market for them."

"As long as we understand each other," the priest said. "Because Mariah is . . . I've known her most of her life, and Mariah is special. . . ."

"You said you attended her mother. . . ."

Father Francis sighed. "I suppose it would be more correct to say that the good sisters at St. Agnes's attended her. But I heard her last confession and administered last rites."

"Was she ill a long time?"

Father Francis scanned the churchyard, then stood up. "Why don't we walk as we talk?"

Kit stood up and the two of them began a stroll through the graveyard.

"Mariah's mother wasn't ill," the priest announced when he and Kit were well out of earshot of the handful of people paying tribute to their loved ones buried in the cemetery. "She was found on the rocks below the ruins of the old tower."

Kit shuddered at the thought. "What happened? Did she trip on the path and fall to her death?" He recalled the narrow path running parallel to the beach above the cliffs. It was slippery in places, but Kit didn't remember it as being particularly treacherous.

"That's what the people of Inismorn think, but Lady Siobhan didn't stumble on the path and fall to her death. She was pushed."

"Are you certain she was pushed?"

"In order to land upon the rocks, she had to be pushed from the path or from the tower," Father Francis said. "If she had slipped on the path, she could have easily saved herself. It's relatively simple to climb down from the path to the beach and back up again. There are dozens of hand and footholds."

"It is possible that she jumped?"

"Never!" Father Francis was adamant. "She was in tremendous pain when we got to her, drifting in and out of consciousness, but she said she was pushed and I believed her. Lady Siobhan would never have willingly abandoned Mariah." He shook his head at the memory of that horrible day. "No, Lady Siobhan was murdered. But, of course, the sisters at the convent and I are the only ones who know it. And Mariah."

"Mariah?" Kit recoiled at the thought.

"Aye. She doesn't remember it, of course. But she saw what happened. Mariah had just started as a day student at St. Agnes's, and every day her mother would walk her to the convent for her lessons, then meet her when they ended. On that day the sister released her from lessons earlier than usual. Mariah waited for her mother for a while, then started home alone. It was spring and clumps of wildflowers were growing along the path. Mariah apparently busied herself along the way by stopping to pick flowers for her mother. But she reached the top of the path at the foot of the ruins in time to see her mother shoved to her death. She couldn't tell us who it was. Nor could she describe him . . ."

"It was a man?"

The priest nodded. "Both Lady Siobhan and Mariah referred to a man. They said he pushed her. But Mariah couldn't say who it was. Poor babe. She was only five at the time. It broke my heart the way she babbled about the bluebells she'd picked while she cried for her mother and for her da."

"Mariah saw him?"

"Yes. Of course, the sisters and I are the only ones who know that. Even Mariah has forgotten. Thank God." He paused in their walk to lean down and replace a bouquet of roses that had blown off a nearby grave. "She used to cry in her sleep and suffer terrible nightmares. The sisters said she woke up at night screaming for her mother and her father. But that passed with time, and she appears to have no memory of it."

"Did you ever discover why someone wanted Lady Siobhan dead badly enough to kill her?"

"No," the priest answered. "There was nothing unusual in her will. It was essentially the same as the one her husband left. In his will, Declan Shaughnessy left everything to his wife, Siobhan, in trust for Mariah. Lady Siobhan sold their house in London, and she and Mariah returned to Ireland, where, according to the old earl's instructions, they were able to live off a comfortable income at Telamor while the bulk of the fortune remained in trust. And if anything happened to Lady Siobhan, Mariah became the earl of Kilgannon's ward."

"So why didn't Mariah grow up at the castle instead of the convent?"

"The old earl was dead, and as far as anyone knew the title was dormant. Martin Bell, your father, Ford, and I were the only people privy to the fact that you had inherited."

"What about Lady Siobhan?"

"At the time of the old earl's death, Lady Siobhan was happily married and living in London, but Lord Kilgannon left instructions with Ford and with me, informing us that should Lady Siobhan ever wish to return to Ireland, she should be allowed to reside at Telamor if she desired to do so until you reached your majority. After that, the decision was up to you, although he asked that we try to persuade you to allow it if you were opposed to the idea. I wrote to Mr. Bell and to your father to tell them of the late earl's request. . . ."

"You mean my father, Andrew Ramsey, the sixteenth marquess?"

"No," Father Francis said. "I mean the fifteenth one. George Ramsey."

Kit glanced down at the ground. He knew George Ramsey, the fifteenth marquess of Templeston, was his sire. His and Drew's. But the fact remained that Kit hated hearing it spoken aloud. He hated to think that his mother and the fifteenth marquess had ever been intimate. And suddenly he wondered how Drew felt about it. . . .

Father Francis realized suddenly that Kit's interruption had nothing to do with a clarification of which marquess was which, and everything to do with the fact that the young Lord Kilgannon didn't want to acknowledge George Ramsey as his father. He waited for Kit to respond, and when he didn't, the priest resumed his story. "Martin Bell and I met to discuss the old earl's instructions, and of course, George agreed to the request. As I said before, George was always a chivalrous sort of fellow. He would not—could not—refuse to help a lady in need."

"Did Mariah's mother know I was to inherit?"

"No. Only Ford, Mr. Bell, George, and I knew that."

"There must have been something her killer wanted, something he was willing to kill for," Kit mused. "But what?" He turned to the priest. "You and the sisters at St. Agnes's aren't the only ones who know that Lady Siobhan Shaughnessy was murdered."

"That's true," Father Francis said. "Mariah knows. But she has no memory of it."

"There is one other person besides Mariah who knows," Kit replied.

"Who?" The priest asked.

"The man who shoved Lady Siobhan off the path and onto the rocks."

Father Francis's eyes widened in shock. Gasping for breath, he clutched at his heart and grabbed a handful of fabric. For a moment Kit feared the priest had suffered an apoplectic seizure.

"Holy Mary, Mother of God," Father Francis whispered, not as a curse, but as a profound prayer. "I never considered that. Do you think ... Surely, he's long gone. ..." He frowned.

Kit shrugged his shoulders. "It depends on what he wanted and whether or not he got it."

"I pray God that he did."

"So do I." Kit found the idea of a serpent in his newly found Eden most unsettling, and the idea of that serpent striking out at Mariah Shaughnessy was too terrible to contemplate. He had promised her a London season, and he'd promised to teach her the things she'd need to know in order to succeed. The last thing Kit needed was to inadvertently invite an unknown killer into their midst. "How did Lady Siobhan come to be the late earl's ward? Did she have any family or friends other than my mother?"

"No family," Father Francis answered. "She was orphaned quite young when a fire swept through a hotel in which her parents, her younger brothers and sisters, and their retinue of nurses and governess were staying while traveling on the Continent. In the Black Forest of Germany, I believe it was. Lady Siobhan was spared because she was here at school at St. Agnes. Knowing that she and your mother were already inseparable, Lord Kilgannon took her in and became her legal guardian. She became his other daughter," Father Francis answered. "She grew up, married, went to live in London, was widowed, and returned to Ireland."

"What about friends? Acquaintances?" Kit asked.

"Oh, there were lots of friends and acquaintances," the priest told him. "Here and in London."

Kit groaned. "Anyone special? Anyone suspicious? Anyone who visited her at the castle, then disappeared after her death?"

The priest heaved a frustrated sigh. "Everyone stopped visiting after her death. Except for an occasional visit by the bishop and the archbishop in Dublin, and the visit you and your family made to Ireland when you were a boy, the castle was closed to all but me and the staff that remained as caretakers."

"There has to be some connection. Some reason for an

otherwise senseless death." Kit frowned, wondering if he should broach the subject of his past.

It was getting close to noon. The sun had disappeared behind the clouds and the wind began to blow. Kit glanced off into the distance toward the sea. Dark clouds hovered on the horizon. A sudden squall had erupted a few miles off the coast. On a day such as this, on the coast not far from here, nineteen years ago, George Ramsey, the fifteenth marquess of Templeston, had gone sailing with his latest mistress and never returned. Their bodies had washed ashore miles away from the port from which they'd sailed, and Drew had suddenly become the sixteenth marquess of Templeston.

"Lord Kilgannon?"

Kit turned his gaze away from the distant storm and focused his attention on the priest beside him. Father Francis's question had given him the opening he needed to probe deeper. "I was thinking about my fath— about the fifteenth Lord Templeston."

Father Francis nodded in understanding. "I heard that he and his companion sailed off on a beautiful day and ran into a ferocious squall, not unlike the one brewing out there." He followed Kit's earlier gaze and watched as the clouds darkened and spread. "They were swept overboard by the swells cresting over the side and drowned at sea. Such a tragedy. Such a loss for you and for your family. Come," he added, pointing to the wheel tracks that encircled the burial ground. The furrows, made by the heavy carts and wagons that brought the dead to their final resting place for centuries, were spaced wide enough apart for two men to walk abreast, and the soft heath that grew in between the furrows made an ideal walking path. "We've time for another round."

They walked in silence for a few moments before Kit inhaled deeply, slowly exhaled, and plunged into the topic weighing heavily on his mind. "So Mariah Shaughnessy's mother grew up with my mother at the castle."

"That she did," Father Francis confirmed. "She wasn't born at the castle. Or in Ireland. But that wasn't unusual.

You see, the late Earl Kilgannon didn't return to Ireland to live in the castle year-around until after his wife died. In the old days Lord and Lady Kilgannon kept a town house in London, another in Paris, and an estate in Normandy."

"Normandy?"

"Yes," the Father answered. "The late countess was French, you know."

"No, I didn't know." Kit frowned. There seemed to be a great deal he didn't know about his Irish inheritance or his long-deceased relatives. Kit had never heard his mother mention her mother being French or that she'd spent her girlhood traversing the Continent. Perhaps he'd misunderstood. It was possible that his mother wasn't the earl's daughter at all. . . . But then how to explain his inheritance?

"Well, I can't say as I blamed them for spending so much time away from Ireland. If my family had been able to leave, I'm sure we would have, too. The English made it very hard for us to remain true to our church. It was easier to be Catholic in France or even London than it was to be Catholic here in Ireland. When the countess died in Paris, the earl returned to Ireland with the girls. I don't remember exactly how old the girls were, but they must have been nine and eleven."

"Ford said there were only two girls," Kit probed.

"That's right."

"My mother and the earl's ward."

"That's right. Lady Siobhan and Lady Alanna."

"Lady Alanna?" The hairs on the back of Kit's neck were standing on end once again.

"Lady Alanna Caitria Frances Kilgannon Farrington," Father Francis said softly. "Your mother."

Kit gasped, turned white, then moved as far away from the priest as he could without falling over a headstone. "You are mistaken. My mother's name is Kathryn."

"The mother you've always known and loved is named Kathryn. But the mother who died shortly after giving you life was Lady Alanna Caitria Frances Kilgannon. I baptized

her when she was born, and I administered her last rites."
Father Francis reached out to touch Kit on the arm. "She
was a beautiful girl with long brown hair and brown eyes.
You look very much like her. Your eyes are the same shade
of brown. She wasn't much older than you are now."

"No."

"She's buried over there." Father Francis pointed to an
elaborately carved stone mausoleum that dominated the
graveyard. "In the Kilgannon family crypt along with her
father, grandparents, and great-grandparents. The countess
is buried at the estate in Normandy, but Lady Siobhan
Shaughnessy and her husband, Declan Shaughnessy, are
buried in the crypt as well as the Kilgannon infants who
died over the years. I'll wait outside if you'd like to pay
your respects. The iron gate is locked, but the key to it is
on the ring I gave you yesterday."

"I'll pay my respects to my family when I visit them
at Swanslea Park," Kit said coldly. "When last I saw
them, my mother and father and my two sisters were very
much alive and well." Turning on his heel, Kit left the
track and cut across the cemetery heading for the gate,
his long strides eating up the distance.

But Father Francis followed, dogging his steps like a
persistent terrier. "I'm sorry that you found the information I've given you so upsetting, Lord Kilgannon." Father
Francis's voice was full of sorrow. "You have parents
who love you and parents you love in return, but they are
not the parents who gave you life."

"They're the only parents who matter," Kit replied tightly.

"If you had been unwanted and unloved by your natural
parents, I would agree with you. But, Kit—"

"I haven't given you leave to address me by my pet
name."

Father Francis reacted as if Kit had struck him. "I was
the first person other than your mother to speak *your*
name. I held you in my arms and consecrated you to God,
then stood helplessly by and watched as your mother's

life bled out. I administered last rites to her and comforted her father. I don't ask or require your leave to address you by your pet name. I'll address you however I choose. It's my right. I earned it."

"Then why wasn't I baptized Christopher George Kilgannon?" Kit lashed out.

"Your mother was a Kilgannon by birth and a Farrington by marriage."

"She was married?"

The priest nodded. "She believed she was a widow when she met your father. Her husband, Michael Farrington, was a young naval officer who had been reported lost at sea when his ship went down. She fell in love with George Ramsey and you were conceived before she learned that her husband was alive. She could have passed you off as her husband's child and pretended not to notice when folks began counting the number of months between Michael's last visit home and your birth. It happens all the time. But when Lieutenant Farrington returned to London, Lady Alanna told her husband the truth.

"It was all quite civilized. The three of them—Lady Alanna, her husband, Michael Farrington, and your father sat down to discuss the situation. No one was to blame. Neither George nor Alanna had meant to cuckold Michael. They believed she was a widow, and since you were not to blame for the circumstances of your birth, Farrington agreed to claim you and raise you as his own if George agreed to step aside and allow Alanna to spend her confinement with her father in Ireland. And that's what would have happened, but Alanna died giving birth. Neither man accompanied her to Ireland. Farrington was assigned to a new naval command, and George remained behind in London. Alanna was, after all, Farrington's wife. But she didn't survive her confinement." He paused to see if Kit was listening. The young man still had his back turned, but he was no longer walking away. He had stopped to hear what the priest had to say. "Your mother died for you. The midwife could have killed you and saved her, but Alanna refused to allow it, and she made her father and me promise not to allow it. You might perish in the end, if that was God's will, she said, but you would not be sacrificed to save her. I held your mother's hand when you were born. I placed you in her arms, and she cradled you until her strength began to fade, then your grandfather placed you in the crook of his arm and held you at an angle so she could see you as I administered the last rites. I'll never forget how he cradled you in one arm and held on to his daughter's hand, or how Alanna opened her eyes, whispered your name, and took her last breath." Father Francis took a deep breath to steady himself. "When it was over, Lord Kilgannon sent for George Ramsey because he was unable to reach Farrington at sea. I thought George would go mad with grief when he arrived. He blamed himself. You see, he'd lost two women in childbirth. He'd lost his wife—Drew's mother—and the child she carried, and he'd lost your mother. But he was determined that he would not lose you."

"What happened afterward? What happened to me?" Kit asked.

"Your grandfather—Lord Kilgannon—wanted you, but he was in ill health, and the loss of his daughter made it worse. With Lady Alanna gone, there was no one here to look after you. So George took you home to England and found a mother for you. I never saw George again. When your grandfather, Lord Kilgannon, died, Ford sent for me. I notified George, through his solicitor, that you were named as Lord Kilgannon's heir."

"I could not inherit Lord Kilgannon's title," Kit protested. "Not if I was born outside the marriage bed."

"But you weren't." Father Francis shook his head. "You were born while your mother was married to Michael Farrington. You were George Ramsey's natural son, but you were Michael Farrington's legal one."

Kit frowned. "What about Farrington?"

"I wrote to tell him the truth—that Alanna had died in childbirth and that we'd sent for George because we couldn't reach him. And we told him George had taken you." Father Francis wrinkled his brow at the memory of the look of sadness on Michael Farrington's face. "He accepted it. He didn't return to London or to Ireland until nearly a year after Alanna died, and when he asked to see the parish registry, I granted the request. I had entered your birth and your mother's death as one entry in the parish registry under Farrington, deliberately smudging the ink a bit, so that anyone reading it would assume that both Lady Alanna Kilgannon Farrington and her infant son had perished. Michael remarked that if you survived, you might need proof of your legal name at birth one day, so he wrote it out. Christopher George Ramsey Farrington. For although Alanna had died and George had taken you away, Michael intended to honor his promise by claiming you as his son. No one would be hurt by the tiny deception and he saw no reason to ruin your life by allowing you to be labeled a bastard because the irony of it all was that if you lived, you would be in line for the title of marquess of Templeston. Although I was unaware of it until Michael Farrington mentioned it that day. There was a family connection. He and George were cousins. George's father and Michael's maternal grandfather were brothers. Michael was second in line to inherit the title of marquess of Templeston behind Andrew Ramsey. Since Andrew was young and healthy, the likelihood of any son of Michael's inheriting the Ramsey and Templeston fortunes was very small."

"How was it possible that I ended up with Mama and Papa and still became Lord Kilgannon's heir?"

"When Michael was reported drowned, George, Lord Templeston, took it upon himself to call upon his widow to relay the news. That's how George and Alanna met. That they fell in love was purely chance.

"I don't know what legal arrangements George and his solicitor made in order to give you to the current Lady Templeston," Father Francis said. "But it was arranged and as Michael's legal heir, you would be next in line.

When George took you to England, you became the son of the one woman George knew would love you like her own." Father Francis looked at Kit. "You have always been greatly loved, Kit. George and Lady Alanna gave you life, and Andrew and Kathryn nourished it."

"What happened to Michael Farrington?"

"He sailed to India to join the East India Company. He died there a few years later."

"Did he remarry?"

Father Francis shook his head.

Kit covered his face with his hands. "Why didn't Mama and Papa tell me?"

"I'm not certain how much they could tell you. I don't know how much they knew until Lord Kilgannon's wishes were made known. But Telamor Castle was rightfully yours. Your inheritance actually came from Lady Alanna. She was her father's legal heir."

"A peeress in her own right?"

"Yes," Father Francis answered. "Had she lived, Lady Alanna would have inherited as countess of Kilgannon. As her only child, you inherited what would have been hers."

"But everyone thought that Lady Alanna's child died with her. No one knew *I* was that child."

"Lord Kilgannon, your father, and your solicitor, Martin Bell, knew. That was enough. They arranged it." Father Francis reached out a hand and patted Kit on the back. "I know you're shocked and confused and angry and feeling betrayed because your parents loved you enough to try to protect you from gossip and pain. But you should fall to your knees and give thanks to God for allowing you to be twice blessed." Father Francis placed his hand on Kit's shoulder. "You were born to loving parents. Look around at your friends and acquaintances and see the ones who were born within the bonds of matrimony to unloving and unlovable parents and give thanks. Everyone has a cross to bear. You've been fortunate. Your cross has been far lighter than most." He patted Kit on the shoulder one last time, then turned and started toward the church. "Think about it."

Chapter 16

She moves a goddess, and she looks a queen.

—ALEXANDER POPE, 1688–1744

Think about it.

He couldn't stop thinking about it. Kit had spent the remainder of the morning and afternoon riding over the estate, racing his horse across the moors, pushing himself and his horse to the limits of their endurance, before returning to the castle well after afternoon tea. But his mood had not improved with his ride. If anything, it had worsened. He couldn't stop thinking about the priest's revelations. He couldn't stop wondering, couldn't stop the doubts.

Kit cursed. He was cold, tired, hungry, and wet from getting caught in a cloudburst from a squall that had rapidly moved ashore, and he was in no mood to see or speak to anyone. It didn't seem possible, but a few minutes of conversation with a parish priest had shaken the foundation of his whole world. The man who sired him wasn't the man he wanted as a sire. The woman who bore him wasn't the mother he adored. And he wasn't really who he thought he was—or thought he should be. Drew had adopted him and made him the heir to the title and to Swanslea Park knowing that as their father's younger bastard son, Kit wasn't entitled to any part of Swanslea Park.

Be careful what you wish for, he reminded himself, because you just might get it. He had wanted answers, and by God, he'd gotten some. Unfortunately, none of the answers were what he wanted to hear.

Christ! What a tangle! But the worst thing of all was that his mother had lied to him. The woman he loved above all others wasn't his mother at all. His birth had killed his mother. Kit sighed. No wonder George had instructed Drew to adopt him and raise him as his own. The man he had always called grandfather had died before Kit reached his fourth birthday, and Drew had married Kathryn shortly afterward. Kit didn't remember George. He didn't remember seeing him or hearing the sound of his voice. His earliest memories began with Drew and with Kathryn. They were all his family. All he'd ever known. All he ever wanted.

He felt as if he were drowning in a quagmire of anger, self-pity, and doubt. And the only cure he'd ever needed for any sort of doldrums—an hour or two spent on the back of a fine horse—didn't seem to be working.

He was beginning to wish that he'd never come to Ireland, that he'd never heard of Telamor Castle, or the earldom, his dead relatives, Father Francis, or Mariah Shaughnessy. He was beginning to think his mother—the live one—the one he adored—had been right in trying to persuade him to stay home where he belonged. Except now he wondered if he belonged there at all, or if Swanslea Park would be better served if someone else inherited it.

Suddenly it seemed that the best and most logical thing for him to do was to collect Everleigh and Mirrant and go back to London. There was nothing to do in Inismorn anyway, and London offered a host of amusements—drinking, gambling, carousing—all of the things young men of his age and station in life were accustomed to doing. He didn't need to live at Telamor Castle to inherit the title or the money that went along with it. And the castle staff and the village of Inismorn could do very well without a lord in residence. They seemed to have managed quite well without him these past twenty years. Even his ward was perfectly capable of managing without him. She was neither poor nor a child. She was a grown woman with a trust fund. He could simply instruct Martin Bell to set up a generous allowance from her trust fund—one that would keep her quite comfortable until she married. Hell, she could stay in the castle for all he cared. Or marry the squire or do whatever she wanted. It wasn't as if she were part of the family. . . . He'd only known her one day. . . . It wasn't as if he owed her anything. . . .

"Cool him down slowly," Kit ordered as he dismounted, tossed the reins of his lathered horse to the waiting stable boy, and took the front steps two at a time. He opened the front door, removed his hat, raked his fingers through his hair, and stepped over the threshold into the vestibule before Ford could assist him.

Kit dropped his hat and gloves on the small gilt table by the front door and headed toward the breakfast room.

"Good evening, my lord." Ford followed at his heels. "I trust you enjoyed the morning service."

"Where's Everleigh and Mirrant?" Kit glanced around. The breakfast room was empty, but the sound of several voices in excited conversation drifted from somewhere close by.

"You were gone so long and the hour grew so late that they decided not to wait for you. Your guests have already broken their fast, eaten luncheon, and enjoyed afternoon tea."

"Good," Kit pronounced. "Find them and tell them to pack their things. I'm leaving."

Ford froze. "Sir?"

Kit whirled around and glared at the butler. "I'm leaving. Packing up. Going back to London."

"But, sir . . ." Ford sputtered, his composure slipping for a mere second. "I don't understand, you've only just arrived . . ."

"One day in Ireland is plenty long enough for me," Kit snorted in contempt. "What the devil are you waiting for, man? Get cracking! Find them!"

"The gentlemen are in the main salon," Ford answered. "Pardon me, sir, but you're dripping wet. Let me take your coat and have someone draw you a bath. You barely had breakfast. You must be famished. Shall I prepare a plate for you? Tea? Coffee? A glass of brandy?"

"No, thank you." Kit paused, trying to get his bearings. He'd only been in residence at Telamor one day and had yet to explore it. So far, he'd been in the vestibule, the second-floor study, the dining room, the yellow salon, his bedchamber, and the breakfast room. He knew where Ash's and Dalton's rooms and Mariah's and Sister Mary Beatrix's rooms were located, but all of the other rooms and their locations remained a mystery. "Where the hell is the main salon?"

"The second door down from the dining room. The main salon, the dining room, and the breakfast room connect to form half of the ballroom," Ford told him. "The yellow salon, the blue salon, and the music room across the hall connect to make the other half of the ballroom."

Kit entered the main salon and stopped in his tracks. Bloody hell! He had forgotten all about Mariah's appointment.

He had expected a larger version of the yellow salon across the hall. He had expected the main salon to be a big, airy room with the usual collection of sofas, chairs, and tables sitting on floral carpets and neatly arranged in conversational groupings in front of the windows and the fireplaces. What he found was a dressmaker's shop to rival anything to be found on Bond Street in London.

A half dozen women scurried back and forth from the dining room to the main salon carrying bolts of silk and satin fabrics, spools of threads, boxes of buttons, beads, paste jewels, trims, and ribbons. Some of the women held the heavy bolts, wrapping and unwrapping yards of material, as the seamstress offered suggestions and Mariah made selections. Others traced dress designs onto heavy brown paper, then disappeared in the dining room only to return minutes later with paper patterns that the dress-maker fitted to Mariah's body.

And the chaos didn't end there. Several crates filled with pattern books were stacked near the only visible piece of furniture in the room—a brocade sofa with a multitude of paper-pattern cutouts scattered upon it.

In the center of the room sat a box, and on top of the box stood Mariah Shaughnessy, dressed in a low-cut evening gown of pale, almost translucent blue silk.

The soft blue silk shimmered in the light. The full skirt was fit tightly at the waist and then draped over a small crinoline. The neckline was wide and scooped to frame the collarbones and breasts, and the sleeves were bare wisps of silk trimmed with silver embroidery. The dress fit her like a second skin. It molded to the curves of her body, making her waist appear to be smaller than it was while it thrust her breasts into prominence.

A small, birdlike woman in a day dress of dark blue wool trimmed in black velvet, with a measuring tape around her neck and a mouth full of straight pins, fluttered about Mariah, tucking, pinning, adjusting, measuring, like a sparrow building a nest.

As Kit stood in the doorway and watched, Madame Sparrow whipped the measuring tape from around her neck, wrapped it around Mariah's waist, and called out the number in heavily accented English: "Seventeen."

Her assistants dutifully recorded Mariah's measure-ments in a big, black leather ledger as the seamstress pro-duced a needle and matching blue thread and adjusted the seams along the side to make the dress fit more snugly.

Seventeen? That had to be a mistake. What woman had a seventeen-inch waist? Kit looked at Mariah and found his answer. A woman built like a goddess. He blinked, amazed that he hadn't noticed it before. Amazed at how much an ugly black dress could conceal.

"Turn," the sparrow lady ordered.

Mariah turned.

The dressmaker clapped her hands in rhythm. "Again.

Again. More." She knelt on the floor and looked up at
Mariah. "Again. We must see how the crinolines move so
we know how much of the lace on the hem of your pantalets to let show when you dance."

Mariah turned again, executing a perfect pirouette on
the box. The pale blue silk of her crinoline skirts fanned
out around her, exposing her stockinged feet and a fair
amount of ankle.

Sensing his presence, Mariah looked up as Kit walked
through the door. "What do you think? Isn't it lovely?
Isn't it the most beautiful dress you've ever seen?"

The dress wouldn't have been anything special by itself. He had seen lovelier ball gowns on even lovelier
women. But something about the way this particular silk
ball gown looked on Mariah made it one of the most
beautiful dresses he'd ever seen. The lightweight silk caressed her body, revealing as much as it concealed. And
it revealed a great deal.

Kit was fascinated by the change. He couldn't seem to
keep his gaze off her. He made a valiant effort, but he
failed.

There was no doubting the fact that the gown was simply made. Simply made to torture him, Kit thought as he
attempted to focus his gaze on something other than her
silver-edged décolletage. His sudden fascination was centered there upon the soft, creamy white expanse of cleavage the dress exposed. Cleavage he hadn't realized Mariah
possessed.

The neckline was modest compared to some of the
necklines he'd seen recently. But not modest enough. His
height gave him a unique vantage point and were it not
for the fact that she was standing on a box, Kit knew it
would be almost impossible for him to look down at her
and not feast on the enticing display of cleavage.

The idea annoyed him. How the devil had everything
gotten so turned around so fast? The day had started off
normally enough, but everything had changed. And some
things had changed beyond recognition. She was his ward,

dammit. He wasn't supposed to want to kiss her. He wasn't supposed to look at her cleavage. Nor should she be exposing it that way.

"I think the bodice is cut too low." Glaring at the offending part of the dress, Kit swallowed hard. Perspiration dotted his upper lip. His body felt tight and hot and achy. He needed a drink. Hell, he needed several.

"Oh, no, my lord," the dressmaker protested. "This style of bodice is the height of fashion in Paris and in London."

"We aren't in Paris or London," he snapped. "We're in Ireland and she's showing too bloody damn much bosom. And she shouldn't be showing any lace on her pantalets when she dances. Unless you want all the men at the dances to refrain from partnering the ladies in order to sit on the sideline and stare at it."

"Kit!" Mariah struggled to keep from stomping her foot.

"You, madame, are supposed to be engaged in the business of creating a wardrobe suitable for a young lady, not some dockside whore."

"You go too far, Kit! How dare you?" Mariah's voice vibrated with outrage. She turned to the seamstress and began to apologize, "Madame Thierry, I beg your pardon for His Lordship's rude behavior—"

"How dare *I*?" Kit's voice rose. "How dare you, Miss Shaughnessy? I don't recall granting you permission to address me by my pet name. Nor is it your place to offer apologies for my behavior!" he shouted.

"Someone needs to!" she shouted back. "Because your manners are appalling."

"You presume to lecture me on manners? A girl who hasn't yet learned to identify the proper eating utensil to use much less . . ."

Mariah blanched, recoiling as if he'd struck her.

Realizing what he'd done, Kit turned nearly as white as she did.

"How could you?" Mariah backed off the box she was

standing on and would have fallen if the dressmaker hadn't reached out to steady her. She righted herself, then lifted the hem of her skirt, turned her back, and walked out of the room.

"Mariah!" Kit started to run after her, then thought better of it and stayed where he was. "Miss Shaughnessy! Come back here! Stay and fight! Don't walk away from me! I'm not a fool, you know!" he yelled up the stairs after her. "There is no Saint Elizabeth of Bohemia! And whether you know it or not, your hair smells like freshly baked bread."

Her gasp echoed down the stairs.

Kit allowed himself a smug smile, then turned and discovered that Madame Sparrow and her assistants continued to go about the business of selecting patterns and fabric, all the while pretending they hadn't noticed that he was behaving like a madman.

The news would most likely be all over the village come morning. It seemed he was carrying on the family tradition by providing the gossips with a juicy bit of scandal of his own.

"Bloody hell!"

Chapter 17

Friendships multiply Joys and divide Griefs.

—THOMAS FULLER, 1654–1734

"*That's enough, Kit!*"

Kit turned to find Ash standing in the doorway to the dining room with Dalton and Ford at his back.

"How the devil do you know what's enough?" Kit lashed out. "And what do you know about it anyway? You're my friend, not my bloody father!" He looked at Ash. "Of that, I'm certain."

"Have you been drinking?" Ash asked incredulously.

Kit shook his head. "Not yet, but it sounds like a fine way to conclude what's become one bitch of a day." He looked around for a drinks table.

"I beg your pardon, ladies," Dalton acknowledged the mixed company before nodding to the butler. "Ford, make arrangements for Madame and her assistants to spend the night."

"Very good, sir." Ford bowed, then withdrew to speak to the dressmaker.

Dalton waited until the butler and the dressmaker were out of earshot before continuing in a fierce whisper. "Blast it all, Kit! What the devil is going on here? We haven't seen you all day. When we left you last night, you were scribbling a letter to your father and planning to attend church this morning. Where the blazes have you been?"

"Mind your own business!" Kit shot back.

"This *is* our business," Ash retorted. "We're your

friends. If we don't tell you when you're acting like a horse's arse, who will?" He walked over to Kit, gripped his arm, and hustled him out of the salon, up the stairs to the second-floor study. Ash opened the door, shoved Kit inside and onto one of the leather chairs.

Dalton followed, closing the door behind him, twisting the key in the lock, and leaning with his back against the door for good measure.

"Who the hell do you think you are?" Kit gave Ash a bone-chillingly cold stare. "This is my house."

Ash wasn't intimidated by it. "I know precisely who I am," Ash replied. "I'm the ninth marquess of Everleigh. I outrank you. And I'm exercising my prerogative to make myself at home. The question is: Who the hell do you think you are to treat a lady and a shopkeeper in that manner? What's the matter, Kit? What happened to put this kind of burr up your arse?"

Kit propped his elbows on his knees and buried his face in his hands. He leaned forward in his chair, and his shoulders began to shake.

Ash and Dalton exchanged looks. They didn't know whether Kit was laughing or crying, and they found the idea of him doing either horrifying.

Kit sat up.

He was laughing. But it was laughter born of pain and confusion. "Well, Lord Everleigh, you always hit the nail on the head. That is the big question of the day. Who the hell do I think I am? Christ! I wish I knew!"

He hadn't meant to spill his guts to his friends, but before Kit knew what was happening, he'd related his conversation with the parish priest to Ash and Dalton. "What have you heard?"

Dalton sighed. "We've heard the same rumors you've heard."

"Kit," Ash said gently, "this can't have come as a complete surprise. You've always known something unusual happened."

Kit nodded. "I just can't believe that my parents didn't tell me the truth."

"Perhaps they did," Dalton suggested. "You've only heard one side of the story today. Who's to say that Lord and Lady Templeston haven't told you theirs? It may be that you chose not to believe them. Or that you've forgotten."

Both Kit and Ash turned to look at him. Dalton wasn't normally given to making such profound observations. "Well, like Ash said, you've always known there were unusual circumstances surrounding your birth. For one thing, there's always been gossip about the fifteenth marquess." He paused. "I mean, we've all heard those rumors for *years*. It's the part about your mother that's come as a surprise. But perhaps it isn't as big a surprise as you think. I mean, we all know things that no one has ever actually spoken aloud. I know my father and mother always detested the sight of each other." Dalton continued, "I've known it all my life, and no one ever had to explain it. Or the fact that my eldest brother and my second eldest brother are most likely the only two sons my father has."

"He's right, Kit," Ash agreed. "Every family has skeletons in its closets. Like the father who sleeps with a succession of governesses and household servants. The brother who drinks to excess. The ancestor whose carnal tastes ran to farmyard animals. No family is without their secrets. But your life isn't what happened when you were born or what was done to it when you were a child. Your life is what you make of it. Your family's skeletons have been seen in public more often than most, but no family is perfect. No one's parents are perfect."

"Even though you want them to be," Kit said softly, before rubbing at the ache forming in his left temple.

"Yes, well, everyone wants their parents to be perfect," Dalton said. "Everyone wants their parents to be good parents and to love their children." He looked at Kit. "But few of us ever get that. You've been lucky."

Ash leaned against the edge of the Hepplewhite desk.

"We live in a system that pits fathers against heirs, eldest sons against the younger ones, and the females against their husbands and male relations. It's no wonder our families are so buggered." He lifted a heavy stone paperweight cut in the shape of Ireland off the desk. The family name of Kilgannon and the family crest were carved upon it. Ash stared down at the stone and sighed. "We promise ourselves that it will be different when we marry, but the truth is that it rarely is. Too often we marry for all the wrong reasons and none of the right ones."

"In that, your family is different. It's obvious that both the fifteenth and the sixteenth Lords and Ladies Templeston married for love," Dalton pointed out. "Perhaps they made mistakes. Perhaps they tried to protect the children they loved. Perhaps . . ."

"They did what they did because they loved me," Kit finished Dalton's thought. "And if that's the case, they certainly deserve the benefit of the doubt. If anyone deserves the benefit of the doubt, it's the parents who loved me. And if I require answers to my questions, they are the ones I should ask."

"Precisely," Ash replied and put the paperweight down to punctuate his word.

"Damnation, but I'm an idiot."

"At times," Dalton agreed cheerfully. "But not very often."

Kit stood up and walked over to give Dalton an affectionate poke in the arm. "My friends, I owe you an apology for my behavior this afternoon."

"No, you don't," Ash told him. "We've seen you like this before. Your apologies should go to the people who haven't."

Kit weighed Ash's advice and took his time answering it. But he didn't disappoint them. "You're absolutely right. My behavior today was most ungentlemanly."

Dalton chuckled. "Reminds me of the time you pounded that Pool fellow. The rector's nephew. What was his name? Albert? Alton?"

"Alden," Kit pronounced, remembering. "He composed some nasty little verse about my mother."

"He was nearly twice your size, and you socked him right in the eye before Dalton could get the chance." Ash laughed.

Kit had always been small for his age. And the boys at school had tried repeatedly to take advantage of that. It wasn't until he entered university that Kit had finally matched Ash in size and strength and surpassed Dalton. Now that he stood well over six feet tall and weighed in at twelve and a half stones, it was hard to believe that he'd ever needed Ash and Dalton to defend him. But he had. And Dalton and Ash had always been there to protect him.

"You and Dalton were sent to the headmaster's office for a caning," Ash continued.

"Where I was also subjected to the *'Lord Ramsey, your conduct today was less than gentlemanly'* speech."

"You didn't get your caning until later," Dalton remembered, grinning at Ash.

"That's because I generally refrain from brawling and fisticuffs in public," Ash said, in a perfect imitation of the headmaster's voice. "I'm subtle."

"That's why you're a diplomatist," Kit said.

"I don't think that filling the Pool chap's rinse pail with piss was all that subtle," Dalton remarked. "I'd say it was decidedly less than subtle."

"Maybe," Ash agreed. "But you must admit that the punishment fit the crime. You did say *'Piss on that and piss on him'* when the headmaster told you to shake hands and apologize."

"Piss on that and piss on him!" The three of them chanted in unison. "I don't shake hands with or apologize to anyone who insults my mother."

Dalton laughed. "We got another caning for that."

"It was worth every swipe of that old hypocrite's rod," Kit said. He pointed to Ash. "And the next morning you bribed Sanders into letting you take his place in the bucket brigade so that you could pump the rinse water into the bath pails."

Ash bowed from the waist and smiled. "I worked damned hard that morning. I had calluses on my hands from all the other buckets I had to fill just to get to Pool's. But I'll never forget the look on Pool's face when he realized he'd just rinsed the soap off his body with the bucket full of piss. Or that he'd have to go to chapel that way because there was no time to fill another bucket."

"Or the look on his face when he walked into the chapel stinking to high heaven and the entire assembly shouted, *'Piss on that and piss on him. I don't shake hands with or apologize to anyone who insults my mother.'*"

As punishment for their disobedience, all of the boys assembled in the chapel that day, except Pool, had all received three stripes of the cane and the forfeiture of dessert puddings for a fortnight.

But even that had been worth it.

Kit looked at his friends. "Thank you for protecting me from my enemies and from myself and for always persuading me to see the error of my ways."

"That's what friends are for, old man," Dalton reminded him. "Now, go do what must be done and apologize to the girl. You hurt her badly."

"I humiliated her in front of everyone," Kit said. "I think it best if I offer my apologies the same way." He took a deep breath and slowly expelled it. "Now all I have to do is persuade her to come back downstairs."

Chapter 18

Fine words dress ill deeds.

—George Herbert, 1593–1633

Mariah rolled off the bed and walked to the dressing table, looked in the mirror, and frowned. Her eyes were puffy and her nose was red from crying, and she was glad that no one could see her. She wasn't a vain person by nature, but she couldn't stop staring at the reflection she made wearing that blue silk ball gown. She touched the silvered glass, amazed at the luxury of having a looking glass in her room.

To the sisters at St. Agnes's, vanity was a sin and mirrors, the devil's handiwork. And there had been no need for mirrors in the convent. No reason to preen and primp, for the only man with access to it was Father Francis. Besides, everyone in the convent wore black. The sisters wore black habits with scapulars, coifs, white wimples, and black veils. The orphans wore black frocks with black bonnets for outdoors and black caps for indoors, and their hair was always tightly plaited. Black was practical. It was sturdy. It was ugly. Nothing like the wonderful blue silk evening gown she was wearing now.

Nothing like the wonderful blue silk evening gown Kit had despised on sight.

Mariah sniffled and blinked back the tears that were hovering at the base of her eyelashes. How many times must she remind herself that crying never did any good? Crying never changed anything. It made her eyes and her throat burn, stuffed up her nose, and left her with a throbbing head, but it never solved any of her problems.

And it did nothing to alleviate the pain that Kit's unexpected reaction to the sight of her in her ball gown had caused or the way his hateful words seemed to embed themselves on her heart and in her mind. So she'd never had to use any but the most basic of eating utensils like the knife, fork, and spoon. He'd probably never baked six-dozen loaves of bread in a day. Or strawberry tarts. Or dreamed of having the most wonderful white layered wedding cake covered in pink confectioner's sugar rosebuds . . . Or dreamed of a wedding at all . . . At least, not a wedding in which she was the bride . . .

Mariah reached up and traced the outline of her bodice. It was daring. After so many years of covering up everything except her hands and face, she'd never dreamed it was not only possible, but permissible to expose this much of her bosom, but Madame Thierry had assured her that all the fashionable ladies in London and Paris wore their dresses this way. Mariah sat perfectly erect. Madame Thierry had praised Mariah's regal bearing and told her that she wore her clothes like a duchess. Mariah smiled. She could thank the nuns for that as well. Perfect posture was a sign of discipline. And Mariah understood discipline better than most. Reverend Mother had insisted upon it.

Mariah stared at the reflection in the mirror and saw her mother. She'd spent the past fifteen years staring up at the stars from the tower ruins hoping to find her mother. Hoping to catch a glimpse of her mother smiling back at her. All those years she'd wished upon the stars for her mother to come back and get her. Mariah swiped at the solitary tear rolling down her face with the back of her hand. All those years she had followed her mother's advice and looked to the stars, but all she'd ever really needed was a mirror.

For the face staring back at her was the one she remembered. They shared the same hair and eyes and nose and mouth and chin, the same bone structure. The same firm jaw.

Her mother had worn dresses similar to this one, colorful dresses made of muslin and lightweight silks and satins in summer and soft warm velvet and wool in the winter. And jewelry. Her mother had worn jewelry.

Mariah stood up and walked over to the wardrobe. There, in the top drawer, in the back behind her extra set of unmentionables and the little monogrammed handkerchief, was the linen drawstring sack Reverend Mother had given to her. The linen drawstring sack that contained the jewelry her mother had been wearing the last time Mariah had seen her.

She pushed the wardrobe drawer closed and walked back to the bed. She climbed up onto it, sat down, untied the drawstring bag, and poured the contents onto the coverlet. Out tumbled a pair of diamond stud earrings, two pins, one an ivory cameo on a pink background, and the other a gold chatelaine with a lady's timepiece attached. The last piece of jewelry was her mother's betrothal ring—a single large blue stone set in gold and accented by a ring of diamonds. Mariah stared at the mound of jewelry. Her mother's jewelry. Her jewelry. She picked up the ring and slipped it onto her finger, then pressed her hand against the folds of her skirt. Slightly darker than the pale blue of the silk, the color of the stone looked lovely against the fabric of her dress.

Mariah suddenly wondered how Madame Thierry had managed to construct a ball gown to fit her on such short notice. She shrugged her shoulders at the thought. Making dresses was Madame's occupation, just as baking bread and pastries had been hers. A good baker always kept the needed ingredients at hand, and Mariah supposed a dressmaker was no different. She studied the remaining cache of family heirlooms and decided that she would have Madame Thierry fashion dresses to match all of her jewelry. A pink one to match the cameo and others in blue and green and red and yellow and lavender and purple . . .

She wanted dresses in every color of the rainbow. She wanted dresses in every color except black. She never wanted to wear black again as long as she lived.

Mariah picked up the diamond earrings. She remembered her mother wearing them. She remembered the diamonds; only Mariah hadn't called them diamonds back then. She had called them twinkles. Because they twinkled like stars. She always thought of her mother when she looked at the stars.

But Mariah wasn't thinking of her mother now. She was thinking of Kit.

Kit who had accused the dressmaker of making her look like a whore instead of a lady. Kit, who regarded her as an obligation to be endured and then discharged. Kit, who didn't remember who she was or care that he had wounded her so badly. If only he hadn't taken such a dislike to her evening gown . . . If only she hadn't had such high expectations . . . If only he had remembered and kept his promise . . .

She glanced over at the bedchamber door. She wasn't sure she would forgive Kit if he did come knocking at the door. He was already late. He was supposed to run after her, fall to his knees, kiss the hem of her skirt, and beg her forgiveness. That's what always happened in the stories her mother used to tell her, and in the copy of *Grimm's Fairy-Tales*, her mother used to read to her, the prince always did everything he could to make the princess happy. And perhaps that was the problem. Mariah frowned. Kit wasn't a prince. He was an earl. Perhaps earls were different. Perhaps the rules governing princely behavior didn't apply to earls. Or perhaps the rules governing princely behavior only applied if the female in question was a princess.

And if that was the case, Kit might never run after her or fall to his knees and kiss the hem of her skirt and beg her forgiveness because she wasn't a princess. She wasn't really even a lady. She had been born one, but she didn't remember how to be one. The best she could hope for, at the moment, was that he consider her to be almost a lady.

Mariah glanced down at the blue ring on her hand. Looking at it made her feel good and wearing it made her feel closer to her mother. Her mother had been a lady, and a lady always wore jewelry.

She smiled at the thought, then picked up the pink cameo and pinned it in the center of her bodice, below her breasts, taking great care not to damage the silk. When that was done, she took great care in pinning the lady's timepiece on the left side of her bodice. All that remained was the pair of diamond earrings. She scooped up the diamond studs and rolled off the bed. Her mother had worn them all the time. They had been her favorite pair, and Mariah always loved the way they caught the light and sparkled. She walked to the dressing table and sat down on the stool so she could put them on in front of the mirror and see if they sparkled on her. But the earrings wouldn't go on. They were made to go through the earlobes. She couldn't wear them. Her earlobes didn't have holes for them. She had no choice except to do without them.

She was disappointed, but she would get over it. Disappointment was a part of life, and she had already learned to manage fifteen years of disappointment. One more wouldn't matter.

Kit took a deep breath, murmured a fervent prayer of contrition, and knocked on Mariah's door.

"Who is it?" came the muffled reply from the other side of the door.

"Kit."

"I don't know anyone named Kit."

Her words were precise and clipped, the tone very cold, very English. The Irish lilt he found so enchanting was gone, and Kit deeply regretted the loss.

"That's right," he agreed. "You've never been introduced to Kit. You've only met the dunderheaded fool who goes by the name of Lord Kilgannon." He pressed his forehead against her door. "I know that you're—"

Mariah cut him off. "You know nothing about me."

"I know that you're angry with me," he said. "And you've every right to be. My behavior this afternoon was appalling."

"That it was."

A hint of the Irish lilt had returned.

"I'm trying to apologize."

"Not very successfully," she retorted.

"Does that mean you're not going to forgive me?" Kit asked.

"It means you're going to have to try harder."

"I'm standing in the hallway shouting through a door trying to tell you that I'm sorry," Kit said loudly. "The entire household—even Sister Mary Beatrix—can hear me."

"I suppose that's only fair," Mariah reminded him. "Since the entire household heard you insult Madame Thierry and the beautiful dress she brought for me to try on, I suppose it's only right and proper that they hear you offer your apologies."

"My sentiments exactly," Kit told her. "I'm sorry. I apologize. I love the dress. It's a beautiful dress and you look beautiful in it. Now, won't you please open the door and allow me to introduce you to Kit Ramsey?"

"No."

"Why not?"

"I've no guarantee that Lord Kilgannon won't return."

"You have my word as a gentleman . . ."

"A fat lot of good that does me!" The Irish in her voice returned with a vengeance. "Seeing as how you were such a *gentleman* to me earlier."

"Miss Shaughnessy," Kit pleaded. "Mariah, I promise—"

The door to her bedchamber opened so quickly Kit nearly fell into the room. He collided with her, placing his arms about her waist to keep them both from falling.

With his hands nearly spanning her waist, Kit felt the soft silk beneath his palms and the curve of her hips below it. She still wore the blue silk evening gown. *Seventeen.* The number popped into his brain and Kit realized that both he and the dressmaker had been right. Mariah's waist *was* that small, *and* the bodice of her dress was cut too damned low. So low that it easily afforded any man who towered above her an incredibly provocative look at her bosom.

Don't look down, he told himself, don't look down. But not looking down took more willpower than he possessed. Especially when the pink cameo she was wearing drew his attention like a big, red X marked on a treasure map.

Kit looked and the sight of her beautiful, creamy white breasts was one he would remember the rest of his life.

"You promise? You promise?" Mariah gave an unladylike snort. "Don't be promising me anything else as Lord Kilgannon or as Kit Ramsey because I don't believe your promises anymore."

"When have I ever made you a promise I didn't keep?"

Mariah almost told him, but the genuine look of righteous indignation on his face was a thousand times more painful than the hurt he'd caused her earlier. "If you don't remember," she whispered, "I'm not going to remind you."

Kit pulled his gaze away from her bosom and looked into her eyes. The expression of raw pain on her face cut him to the bone. "All right," he surrendered. "I admit that I promised you a London season, and I was about to renege on the promise by packing my bags and heading back to England. But I've changed my mind and I'm standing good for it."

Mariah gave him a look of haughty disdain. "I'd rather marry the squire, receive my fortune, and have done with it."

"Not on your life!" His whole body vibrated with anger. "I promised you a London season, and that's what you're going to get."

"I don't want it."

"That's too damned bad. The dressmaker will be staying here at the castle until she completes the fittings for your wardrobe. Your lessons begin in the morning. Be dressed and downstairs at seven." He turned on his heel and started down the stairs. "We have a lot of work to do and only a few short weeks in which to accomplish it."

"Why not save yourself the work?" she challenged. "I doubt the squire will mind."

"Believe it or not, that's exactly what I planned to do when I returned from the village this afternoon."

Mariah held her breath, closed her eyes, and began to pray. Be careful what you ask for because you just might get it.

"I planned to pack my bags, cut my losses, go back to England, and leave you and the castle to its fate."

"What stopped you?"

Kit didn't know what had stopped him or when he'd changed his mind. All he knew was that, suddenly, he had no desire to run home to Swanslea Park unless Mariah Shaughnessy was with him. When he returned, it would be to help her make her debut. Last night, he'd been planning to send her to London and let his mother and sister teach her what she needed to know. And this afternoon he'd decided to toss it all and leave her to the squire or whoever else took a fancy to her. But all of a sudden he was excited by the challenge of molding her into a lady that anyone would be proud to offer for. Maybe it was something Ash had said about promising oneself that things would be different, but all at once he wanted to give her the opportunity to try. "Let's just say I like a challenge."

"Let's just say that's a horrible thing to say. I may not have grown up with the same opportunities you've had to learn the rules of society, but I'm no dockside whore, either, and I resent being treated as if I were a project you must accomplish."

"I apologize once again," Kit said. "I didn't mean to imply that you were a project or compare you to a prostitute. The challenge to which I refer is the time constraint. My mother and sister have been planning Iris's coming out for nearly six months. We have less than half that time."

"You threatened to marry me off to the squire without a backward glance if I uttered a single complaint," she reminded him. "And in all honesty, I must admit that I complained about your manners."

"A minor slip of the tongue, I'm sure." He smiled at her. "And one I've chosen to overlook."

"Why?"

"Because I like a challenge and because Father Francis promised your mother he'd see to it that you had your coming out."

"My mother isn't here any longer," Mariah said softly. "She isn't going to be disappointed."

"What about you?" he asked. "Aren't you going to be disappointed? You told me a London season was what you wanted, and I promised you and Father Francis that you would have it, and by God, I'm going to keep that promise if it kills me." He turned on the stair and met her unflinching gaze. "I'm going to keep that promise if it kills us both. You can serve yourself up to the squire like a sacrificial lamb if you want to, but it's going to be after you've made your bow and had your coming out, because I always keep my promises."

Mariah looked him right in the eye. "I'm heartened to hear it, Your Lordship," she retorted. "Because I intend to see that you do!"

Taking a step back, Mariah punctuated her intention by slamming her bedchamber door so hard it rattled in its frame.

Kit met Ash and Dalton at the foot of the stairs. "I apologized," he snapped.

"Is that what you call it?" Ash's eyes twinkled with mirth.

"Why?" Kit demanded. "What would you call it?"

"A prelude," Dalton answered.

"A prelude to what?" Kit was rapidly losing patience with the wordplay.

"That remains to be seen." Ash grinned. "But from what I can discern about the topic, I'm fairly certain that what just took place here is a prelude to a rather passionate marriage."

Dalton nodded his head in agreement and began to laugh.

Kit gritted his teeth, then stalked off toward his office with the sound of his friends' laughter ringing in his ears. "Go to hell. Both of you."

Chapter 19

We forgive to the extent that we love.

—La Rochefoucauld, 1613–1680

Kit thought that he and Mariah had finished with each other for the evening. She hadn't appeared at supper, and Kit hadn't had the stomach for forcing her. He'd simply instructed the housekeeper to have Cook send a tray to her room.

He hadn't seen Mariah's chaperone since their confrontation the previous morning, either. The fact that she hadn't appeared at any meal at which he was present gave Kit a measure of alarm. The nun looked to be eighty if she was a day, and the last thing he wanted to discover was that the sister had decided to meet her maker while in residence at Telamor.

But Mrs. Kearney assured him that one of the maids had delivered a supper tray to Sister Mary Beatrix's room. The master could rest easy knowing that Miss Mariah's chaperone had a healthy appetite and was very much alive and on duty. Kit found the sister's usefulness as a chaperone questionable, since she hadn't acted in that capacity since she arrived, but he was relieved to know she was still breathing.

Tonight's supper had been a decidedly masculine affair with Kit, Dalton, and Ash the only participants. Mariah and Sister Mary Beatrix had had trays delivered to their rooms, and Madame Thierry and her four assistants had elected to dine in the housekeeper's quarters with Ford and Mrs. Kearney.

Dalton and Ash had retired to their rooms after challenging Kit to a game of chess and several hands of cards. Kit had won the chess match and lost all three hands of cards. He was alone in his second-floor study sitting at his desk composing another letter to his father when a flash of pale blue silk caught his eye. He glanced up at the mantel clock and saw that it was ten minutes after eleven. He stood up and walked to the door.

"Mariah?"

She froze at the sound of her name.

"What are you doing wandering the castle at this time of night?"

She dropped the book she was holding, but managed to hang on to the old-fashioned brass lantern she'd been using to light her way. Mariah turned to find Kit standing in the doorway of the study. He'd removed his coat, waistcoat, and necktie since she'd last seen him. His white shirt was opened at the throat. Although she'd never seen one before, she recognized the garment he was wearing over his shirt and trousers as a man's robe. It was long, reaching almost to his ankles, and the dark bronze color complemented the chocolate brown of his eyes. Mariah liked the way he looked in it.

She watched as he moved forward, then bent to retrieve the book. *"Grimm's Fairy-Tales?"*

She nodded and her eyes widened as Kit stepped back into the room and beckoned her to follow. He placed the book on the corner of the Hepplewhite desk and took the lantern from her, lowered the wick, and set it on the desk beside the book while he waited for Mariah's explanation. "I heard Lord Everleigh and Mr. Mirrant come upstairs hours ago," she said. "I thought you had retired as well."

"I thought the same of you," he said. He hadn't seen her go by, but it was quite possible that he'd missed her because up until a few minutes ago, he'd been silently

exploring the house. "What were you doing? Reading in
the library?"

She shook her head. "I came to get it because I couldn't
sleep."

He smiled at her. "That much is obvious."

Mariah blushed.

"I'm sorry," he told her. "I spoke my thoughts aloud."
He reached out and tilted her chin up with the tip of his
finger so that he could look her in the eyes. "I didn't mean
to mock."

She raised an eyebrow in disbelief.

Kit chuckled. "It's true. I just meant that since we seem
to be the only two souls creeping about the castle in the
middle of the night, the obvious reason is that neither one
of us can sleep." Her eyes were extraordinarily blue. A
deep, dark, almost violet shade of blue fringed with thick
black eyelashes and framed by nicely arched brows. He
was struck once again by how lovely she was. Especially
with her long, wavy black hair loose and falling about her
shoulders. When he had last seen her, it had been confined
to one long plait hanging down the center of her back.
She reminded him of someone. "*Grimm's Fairy Tales* is
rather gruesome reading for bedtime."

"Not the ones I read."

"Let me guess," he teased. " 'Snow White and the
Seven Dwarfs' or 'The Sleeping Beauty in the Woods'?"

"Both."

"You like stories about princes and princesses?"

"Of course," she replied. "Meeting and falling in love
with a handsome prince is every girl's dream."

Kit stared at her. "Is it yours?"

Mariah lowered her gaze once again.

"Do you dream of meeting and falling in love with a
handsome prince?"

"No."

That surprised him. He would have sworn that she was
the romantic type. He would also have sworn that he'd
just seen her likeness on a portrait hanging in the third-

floor gallery. "Come with me." He took her by the hand, and Mariah had no choice but to follow him out of the study and down the passageway.

"Where are we going?"

"Have you ever been to the third-floor gallery?"

"I don't think so."

"Neither had I until ten minutes ago, but there is something there I think you should see." He quickened his pace. Mariah stumbled on her way up the stairs, and Kit stopped to steady her. He watched as she gathered her skirts in her hand and lifted them a fraction higher to keep from stepping on the hem. She was barefooted.

As he pulled her up the stairs to the third-floor gallery, Kit was struck by the contrast. He'd never seen a girl wear a ball gown without stockings and shoes. The sight of Mariah's bare feet and ankles beneath the silk ball gown was proving to be quite arousing.

He breathed a sigh of relief when they reached the gallery and Mariah let go of her skirts.

"There." Kit pointed to two large gilt-framed portraits hanging side by side on the gallery wall. "Recognize her?"

Mariah looked up at a portrait of a young woman wearing a dress the color of freshly made butter. She wore no jewelry, except a small gold circlet perched atop her rich chestnut-colored hair. Her eyes were a warm shade of chocolate brown, and her smile was slightly mischievous, as if she had a secret no one else knew. She reminded Mariah of someone, but Mariah didn't recognize her. She shook her head.

Kit followed her gaze. "No, that's my—the late earl's daughter," he broke off. He'd almost said *my mother*. But to do so seemed wrong somehow. Disloyal. The woman in the portrait may have given him birth and gifted him with Telamor, but he didn't remember her. She was simply a lovely face painted on canvas. She wasn't Kathryn, Lady Templeston. She wasn't his mother. "I meant the other lady."

Mariah turned her attention to the other portrait.

"Mama," she breathed, tears forming in her eyes as she stared up at a portrait of a woman with black hair and blue eyes wearing a lavender dress, diamond earrings, and a gold and diamond locket, a woman who bore a remarkable resemblance to the reflection Mariah had seen in the mirror earlier in the evening. She turned to Kit. "That's my mother."

Kit smiled. "Without a doubt. You could be twins."

Mariah's face lit up like a Roman candle, and her smile was the most beautiful smile he had ever seen. "Truly?"

"Well, perhaps not *identical* twins . . ."

Mariah's face lost a fraction of its glow as she struggled not to show her disappointment. "Oh . . ."

"But only because you're lovelier."

"Oh, no," Mariah shook her head. "I couldn't be. My mother was a lady." She looked up at the portrait. "The most beautiful lady I've ever seen."

Kit reached out, placed his index finger beneath her chin, and gently turned her to face him. "Your mother was lovely," he said. "But she isn't the most beautiful lady *I've* ever seen." He stared at her lips and fought the almost overwhelming urge to taste them.

There was no mistaking the look in his eyes. "I'm not a lady," Mariah protested. "I may have been born one, but—"

"Blood always tells," Kit interrupted. "Once a lady, always a lady." He brought her face closer to his and bent his head.

He was within a hair's breadth of touching her lips, when Mariah stepped back.

Kit let her go.

"I remember Mama just like that," Mariah said suddenly, nervously worrying her bottom lip with her teeth. "I remember her smile and the way she always wore sparkly things."

A precious memory from his childhood flashed before Kit's eyes. A little girl in the crumbling tower baring her heart to an eight-year-old boy. *"My mummy's gone to heaven, too. She's a star. See that one up there? The shiniest one? I think that one must be my mummy 'cause she used to wear lots of sparkly things."*

"You must miss her very much," Kit murmured.

Mariah nodded.

"How did she die?"

"Reverend Mother told me she had an accident. She tripped on the path that leads from the convent to the castle and fell to her death on the rocks below."

"I'm sorry," Kit replied sincerely.

Mariah shrugged her shoulders. "I don't remember when she died. I only remember her alive and beautiful."

"I think it's best to remember the people we loved as they were when they were alive, not the way they died," Kit said softly.

Mariah nodded. "And I have other things to remember her by."

"Like your accessories." Kit noticed that Mariah was wearing jewelry she hadn't been wearing while standing on the box in the dining room.

"I beg your pardon?"

"Your jewelry." He focused his gaze on the pink cameo. "It's lovely. I didn't remember seeing it when you were standing on the box being fitted."

She looked at him as if she thought he was going to accuse her of stealing his family jewels. "Reverend Mother gave them to me before I left the convent. My mother was wearing these the day she . . ." Mariah bit her bottom lip. "The last time I saw her."

She extended her right hand so that he could admire the ring on her finger. "I don't know what it's called, but it was my mother's betrothal ring and it's a pretty shade of blue," she said. "See? It almost matches my dress." She narrowed her gaze at him, daring him to make any more hateful comments about her dress.

"Yes, I believe it does." Kit was caught in her spell. A spell he was sure Mariah wasn't deliberately conjuring. He smiled once again. "And I'm no authority, but I believe the stone in your ring is called an aquamarine."

Mariah looked up at him, and the light in her eyes sent his heart racing.

"Aquamarine," she repeated. "Sea water."

"That's right," Kit said. "Named for the color, I suppose." He couldn't take his eyes off her. She was as excited as a child, and the pleasure she found in showing off her mother's jewelry was contagious. Kit found himself equally excited, but in a manner that was decidedly unchildlike. He felt his body react. If she were his, he'd buy her jewelry every day just to see that look on her face. Kit swallowed the lump in his throat. If she were his . . . "It's very pretty."

"Isn't it? And look . . ." She reached up to show him the gold chatelaine and the little watch attached to it. "Here's a lady's timepiece. . . ." She touched each item as she called it by name and Kit followed the progress of her fingers. "And a cameo. Isn't it pretty?"

"Very."

Mariah tilted the brooch at an angle so he could get a better look at the ivory relief. "Look at the carving and the tiny diamond marking her necklace. Have you ever seen anything as exquisite?"

"I think, perhaps, I have." He gazed past the cameo and focused on the soft curve of her breasts. Mariah's skin was the same warm ivory color as the face of the woman carved on the cameo and he imagined that the tips of her breasts would match the pink background of the cameo. Kit groaned.

"Lord Kilgannon?" She moistened her lips with the tip of her tongue.

"Kit."

"Are you all right?"

"Yes." He bit back another groan. "Why do you ask?"

"I thought you might be in pain," Mariah ventured.

Kit chuckled. "I am." He read the concern and the confusion in her eyes. "And here I thought you were probably still angry with me."

Mariah smiled. "I never stay angry very long. I've decided to forgive you."

"Why?" he asked.

The look she gave him was completely earnest. "Because you're an earl, not a prince. And I don't think you
know what the rules are any more than I do."

"Is that all?"

"And because you're looking at me the way Father
Francis looks at my strawberry tarts," she whispered.

"I suppose that's because you look good enough to
taste." Kit heard the warning bells go off in his head and
knew that he was in danger, knew that he was about to
compromise his morals, knew that he was about to jump
off the precipice of all that was comfortable and familiar
to him into uncharted territory. But he ignored the warn-
ings and jumped anyway. And discovered that he could
fly. He lowered his head and touched his lips to the top
of her breasts. He had meant to kiss her mouth before he
journeyed on to her neck and then to her bosom, but the
curve of her breast called to him like a siren. He kissed
it again, tracing her cleavage with the tip of his tongue.

Her heart began to race. He could feel it beating beneath his palm as he molded her breast in his hand.

Mariah gasped as her breast slipped free of her bodice.

Kit appeared as stunned at she was for a brief second
before a cat-that-ate-the-cream smile appeared on his face
and his eyes changed from the color of melted milk chocolate to that of dark chocolate.

Her knees buckled when he pressed his lips over the
tip of her breast. She would have fallen if she hadn't tangled her hands in his hair and held on and if Kit hadn't
reluctantly broken off his kiss long enough to scoop her
up in his arms. "K-Kit," she breathed, when Kit turned
and carried her down the stairs and back down the passageway.

"Hmm?" She still had her fingers tangled in his hair,
and Kit's reply was muffled against her upper arm. The
half sleeve of her evening dress exposed her soft skin and

Kit took advantage, kissing as much naked flesh as he could reach as he carried her.

"W-what are we doing?"

"Kissing."

"My arm?" she asked.

"For now," he murmured. "Kissing other places can come as soon as we get where we're going."

"Where are we going?"

"Someplace private." He didn't realize where he was going either until he found himself standing in front of her bedchamber—the bedchamber that connected to the one where Sister Mary Beatrix kept a less than vigilant eye on her charge. He set her on her feet, kissed her one last time—a long, lingering, passionate kiss that foretold of the delights to come—then opened the door and gently urged her inside.

He broke the kiss and closed the door. He stood in the hallway silently cursing himself for being a fool, cursing himself for being a gentleman, cursing himself for not being more of a gentleman, when the door opened once again. "Mariah, please, go to back inside and go to bed and lock the door behind you."

"I can't." She looked up at him. "I didn't just go to the library to get the book," she explained. "I went looking for Mrs. Kearney or Madame Thierry or one of the maids, but I got all turned around in the maze of passageways, and I ended up at the library."

Kit's eyes filled with tenderness, remembering how excited she'd been to show off her mother's jewelry. "What was so important that it couldn't wait until morning?"

"I need help getting out of this dress."

Kit looked down. She was already half out of it.

"It fastens down the back." She turned around and moved her hair out of the way so Kit could see.

"There aren't any buttons," he said in confusion.

"There will be," Mariah answered. "Tiny bead ones, but for now, I'm sewn into it."

"Why didn't you ask your chaperone to help you?" Kit asked.

Mariah looked mortified. "I couldn't let Sister Mary Beatrix see me in this. Besides, she's old. She needs her sleep. I didn't want to wake her. Could you hurry, please? What isn't sewn is pinned and the pins are beginning to hurt."

"Why the devil didn't you say so earlier?"

"You didn't give me a chance."

He glanced around the room. A pair of diamond earrings and a small handkerchief lay on the dressing table alongside a wooden hairbrush, but those were the only personal items he could see. "Where do you keep your embroidery basket?"

"I don't have one."

"No embroidery scissors?"

She shook her head.

Kit thought for a moment. "Stay here. I'll be right back." He walked down the hallway to his bedchamber, grabbed the waistcoat he'd left hanging on the arm of a chair, and retrieved a small penknife. He returned to find Mariah standing exactly where he'd left her. Kit placed his hand on the small of her back and propelled her to the little stool in front of the dressing table. "You might as well sit. This may take a few minutes."

She nodded her assent, and Kit began to cut through the stitches holding the dress in place. "Be careful," she cautioned. "Don't tear it. It's the only dress I've got that isn't black."

"Don't worry." He leaned forward and pressed a kiss at the nape of her neck. "I won't damage it."

It took a bit longer, but Kit was as good as his word. He carefully sliced the threads holding the back of the dress together, and then helped her ease the evening gown off her shoulders. Mariah stood up so he could slide the fitted waist over her hips and Kit was treated to a marvelous view of Mariah, naked except for the sheer dressmaker's chemise, in the flesh and reflected in the dressing table mirror.

She instinctively crossed her arms over her breasts, but lowered them when she saw the expression of wonder on his face. Mariah drew herself up to her full height and met his gaze in the mirror, watching him look at her.

Realizing he still had the blue silk dress in his hand, Kit carefully laid it across the top of the dressing table. He moved behind Mariah, pressed his front to her back, and reached around, cupped her breasts in his hands, and pressed his lips against her hair.

"I'm honored," he said, at last, his voice hoarse with emotion. "Thank you." He backed away from her.

Mariah started to turn around, but Kit stopped her. "No, don't." He smiled a self-deprecating smile. "If you turn around, I may not be able to walk away. Do you understand?"

Mariah nodded.

He traced the indention of her spine with his index finger from the nape of her neck to the curve of her buttocks, then reluctantly backed his way to the door without taking his gaze away from her.

Reaching behind him, fumbling for doorknob, Kit gently eased the bedroom door open. "Good night, Mariah. Don't forget to remove your jewelry from the dress."

"I won't," she whispered.

"Sweet dreams." He backed into the hall and began to close the door, but halted when she said his name.

"Kit?"

"Yes?"

"I love you."

"Mariah . . ."

"I always knew you would come back for me."

Chapter 20

By all means use some times to be alone.

—GEORGE HERBERT, 1593–1633

*K*it didn't sleep that night. He returned to the second-floor study in order to sit and think—how he could have been so extraordinarily blind?

For years he had kept the little girl in the tower a secret. He had never breathed a word of his meeting with her—or his spontaneous offer of marriage. Growing up, he had led the usual sort of life that the heirs to great family fortunes lived.

He had gone off to school, made lifelong friends with Dalton and Ash, gone to university, completed his Grand Tour, and spent a few months languishing in London before returning to Swanslea Park to concentrate on learning the family business—which in his case included managing an enormous amount of real estate and cash, breeding Thoroughbred horses, and learning the game of politics and statesmanship.

At two and twenty, Kit had planned to begin his bachelor life on the estate he'd inherited in Ireland, to spend a few years setting up a fine stable where he'd breed and train Thoroughbred horses before settling down to marry and raise a family of his own.

But fate, it seemed, had other plans for him.

Mariah Shaughnessy had reentered his life and reminded him of the promise she thought he had forgotten. But the truth was that Kit hadn't forgotten it. Or her. He realized now that the eight-year-old boy who made that impulsive offer of marriage had been as steadfast in his resolve to keep his promise as she had been in hers. The proof was in the fact that he had never kept a mistress or seriously entertained the notion of doing so.

While other young men at university had set demireps and actresses up in discreet houses in London or near the university, he hadn't felt the need.

Kit inhaled, then blew out the breath. Oh, there had been a few women in his past—a demirep or two, a slightly older widow in need of companionship, and surprisingly enough, a friend, and a young lady of good family who had eloped to Gretna Green with a soldier and been abandoned and disgraced. He had enjoyed all of them, but there had never been anyone who captured his heart until now.

Kit smiled, remembering how he'd approached his father with the question of what to do about the need for a certain sort of female companionship. He had been fifteen at the time, and he and Drew were supervising the breeding of his father's prized Thoroughbred stallion to Felicity, his mother's favorite mare. As they watched Zeus go through the mating dance, asking and receiving permission from the mare before he finally covered and mounted her, Kit had timidly asked his father how he should manage his urge to mate.

And he had never forgotten Drew's succinct answer. "With your hand."

"Sir?"

"Use your hand," Drew told him. "In the same motion Zeus is using, and you'll receive the same satisfaction with none of the consequences."

"Ash's father has already provided him with instruction from a wh—"

"I'm sorry to hear that," Drew answered.

"Why, Papa?"

"Because you're *fifteen*," Drew said. "And at fifteen you're too immature to appreciate the experience or to handle the consequences of such intimate relations."

"You mean a baby?"

"A baby or venereal disease, or a host of other complications, including the emotional attachment you will feel for the woman who shares your first experience."

"You think that I would form an emotional attachment to a *whore*?"

Drew's eyes flashed fire. "Don't ever let me hear you say anything like that again! Do you not have a mother, two sisters, and a governess you dearly love?"

"Yes, sir."

"Then you need to know that in our world, few options are open to women. We are fortunate in that we have land and position and capital, but not all families are so fortunate. For some families, the difference between living and dying depends upon a woman who willingly—or unwillingly—offers herself up for men to use in exchange for cash. Listen carefully, Kit. If you learn nothing else from me, I want you to understand that every *whore* you see on the streets, every demirep, fallen woman, governess, shop girl, or servant is someone's daughter or sister or mother or aunt or cousin or friend. They belong to a family just as your mother and sisters and governess belong to our family. They do not deserve your contempt or need your pity. They *are* in need of your consideration and your understanding."

"Yes, Papa."

"And the answer to your question is no. I don't *think* you'll form an emotional attachment to the woman who shares your first experience. I *know* you will. We all do." Drew smiled. "We all remember our first time. Usually with equal measures of pride and chagrin, and bittersweet regret." Drew reached down and patted Kit on the shoulder. "You cannot let go of your emotional attachment to Lancelot. And he was only your first pony. How do you think you will feel about your first time with a woman?"

"I see your point, Papa. But . . ." Kit frowned.

"You aren't going to hell," Drew said. "And you aren't

going to go blind. Trust me, son. Everyone does it. They just don't speak of it."

"Even?"

"Yes." Drew nodded. "When the time is right for you to expand your knowledge with a female, you'll know it. And if you do as Zeus did and wait for permission and follow her lead with tenderness and care, you'll be fine."

"Why does Zeus always wait for permission? He's the stallion. He's bigger and stronger. He could easily mount Felicity and spill his seed whether she was ready or not. But he waits."

"He waits because nature gave Zeus more sense and more manners than he gave most men. Zeus wants a mare who is his equal in heart and in strength. He can subdue her and force her to submit, but if he does that he runs the risk of having other stallions or mares do the same to her." He looked at his son. "Have you ever noticed that he doesn't always cover all the mares we offer him?"

Kit nodded. "And you always let him have his way."

"I do it because he's a horse and I believe he understands better than I do which mares will throw the strongest foals." He reached over and ruffled Kit's hair as he had done when Kit was little. "And I also believe he has the right of refusal. Lord knows I've never had the inclination to mate with everything that was offered to me. And Kit, always remember that a true gentlemen doesn't indulge his carnal appetites with children, animals, or those who do not wish it."

Kit nodded. "Papa, how old were you?"

"Nineteen."

"That old?"

"That old," Drew confirmed. "And even at nineteen I was unprepared for my feelings." He winked at Kit. "I should have listened to my father."

"What did he say to do?"

"He said to use my hand."

Kit smiled at the memory. The day after their talk a discreetly wrapped package appeared in Kit's bedroom. It contained several packets of French letters, a sea sponge and vinegar, a pessary, and two very informative sources of information from Drew's personal library. One was an outlawed pamphlet that explained the purpose of the birth-control devices contained in the package and detailed instructions for their use, and the second was an exquisitely illustrated book of color plates of the male and female anatomy and plates showing couples engaged in intimate acts. The plates were tastefully drawn, and the text accompanying the plates described each intimate act and the pleasure to be gained from it for male and female.

A letter from Drew accompanied the unusual gift. "My son," Drew had written, "I hope these will be of help to you in preparing for the future. Trust your instincts. When the time is right and the opportunity presents itself, you will know it and be the better lover for having taken the time and the care to learn. Also remember that there is no shame in taking instruction from your partner. Indeed, that is the most enjoyable way to learn, and there will always be wonderful, fascinating women who care enough to nurture and further your instruction. Treasure them, my son, appreciate, admire, respect, and protect them as they have appreciated, admired, respected, and protected you in the moment of your greatest vulnerability. Love, Papa."

Kit still had those books.

His father had been right. About everything. The opportunities that had presented themselves were experiences to be treasured. Experiences that had all led him to the place he found himself in now. Falling in love for the first time in his life with a girl who had waited fourteen years for him to remember.

Kit shook his head in wonder and stared at the little brass lantern sitting on his desk. The same little brass lantern he had given her to light her way on her journey to and from the tower all those years ago.

He knew it was the same lantern, not because Mariah had used it to light her way through Telamor Castle's maze of passages last night, but because the words *Kit's Light* were engraved upon the side.

The lantern had been a birthday gift from his mother. A lamp to light Kit's way as he explored Swanslea Park and all of its surroundings. It was a child's lantern. Smaller than the normal lanterns, easier for a child to manage, and his father had patiently taught him how to light it, trim the wick, and how to clean it, preparing it for the next day's adventures. Kit had carried it with him on the family's Irish holiday, but he hadn't brought it home.

Weeks later his father wondered what had happened to it, and Kit had truthfully replied that he had left it at the tower. Drew assumed Kit had forgotten it and replaced it with a new lantern the following week.

But Kit hadn't forgotten it. He had given it to the brave little girl who sneaked out of the convent at night and walked a mile or so down the narrow path that ran along the cliffs in order to climb up to the tower and sit and wish upon the stars.

To wish for the return of a mother who had been murdered. To wish for cake she wouldn't eat because a spoiled, thoughtless boy had told her no one would marry her if she got fat from it. To wish for a handsome earl instead of a handsome prince because the earl had impulsively promised to marry her.

Kit squeezed his eyes closed to keep the hot sting of tears burning them from falling. She had been as constant as the sun and had waited fourteen years for her earl to appear. And that stupid ass of an earl had come within a hair's breath of marrying her off to some country squire to save himself a bit of inconvenience. She must think him a heartless blackguard and yet . . .

I love you. I always knew you would come back for me.

Kit looked up and glanced at the clock on the mantel. It was forty-one minutes past the hour of six. He pushed back from the desk, stood up, and walked over to the bellpull to ring for Ford.

The butler appeared at fifty-two minutes past the hour. He carried with him a tray containing a pot of hot coffee, a cup and saucer, a plate of buttered toast, and a freshly ironed newspaper. "I took it upon myself to bring you a bit of breakfast, sir." Ford entered the study, set the tray on a side table, and poured Kit a cup of coffee.

"Thank you, Ford."

"You're welcome, sir."

"How long have you been in service here?" Kit asked.

"A score and six years, my lord. I began as a footman and worked my way up to my current position."

"So you were in service here when Lady Siobhan and Miss Mariah came to live here after Lady Siobhan's husband died."

"Yes, sir."

"How did Mr. Shaughnessy die?"

"His carriage overturned, sir. In London."

Kit exhaled. Carriages frequently overturned, and the occupants often died as a result of it. "Was there anything to suggest that Mr. Shaughnessy's accident was anything but an accident?"

"Not that I am aware of, sir."

"What about Lady Siobhan?" Kit asked.

"She slipped on the path and tumbled to her death." Ford paused. "Permission to speak frankly, sir?"

Kit nodded.

"We've always been very fond of Miss Mariah, sir, and found it quite sad that she should have to grow up at St. Agnes's. The staff and I are very happy to see that you have restored her to her rightful home."

Kit picked up a slice of buttered toast and bit into it. "Where is Miss Mariah this morning?"

Ford hesitated a second too long.

"Don't tell me. Let me guess. She's in the kitchen baking bread for Saint Elizabeth of Bohemia's Second Day."

"Quite so, sir," Ford answered.

"Blast it!" Kit set his cup down with enough force to rattle the saucer. "I didn't bring her here to work."

"For Miss Mariah, baking is a labor of love, sir. It's something at which she excels and something she enjoys immensely. And, indeed, sir, if she were not in the kitchens baking, we would have no bread." Ford quickly explained that the castle had been buying its bread from the convent, and as the convent had recently lost its head baker, it was not able to fulfill the orders.

"Damnation," Kit muttered. "If it makes her happy, she has my permission to continue so long as she doesn't miss her fittings or her lessons." He looked at Ford. "She will soon be one and twenty. If she's to have any chance at all to succeed in society, she must make a good showing." Kit knew that Mariah's debut into society would be successful because he knew that she would conclude her season by marrying the very wealthy earl of Ramsey and Kilgannon, heir to the marquess of Templeston. But he didn't want that to be the only reason her season was successful. He wanted it to be successful because she'd earned her place, not married it. "Agreed?"

"Agreed, sir."

"Now"—Kit poured himself another cup of coffee—"I noticed when I was in Miss Mariah's room last night . . ."

Ford's usually impassive expression was clearly disapproving.

"That's right," Kit said. "I was in Miss Mariah's room last evening. I mention it now because I noticed that other than a hairbrush, a handkerchief, and the few pieces of jewelry her mother was wearing the day she died—jewelry the abbess turned over to Mariah the day she left the convent—there were no personal items in the room at all. No jewelry box, no pin boxes, no embroidery baskets or perfume bottles, none of the items one would expect a young woman of her station to have. What happened to her mother's things? Surely, Lady Siobhan possessed those sorts of personal items. Items her daughter might like to have."

"Of course, sir." Ford shook his head as if to clear it. "How thoughtless of us. We stored everything away years ago in preparation for whoever would succeed the old earl. You see, sir, we had no way of knowing if that person would be you or if you would bring your family with you. Lady Siobhan's jewels are locked in the safe in the master bedchamber, sir, along with Lady Alanna's, and I believe the remainder of Lady Siobhan's things are stored in the attic for safekeeping."

Kit nodded. "See that they are removed from storage and placed in Miss Mariah's room. And see to the immediate hiring of a lady's maid for her."

Ford winced. "Lady's maids are hard to come by in Inismorn, sir. I may have to use an agency in Dublin or London."

"Nevertheless, Miss Mariah should have one. The reason I entered her room last evening was to help her remove her evening gown."

Ford coughed suddenly.

"She came looking for someone to help her and found that everyone had retired for the night. I was the only one awake at that hour. If you cannot locate a lady's maid right away, please see to it that someone is available to help Miss Mariah the next time the dressmaker pins and sews her into one of her creations."

"Indeed, sir." Ford bowed. "Lord Everleigh and Mr. Mirrant are at breakfast below and have asked when they might join you, and the dance master you asked me to secure will be arriving later this morning in time for Miss Mariah's afternoon lessons. If there is nothing else you require of me, I will see to your instructions."

"Thank you, Ford. Please inform Everleigh and Mirrant that they may join me here now. When the dance master arrives, have him await me in the morning room. And have someone drive Mariah to mass in the carriage and send a footman along to accompany her." The butler bowed and would have withdrawn from the study, but Kit stopped him. "Oh, and Ford?"

"Yes, sir?"

"Do you happen to play cards?"

"I have in the past, my lord, but not lately."

"I understand that you and Lord Everleigh will be instructing Miss Mariah on table settings and the etiquette concerning dinner parties, luncheons, at homes, and teas."

"Quite so, sir."

"Then plan to join us for her instruction in cards. In order to instruct her, Miss Shaughnessy and I will play as one person, so we need another to make a foursome. We play for money just as we do in society. Don't worry, I'll stake you." He smiled at his butler. "I wouldn't ask you to gamble your own money away just to further Miss Mariah's education." Kit handed Ford a duplicate key to the one on his key ring. "That key fits this cashbox." He opened the top drawer of the desk and showed Ford the cashbox he had installed in the false bottom of the desk drawer. "You and I have the only keys to it. Take what cash you need from here. I would like you to keep half of anything you win. If that's acceptable to you."

Ford blinked. "I beg your pardon, sir, but that doesn't seem quite the thing since I will be using your money instead of my own."

"You're entitled to recompense for time spent away from your other duties. Duties that will have to be attended to no matter how late the card game. I was going to suggest that you keep everything you win from Lord Everleigh or me and return what you might win from Mr. Mirrant to the cashbox as Mr. Mirrant can't afford the losses, but that would entail keeping track of who lost what to whom. This seemed the best way. Keep half of whatever you win and don't worry about any losses. I'll see that your losses are covered and that Mr. Mirrant is able to recover his. Agreed?"

"Agreed, sir."

Chapter 21

One father is more than a hundred schoolmasters.

—George Herbert, 1593–1633

SWANSLEA PARK
Northamptonshire, England

"*Drew, the morning post has arrived with a* letter from Kit." The marchioness of Templeston greeted her husband as soon as he entered the breakfast room.

The sixteenth marquess of Templeston smiled at her as he walked to the sideboard and helped himself to a cup of coffee from a large silver urn. He crossed the room, set his cup and saucer on the table, and leaned down to kiss his wife. "How is it that you managed to bathe and dress and beat me down to breakfast?"

They had returned from their morning ride a half hour earlier. "You lingered to chat with the grooms and to talk to the horses. I did not."

Drew sat down beside her. "You could not," he said softly.

They exchanged knowing looks.

"I daren't get too close to the stallions or the grooms with your scent still upon me."

"And that is precisely the reason I stayed to distract the grooms."

"Do you think they notice?"

Drew had no doubt that they noticed. His and Kathryn's

private morning rides were the stuff of legends among
Swanslea Park's grooms and stable boys. But Drew also
knew that none of the grooms or stable boys would ever
be indiscreet or risk embarrassing Kathryn. The fact that
they rode out nearly every morning they were in residence
at Swanslea Park and returned slightly disheveled and
very satisfied was nothing remarkable. But the fact that
they had been doing it for nineteen years was.

He wouldn't lie to her, but neither would he embarrass
her nor jeopardize their private time together, so Drew's
reply was carefully worded to set her mind at ease. "I
shouldn't think so, for no one has ever breathed a word
of it to me." He kissed her again, then took a sip of his
coffee. "Where are the girls this morning?"

"Still sleeping." Wren waved the letter in the air, but
Drew made no move to take it from her.

"And Ally?" He asked about the governess who had
been with the family since before he and Kathryn were
married.

"You know Ally takes her breakfast in bed while we're
out riding and takes her own morning ride once we return.
You probably met her in the stables."

Drew grinned. "I did. She looked quite fetching this morning in her new riding habit. Riley rode out with her." He
looked at Wren. "I wish the man would offer for her. He's
been in love with her since the first time he saw her sit a
horse."

Wren waved the letter beneath his nose once again. He
pretended to look surprised. "What's that?"

"You know what it is," Wren said in exasperation. "It's
a letter from Kit, and it's addressed to you or I would
have already opened it."

"Well, why didn't you say something instead of waving
it beneath my nose?" Drew winked, then took the letter
out of her hand and broke the wax seal. He was relieved
to see that it was the seal of the earl of Ramsey and not
the seal of the earl of Kilgannon. The boy had inherited

the Irish earldom first, but he would always be Drew's
beloved son and heir.

"Go on, read it!" Wren was practically bouncing in her
chair.

12 April 1838
Telamor Castle
Inismorn, Ireland

Dear Papa, Mama, and sisters,
   I am writing to inform you that Everleigh, Mir-
rant, and I arrived safely in Ireland two days past.
We spent the night aboard ship, disembarking early
the following morning. We arrived at the village of
Inismorn before the nooning hour, and I met with
the parish priest, Father Francis O'Meara, upon
arrival.
   The priest has been most helpful in explaining the
earl of Kilgannon's responsibilities to the village
and the parish. I was surprised to learn that in ad-
dition to inheriting the earldom, the castle, and the
surrounding acreage, I have also inherited the role
of guardian. . . .

Drew stopped reading aloud and began to laugh.
"Drew!"

"I can't help it," he told her. "If I didn't know better,
I would say that this was my father's doing."

"Do you think that's possible?"

"Anything's possible," Drew said. "It's not very likely,
but it does sound familiar, and it certainly bears my father's signature."

"Or Martin's," Wren reminded him.

Drew nodded thoughtfully. "Martin did know about the
earl of Kilgannon and Kit's inheritance. And he had to
have known about Kit's other mother."

"Well, go on," Wren urged. "Don't keep us in suspense.
Read the rest of it."

> *My ward, Miss Mariah Shaughnessy, has lived at St. Agnes's Sacred Heart Convent for the past fourteen years. It seems that Miss Shaughnessy's mother was the ward of the previous earl of Kilgannon and, in the event of her death, entrusted her daughter to the earl's care. As neither the number or the Christian name of the earl is mentioned, (an omission Martin would never have made), I became Miss Shaughnessy's legal guardian when I inherited the title. . . .*

Wren and Drew looked at each other. "Martin," they pronounced.

> *Miss Shaughnessy arrived with her chaperone, a nun from the nearby convent, shortly before I took up residence. The castle is thinly but adequately staffed and with a chaperone and Everleigh and Mirrant in residence with me, there is no cause for concern for Miss Shaughnessy's reputation. There is, however, concern on my part. As her guardian, my duty is to see that her mother's dying request—that her daughter be presented at court and make her bow to the queen before her twenty-first birthday—is granted. . . .*

This time, Wren began to laugh. "Serves him right," she said. "He couldn't wait to leave Swanslea Park to escape the preparations for Iris's coming out. He couldn't wait to be free from the tedium, as he called it, of practicing dance steps with his sisters and helping with their memorization of who's who among the peerage." She turned to Drew who was fighting to keep his own laughter under control. "Iris and Kate have been struggling with the who's who for weeks and they were born into the peerage. Imagine how much instruction Miss Shaughnessy will need."

"I still have trouble telling who's who," Drew said.

"Yes, well, so do I," Wren admitted. "And that isn't all—" She covered her mouth with her hand to smother a flood of giggles.

"What?" Drew demanded.

"I don't imagine they do much dancing in convents. . . ."

Drew gave up all pretense of composure. He let the letter fall to the table and roared with laughter. "I almost feel sorry for the boy."

Wren retrieved it and continued reading:

> As Miss Shaughnessy's natal day is a mere three weeks from today, I thought that I might send her to you for instruction. Although she was born a lady, Miss Shaughnessy has come of age at St. Agnes's convent and had not been schooled in ladylike pursuits or the rules of conduct of society.
>
> As her guardian, I wish to do well by her and can think of no better education in the ways of society than the one that she might gain if you would but allow her to travel to Swanslea Park and share in Iris's instruction. . . .

"That little rapscallion." Although Kit now stood eye to eye with his father, Drew still thought of him as the little boy who had stolen his older half brother's heart so long ago and had become his adopted son. "He's got some nerve trying to pawn her instruction off on us after rushing to Ireland to escape the tedium of partnering his sisters and helping them memorize Debrett's, leaving me to do it."

"You're the one who encouraged him to go to Ireland," Wren reminded him.

"That's right, I did," Drew said wryly. "Because I thought it was time he became his own man."

"A London season is expensive and can be overwhelming," Wren offered.

"He's got plenty of money, and he's a hell of a lot younger than we are. He'll survive it."

"You're not going to help him?" Wren was surprised. Drew had always spoiled Kit more than she had. She thought it was Drew's way of making up for Kit's loss, for the fact that Kit was never going to know the father they shared.

"I'm not going to lift a finger," Drew told her. "Except to write to say that Miss Shaughnessy is welcome to share Iris's debut provided she receives the necessary instruction before she arrives. You have enough to do with your work on the *Flora and Fauna Native to Gibraltar* and with all the to-do with Iris's wardrobe and the myriad social engagements we'll have to host. Not to mention getting the London house fully staffed and in order. And I have Swanslea Park and the rest of our holdings to look after and the next session of Parliament to prepare for. I've been asked to join Lord Melbourne's staff."

"Oh, Drew! How wonderful!" Wren was thrilled that the prime minister had recognized Drew's talent for diplomacy and leadership.

"Most of the time it's going to be a bloody nuisance," Drew said ruefully. "I hate playing politics. But it's where my talents lie. And at the moment I would say that this appointment couldn't come at a better time." He drank a bit of his coffee, realized it had grown cold, and stood up to refill it. "Does Kit have anything further to say in the letter?"

Wren scanned the remainder. "He sends his love, hopes that we are well, and looks forward to hearing from you soon. *Soon* is underscored twice."

"I'm afraid that the new earl of Kilgannon isn't going to like my reply at all," Drew said. "He's about to learn one of life's hardest lessons."

"And that is?"

"Everything comes at a price."

Chapter 22

*Thou art the book,
The library whereon I look.*

—HENRY KING, 1592–1669

*L*ord Everleigh and Dalton Mirrant were in the study helping Kit devise the lesson schedule for the week when Ford delivered his father's letter. After speaking with Ford, Mrs. Kearney, and Madame Thierry, they were working on a way to arrange Mariah's week to everyone's satisfaction.

"A letter arrived for you by special messenger, sir."

Kit took the letter, broke open the marquess of Templeston's seal, unfolded the letter, and began to read it:

> *14 April 1838*
> *Swanslea Park*
> *Northamptonshire, England*
>
> *My dear Kit,*
> *Miss Shaughnessy is welcome to join your sister when she makes her curtsy to the queen, provided that she has received all the necessary instructions.*
> *We shall remain at Swanslea Park until the first of May, when we shall remove to London.*
> *Shall I open your London town house or will you be residing with us at Templeston Place?*
> *We look forward to meeting Miss Shaughnessy.*
> *Your mother's and your sisters' love is enclosed with mine.*
>
> *As ever, Papa*

"What's the verdict?" Dalton looked up from the newspaper he was reading.

Kit closed his eyes for a moment, then opened them and slowly exhaled. "Typically Papa."

"He said yes," Ash guessed.

"He said no," Kit answered.

Dalton turned to Ash. "You owe me a tenner."

Ash frowned. "I can't remember if Lord Tarleton is a baron or a viscount." Ash had volunteered to help Mariah memorize the titles and forms of address she'd need to remember for her presentation. He'd been engaged in his listing of the peers and their titles along with bits of common information about them that Mariah would be expected to know.

"Baron," Kit and Dalton answered in unison.

"Lord Carleton is the viscount," Kit added.

"Thanks," Ash made a few notations on his list.

"Stop evading the issue," Dalton told him. "And admit you owe me the ten pounds we wagered."

"I owe you ten pounds." Ash took out his wallet and handed Dalton the same ten-pound note Kit had lost to him the day they arrived at Telamor. "I assume a note will serve in lieu of guineas."

"A ten-pound note will do very nicely." Dalton folded the money and tucked it into his own wallet.

Ash shook his head. "I was sure he would do it. It's not like Lord Templeston to refuse any reasonable request."

"Ha!" Dalton proclaimed. "That's why you lost. Kit's request wasn't the least bit reasonable. It was a damned imposition. Even for parents." He glanced at Kit. "Why are you looking so relieved? I thought you *wanted* to send Miss Shaughnessy to Swanslea Park. In fact, I offered to accompany her."

"When I wrote the first letter, I thought it would be best," Kit admitted. "For all of us. But we've already made a good start by hiring the dressmaker, and the dance master will be arriving later this morning, and since we've all spent a good deal of time in planning her curriculum, I have reconsidered. . . ."

They had planned her schedule of lessons with the same amount of care and attention to detail that Wellington had given to his campaign against Napoleon. Because time was short and because Mariah insisted on baking, her days would be extraordinarily long. But at the moment that was unavoidable.

Kit had done his best to combine lessons to accommodate her, but he knew she would eventually have to concede to allowing Ford to hire a baker for the castle. Mariah simply couldn't bake all the bread and cakes and pastries they needed and do all of the other things she needed to do before the season began.

Mariah's early mornings were to be spent in the kitchens baking. After mass came fittings with Madame Thierry and her assistants, and after luncheon and an hour's nap, Mariah's afternoons and much of her evenings would be spent in lessons.

The schedule was incredibly difficult to keep for someone who rose at four in the morning in order to bake. But so was the endless round of entertainments of the season. During the season, breakfast began at eleven, followed by shopping and morning calls that generally began around two or three in the afternoon and lasted until tea.

The hours after tea were spent preparing for the evening's entertainment. Balls rarely began before nine in the evening, almost always included a midnight supper, and often lasted until four or five in the morning. A few hours of sleep and the whole cycle began again.

The hours required for a lady baker would prove to be an excellent test of her ability to survive the season.

"And I've already written to tell Papa I've changed my mind." Kit picked up his cup and took a sip.

"He shall be quite happy to hear that," Dalton declared.

"Yes," Ash added. "Because he knows what we're letting ourselves in for." He looked at Kit and winked.

Dalton dropped the newspaper and leaned back in the leather armchair. "Well, I never thought I'd say it, but the truth is that after years of being molded into the gentleman

I've become, I rather like the idea of molding a young woman into my image of what a lady should be. Lord knows, their mamas seldom teach them the things they really need to know."

Kit choked, spewing coffee everywhere.

Dalton leapt up and began pounding Kit on the back. "Not to worry, old man," he said. "I'm not molding her entirely in my image of the perfect lady, you and Ash are contributing."

"Thank God," Ash said dryly. "Because your tastes in women are a little less discerning than ours."

"You're talking about what I like in women who are not ladies," Dalton protested. "I'm talking about my opinion of what true ladies should be and what they should know." He sighed. "Take Lady Templeston, for example . . ."

Ash rolled his eyes and gave Kit a knowing smile. "Lady Templeston may be your shining light of what a true lady should be, but you aren't likely to find another one like her. And she's already taken."

"I'm simply saying that Lady Templeston is an intelligent well-educated woman, able to converse on a variety of subjects. She is her own woman with her own sense of style and grace and an unfailing instinct for what suits her. And there is nothing artificial about her. She makes you feel at home and comfortable." Dalton sighed again. "I enjoy taking tea with Lady Templeston and Iris and Kate and Miss Allerton, and I can't say that about any of the other ladies I've called upon. When I'm at Swanslea Park, I never feel as if I want to escape."

"If that's the case, you should offer for Iris," Kit replied offhandedly as he mopped up droplets of coffee with his handkerchief. "Except for the fact that she has no apparent talent for painting, she's Mama made over."

There was complete silence in the room.

Kit looked up from his task and over at Dalton.

Dalton was blushing.

"Iris?" Kit asked as realization dawned.

Ash began to laugh. "It took you long enough to notice."

"Do you intend to offer for her?"

Dalton stood up and began to pace the room, then finally stopped before the window. He stared out of it for a long time before he finally shook his head.

"Why not?"

"Because your father would have to be a fool to allow his eldest daughter to marry a younger son with no prospects." He turned around to face his two friends. "I was trained to be a clergyman, though I haven't a true calling for it, but it's a gentlemanly profession, and as a clergyman I could eventually take a wife, unlike my brother who chose the army, provided I attain a suitable living. I'm a gentleman and the younger son of a viscount. I've three other brothers in line before me, so the likelihood of my inheriting is very slim. I have no money of my own, and I live off the largesse of my friends. What young lady is going to look twice at me? And what father would consider me if she did?"

"But, Iris—"

"I'm not good enough for Iris," Dalton said flatly.

"You love Iris and yet you're willing to stand by and say nothing while she makes her coming out? You're willing to watch while some other man courts her? While some other man proposes?"

Dalton looked Kit in the eye. "Why not? Isn't that what you're about to do with Miss Shaughnessy?"

"Not at all," Kit told them. "I'm going to marry her."

"What?" Ash asked the question, but both he and Dalton were staring at Kit. "When?"

"Once she's celebrated her birthday and no longer has to worry about losing her fortune. And if I can wait that long, after the season," Kit said. "Personally, I don't care to wait, but Mariah's mother wanted her to have a London season, and I'm going to do my best to see that she gets the entire thing. Then we'll cap it off with a wedding."

"Congratulations, old man!" Dalton was genuinely happy for Kit.

Ash was happy as well, but his happiness for Kit was tempered with his usual caution. "Are you certain she's the one? You've only known her a few days."

Kit grinned. "I've known her much longer than a few days," he said. "I just didn't know her name. I've carried the memory of her in my heart for the last fourteen years. You see . . ." Kit related the story of how he and Mariah had first met, of how he had offered to marry her, and how she had accepted, then waited for him to return.

"You gave up eating sweets after that trip to Ireland," Ash remembered.

"And when you discovered you'd inherited this place, you told us you wanted to come to Ireland to find your destiny."

Kit nodded. "I think I've somehow always understood that *she* was my destiny." *Like Zeus, he had somehow instinctively recognized his mate.*

"Does she know?" Ash asked.

"She's known since she was six."

Ash laughed. "A lot has changed since then. Have you asked her to marry you again? As man to woman?"

"Not yet," Kit told him. "But I will."

"Hopefully, after you've spoken with the squire," Ash reminded him. "If he is serious about marrying Mariah, things could get nasty, and you don't want to run the risk of breaking her heart."

Kit slapped his palm against his forehead. "Bugger me! But so much has changed in the last couple of days that I forgot all about the squire's claim to Mariah."

"I'll wager *he* hasn't," Dalton said wryly.

*His words proved prophetic, for when Ford en-*tered the study fifteen minutes later, he carried a silver salver with two white calling cards on it.

Kit lifted the first calling card off the tray. "Terrence Reardon," he read.

"The dance master, sir. He arrived a few moments ago. I've shown him into the music room to await your arrival."

Kit frowned. "The music room?" He didn't want the man wandering about the music room assuming he had the job when Kit fully intended to see the man in action before he hired him. He'd seen a great many dance masters come and go in the past few months—so many, in fact, that his father had finally determined that he and Kit could better teach Iris and Kate how to dance. From that experience Kit had learned that one simply didn't allow a strange man to waltz into a room and take one's sisters or one's loved one into his arms without having had the opportunity to meet and observe the man beforehand. And he had instructed Ford to show him into the morning room before bringing him up to the study. "Why not the morning room?"

"I took the liberty of showing your other visitor into the morning room, my lord."

Kit picked up the other card and read it aloud. "Sir Nathan Bellamy, Esquire." He looked up at the butler.

Ford nodded.

"Oh, *hell*. The squire."

Dalton glanced over at Kit. "Speak of the devil . . ."

"And he appears," Ash concluded.

Chapter 23

For evil news rides post, while good news baits.

—John Milton, 1608–1674

"The earl of Kilgannon," Ford announced as he opened the doors to the morning room.

The squire stood up and sketched a flawless bow as Kit entered. "My lord."

"Sir Nathan." Kit's mental image of a country squire was a short, squat, and toady sort of fellow who blustered about pretending to be something he was not. One whose lack of looks and social standing garnered him only the barest degree of acceptability.

He expected a middle-aged man with a potbelly, receding hairline, and nose reddened from hard living and drink. What he saw was a middle-aged man whose looks and bearing were nearly equal to his father's. A man with dark eyes and a handsome, sun-bronzed face who stood as straight and as tall as a lance, without an ounce of spare flesh about his middle and one whose full head of thick, shiny dark hair, graying slightly at the temples, was probably the envy of most fellows his age.

No one, upon seeing this man in a drawing room, would ever mistake him for a country squire. Bellamy looked nothing like a country rustic. He gave the appearance of being urbane in nature and much more refined and important than his standing would indicate.

Kit disliked him on sight.

"I beg your pardon for calling uninvited," Bellamy began, "but I've come on a matter of some importance, as I am certain you are aware."

"I am." Kit did not sit or offer the squire a chair, but remained standing, using the advantage his extra inch of height gave him.

"Then you must also know that some months ago, I spoke with the abbess of St. Agnes's about a matter of the heart regarding Miss Mariah Shaughnessy."

Kit narrowed his gaze at the choice of words. "A matter of the heart?"

Bellamy smiled.

Kit was disgusted to find that in addition to appearing youthful and handsome, Bellamy still possessed all of his shiny white teeth.

"Indeed, Lord Kilgannon. When one is speaking to a nun about the possibility of marriage to one of her charges, are not all marriages matters of the heart?"

He didn't like Bellamy's oily answer any better than he liked his looks or his patronizingly false smile. "What sort of matter is it when one is speaking to a peer of the realm?"

"It is still very much a matter of the heart, but I suppose one must also admit to a certain familial obligation."

Kit deliberately misunderstood. "I was not aware that you are in any way related to Miss Shaughnessy."

Bellamy smiled again. "I am not currently related to Miss Shaughnessy in any way but I should like to be, shall we say, related by marriage in the near future?"

"How near into the future?" Kit asked.

"Within the month."

"So soon?"

"Not soon at all, Lord Kilgannon. Look closely and you shall see that I am not quite the age my youthful appearance would suggest. I did not rush into the matter of marriage as many of my contemporaries did. I took the time to sow all of my wild oats, preferring to wait until the perfect young lady came of age."

"And Miss Shaughnessy is that perfect young lady."

"But of course, my lord, or I would not have proposed

such an advantageous alliance—made such a tender offer of marriage to her guardian."

"You mean the Mother Superior," Kit said, deciding to cut to the chase and put an end to the squire's visit. "Because I have not entertained an offer of alliance—tender, advantageous, or otherwise. Nor would I consider doing so as I cannot help but think that any advantages of such an alliance would be yours. I see no advantages for *my ward*."

"She was not your ward when I spoke to the Mother Superior regarding my intentions."

"I beg to differ."

"Nonetheless," the squire continued as if he had not heard Kit's response, "the Mother Superior accepted my honorable proposal of marriage on Miss Shaughnessy's behalf."

"She did not have the authority to do so."

"I had no way of knowing that when I made my offer," Bellamy reminded him. "I made the offer and was accepted, and as such, I am entitled to see that my expectations are satisfied."

"Your expectations do not concern me."

"The release of her fortune concerns you," the squire sneered.

At last Kit allowed himself a tiny smile. "A fortune you told the Mother Superior was of no interest to you," Kit retorted. "Did she hear in error? Or did you deliberately mislead her by lying?"

The squire glared at Kit. "You misinterpret my intent. I said what the Mother Superior wished to hear. The purpose being to reassure her."

Kit didn't blink. "You lied."

"I did," the squire admitted. "But my intentions were honorable."

"We have reached the *heart of the matter* at last," Kit said. "I submit that you lied to the Mother Superior in order to further your personal aims. And as such, I submit that whether you intended it to or not, your claim holds true. Miss Shaughnessy's fortune is of no interest to you. Your claim to Miss Shaughnessy is nullified and your presence here no longer required. Good day, Sir Nathan."

"I have the prior claim to her." The squire shook with impotent rage. "I will take my case to the courts."

"Do what you will," Kit informed him in a dismissive tone. "But Miss Shaughnessy and I have been betrothed to one another since we were children."

Bellamy smiled then. "Be warned, Lord Kilgannon, you have not heard the last of me."

"That may be true," Kit allowed, "but I have heard the last of you *today*. Ford will show you to the door."

"I hope that wasn't the dance master," Mariah said moments later when she entered the morning room after returning from mass.

"Who?" Kit asked.

She removed her bonnet and looked around for a place to put it, before finally deciding just to hold on to it by its ribbons. "The man I met on the walkway leading up to the front door. The one with the disagreeable look on his face."

"Oh, that man." Kit laughed. "No, that wasn't the dance master. The dance master is waiting for us in the music room. You're late."

Mariah smiled. "I stopped in at the rectory. Father Francis insisted that I go show Mrs. Flynn my new dress." She took a few steps forward, then twirled around in a graceful pirouette. Mariah was wearing the first dress Madame Thierry and her assistants had completed. A day dress made of lightweight blue wool, with matching gloves, bonnet, and half boots.

"And what did Mrs. Flynn have to say about the new addition to your wardrobe?" Kit asked.

"She said I looked like a princess. And that the color of my dress reminded her of the wild bluebells that grow along the cliffside path in the spring." She waited for Kit to catch up to her, then smiled up at him. "What do you think?"

"I think the color pales in comparison to the blue of your eyes."

"Truly?"

"Cross my heart." He did just that, sketching a cross over the left breast pocket of his coat.

His eyes darkened as he looked at her.

"What are you thinking now?" Mariah asked, recognizing his intent, but wanting him to say it.

"I'm wondering where the devil your chaperone is when I need her?"

"In her room, of course. When she's away from the convent, Sister Mary Beatrix practices strict solitude," she answered, glancing around to see if any of the household was watching, before she moved closer to him and tilted her face up for a kiss.

"What good is she as a chaperone?"

"She doesn't need to chaperone," Mariah answered. "She knows she can trust you."

"Wonderful," Kit grumbled.

"Well?" she hinted broadly.

"Well what?"

"We're alone. Aren't you going to kiss me?"

Kit obliged. Kissing her quite thoroughly until footsteps sounded outside the morning room. "So much for Sister Mary Beatrix's misplaced trust."

"It isn't misplaced," Mariah corrected. "You haven't been trying to kiss her, have you?"

"Not yet," Kit said, planting a kiss on her nose before releasing her. "But I will if you don't stop teasing me."

"Uh-hmm." Ford appeared in the doorway. "Excuse me, sir, miss. But the dance master and Lord Everleigh and Mr. Mirrant are awaiting Miss Mariah in the music room."

Kit offered Mariah his elbow.

She put her hand on his arm. "You never did tell me who that man on the front walk was."

"That was your erstwhile betrothed," Kit told her. "Sir Nathan Bellamy, Esquire."

"Ooooh." She shivered involuntarily.

"Didn't you find him handsome?" he asked. "Mother Superior apparently did."

"Mother Superior is welcome to him," Mariah retorted. "I hope you refused him."

"He didn't offer for *me*," Kit teased. "He offered for *you*. But I sent him packing anyway. On your behalf, of course." He smiled down at her. "I suppose that must have accounted for the disagreeable look on his face."

Three quarters of an hour later the dance mas- ter, Mr. Terrence Reardon, followed the squire out the front door.

And everyone who'd been present for the dance lesson was glad to be rid of him.

He had turned out to be a shorter, oilier version of the squire. He oozed counterfeit charm from every pore, and his obsequious bowing and scraping set Kit's and Ash's teeth on edge.

The domestic employment agency Ford had sought when Kit asked that he secure the services of a dance master and a lady's maid had sent Mr. Reardon to see His Lordship at Telamor Castle. Since Ash was the highest-ranking lord in the house, Mr. Reardon assumed he was the lord looking to employ him. Kit did nothing to correct that assumption. And neither did anyone else.

Kit simply used Mr. Reardon's incorrect assumption as an opportunity to observe the dance master and measure his character and his level of competence. Kit sat on a chair beside Dalton behind the pianoforte, watching the dance instruction and turning pages while Dalton played. The first thing he noticed was that Mr. Reardon's knowledge of the dances currently in vogue in London was limited. His dance steps were sloppy and his instructions impossible to follow. "Begin the steps of the quadrille, Miss Shaughnessy."

"She can't begin the steps of the quadrille, Reardon," Dalton called out from behind the pianoforte. "She doesn't know how."

Reardon ignored him. "Music!" he ordered. "Begin, Miss Shaughnessy."

"I can't," she told him. "I don't know the steps."

Reardon clucked his tongue, shook his head, rattled off names of the steps, almost barking them at her.

Mariah looked to be on the verge of tears until Ash suggested that the dance master *show* her how to perform the steps rather than how to *recite* them.

The dance master showed her the steps once and demanded she repeat them. Mariah tried. But the harder she tried, the worse it became. First she turned the wrong way, then she tripped and stepped on his toes, and the more mistakes she made, the angrier Mr. Reardon became. "You clumsy, ignorant young woman," he scolded. "Again!"

"No," Ash interrupted. "Try another dance."

Mr. Reardon nodded and then clapped his hands and demanded Dalton play a minuet.

Dalton looked at Kit. Kit shook his head and Dalton began a waltz.

"Stop!" he shouted at Dalton who was playing the pianoforte. "I want a minuet. If she cannot do the steps to the quadrille without stepping upon my toes, I will not have her waltzing on them lest we both go tumbling to the floor."

Kit stood up and started toward the dance master.

Ash took one look at him and attempted to diffuse the tension. "You are the dance master," he said. "Your job is to teach her, not berate her."

But Mr. Reardon sealed his own fate. "My lord, I beg your indulgence, but I cannot teach this young woman to dance under these conditions. The accompaniment is amateurish and without the necessary rhythm, and your ward . . ." He threw up his hands. "I fear she is too far lacking in grace and intelligence to even begin to learn to dance."

As they watched, tears began to roll down Mariah's face. She didn't make a sound. She simply stood there with her head bowed in shame at her inability to master a single dance.

"Kit! Wait!" Ash shouted a warning.

But the warning came too late for the dance master. He executed the only graceful turn he'd made during the lesson and received a fist in the eye for his effort.

"I wanted to do that," Ash complained.

"What stopped you?" Kit rubbed his knuckles.

"You." He looked from Kit to the dance master on the floor. "Now what? Once word of this gets around, we aren't likely to have any more dance masters appear at the door looking for work."

"We won't need one," Kit said grimly. "I'll do it."

"You?" Ash raised an eyebrow in query. "When we left Swanslea Park, you swore you'd never dance another step as long as you lived."

"With Iris or with Kate," Kit hedged. "I'm willing to make an exception in this case."

"Oh?" Ash's eyebrow rose another fraction. "And why is that?"

"This is a matter of defending Mariah's honor. Now, get him off the floor and onto that chair." Kit pointed to the chair in question. "He's going to have the pleasure of watching Mariah dance, and then he's going to get the devil off my property."

Ash grinned. "Whatever you say, Lord Kilgannon." He jerked Mr. Reardon up by his collar, dragged him off the dance floor, and over to the chairs lining the wall. He set the dance master on the chair Kit indicated, then sat down beside him.

Holding his hand over his eye, Reardon attempted to make a run for the door, but Ash caught him by the coat-tails and pulled him back onto the chair. "I wouldn't if I were you," he warned. "You're skating on very thin ice already. Now, sit still and keep your mouth shut."

Kit walked over to Mariah, gently wiped her tears away with the pad of his thumb, and then bowed at the waist and held out his hand. "May I have the pleasure of this dance, Miss Shaughnessy?"

She shook her head. "I can't dance. I don't know how."

"Yes, you do," he insisted gently. "All it takes is the

right partner." He put his hand on her waist, gently pulled her forward, and took her hand in his. "Gather your skirt in your hand and spread it out like a fan." He shook his head at her first attempt and praised her on her second. "There, like that. That's right." He turned to Dalton and nodded. "I'll lead you," he promised. "All you have to do is take a deep breath, look me in the eye, listen to the rhythm of the music, and step. . . ." Kit stepped into the dance, and Mariah followed, and suddenly, as if by magic, she was dancing. Flying. Waltzing around the room.

They waltzed around the room until Mariah was breathless and giddy with excitement and Dalton was tired of playing. When the music stopped, Kit bowed to her, and Mariah sank down into a graceful curtsy.

"Genuflecting, my lady?" Kit teased.

"No." She looked at him with joyous wonder. "Simply honoring a true master of the dance."

"All it takes is the right partner." He offered her his hand and helped her up, then walked with her over to the dance master.

"*That*, Mr. Reardon, is how a gentleman teaches a young lady to dance. And as this young lady has proved to be such an accomplished dancer, I don't believe we require your services. Good day."

"What about the fee? And my eye?" Mr. Reardon demanded.

Kit smiled. "I don't believe you should pay me a fee for blackening your eye. It was my pleasure to do so."

"I recommend ice for the first day." Ash offered his opinion to the dance master. "And the application of leeches thereafter."

"Amateurish accompaniment, my arse!" From behind the pianoforte, Dalton launched into a stylish performance of Frederic Chopin's Concerto for the Piano in E Minor.

"And I suggest you offer Mr. Mirrant your apologies on your way out," Ash offered another helpful opinion. "Or you may find your other eye blackened before he finishes this concerto."

Chapter 24

The lark now leaves his wat'ry nest
And climbing shakes his dewy wings.

—Sir William Davenant, 1606–1668

Swanslea Park
Northamptonshire, England
Two days later

"We've another letter from Kit," Wren announced as Drew entered the Dowager Cottage where Wren kept her studio. If she was working and he was in the neighborhood of the cottage, Drew always made it a point to join her for tea. "Newberry just sent it over. It arrived with the afternoon post."

"Have you opened it?" he asked as he walked over to the easel by her worktable.

"No." She shook her head. "I've been tempted, but I hadn't yet reached a stopping point." Her work as a botanical and zoological illustrator was exacting, and she prided herself on the quality of her drawings and paintings. "It's on the table by the door. Give me a second. I've almost reached a stopping point."

Drew retrieved the letter, then walked over to view her progress. "Very nice." He complimented her renderings of the front, back, side, and cross-section views of one of a species of butterflies found on the island of Gibraltar.

"I like it," Wren murmured.

"Enough to start work on a miniature of it on silk?"

Wren pursed her lips in thought. "I'm not sure. I may just wait and surprise you."

Drew leered at her. Kathryn had been surprising him with tiny works of art painted on her silk stockings for nineteen years, and her surprises never failed to excite and arouse him. "I'll look forward to it." He walked to the tea table, poured the tea, and arranged Kathryn's favorite sandwiches on her plate. "Done yet?"

Wren nodded. "All done." She dropped her brush in a jar of cleaner, cleaned her hands, removed her painter's smock, and smoothed her hair into place. She knew she smelled of perfume and turpentine, but Drew had never seemed to mind.

She sat down on the small love seat beside him and accepted the plate he handed her. Like their morning rides, this was a ritual they observed while at Swanslea Park, and everyone in the household knew that interruptions were forbidden except in the case of an emergency.

"Well, go on," she urged. "Open it."

"Finish your tea like a good little artist and I will." He leaned over and kissed her soundly. "I venture to say the boy probably wasn't too pleased to receive my letter. It will be interesting to see how he responds."

Drew devoured three tiny sandwiches, drank his tea, and bit the head off a gingerbread boy before he set his plate aside and picked up the letter and broke the wax seal.

It was the Ramsey seal once again, and Drew smiled in spite of himself.

"I'm being very patient," Wren announced. "But I won't put up with this deliberate dawdling much longer. Read it!"

13 April 1838
Telamor Castle
Inismorn, Ireland

Dear Papa, Mama, and sisters,

I hope this letter finds you well. I haven't had time yet to receive your post and this letter may cross it along the way, but I felt an urgent necessity to let you know that I have decided to keep Miss Shaughnessy.

Wren frowned. "That's not a good sign."

Drew met her gaze. "I think it's a very good sign," he disagreed. "It means he's accepting the responsibility he inherited along with the title."

"If he's decided to keep her, there's an emotional attachment already," Wren fretted. "And you know how hard it is for Kit to let go of anything he becomes attached to. What will he do when she comes out and someone else offers for her?"

I've arranged for a dressmaker and a lady's maid and a dancing teacher to join us here at Telamor, for we have decided to prepare Miss Shaughnessy for her presentation before we leave for Swanslea Park.

I hope my change of heart has not adversely affected your schedule, and I offer my sincerest apologies if it has done so. But I have come to realize that Miss Shaughnessy is my responsibility, and I did you and Mama and Iris and Kate a great disservice in asking you to shoulder it for me.

Miss Shaughnessy is a very quick learner, and with Everleigh and Mirrant's help and knowledge, I am certain that she will be most presentable.

My love to you all,

Kit.

"Oh, my stars," Wren said. "Ally and Iris and you and Kate and I have been laboring for *months* to prepare Iris. And Kit thinks he and Ashford and Dalton are going to do it in three weeks? He must have lost the good sense he was born with."

"Or his heart," Drew murmured. He folded the letter. "He made the right choice."

"For us or for him?"

Drew glanced down at his wife and saw that she was crying. "Oh, Kathryn, my love . . ."

"He's grown up, Drew," she wept. "Our precious little boy is grown. Nothing will ever be the same."

"No," he said gently, pressing his lips to her soft hair. "I don't suppose it will. But we always knew it had to happen someday."

"It's happening too soon." She looked up at Drew. "I told you not to let him go to Ireland. I was afraid we would lose him if you let him go."

"And I was afraid we would lose him if I didn't," he admitted. "We always knew the day would come. This is the way it's supposed to be. We gave him wings so he could fly. And if everything works out the way it should, one day Kit will present us with another precious little boy to love."

"And then I shall be a grandmother." Wren looked up at him and cried even harder.

"The grandest," he pronounced, with more than a touch of humor in his voice.

She glanced up at him between sniffles. "I fail to see what's so amusing."

Drew shrugged. "I was thinking that I've never been seduced by a grandmother."

Wren let out a sigh of exasperation. "Is that all you can think about?"

Drew nodded and gave her a boyish grin. "It is when I'm with you."

Chapter 25

The hand that hath made you fair hath made you good.

—WILLIAM SHAKESPEARE, 1564–1616

Her lessons began in earnest the day after the dance master departed.

From Lord Everleigh, Mariah learned the conventions of English society. Mariah struggled to memorize Debrett's and the rules governing every aspect of life in London society. She practiced conversation and forms of address, curtsies, and the all-important rules of behavior, including those concerning her presentation at the drawing room at St. James's Palace where she would make her curtsy to the queen.

Lord Everleigh had a gift for remembering details, the things a hostess and wife was expected to know, from the wines to serve with dinner to the proper selection of the gentleman's cigars. He was an excellent arbiter of all that was proper and in good taste, and he taught her as much about the world as he knew it as she could absorb. There were rules and etiquette for every aspect of English society, and Lord Everleigh knew them all.

Lord Everleigh and Ford began instruction in table manners, the proper way to lay a tea table, how to pour, and how to engage in small talk. Ford generally instructed while Lord Everleigh took the opportunity to engage Mariah in the small talk, regaling her with the latest bits of gossip and personal tidbits about members of the peerage, testing her powers of recall. He made it into a game, trying to trick her by using the wrong names or improper titles or forms of address, but Mariah persisted, refusing to be daunted.

Lord Everleigh offered his bits of wisdom to Mariah and she soaked up the knowledge like a sponge. She likened it to learning the catechism she had learned at the convent, where the rules of society were every bit as strict as anything she might find in London.

From Dalton Mirrant, she gained a sense of style and of polish. He was a charming companion, intelligent, witty, entertaining. He had a fine singing voice and an ear for music and languages. He played the pianoforte like a dream and decided to teach Mariah the basics as well as all of the songs she needed to know in order to mix with other young people on musicale evenings. He told her stories and jokes and conversed with her in French and Italian, allowing her to practice the languages she had learned at school, adding a smattering of German to her repertoire, and patiently correcting her pronunciation and refining her accents.

Lord Everleigh could not distinguish colors, while Dalton had a flair for it, so Dalton began consulting with the dressmaker in the cut and color of Mariah's wardrobe, but did not attend the fittings since he was neither her guardian nor her betrothed.

Dalton had to console himself with the knowledge that he would be allowed to view the wardrobe he had had a hand in creating as she made use of it during the season.

As her guardian, Kit could attend her fittings, but he didn't. Watching her being fitted for her new wardrobe would have been sheer torture for Kit, who was finding it hard to keep a correct posture and distance during her dancing lessons.

From Kit, Mariah learned confidence. The confidence of knowing she was loved. He hadn't yet said it to her aloud, but Mariah knew it. She felt it in his touch, in his voice, in the way he looked at her, and in the way he looked out for her. Kit wasn't as smooth a talker as Dalton or as stern a taskmaster as Lord Everleigh, but he was by far her greatest teacher. She endured the long days of endless fittings, recitation, practice, and drilling in order to share her leisure time with Kit.

With Kit, she danced and painted and explored Telamor Castle and its surroundings. With Kit she shared her dreams and learned of his. He told her of his plans to build a stable at Telamor and to raise Thoroughbreds. She told him of her dream to construct a three-foot-tall wedding cake covered in pink rosebuds. Together, they sketched designs for the stables and the grounds. They mixed the perfect shade of pink for candy rosebuds and the perfect colors for racing silks and selected the names for the generations of horses that would be born at Telamor Stables.

Kit shared his childhood memories and gave Mariah the childhood she had missed. He allowed her to play and helped her remember the childish pursuits she had long since put away. And there seemed to be nothing he wouldn't do to please her. They walked along the beach, collecting shells and playing tag with the waves. They gathered wildflowers on the moor and sat for hours talking while they wove wildflower garlands for her hair. He taught her to sketch and to paint with watercolors.

Kit was a highly skilled watercolorist. And it only stood to reason that he would have the knowledge, if not the talent, after having grown up in Wren's studio. But he had talent to go along with the knowledge. He was an artist.

Every afternoon he and Mariah set off to sketch and paint. Mariah's talent was in landscapes, while Kit's was as a gifted portraiture artist for both humans and animals. Only a portion of the art lessons was given over to art. The rest of the time was spent in the serious pursuit of play, but Kit made sure Mariah had a box of paints and brushes, a palette, a smock, an easel, paper or canvas, and a minimum of instruction. But the art lessons gave them a reason to escape from the other lessons and concerns of the castle and to run wild, exploring the estate.

Three days after the departure of the dance master, Mariah and Kit set off to paint and to explore the castle grounds. They were playing hide-and-seek in the maze, stealing kisses behind the statuary when all at once Mariah rounded a corner and stumbled out of the maze at the opposite end of the garden from where they started. There, in the far corner of the original garden, was a stone wall over six feet tall with an arched door set into the wall.

"Look, Kit." Mariah set her paints and easel down and hurried to the wooden door.

"What is it?" he asked.

"My garden," she answered.

"Yours?"

Mariah blushed. "Well, it's really yours because the castle belongs to you, but I remember when I was a little girl, I used to play in this garden. My mother had the stonemasons and the gardeners build it for me."

Kit was puzzled. "Why?"

Mariah laughed. "Because I could get out of the big one. I could climb over the walls or simply unlatch the gate and walk away. She built this one for me so I would be safe." She reached for the door handle and pushed. "It's locked."

She was so disappointed that Kit pulled out his key ring and handed to her. "Try these."

Mariah took the keys from him and inserted them, one by one, until she reached the key that unlocked the door. She returned his key ring to him, then pushed the door to the garden open.

The garden inside was lush, slightly overgrown, and because the weather had been so mild, in early bloom. The air in the enclosed garden was filled with the salt-air tang of the sea and the heady scent of roses and gillyflowers and lilies—none of them hothouse varieties, but flowers that grew and had grown on the estate for years. At one end of the garden was a child-size cottage complete with a bricked walkway and a sandbox. And at the other end beneath the limbs of a massive shade tree hung a swing.

It was a child's paradise of a garden, and when Kit looked at it, his mind filled with pictures of children playing here. Not just one lonely little girl, but three or four—all with dark hair and blue eyes like their mother.

Their mother.

He glanced over at Mariah. "I never forgot that evening."

Puzzled, Mariah frowned. "What evening?"

"The evening I met you," he said. "In the tower. I remembered every detail of that night."

Mariah laughed. "Except my name and my face."

"The only time I got a proper look at your face was when I kissed you," he said. "And your eyes were closed. All I knew was pale complexion, dark lashes, dark hair, and soft lips. And you never told me your name. But for all these years, you've been my little girl in the tower."

"Yet you didn't recognize me."

The corners of Kit's eyes crinkled when he smiled and a dimple appeared in one cheek. "You've changed a bit." He stole a peek at her bosom.

"So have you," she replied. "You're a much better kisser now."

"I've had more practice," he admitted. "You were the first girl I ever kissed."

"You're the only boy I've ever kissed," she said softly.

"I'm glad," Kit told her. "Because I meant what I said when I promised to marry you. I never forgot that I made that promise. I dreamed about you and the tower. I dreamed of rescuing you and marrying you. I didn't know your name, but I've carried a memory of you in my heart ever since."

"I didn't recognize you, either—until Mr. Mirrant called you Kit."

"Then, I'm forgiven?" he asked.

"Always." Her heart overflowing with emotion, Mariah brushed at the tears brimming in her eyes and focused her attention on the swing in order to keep from crying.

Kit leaned over and brushed her lips with his. "I believe that's reason to celebrate," he murmured, reaching over and gently caressing her cheek with the palm of his hand. A strand of her hair was caught on her eyelashes, and he carefully pulled it free.

Mariah caught his hand in hers and pressed a kiss against his palm before she released it. "What do you have in mind?"

"Would you like to swing?"

His question surprised her, but Mariah nodded her head. "Very much."

Kit took her by the hand and led her to the swing. He tested the ropes and found them to be strong and secure and then lifted the seat and checked the underside. Although not as clean or as comfortable as it had once been, the silk that covered the padded wooden seat was intact.

Kit removed his handkerchief from the breast pocket of his jacket and brushed the seat off before he sat down on it, testing its strength against his weight. If the swing decided to collapse and break, he would just as soon have it do it while he was sitting on it and not when Mariah was flying toward the sky.

"All right," he said when he completed his inspection. "It's safe." Kit patted the seat. "Come sit down."

Mariah didn't need further prompting. As Kit watched, she politely lifted her skirts and petticoats and sat down on the swing so that her bottom, clad only in silk drawers, touched the surface of the swing, not the fabric of her dress, then she carefully fanned her skirts out around her.

"I wiped the grime off the seat as best I could," he told her.

"I know," she told him. "But you've a dusty rectangle on the seat of your trousers." She smiled. "I didn't want the same thing to happen to my new dress."

Kit dusted the back of his trousers with the palm of his hand and walked around the back of the swing to push her.

"Higher," she demanded once her feet cleared the ground.

"Your wish is my command, Miss Shaughnessy." He complied, laughing as her skirts flew up over her legs and into her face and down again and into his face. Strands of her long black hair came loose from its bun and whipped back and forth in the wind. She was beginning to look thoroughly disheveled and thoroughly happy, and Kit thought that he might search his entire life and never find a better match.

"More, Kit! Higher!" Laughing with delight, Mariah urged him to push her higher and farther until she was soaring almost as high as the top of the wall.

She kicked her legs, pumping as the swing arced higher, then plummeted once again, bringing her back down to earth.

"Have you had enough?" he asked as she put her feet down and slowed the swing to a stop.

She shook her head.

"Then what is it? What's wrong?"

"Nothing's wrong," she told him. "I thought you might want a turn." She smiled at him. "There's only one swing and I wanted to share it with you."

He shook his head. "That's all right, sweetheart. It's your swing. Enjoy it."

She reached back, caught him by the hand, and pulled him around to face her. When he stood before her, she reached for him, pulling him close enough to kiss.

Mariah put her heart into her kiss. She teased and taunted him and led him on a merry dance as their tongues met and clashed and mated, and in the end she rewarded him with a sweet, hot, enticing kiss that promised him paradise.

Kit's heart began to race, his pulse throbbed, and the tightening in his groin grew so intense that he wondered if his trouser buttons would contain him. He knew Mariah was treading in very dangerous territory and only an effort of will would save her. He softened the kiss, then gently pulled away.

Mariah stared at up at him. "Please?"

His eyes were closed and his breathing heavy. "Hmm?"

"Won't you share my swing with me?"

He opened his eyes and looked into her blue ones. "I'd be delighted."

Mariah climbed out of the swing and started around the back to push, but Kit caught her by the hand and stopped her. "There's a better way to share," he murmured. "I saw it in a book once."

"How?"

He sat down on the swing. "Come here and I'll show you." He spread his legs to brace himself and steady the swing, then put his hands on Mariah's waist and lifted her onto his lap.

"Like this?" she whispered, shocked and more than a little excited.

The feeling was such an exquisite kind of torture that Kit had to increase it. "Not quite." He lifted her once again as he issued instructions. "Put your right leg on one side of me and your left leg on the other."

She maneuvered into position and increased the exquisite torture tenfold.

Kit cupped her silk-clad bottom and held her close against him. "Now, raise your skirts and fluff them out around us."

She did.

Kit rocked the swing back and forth with his foot.

Mariah burrowed against him, enjoying the feeling of being close against him and the slightly wicked cachet of being held in such a manner. She pressed her lips to his neck where his pulse beat in the hollow beneath his ear and felt it throb against her lips and in the secret part of her he held pressed against him. She shifted against the madness she could feel down there, and Kit shuddered. "What sort of book?"

"The sort that's never mentioned in polite company."

She lifted her head to look at him. "You own a banned book?"

"Shocking, isn't it?"

"Was this the only picture?"

"No," he whispered. "There were lots more. Different kinds. All with exotic names."

"What's this one called?"

"Swans in Flight."

"I don't suppose you'd like to share that book?" she asked, settling more firmly against him.

"I might be persuaded to," he drawled. "With my lover and my wife."

"Both?" she asked. "Your lover and your wife?"

"In the same person," he said. "Isn't that what marriage is supposed to be about? Finding a lover and a wife and a best friend and a confidant all in the same lovely form?"

"I thought it was about finding a lover and a husband and a best friend and a confidant all in the same handsome form."

"Isn't it fortunate that we feel the same way?" He kissed her tenderly.

"Kit?"

"Hmm?"

"I feel like a swan ready for flight."

"Lock your legs around me, love, and I'll do my best to oblige." He slipped his hand beneath her skirts until he located the convenience slit in her silk drawers, then pressed his fingers against her most secret place and pushed the swing as hard as he could with his feet.

Kit worked magic with his fingers. He slid his fingers inside her, feeling the slippery warmth as her body prepared the way for him.

Mariah sighed her pleasure, wiggling against him, as he touched her in ways she could not have imagined.

"Kit?" Her voice was higher than normal, her breathing ragged.

"I'm here, sweet." He skimmed the pad of his thumb

through her slick womanly folds, then pressed it against the hard little bud, hidden there.

Mariah gasped. Her eyes fluttered open, then closed again.

Kit increased the exquisite pressure ever-so-slightly, before covering her mouth with his own, swallowing her scream of pleasure and surrender as she shuddered against him.

Seeking to prolong her moments of pleasure, Kit removed his hand from between their bodies and held on to Mariah as he pushed the swing into a higher arc as they left the ground and began to soar.

High above them in the second-floor study, Ash looked up from a copy of Debrett's. "Stop pacing. You're driving me mad."

"I can't help it," Dalton muttered.

"Then pace elsewhere."

"Fine." Dalton opened the full-length Palladian window and stepped out onto the balcony and resumed his pacing.

"That's it!" Ash slammed the book closed, stood up, and walked to the window to watch Dalton pace. "All right. What's bothering you?"

"I keep thinking about Kit asking if I planned to offer for Iris." Dalton stopped pacing and began fiddling with the telescope.

"Why don't you?"

"You know why," he muttered, staring into the eyepiece of the telescope. "You can see the ocean from here."

"That's most likely why there's a telescope there," Ash replied. "You refuse to offer for Iris because you're a younger son with no prospects."

"That's right." Dalton turned the telescope.

"And she's an heiress with a large dowry. Marry the girl and live off her money."

"I can't."

"Why not? People do it all the time." Ash snorted. "Our whole society is based on it."

"I'm not going to go to Iris with nothing more than the shirt on my back." He focused the telescope, looked into it, then readjusted its position.

"Would you take her if she came to you with nothing more than the dress on her back?" Ash asked.

"Yes," Dalton answered. "In a heartbeat."

"Did it ever occur to you that Iris might feel the same way? Stop letting your pride get in the way of your happiness. Iris knows you're a younger son with no prospects. You're not hiding anything from her or betraying her trust. If she loves you and wants to marry you, do it. You're not going to be a kept husband. There's no place on earth you love more than Swanslea Park. You'll work your arse off for the good of the place and love every minute of it. Lord Templeston and Iris and Kit know that."

"Swanslea Park will be Kit's one day, not Iris's."

"Kit's got this place and several others. He can't be everywhere at once, and he'll probably want to spend a large part of the year here. You heard him. He's planning to marry at the end of the season, and I'll wager it'll be sooner than that."

A flash of rose-colored wool caught Dalton's eye. He bent at the knees and looked through the telescope. "How soon?"

"Within a month."

"I'll wager a fortnight," Dalton countered.

"Done. Because a fortnight from now, Mariah will barely have had time to make her curtsy," Ash reasoned.

"Fine." Dalton stepped back from the telescope. "Now, look at this."

Ash peered through the telescope. "I'll be damned if it isn't *Swans in Flight*."

"That's right, old man." Dalton whistled. "I've never seen it performed, but I've seen the pictures."

"Let's hope no one else has," Ash said wryly. "I didn't

know there was a garden back there, let alone a swing."
He turned to Dalton. "Unbolt that telescope."

"And do what with it?"

"Lock it in your trunk or pitch it in the ocean. I don't
care. Just get rid of it before someone else happens to see
what Kit and his betrothed are doing during their art lessons. We've worked too bloody hard to have her reputation ruined now."

Dalton unbolted the telescope. "Especially by the man
who's supposed to be her guardian."

Chapter 26

On with the dance! let joy be unconfined;
No sleep till morn, when Youth and Pleasure meet
To chase the glowing hours with flying feet.

—GEORGE GORDON NOEL BYRON, LORD BYRON, 1788–1824

25 April 1838
Telamor Castle
Inismorn, Ireland

Dear Papa, Mama, & sisters,
We are leaving Ireland today for London. Ash
has pronounced Mariah as prepared for her coming
out as any young woman can be.
Mariah and I shall be delighted to join you in
London at Templeston Place if the invitation still
stands. As my town house is a bachelor establish-
ment, and unsuitable for Mariah's needs, I am lend-
ing it to Mirrant. Ash, of course, will stay at his
own town house.
I look forward to seeing all of you and in having
you welcome Mariah into the family. I intend to ask
Mariah to marry me as soon as I am absolved of
my duty as her guardian. She will obtain her majority on the fifth day of May, and I shall offer her
my ring. If Mariah agrees, I should like to be married at the end of the season.
As ever,
Your loving son,
Kit.

Mariah expected London to be a bright shining city, full of beautiful buildings and parks and

acres of green. She wasn't prepared for the dank, dreary, fog-shrouded city swathed in layers of smoke and soot and grime that greeted her when they arrived.

"It isn't at all the way I imagined it," she said as they boarded the carriage that would take them from the docks to the marquess of Templeston's Mayfair town house.

She looked around at the dockworkers and the ragged mudlarks running barefooted in and around the shoreline of the Thames. Where were all the wondrous palaces and town houses Lord Everleigh had described? No wonder Kit had come to Ireland. No one could live in this cold dreary place and be happy about it.

Kit gave her a reassuring smile. "Don't worry," he said. "It gets prettier as we get closer to the house."

She took a deep breath and began picking at a string on the index finger of her glove.

Kit placed his hand over hers to stop her fidgeting. "I hope you're carrying an extra pair of gloves," he teased. "Because you're going to have those unraveled if you keep pulling at the seams."

She had already pulled open the seam of one glove. Fortunately, Madame Thierry had insisted she carry extras. "For what the glover charged to make all these pairs of gloves, one would think that they would hold together better," came Mariah's waspish reply.

"The gloves are fine," Kit said. "You're suffering a case of nerves at the prospect of making your curtsy at the drawing room at St. James's."

"I'm not nervous about bowing to the queen," she said. "I'm worried about meeting your mother and father."

Kit smiled, then lifted her chin with his index finger and turned her to face him. "You've nothing to worry about. They're going to love you."

"But he's the marquess of Templeston and your mother is a famous artist."

"And you're the famous lady baker of Inismorn."

"Kit, please. What if they don't like me? What if they

have some other lady in mind for you to marry?"

"They will just have to change their minds," he told her tenderly. "Because I'm going to marry you."

Mariah bit her bottom lip and looked down at her lap. She had given him every opportunity to change his mind and every opportunity to tell her he loved her, but Kit had done neither. He had simply decided to keep the promise he'd made to her when they were children. But merely keeping his promise wasn't enough. There had to be a better reason for marriage than that. "What if I do something wrong? What if my manners aren't good enough for London society? What if I trip on my train and fall on my face? Or drop another soupspoon or use the wrong knife? What if the queen decides to hold my Irish heritage against me? What if the dance master was right? What if you are the only person in London with whom I can dance?"

"Then you'll scandalize society by dancing all your dances with me, and the day after the ball, everyone in London will read about it in the *Morning Post*. And I'll be forced to marry you to save your reputation."

The carriage rolled to a stop in front of an elegant Georgian town house.

"Don't worry," he said once again. "Everything is going to be fine. Nothing is going to spoil your debut into society. Chin up. Smile prettily. As long as you don't tumble over when you curtsy to my father, everything will be fine."

She looked up at him, panic in her eyes.

"Relax, sweet." He brought her gloved hand to his lips and gently kissed her fingers. "I was teasing."

"That's nothing to tease about," she wailed. "Now I'll worry about doing it."

"It wouldn't matter if you did," Kit promised. "Papa would help you up without batting an eye. In his line of work, it happens all the time." He opened the door of the carriage and leaned forward, preparing to climb out.

Mariah placed a hand on his arm. "You're sure your parents won't object to me?"

"Object to *you*?" Kit stepped down from the carriage and held up a hand to help her alight. "Impossible."

⟡

Mariah worried needlessly.

She executed a flawless bow to Lord and Lady Templeston as Kit introduced her to his parents and was warmly greeted by his sisters, Lady Iris and Lady Kate.

Everyone in the household was present to welcome Lord Kit and his young lady home. In addition to his parents and sisters, his friend and former governess, Miss Harriet Allerton, was there along with the butler, Horton, the housekeeper, Mrs. Brinson, and a host of maids and footmen and grooms, whose names Mariah had trouble remembering.

After a quarter of an hour spent getting acquainted, Wren escorted Mariah to a bedroom down the hall from Iris's and Kate's.

"You must be exhausted after your journey," Wren said. "The coachmen are still unloading your things, so there's no need to rush to change for tea. Why don't you try to rest a bit?"

"Thank you, Lady Templeston." Mariah removed her bonnet and unbuttoned her glove.

"Allow me," Wren said, taking the bonnet and the glove from Mariah and placing them on the dressing table.

"Thank you." Mariah smiled at Kit's mother.

Wren smiled back. "You're welcome, Miss Shaughnessy."

"Mariah. Please."

"You're welcome, *Mariah*." Wren glanced down at the timepiece pinned to her dress. "You'll probably think us unforgivably rude, but Iris has one last fitting scheduled for her presentation gown, and this afternoon was the only time the dressmaker could come to the house to do it. I've got to collect her and see that she gets downstairs on time.

Everyone is returning to town from their country houses, and every seamstress in town is working around the clock preparing wardrobes for all the girls who will be coming out. Your invitation to your drawing room arrived yesterday morning with Iris's. You are to be presented to Her Majesty at St. James's palace at three o'clock on Wednesday, and at the conclusion of the drawing room, we're to attend a dinner party at the Duchess of Kerry's. When your trunks arrive, have your abigail send whatever needs pressing downstairs."

"Where *is* your abigail?" The voice came from somewhere behind her.

Mariah turned around and discovered Kate had followed them up the stairs and had plopped down on the bed. "My what?" She unbuttoned her other glove and placed it beside its mate, on top of the dressing table.

"Your lady's maid," Iris answered from the doorway. She entered the bedroom and went to sit beside Kate on the bed.

"I don't have one."

"What?" Wren was surprised. "Who has been dressing you? Who has been helping you dress?"

"At St. Agnes's, where I lived before I went to live at Telamor, I generally dressed myself," Mariah explained.

"How?" Kate blurted.

"It isn't hard when all you have to wear are ugly black dresses that button down the front. When I arrived at Telamor, Lord Kil—I mean, Lord Ramsey, hired Madame Thierry, the dressmaker to create a wardrobe for me. Either she or one of her assistants helped me dress."

"What about the journey?" Kate asked. She had the same chocolate-brown eyes as Kit, and though her hair was light brown, Mariah thought that it would one day be the same lush coffee color as Kit's.

Mariah blushed.

"You traveled all the way from Ireland with Kit without an abigail? Alone." Kate's brown eyes widened at the thought of a juicy scandal. "How wonderful!"

Mariah reached up and untied the strings of her traveling cape.

"How irresponsible!" Wren exclaimed. "What was Kit thinking?"

"He was thinking that since lady's maids were in short supply in Inismorn, that it might be possible to hire one once we reached London," Mariah answered, unwilling to let anyone, even Kit's mother, accuse him of not observing proprieties. "Ma'am," she added, curtsying for good measure.

"When Kit wrote to us explaining that he had become your guardian, he said that you arrived at Telamor Castle with a chaperone. Why did she not accompany you to London?"

"Sister Mary Beatrix refused to leave Inismorn." Mariah didn't think it prudent to explain that Sister Mary Beatrix had refused to leave her room during the weeks they had been in residence except to go to seven o'clock mass. "And nothing Kit—I mean—Lord Kil—Ramsey said would persuade her otherwise. In the end Lord Everleigh decided that since Lord Ramsey was my guardian, it would be more prudent for me to travel alone with him than to travel in the company of Lord Everleigh, Mr. Mirrant, and Lord Ramsey without a chaperone in attendance."

"Lord Everleigh is probably right," Wren conceded. "But I'm afraid it's going to be impossible to find an abigail to attend you at this late date. Iris's lady's maid can't possibly take on the added responsibility. . . ."

"Did Madame Thierry fashion that for you?" Iris asked.

Mariah glanced down at the traveling dress she wore. It was made of indigo kerseymere. The bodice was fitted at the waist, the skirt full and flared. Both the bodice and the skirt were trimmed with black braid. An indigo-colored reticule matched her kid gloves and her dyed half-boots. "Yes," she answered. "Is there something wrong with it?"

Iris shook her head. "It's wonderful and that shade of

blue is divine." Iris didn't look a thing like Kit, but she was the spitting image of her mother, with dark blond hair and gray-green eyes.

"Mr. Mirrant chose it," Mariah said.

"Dalton Mirrant?" Iris was surprised.

"Yes," Mariah answered. "He helped Madame Thierry select the fashion plate and chose the fabric. He has a very good eye for color and, according to Madame Thierry, quite a flair for design. He seems to be able to look at a fashion plate and know exactly what clothes will suit. As a matter of fact, he chose several of the designs that Madame Thierry created for me."

"I can't believe it of Dalton," Iris mused. "He has always dressed very well, but I've never heard him breathe a word about ladies' fashions. He's always talking about riding and hunting and the estate. I can't believe he never said anything."

"I think Mr. Mirrant was rather surprised by it and, perhaps, a bit embarrassed. I heard him tell Madame Thierry that he had never thought about it much, but he'd always hated to see women in colors that didn't suit them."

"You will point out the dresses that Mr. Mirrant selected for you, won't you?" Iris asked. "I should hate to have a completely new wardrobe made for the season, only to learn that Dal— I mean, Mr. Mirrant thought it all wrong for me."

"I'm sure he would never dream of finding fault with your wardrobe," Wren said. "Dalton has far better manners than that." She bit her bottom lip. "And even if he did find fault with your wardrobe, I know he'd be too much a gentleman to mention it." She checked the time again. "Please excuse us, Mariah." Wren motioned her daughters off Mariah's bed. "We must get Iris downstairs. You make yourself comfortable. I'll send my abigail to help you settle in. In fact, I'll share my abigail with you for the season. It will give her something to do. She de-

spairs of me because I always smell of turpentine and
paints. . . ."

Mariah laughed. "Madame Thierry says I always smell
of baked bread and sugar frosting."

Wren nodded her head. "It will make Nealy quite happy
to attend to you for the season. She never has the opportunity to do anything for me except arrange my hair upon
occasion because Drew—I mean, Lord Templeston—prefers to see to my dressing and undressing himself. . . ."

"Mama!" both her daughters exclaimed.

Wren blushed bright red, then looked at her girls. "I
know I shouldn't say things like that in front of you. But
it's true. And you might as well hear it from me than
from the servants. You're young ladies and getting to the
age where you need to understand some of what goes on
between husband and wife. And your father and I have
never made any secret of the fact that we love each other
and enjoy each other's company."

Mariah smiled. Everything was going to be all right.
Lady Templeston wasn't the frivolous sort of lady at all.
Mariah thought they might one day become close friends.

"Come, Kate. Iris. Let Mariah rest for a bit. Then we'll
bring Nealy and come back and help her dress for dinner.
She can show us all of her new things, and we can decide
if we've more shopping to do."

Kit stood at the bottom of the staircase and
watched as his mother led Mariah upstairs.

"She seems like a charming girl," Drew said as he
watched Kit watch Mariah Shaughnessy ascend the main
staircase of Templeston Place.

If Drew had had any doubts about Kit's sincere desire
to marry Mariah, they were laid to rest in that moment.
Kit looked at Mariah the way he still looked at Kathryn.
The way he would always look at Kathryn. "Come into
the study." Drew opened the door and motioned Kit inside. "We'll have a drink while the ladies are upstairs,

and you can tell me all about your inheritance and your Miss Shaughnessy, and don't omit any of the details, for your mother is sure to grill me on the subject later."

Kit entered the room and was immediately surrounded by the familiar smells of sweet tobacco, lemon beeswax, and old leather. A hundred memories flashed through his mind. Memories of the times he had sneaked into the study when he was a child, just to be near his hero, of waking in his father's arms as Drew carried him up the stairs to bed. Memories of standing before Drew's massive oak desk and reciting lessons, of listening as Drew patiently explained whatever he happened to be working on. Memories of standing with bowed head and downcast eyes, staring at the Turkey carpet as Drew chastised him for boyish infractions against the rules.

"Have a seat." Drew waved Kit into his customary chair, then walked over to the cellaret, removed a decanter and two glasses, and poured two fingers of whisky into each. He handed a glass to Kit, then lifted the other and raised it in a toast. "Here's to you, Lord Kilgannon."

Kit hesitated. It was the first time his father had ever offered him a drink of anything stronger than claret or port.

"Go ahead." Drew smiled. "A man who has inherited an estate and a title and is contemplating marriage is certainly old enough to share a drink with his father."

"Did you share a drink with your father when you proposed to Mama?"

Drew raised an eyebrow. "We did the first time," he answered honestly. "He was gone by the time I proposed the second time. If I remember correctly, I probably shared a drink with you. Milk, I believe it was."

Kit was puzzled. "I don't remember."

"There is no reason you should." Drew's brown eyes sparkled at the memory. "You were about four years of age at the time. But you've been to Ireland and spoken with Father Francis, you must have some idea of how you came to be the late earl of Kilgannon's only male relative," Drew said softly.

Kit nodded.

"We expected you to ask questions when Martin presented you with the documents," Drew continued. "Your mother and I held our breaths, wondering what you would want to know and how we would answer you, since there was still a great deal we didn't know ourselves, but you've never asked." He drained the whisky from his glass and poured himself another. "So now I'm asking you."

"I know that George Ramsey was my father," Kit told him. "Just as he was your father. You told me that yourself when I was little. And I remembered it even though I never wanted to admit it." He looked at Drew. "I know that when he died, you married Mama, and managed somehow to legally adopt me as your son and heir." He paused as if debating how much he should reveal. "I heard the rumors about you and Mama when I was growing up. I heard them from the boys at school and at university."

Drew frowned at the thought of schoolboys tormenting Kit. "I brought a few things from Swanslea Park to help explain." He turned and unhooked the latch on a Sir Joshua Reynolds's landscape, and swung it open on its hinges to reveal the door of the safe concealed behind it.

Drew spun the dial to a series of numbers, opened the door, and removed a sheepskin packet of documents and a black velvet jewelry pouch. He handed the packet to Kit. "Read these and then I'll do my best to answer your questions."

Kit took out the first letter and opened it. A chill went through him as he read the first line:

My dearest son,
    If you're reading this letter, then I've met my Maker a bit sooner than I'd planned. If everything is as it was meant to be, either Martin or I would

have already destroyed it, but if you're reading it, that is not the case.

I cannot rest easy in my grave until you know that I never meant to fail you. You counted on me, and my momentary thoughtlessness drastically altered your life's path in a manner neither of us could have foreseen. I hope, one day, that you'll forgive me. I bear a heavy guilt for my misplaced trust.

Because I love you, son, and I have always been so very proud of you—as a boy and as the man you've grown up to be. Your mother and I always knew that you were our shining accomplishment and our greatest joy. You were the light of her life, and you've been the light of mine.

I have entrusted to your care my second shining accomplishment and the joy of my old age, my son, Christopher George Ramsey. Kit. He needs you, Drew. He needs a father to love and to look up to. Be that father. He cannot help the circumstances of his birth, nor should they matter. But in a country like ours, the order and circumstance of one's birth is everything. I claim him as my son because he is my son. He cannot claim legitimacy; but he can lay claim to something more important, blood. He is your half brother, but I would ask that you raise him as your son, for I do not want him to suffer for the actions (not the sins) of his parents.

I did not sin in loving his mother, nor did she sin in loving me. My sin was in putting a solemn promise to one love ahead of the needs of another. There are those who will view Kit as an accident or a mistake. He was never an accident or a mistake. I wanted him—loved him—just as much as I wanted and loved you. Accept him, with my blessings, and give him the family he deserves.

For you see, Drew, my fondest wish for you was that you would meet a young lady and have what

*your mother and I shared. I thought you had found
it with Wren, but something terrible happened to
prevent her from marrying you.*

*Don't blame her. She did what she did to protect
you. She has never confided it to me. I guessed the
truth. I didn't want to believe it, but I know it was
true.*

*It is not my place to divulge her secret. She must
be the one to do that. I can only say that no matter
what you believe of me at this moment, know that I
loved you and that I tried to atone for my mistake
by watching out for the one you loved.*

*You should also know that all of the ladies with
whom I have been intimately acquainted have my
locket. The locket that accompanied this letter is the
one I gave to Kit's mother. All of the ladies with
whom I've shared a bed and pillow—including Kit's
mother—have something else in common—a trait
you cannot fail to notice should they decide to present themselves to you.*

*Trust in your heart, my son. Follow it. Let it lead
you to Wren's door. Don't grieve too much for me,
for I am with your mother now, and we are both
looking out for you and your family.*

My love to you and to Kit and to Wren.

Your loving and proudest of fathers, George.

Kit refolded the letter and handed it to Drew.

"The letter was meant for my eyes alone. For your pro-
tection, I should have burned it years ago, but I saved it
because it was from my father—our father—and I thought
that you should be able to read it to see how much he
loved you. How much he loved us both. And I kept it as
a remembrance of how I came to be your father instead
of simply your older half brother," Drew said softly.

"How did you manage to make me your heir?" Kit
asked. "Even he says I'm a bastard."

"No, you're not," Drew denied. "You were our father's

natural child. Technically, he could not lay claim to you, but you were not illegitimate in the eyes of the law. Although he did not reveal your mother's name or the circumstances of your birth, Martin assured me that your Irish inheritance was quite legal because your mother was a peeress in her own right and that while you were Father's natural son, you had been born within the bonds of marriage. Otherwise, I could not have secured the letters patent from the king allowing you to become my legal heir."

"That's possible?"

Drew smiled. "It's unusual. But with a great deal of money and the right motivation, it's possible. Titles have always been bought, sold, and awarded. And our late sovereign was always in need of cash."

"What if you and Mama had had a son?"

"We did," Drew answered. "You. And anyone searching for proof to that fact will find it."

"But, Papa—"

"We all had our reasons for doing what we did," Drew said. "But our father's reasons were probably the purest reasons of them all. He was trying to make amends. Trying to set things right. And he knew that I would never refute you or refuse him the chance to try to make things right."

Kit looked at the man who had been the only father he had ever known. "There were always rumors about my paternity. Rumors as to whether I was your son or your father's. What I didn't understand was that there were questions about my maternity as well." He took a deep breath. "Why didn't you and Mama tell me about Lady Alanna before I went to Ireland?"

Drew sighed. "We didn't know her identity until we learned you had inherited the old earl's title. I knew some things—that she was a peeress in her own right and that she was married when you were born—but I didn't have all of the facts. Apparently, Martin and the priest, Father

Francis, were the only two people alive who knew the true circumstances of your birth."

"And Ford," Kit added.

"Ford?"

"The late earl's butler. He was privy to a great many family secrets, and he was the one who summoned the priest after the late earl died."

"Well, except for those three, everyone else took your secret to the grave. Your mama told me that Father appeared at her door one evening with you in his arms. He told Kathryn that you were in need of a mother, and since she was in need of a son, he could think of no one better suited to be your mama. Because your mother and I had no idea who your *other* mother was, we decided to make certain no one would ever believe you were anything except our son. And since Father's will excluded you from inheriting Swanslea Park because it was a legacy from my mother, I had Martin change *my* will and arrange the amendment to the letters patent to make certain you did inherit it—as all sons and heirs should do."

"All these years, you and Mama have endured the rumors. All the things they've said about your liaison with her . . ."

Drew laughed. A bitter-sounding laugh that told Kit a great deal about the variety of vicious rumors Drew had heard repeated and embellished over the years. "There have been many things said about my liaison with Kathryn over the years. Most of them false, but we allowed the rumors to circulate—even circulated a few ourselves about an elopement to Gretna Green because we knew the truth and the rumors were less painful and damaging."

"Even for me?" Kit asked.

"Especially for you." Drew inhaled, then slowly expelled the breath. "We had that"—he nodded toward the jewel pouch that held the locket that George had given to Kit's mother—"but we didn't know to whom it had once belonged. We felt it was better to have everyone believe you were the product of our union than to increase speculation." Drew handed the second document to Kit.

Kit read it. "Codicil to the Last Will and Testament of George Ramsey, fifteenth Marquess of Templeston. My fondest wish is that I shall die a very old man beloved of my family and surrounded by children and grandchildren, but because one cannot always choose the time of one's Departure from the Living, I charge my legitimate son and heir, Andrew Ramsey, twenty-eighth earl of Ramsey, Viscount Birmingham, and Baron Selby on this the 3rd day of August in the Year of Our Lord 1818 with the support and responsibility for my beloved mistresses and any living children born of their bodies in the nine months immediately following my death.

"As discretion is the mark of a true gentleman, I shall not give name to the extraordinary ladies who have provided me with abiding care and comfort since the death of my beloved wife, but shall charge my legitimate son and heir with the duty of awarding to any lady who should present to him, his legitimate heir, or representative, a gold and diamond locket engraved with my seal, containing my likeness, stamped by my jeweler, and matching in every way the locket enclosed with this document, an annual sum not to exceed twenty thousand pounds to ensure the bed and board of the lady and any living children born of her body in the nine months immediately following my Departure from the Living.

"The ladies who present such a locket have received it as a promise from me that they shall not suffer ill for having offered me abiding care and comfort. Any offspring who presents such a locket shall have done so at their mother's bequest and shall be recognized as children of the fifteenth Marquess of Templeston and shall be entitled to his or her mother's portion of my estate for themselves and their legitimate heirs in perpetuity according to my wishes as set forth in this, my Last Will and Testament. George Ramsey, fifteenth marquess of Templeston."

Kit took out the locket, opened the lid, and stared down

at the miniature portrait of his father. He closed the lid and studied it. He didn't remember the locket, but it seemed familiar—as if he'd seen it somewhere before.

Drew walked to the bell and rang for Horton. "Please ask Lady Templeston to join us in the study," he instructed when the butler appeared, then waited until Horton left the room to continue. "It's her story as well as mine. She should she be present for the telling of it."

Wren knew when Drew summoned her what was to come. The thing she had dreaded all these years had come to pass. Kit had grown into a man, and the answers that had satisfied him as a child would no longer suffice. Now he wanted to know the whole story of who he was and how he had come to be her son.

She entered the study and ran straight to Kit. He stood up and caught her in his arms as she hugged him the way she'd wanted to do when he arrived. "Oh, Kit, it's so good to have you home."

"It's good to be home with you and Papa and Ally and the girls." Kit hugged her tightly.

"Kathryn," Drew said gently. "It's time."

Wren took a shaky breath, and Drew walked over and put his arms around her. "Does he remember that terrible, terrible day?" she asked.

"What day?" Kit wondered.

"The day you were stolen away from us by the people who thought they had a right to you." She glanced at Drew. Once Kit had been safely returned to her, Wren had never again spoken aloud the names of the people who had taken him. But for years thereafter, Kit had had bad dreams and nightmares about the people who had taken him away from his mama and Drew.

Both Wren and Drew had sworn that that would never happen again. They set out to make certain no one would ever have reason to question Kit's place in the world as Drew Ramsey's son and heir.

"Start at the beginning and tell him everything," Drew told her.

"I don't know if I can," Wren said. "But I'll try." She met Kit's gaze. "What I am about to tell you changes nothing. I am your mother. You are my son. That's all that matters to me."

"Of course, Mama." Kit lowered his gaze. The last thing he wanted to do was upset his mother.

"You know that I was married before I married Drew?"

"To Stafford. The celebrated biologist," Kit answered.

"Yes, that's right." Wren nodded. "To Bertrand Stafford, a sweet, gentle *old* man who offered to marry me and give my child a name."

"What?" Kit was stunned.

"Drew and I were engaged to be married before I married Bertrand, but something happened two days before our wedding that changed the course of our lives." Wren stopped speaking, visibly struggling to find the words and the courage to say what she had to say next.

"He's a grown man, Kathryn, my love. Tell him."

She looked at Drew with tears in her eyes. "I can't."

Drew took a deep breath. "Two days before our wedding, your mother was attacked and her virginity was forcefully taken from her. Kathryn failed to appear in church the morning of our wedding. I tried to find out what had happened, but she refused to see me—couldn't let me see her, for her assailant had struck her and bruised her face. Her failure to show up made me a laughingstock in town. The earl of Ramsey was left standing at the altar. Hurt and angry, I rode off to join Wellington on his campaign to corral Napoleon."

Wren resumed the tale. "By the time I was sufficiently recovered to face Drew, he was gone to war. I thought I would die from the pain and the heartbreak and the humiliation of what had happened to me. I wanted to die. And then a miraculous thing happened to make something horrible bearable. I discovered I was with child. I couldn't go to Drew, so my father turned to his dearest friends,

Bertrand Stafford and George Ramsey and prevailed on them to save my reputation. Because I would not reveal what had happened, George had no way of knowing if the child I carried was Drew's. Nor could he offer me marriage because he had promised Drew's mother he would never remarry or allow another child to take precedence over hers."

"But there was another reason my father wouldn't marry Kathryn," Drew said. "Because he always held out hope that one day we would meet again and fall in love again and marry, and he knew that if he married her, she would be barred by law from marrying me—her stepson." He smiled at Kit. "We didn't know it at the time, of course, but now we know that Father had another reason as well. He had already met and fallen in love with your mother. And he couldn't marry Kathryn without betraying three of the people he loved most—my mother, your mother, and me."

"So Bertrand married me and gave my son a name. Of course, there were rumors about me. It was impossible to keep my condition a secret. And since I had left Drew waiting at the altar, everyone assumed we'd had a lover's quarrel and that I married Bertrand when I discovered I was carrying Drew's child. I did nothing to quell the rumors, for I would rather have the gossips believe my child belonged to the man I loved than to know what really happened to me. Five months after my son, Ian, was born, Bertrand died."

"Your mama was left with an infant son and facing eviction from the home she had shared with Stafford."

"And then Ian died suddenly, unexpectedly, soon after Bertrand," Wren continued. "I was devastated. My life had been irrevocably changed by his conception, and his birth had been the only thing that made my life worth living." She looked up at Kit. "Losing Ian was a blow from which I thought I would never recover. I thought I might never have another child, because after Ian's death I learned that boys in my family often died in infancy.

Then one night, three months after Ian died, George showed up at my door with you in his arms. It was love at first sight. George gave you to me, saying that the best thing he could do as your father was to give you to me to love. All he asked in return was that I move to Swanslea Park and become your mother. My doing so created a firestorm of gossip. There were those who thought George had made me his mistress and that you were our son and there were people who thought that George had taken pity on his son's discarded betrothed and that he had made me his mistress in order to gain possession of his grandson. I let people think what they would because I was afraid that if anyone found out I wasn't really your mother, someone might try to take you away from me."

Drew continued the story. "And one day, shortly after your mama and I had reunited and married, the family of the man who had assaulted Kathryn arranged to have you stolen from us because he believed you were his child."

"We died a thousand deaths before we were able to rescue you," Wren told Kit.

Kit raked his fingers through his hair in an impatient gesture so reminiscent of Drew that Wren's heart ached to see it. "I was so angry," Kit said. "When Father Francis told me about my birth, I was so angry because I believed you had kept the truth hidden from me. I believed you lied to me."

"Oh, Kit . . ." Wren held out her arms to him, and Kit walked into them, put his head on her shoulder, and wrapped his arms around her waist, the way he had done as a child. Tears rolled down her cheeks as Wren held the man who had been her precious little boy. "If we lied to you, we did so by omission. It hurt so much to talk about what happened. It hurt so much for me to remember and for you as well. You suffered bad dreams and nightmares for years after you were taken from us. You would leave the nursery and come climb into bed with Drew and me because you dreamed the man had taken you away from your mama and papa again. We never really knew how much you heard or how much he'd said to you before we rescued you, and so we tried to forget it and hoped that you would." She pressed a kiss to Kit's forehead and ruffled his soft brown hair. "You are my son, Christopher George Ramsey. I never knew your other mother's name until after you inherited Telamor Castle, but I've said a prayer of thanks to George and to her every day you've been mine." Wren kissed him again.

"Her name was Lady Alanna Farrington," Kit said softly.

Drew nodded. "The wife of Michael Farrington, who was a cousin of ours and was, in fact, next in line to inherit our title. He was reported drowned the year preceding your birth, but turned up alive some months later. I learned that he was married and that his wife died in childbirth. I had no idea that she had died giving birth to you until Martin presented you with your inheritance and I began to ask questions. I do know that Michael Farrington returned to service and that he died of fever and without legal issue in India shortly after Father's death. When his solicitor contacted Martin with the news, Martin realized that with Farrington's death, I had no legal heir, and without one, our title would be extinct unless I could make you my heir. We began petitioning the Crown for an amendment to our letters patent when I married your mama." He smiled at Wren. "And not just to make *you* my legal heir, but to allow you or any other children— male or female—born of my body to inherit. Farrington's untimely death allowed the petition to go through." Drew turned to look at Kit. "Martin and I have spoken and I have managed to piece together a good bit of the facts he could not, in good faith, reveal. Imagine my great pleasure in discovering that you could have inherited anyway." Drew ran his fingers through his hair. "Although, I must admit that at first I was surprised to find that Father had fallen in love and had an intimate relationship with another man's wife. I had never known him to do that before. But once I began to fit the pieces of the puzzle together, I knew he believed her to be a widow."

"They both did," Kit said. "At the time they met." He related the story Father Francis had told him of how Lady Alanna and George met and what transpired once Michael Farrington returned from the dead.

"Poor George to find love again only to lose her," Wren whispered. "And poor Lady Alanna, forced to choose between the men she loved."

Drew nodded in agreement.

"Father Francis told me what he knew about it," Kit said. "Including the fact that she and Mariah's mother grew up together. Lady Alanna was the earl's daughter and Lady Siobhan was the earl's ward."

Wren took a deep breath, and then leaped at the opportunity to change the subject. "Your Mariah is a lovely girl. And she tells me we have much in common." She smiled at her husband. "While I smell of turpentine and paint, she tells me she always smells of baked bread and cake frosting. I take it she bakes?"

Kit laughed. "For the entire village of Inismorn, the castle, and the convent. At St. Agnes's everyone works and Mariah was trained to be a baker. She will be the first to tell you that she is the best baker in all the parish. . . ."

Drew poured Wren a glass of sherry, refilled his and Kit's glasses with whisky, then sat down and motioned for Wren and Kit to do the same. "All right, son, tell us all about the girl who is to become our daughter-in-law."

Chapter 27

The babe whose birth embraves this morn,
Made his own bed ere he was born.

—RICHARD CRASHAW, 1613–1649

"Good morning, miss." Lady Templeston's abigail, Nealy, placed a tray containing a cup and saucer, a pot of hot chocolate, and a plate of toast with orange
marmalade on the table beside the bed.

Mariah opened her eyes and discovered a necklace,
bracelet, and earring set of perfectly matched diamonds
from Kit lying on her pillow. She picked up the folded
piece of stationery and read the note written in Kit's bold
hand: *No young woman can make her curtsy to the queen
without diamonds. Wear these for luck and know that I
will be thinking of you. Your Kit.*

Mariah sighed. Today was her twenty-first birthday.
The day she would make her debut into society and be
presented to the queen. It also marked the day when she
could be legally wed without forfeiting her fortune. And
although Kit had presented her with a gift to honor the
occasion, he had made no mention of his promise nor
wished her a happy birthday. She knew the sting of tears
that filled her eyes was childish, but she had thought that
once she became of age, Kit might formally propose or
at least admit to having feelings for her. She was disappointed that he hadn't signed his note with love, but he
had remembered her love of jewelry and given her a small
fortune in diamonds.

She drank her chocolate, took a bite of toast, and hurried through her toilette in order to thank him before he left for his morning ride. She dressed in a morning dress of the color of damask roses and fidgeted in her seat as Nealy piled her hair into an artful arrangement of cascading curls. When the abigail finished fashioning her hair, Mariah handed Nealy the diamond necklace.

"I'm afraid it isn't done, miss."

"What?"

"Young ladies who've not yet made their bows are not allowed to wear diamonds before afternoon."

"But, Nealy, Lord Kilgannon gave them to me. He expects me to wear them."

Nealy shook her head. "I cannot help you, miss. If you wish to wear them, you will have to seek permission from Lord and Lady Templeston or Lord Kilgannon himself."

Mariah glanced at the ormolu clock on the mantel and sighed. "I overslept. It's past time for Lord Kilgannon and Lord Templeston to leave for their morning rides in the park. I won't be able to thank him or to ask permission."

"You may still be able to, miss, for when I was getting your breakfast tray, I heard that Lords Templeston and Kilgannon had been forced to delay their morning ride because of a loose horseshoe or something. . . ."

Mariah clutched the box to her chest and fairly flew down the stairs in an effort to catch Kit before he left for his ride, hoping for the opportunity to thank him privately.

They had been in London for nearly five days, and Mariah had been swept up in a flurry of last-minute shopping and other activities that coincided with preparations for the season. She had barely had the opportunity to speak to Kit, much less spend time with him alone. He rode early in the morning, but there had been no time to teach her to sit a horse, so Kit rode with Miss Allerton or his father while Mariah breakfasted with Iris and Kate.

Lord Everleigh had been right. In London her reputation was of paramount importance and what might be overlooked in country society could be devastating in

London. She hadn't believed any rules could be more confining than the rules with which she'd grown up at St. Agnes's, but she was wrong.

Although Lord and Lady Templeston had welcomed her into the family and treated her with great kindness and respect, Mariah had not yet come out into society and was, in many ways, relegated to the company of Iris, Kate, and the governess.

She missed Kit. And the freedom he had afforded her in Ireland. She missed their private time together and the way he kissed her and made her feel.

Since coming to London, his behavior had been above reproach.

Mariah couldn't help wishing that it had been a little less circumspect.

"Surprise!"

The shout rang out as she entered the breakfast room.

Mariah stood framed in the doorway until Kit walked over.

"Happy birthday, sweetheart." Kit leaned over and kissed her on the cheek, then took her by the hand and led her to the breakfast table where a small mountain of presents awaited her.

Lord and Lady Templeston, Ladies Iris and Kate, Miss Allerton, Lord Everleigh, Mr. Mirrant, and Kit had risen at an unfashionably early hour and assembled in the breakfast room to wish her happy birthday.

Kit noticed that she was hugging the box containing the diamond set pressed to her heart.

"Don't you like them?" he asked.

"Oh, Kit, they're beautiful!" Mariah breathed.

"If they're that beautiful, I suppose it's silly to ask why you aren't wearing them?" he teased.

Realizing that Nealy's refusal to allow her to wear the jewelry had been little more than a ruse to force her downstairs, Mariah answered, "It isn't entirely proper for me to appear at breakfast in diamonds, unless you're the one who fastens them on."

"Then allow me to do the honors so you can open the rest of your gifts." He took the box from Mariah, opened it, and fastened the necklace around her neck, then followed with the bracelet. When he'd finished, he handed her the earrings.

Mariah shook her head. "My ears don't have holes for them."

Iris gasped. "You can't go without the earrings."

Mariah looked at Kit, and then at Lady Templeston to Lord Everleigh, who told her, "Young ladies customarily wear earrings upon their presentation."

Kit frowned. "I suppose we could return them to the jeweler for refitting with a different sort of clasp—"

"No," Mariah said. "Can't you pierce them?"

Everyone looked at one another and shook their heads.

"Your earlobes may redden and swell before your presentation," Wren told her.

"Surely no one will notice," Mariah insisted.

"They may prove to be rather sore and painful, my dear," Drew told her.

"Oh."

She replied in such a small, disappointed voice that Kate offered, "I'll do it."

"No, little minx," Kit said, giving his young sister an affectionate hug. "I'll do it."

"Truly?" Mariah asked hopefully.

"Cross my heart," he said. "But you must open your other presents first."

Mariah did. And she was overwhelmed by the generosity of Kit's family and friends. There was a pair of net mittens and a set of monogrammed handkerchiefs from Kate, a lace fan and a bottle of cologne from Iris. Miss Allerton presented her with a book of Lord Byron's poetry. Lord Everleigh gave her a set of calling cards engraved with her name. Mr. Mirrant presented her with packets of creamy vellum stationery. From Lady Templeston came a hand-painted silk scarf, and from Lord Templeston came a beautiful black onyx rosary.

"It belonged to one of my great-great grandmothers," he explained. "She was Catholic, too."

Mariah gasped when she saw it and began to cry. "I cannot thank you all enough. It has been the best birthday I ever had."

"Don't cry, sweetheart," Kit whispered. "Or your eyes will be all puffy and red before your presentation. You don't want them to match your ears, do you?"

Mariah dried her tears on one of her new handkerchiefs.

"I have another gift to give you," Kit said. "Several, in fact."

He walked over to the bell and summoned Horton, who entered the breakfast room bearing a carved jewelry box. "I had Ford pack these with my things before we left Telamor. The jewelry box and the jewelry inside it all belonged to your mother. It was stored in the safe at Telamor." Kit handed Mariah the box.

She opened the lid and was immediately immersed in a flood of memories. The jewelry box was musical, and the old-fashioned minuet was one Mariah instantly remembered from childhood. More tears cascaded down her cheeks, and Mariah carefully closed the lid on the box. "Thank you," she breathed. "I thought it must be lost or sold, for no one ever told me what happened to her things."

Kit smiled at her. "Most of her personal items have found their way back to your rooms at Telamor and what hasn't been returned has been kept in storage there." He waited for Mariah to regain her composure, then resumed his gift-giving. There was another jewelry box in the safe at Telamor. Jewelry that had belonged to Lady Alanna, but Kit intended to save it for the honeymoon. But before there could be a honeymoon, he had several more items to be attended to. He took an official-looking document out of his pocket and a large sapphire ring with one pear-shaped stone surrounded by smaller diamonds.

"I purchased a special license," he said softly. "And a betrothal ring to go along with it. I love you, Mariah, and it would please me beyond all measure if you would help me keep a promise I once made to a six-year-old girl and consent to be my wife."

Mariah broke into a dazzling smile. "Yes."

Kit slipped the ring onto her finger.

The girls and Ally rushed to congratulate Mariah. Ash and Dalton slapped Kit on the back and congratulated them both.

When congratulations had all been given, the Ramsey family and friends sat down to breakfast. No one lingered over the meal. There was much to be done and very little time in which to do it.

After breakfast Dalton and Ash left to attend to the betting book at White's, where they had recorded a number of wagers since returning to London.

Drew sent Iris and Kate upstairs with Miss Allerton, while Kit kept his other promise. Wren asked Horton to gather the necessary items, then remained behind with Drew to instruct Kit on the proper procedure and to offer moral support.

Horton delivered the items, and Kit laid out a large needle, a bottle of whisky and two glasses, a bucket of ice, and a cork.

He waited until the sideboard had been cleared of breakfast, then set Mariah up on it so he could more easily reach her ears.

"Are you certain you want to do this now?" Kit asked.

Mariah nodded. "I want to wear my earrings at the drawing room."

Kit inhaled, then slowly let out the breath. "Very well. Here goes." He took a large chip of ice and handed it to Mariah. "Hold this to your earlobe. It will help lessen the pain."

She did as he asked and when her earlobes were pink with cold, Kit poured two glasses of whisky. He swirled the needle around in one and took a huge swallow out of the other. Kit set the glass of whisky down, then picked up the cork, placed it behind Mariah's ear and pushed the needle through her earlobe from the opposite side.

Mariah bit her bottom lip, but managed a brave smile when Wren handed him a diamond earring.

Kit's fingers trembled and his knees threatened to buckle as he fastened the clasp to the back of the diamond stud. He was white-faced, perspiring profusely, and breathing as hard as if he'd run a race by the time he repeated the procedure on her other ear.

Mariah gasped once and bit her bottom lip again as he pierced the second earlobe, but she didn't move until Kit slipped the second diamond earring into place and attached the clasp.

"Is it over?" she asked.

"It's over," he said in relief.

Mariah turned slightly in order to view her new earrings in the mirror. She smiled in delight as the diamonds sparkled back at her. The pain had been worth it. "Thank you, Kit."

"You're welcome," he breathed. Then, "*Christ*, Mariah, don't ever ask me to do anything like that again."

Forgetting that his mother and father were in the room, forgetting everything except the fact that he needed reassurance after his feat of bravery, Kit dropped the cork and needle, took Mariah's face in his hands, and kissed her soundly, thoroughly, until they were both aching for more.

"Uh-hmm," Drew cleared his throat.

Kit broke the kiss.

Mariah blushed.

"Kit, your mother has a few instructions for her."

"You'll need to keep earrings in at all times until the holes have healed. Just turn them several times a day to keep the hole from growing up around the posts," Wren said.

"All right," Drew pronounced. "I'll see you both later in the morning. Many happy returns of the day, Mariah." He turned to Kit. "Don't keep her too long. She has a great deal to do before her drawing room." He took Wren by the arm. "Come, my love."

"We're not going to leave them alone in there," Wren said as Drew led her out the door.

"They're engaged to be married, Kathryn."

"But, Drew, you saw the way he kissed her. . . ."

"That I did, my love," he agreed. "We did the same when we were first engaged."

"But, Drew . . ."

"Kit's a grown man."

"I know he's a grown man," Wren fretted. "A grown man with needs. That's why I'm worried."

"Nothing is going to happen in the breakfast room."

Wren lifted an eyebrow and gave her husband a knowing look. "Oh, really? Since when?"

Kit waited until his parents left the room, then withdrew a velvet pouch from his jacket pocket.

"More jewelry?" Mariah's eyes lit up at the prospect.

Kit nodded and removed a gold and diamond locket from the velvet bag and handed it to Mariah. "It belonged to my mother."

"Lady Templeston?"

"No," Kit shook his head. "Lady Alanna Kilgannon Farrington." He lifted Mariah down from the sideboard, then told her the story. "Drew is really my half brother, not my father. My father was George Ramsey, fifteenth marquess of Templeston. But Drew and Mama adopted me and brought me up as their son when our father died. My father gave that locket to my mother. When she died, he gave it to Drew to keep for me. I'd like you to have it."

"Oh, Kit, I'll treasure it always."

He was about to tell her the significance of the locket when Mariah opened it. "I remember this locket," she said slowly.

"I don't think that's possible." Kit frowned. "It's been in Drew's safe since I was a child."

Mariah looked at the miniature of George Ramsey, then

closed the lid and smiled at Kit. "I don't mean this exact locket," she said. "But one that looked just like it. It even had a portrait of a man inside just like this one."

Kit's heart seemed to stop. "Where did you see a locket like this one?" he asked, but he already knew the answer. He'd suddenly remembered where he'd seen it. In the portrait gallery of Telamor Castle. Lady Alanna Kilgannon Farrington hadn't been painted with any jewelry, but Lady Siobhan Shaughnessy had—and she'd been wearing a locket just like the one Mariah held in her hand.

"My mother used to wear one all the time."

"Do you have it?" Kit asked urgently.

"No," Mariah answered, and a frown started to knit her brow.

"It wasn't among the jewelry I gave you this morning," Kit told her. "Was it among the jewelry the Mother Superior gave you? The jewelry your mother was wearing the day she died?"

"No." Mariah shook her head. "But it should have been because she wore it all the time."

"If you don't have it, the convent doesn't have it, and it wasn't left at Telamor, who has it?"

"Lewbell." Mariah began to shiver. "He was holding it in his hand after my mama fell onto the rocks."

Chapter 28

Thus the whirligig of time brings in his revenges.

—WILLIAM SHAKESPEARE, 1564–1616

"*Lewbell?*" *Kit asked before gently taking* Mariah in his arms. "Sweetheart, is that his name?"

Clinging to Kit as the memories came flooding back, Mariah murmured against his shirtfront, "I don't remember any name but Lewbell."

"Do you remember if he was Irish or English?" Kit asked.

She frowned. "I think English. Mama knew him before."

"Before you went to Ireland?"

Mariah nodded. "Before. When my da lived with us."

"Then he might have been one of your father's friends," Kit speculated. "Do you remember your father? Or anything about him?"

Mariah shook her head. "Not much. The sound of his voice, I think. And the way he smelled." She looked at Kit. "The scent you wear is very like his. It smells of orange spices and vanilla."

"It's called Madeira Spice. I have it mixed in a chemist's shop on Bond Street," Kit told her. "Perhaps your father shopped there as well."

"Lewbell was standing on the path, Kit. I saw him."

It broke my heart the way she babbled about the bluebells she'd picked while she cried for her mother and for her da. Kit suddenly recalled the words Father Francis

had spoken that day in the cemetery. Only Mariah hadn't
been babbling about bluebells. She'd been trying to tell
them the name of the man who had killed her mother.
Lewbell.

Kit led Mariah to a chair. "Can you remember his
face?"

She shook her head again. "I try, but I can't seem to
picture it."

"Don't worry," Kit soothed. "You don't have to remember today. All you have to do is rest." He walked
over to the bellpull and summoned Horton, then turned
back to Mariah. "Sweetheart, I need to talk to Papa about
this. He knows everyone who's anyone in London. He
may know about the locket and the man of whom you
speak. I'll send Horton for Mama and ask her to make
your excuses this afternoon."

"No."

"Mariah . . ." he began.

"I want to make my curtsy this afternoon." She stared
up at him. "Everyone has worked so hard. Please, don't
ask me to delay it."

"If you're certain . . ."

"I'm certain."

"And if you promise to get some rest before your presentation."

Mariah hesitated, then nodded. "All right. But you have
to try to find out what happened to my mother's locket."

*Damnation! How could he have forgotten about the
locket? How could he forget its significance?*

"Agreed." He brushed her lips with his own, then
helped her to her feet, and walked her to the door.

They met Horton in the doorway. "Please ask my father
to meet me in his study as soon as possible. I'm going to
take Miss Shaughnessy upstairs, and then I'll wait in
Papa's study."

"I'm sorry, sir, but Lord Templeston was called away
to Downing Street," Horton announced.

"Do you know when he's expected to return?"

"I'm afraid not, sir," Horton told him. "He's meeting with the prime minister, and one never knows how long those meetings will last. He does expect to return in time for the young ladies' presentations, however." The butler started to withdraw, then suddenly changed his mind. "Lady Templeston is in her salon if you wish to speak with her."

Kit nodded. "Thank you, Horton."

"You're welcome, sir. And may I wish Miss Shaughnessy many happy returns of the day and offer you both my felicitations on your upcoming nuptials?"

Mariah beamed at the butler. "Yes, Horton. And thank you."

Kit didn't get a chance to speak to either one of his parents, and he'd barely caught a glimpse of Mariah all day.

He knew she'd been badly shaken by her memories, but Mariah's refusal to cancel her presentation meant that she was kept busy the rest of the morning and into the early afternoon. And because his mother nervously despaired of them being late, Mariah and Iris, accompanied by Wren, left Templeston Place earlier than expected, arriving at St. James's Palace a half hour ahead of the appointed time.

Equally resplendent in white evening gowns, with the requisite three-foot-long train, shoulder-length gloves, fan, and diamond hair clips with three white egret feathers signifying their status as debutantes, Mariah and Iris waited in line with the other ladies to be presented, with Iris, as daughter of the marquess of Templeston leading Mariah who was presented as Miss Mariah Shaughnessy, ward of the earl of Ramsey and Kilgannon. Mariah handed her calling card to the Lord Chamberlain and waited until her name was called before dropping her three-foot-long train and stepping forward. She managed a flawless curtsy before the queen, kissed her ring, and carefully backed away having had Queen Victoria pronounce her as utterly charming.

The ball that followed the drawing room was held at the duchess of Kerry's London mansion.

While Mariah danced the opening quadrille with Lord Everleigh, Kit was closeted with Drew in the duchess of Kerry's library.

"I thought you'd be dancing with your betrothed," Drew told him. "Instead of dragging me in here to talk. What is it? Have you decided when to set the date? Because if it's any time before the end of the season, your mama is going to kill you."

"I've been looking for you all afternoon." Kit stood rigidly erect and his voice was tight with emotion. "There may not be a wedding."

Drew looked at the young man who had been brimming over with love and happiness hours earlier and frowned. "What is it?"

Kit blurted the news. "Mariah's mother had a locket like mine."

Drew paled. "Are you certain?" he demanded. "Have you seen it?"

Kit shook his head. "I haven't seen it, but when I gave Lady Alanna's locket to her, Mariah told me she'd seen one just like it." He quickly related everything Mariah had remembered and his memory of seeing the portraits in the third-floor gallery of Telamor Castle, then plopped down on the sofa as if his legs would no longer support his weight. He propped his elbows on his knees, then cradled his face in his hands. "Hell, Papa, I may have just proposed marriage to . . ."

"Don't," Drew said firmly. "You've seen a portrait of Lady Siobhan at Telamor, right?"

"Yes.

"Describe her."

"What?" Kit looked up at Drew.

"Describe her, son. Tell me what she looked like."

"She looked like Mariah," Kit told him. "Black hair, fair skin, blue eyes."

"Describe Lady Alanna."

"Brown hair, brown eyes like yours or mine, fair skin."

"Does Lady Alanna bear any resemblance to the portrait of my mother hanging at Swanslea Park?"

"Yes, there is a certain resemblance." Kit answered slowly. "A marked resemblance."

"Does she bear any resemblance to Lady Siobhan or Mariah?"

Kit mentally compared each of the women's features. "None."

Drew heaved a sigh and relaxed, then placed his hand on Kit's shoulder. "It will be all right." He closed his eyes. "I don't know how Lady Siobhan got the locket. Perhaps she borrowed it for the portrait or she had one similar, but I would stake my life on the fact that my father—our father—didn't present it to her. Because all of his mistresses look enough alike to be sisters and they all resemble my mother. They all have brown hair and brown eyes. He promised that in his letter, and he would never go against his word." He sat down beside Kit on the sofa and put his arm around Kit's shoulder. "The quadrille is ending, then there will be an old-fashioned minuet because Barbara, the duchess of Kerry, likes them, and after that, a waltz. I've promised your mama a waltz." He looked at Kit. "Go waltz with Mariah."

"I'm almost afraid to," Kit admitted. "I'm afraid to tempt fate."

"You won't be," Drew told him. "And I wouldn't be encouraging you if I thought there was any danger of that terrible thing coming to pass. But Mariah needs you. It's her birthday and the day you proposed and the day she remembered seeing her mother shoved to her death. Hold her, son. You need it and she needs it."

"Have you ever heard of the man Mariah remembers as Lewbell?"

Drew shook his head. "But that doesn't mean there isn't someone. I'll ask around."

*Mariah danced the minuet with Dalton Mir-*rant, worrying her way through the painstakingly precise steps of the old-fashioned dance in order to glide around the room in Kit's arms during the waltz.

The orchestra began the three-quarter-time music as Kit relieved Dalton to go dance the first waltz with Iris. Kit took Mariah's hand in his and placed his other hand on her waist, then stepped effortlessly into the rhythm of the waltz.

"Whatever happens from this moment on," Kit whispered into her hair, "know that I love you. That I will always love you."

The tone of his voice alarmed her, and Mariah tried to look up at him, but Kit held her fast. "Kit?"

"Sssh," Kit soothed. "It's all right, sweetheart. Everything will be all right."

"I love you, too, Kit," she said. "I always will."

After the waltz Drew was as good as his word. He began circulating through the crowded ballroom, out onto the terrace and back in the smoke-filled card and gaming rooms until he came across Viscount Mirrant, Dalton's father, leaving the card room and making his way toward the refreshment tables set up at the back of the ballroom.

"Templeston," Viscount Mirrant said. "I heard you were paying for information about a man named Lewbell."

"I was *asking* for information," Drew answered. "But I'll be happy to pay your gaming losses tonight if the information is accurate and useful."

"Years ago I used to play cards with an Irishman. A nice chap. Good cardplayer." The viscount nodded, remembering. "He had a friend he called Lewbell. Had some connection to the theater, as I recall. I remember hearing Lewbell was trying to console the widow after the

Irishman was killed in a carriage accident."

Drew raised an eyebrow at that. "Do you happen to remember the Irishman's name?"

"Of course," the viscount answered. "Like I said, for an Irishman, he was a very nice chap. His name was Declan Shaughnessy and his wife was Lady Siobhan, daughter of the earl of Trahearne. She was orphaned early, and because her father died with no surviving male issue, the title is dormant. The gossip going round was that Lewbell thought he could marry the widow and produce a male heir to inherit her father's title. I don't know what happened to him, but I haven't seen him in London in ages." He leaned close. "I'll need fifty pounds."

Drew reached into his jacket, removed his wallet, and handed the viscount a hundred pounds.

Viscount Mirrant disappeared into the card room. Drew scanned the ballroom. Kit was partnering Iris in another quadrille while Dalton was dancing with Mariah.

Mariah followed the steps of the quadrille as she moved from one square to another. She whirled in one direction and Dalton turned in the opposite as they moved into the next square and changed partners.

"Happy birthday, Mariah."

Mariah looked up at the tall, handsome middle-aged man who had just become her partner. "Do I know you, sir?"

"Of course you do, my dear," he said. "I am your betrothed."

"You're mistaken, sir." Mariah tried to step away, but the gentleman grabbed hold of her hand and wouldn't let go. "I am betrothed to Lord Kilgannon."

"Oh, no, my dear. You are betrothed to me. I had the prior claim to you."

Mariah's eyes widened. "Squire Bellamy?"

"In the flesh."

"But Lord Kilgannon explained that Reverend Mother was not my guardian. She didn't have the authority to accept your proposal on my behalf."

The squire smiled at her and tightened his grip. "It matters not at all to me whether she had the authority to accept my proposal on your behalf or not. The fact remains that she did accept my proposal." The steps of the dance called for a bow. The squire bowed but did not let go of her hand. "I've waited fourteen years for my plan to come to fruition. I've waited fourteen years for you to come of age." He led Mariah down the row of dancers toward the door.

"Unhand me, sir!" she exclaimed.

"Don't try it," he warned. "Your father tried to thwart me and he died. Your mother tried to thwart me and she died."

"Lord Kilgannon—"

"Will die as well if he tries to thwart me. Think about it, Mariah. Do you want to lose everyone you've ever loved?"

He danced her out the door, and Mariah never made a sound.

Kit led his sister, Iris, through the maze of steps in the quadrille. He moved from one square to another. Iris whirled in one direction and Kit turned in the opposite as they moved into the next square and prepared to change partners.

"Bloody hell!" Kit swore.

Iris flinched. "Kit!"

"What the devil is *he* doing here?" he demanded.

"Who?" Iris asked in confusion.

"The squire."

"What squire?" Iris asked.

"The one dancing with Mariah." Kit glanced around and discovered Mariah and the squire were gone.

A single lantern illuminated the interior of the carriage as Bellamy shoved Mariah inside it.

He took the seat facing the rear of the carriage and pulled Mariah from the opposite seat to sit beside him. He rapped on the ceiling of the carriage with a silver-knobbed cane, and the vehicle surged forward with enough force to send Mariah tumbling against him.

The squire gripped her left wrist with his right hand and used his left one to remove his watch from his pocket. He opened the lid and looked at the face. "The dance should last another ten minutes or so," he said. "We'll have plenty of time to reach our destination before your Lord Kilgannon realizes you're missing."

Mariah barely heard him. She stared at the gold and diamond locket attached to the squire's watch chain. "Lewbell," she breathed. "You're Uncle Lewbell."

"Very good, sweet Mariah. You do remember me." He reached over and traced the line of her jaw with his thumb. "I wondered."

"Take your hands off me!" she ordered.

He grabbed her chin in his hand. "I will do more than touch your face, sweet Mariah," he said. "You are mine. I trained you to suit only me—Sir Lewis Bellingham."

"Why?" she demanded. "Why me?"

"Because your maternal grandfather left a very nice title dormant and a very large income unclaimed. I intend to marry and get my heir on you so that I might claim it before the earl of Kilgannon does."

Mariah screamed then. And she continued to scream until the squire turned on the seat, placed his hand around her throat, and squeezed.

❧

Kit searched the duchess of Kerry's ballroom from top to bottom, but there was no sign of Mariah.

"We have to find her, Papa."

"We will, son." Drew looked at Kit and recognized the agony he was suffering. Drew had suffered it himself when Kathryn failed to show up for their first wedding

and again when Kit had been stolen from the safety of
Swanslea Park.

Drew turned to Barbara, the duchess of Kerry. "Your
Grace, I need to borrow a brace of His Grace's pistols."

The duchess nodded toward a footman. "Fetch them."

"And I'll need a coach and coachman as I sent my wife
and daughter home in ours."

"Done," she said. The duchess of Kerry had always
been partial to the fifteenth marquess of Templeston, and
she had transferred that affection to the sixteenth. With a
discreet flick of her fan, the duchess summoned her butler
who hurried to her side. "Please see that the marquess of
Templeston gets whatever he requires. His word is the
same as mine."

"Thank you, Your Grace," Kit said. "Is there anything
you can tell me about a man called Lewbell? He was here
at the ball. A man who is known in Ireland as Squire
Nathan Bellamy."

The duchess looked up at Drew. "Lewbell? I haven't
heard that name in years. He wasn't on the guest list, and
I can't imagine him rusticating in Ireland. Why, the very
thought is incredible."

"Who?" Drew asked.

"Sir Lewis Bellingham. The celebrated actor. Lewbell
was our nickname for him. Lady Siobhan Shaughnessy,
Lady Kerseymere, Lady Emberson, and I were patron-
esses of his theater company. You see, Lady Siobhan's . . ." She paused. "Lady Siobhan. Good heavens!
Your Mariah is Siobhan's little girl. Dear me, but she
looks like her mother. I should have seen the resemblance
right away. But Siobhan . . ."

"Yes?" Kit prompted

"Siobhan has been gone so many years. Her husband,
Mr. Declan Shaughnessy, managed the property her father
had owned here in London including several theaters Sir
Lewis's company leased."

"It's too far for him to take her to Ireland," Kit said.
"He must have a place nearby."

"And a special license," Drew added grimly. "Otherwise, what is the point of kidnapping her on the day she reaches her majority and can claim her fortune?"

"He means to marry her," Kit's tone was urgent. "We have to stop it. Where would he take her?"

"Try Number Twelve Berkley Square," said Viscount Mirrant, whom Dalton had recruited from the card room to help in the search for Mariah. "That's where Shaughnessy lived. I heard it sold to someone in Ireland a few months ago."

Mariah awoke in the parlor of the home in which she had been born. She was sitting on a chair, her wrists tied to the wooden arm of the chair with a silk scarf.

"Welcome home."

Mariah looked around. The house seemed vaguely familiar, but she had no real memory of it. "This is not my home." Her throat hurt and her voice was little more than a painful croak.

"It was, sweet Mariah, and it will be again. After tonight." He leaned so close his warm breath brushed her cheek.

She stared into his eyes and saw the madness living there. "You killed my mother."

He shook his head. "Most unwillingly, I assure you, but she refused to marry me. After I had gone to all the trouble of arranging your father's unfortunate accident. She recognized the snuffbox I took from him as a keepsake, and she refused to allow me to become your papa. She told me she was going to put you in the convent where I could never get my hands on you again."

Mariah began to shudder as a barrage of memories came rushing back. She remembered Lewbell reaching beneath her skirts. Lewbell threatening her, promising her something bad would happen to her mama if she said a word. And Mariah hadn't said a word, but he had killed

her mama anyway because her mama had seen the blood
Lewbell had left. Mariah had tried to wash it off, but it
had left a mess and Mama had seen it. Her mama had
sent her to St. Agnes's to protect her. He had killed her
mama and taken her locket.

"The reverend is waiting in the study. Shall we invite
him in?" Lewbell opened the door to the parlor and called
for the reverend.

"You are wasting your time, sir," Mariah told the minister as he walked into the room. "Because I won't marry
him."

"Yes, you will," Lewbell contradicted her. "Because if
you do not, Lord Kilgannon will die." He opened his coat
to reveal the pistol secreted in the waistband of his trousers.

"You will die before he does," she said fiercely. "I
promise."

Lewbell laughed. "No need to protect him, my sweet
little girl, because he won't want you once he knows the
truth about you." He stood in front of her facing the parlor
door, his back to the window as he looked down at her.

Mariah tilted her chin up a notch higher. "And what
truth is that?"

"That you were mine first and that you'll always be
mine first," Lewbell said, and Mariah shuddered in re-
vulsion at the look in his eyes.

"I was never yours," Mariah spat. "I will never be
yours."

Lewbell turned red in the face and shouted at the minister, "Begin!"

"Stop!" Kit burst through the front door of
Number Twelve Berkley Square and raced up the stairs
to where the sound of voices could be heard. His father,
Dalton Mirrant, Ash Everleigh, and Viscount Mirrant followed close behind him to the front parlor.

Mariah was seated, her wrists tied to the arm of the chair. She turned to look at him.

"Keep going," Lewbell ordered the minister.

"Do you, Mariah Shaughnessy, take this man—"

"No, I do not."

"Yes, she does," Lewbell corrected. "Keep going."

Kit walked into the parlor. "No, she does not. Stop this ceremony at once!"

"Take one more step and she dies." Lewbell raised his .pistol and pointed it at her.

Kit froze.

Mariah did not.

She saw the gleam in Lewbell's eyes as he stared at Kit and knew he intended to kill Kit the way he had killed her mother and her father. Leaning back in her chair, Mariah lifted her feet and kicked Lewbell as hard as she could in the groin.

He cried out and stumbled against the windowsill behind him. The pistol fired and shattered a vase by Mariah. For an endless moment Lewbell teetered, fighting for his balance, before the latch on the window gave way and there was nothing but air to cling to. He tumbled through the window and fell onto the cobblestone street below.

Mariah heard his shout of terror die as he hit the cobblestones. She heard a warning cry from someone below and the frightened neighs and the clatter of shod horses as they scrambled to regain their footing on the slippery street. And she heard the thick, heavy crash of a carriage overturning.

Lord Templeston rushed to the window, looked out, then quickly exited the room.

"He killed my mother," Mariah whispered. "He killed my mother and my father. He has my mother's locket. She put me in St. Agnes's to protect me because she knew he killed my papa." She was babbling and she knew it, but she couldn't seem to stop.

Kit ran to her, untied her wrists, and then covered her

face with kisses. "Shh, sweetheart." He held her close. "It's over."

"He killed them, Kit. And he would have killed you, too. I had to stop him."

"You did stop him, my love," Kit murmered. "You saved my life." His hands were trembling as he framed her face between his palms and kissed her lips before he lifted her wrists and gently rubbed the circulation back into them. "Mariah, sweet Jesus, Mariah. Are you all right? Did he hurt you?"

"No," she managed.

But he had. Kit saw the bruises his thumbs had made as he pressed them against her throat.

"He's dead." Lord Templeston reentered the parlor a quarter of an hour later. "He landed on the street in front of a hansom. The driver overturned the carriage trying to keep the horses from trampling him. The driver and the horses are fine, but the carriage landed atop Bellingham. The passengers were a bit shaken up, but luckily, none of them were hurt. After we loosed the horses and righted the carriage, I retrieved this." Drew walked over to Kit, and handed him the gold and diamond locket that had belonged to Mariah's mother. It was similar to be sure, so similar it was almost identical, but there was no seal or jeweler's mark and the picture inside it was not George Ramsey. On one side was a miniature of a man and on the other side was miniature of a little girl. Declan Shaughnessy and his daughter, Mariah.

The only legacy attached to Lady Siobhan's locket was a legacy of love and remembrance from a loving wife and mother.

"I love you," Kit said, kissing her gently. "Mariah, I love you."

"I love you, too," she answered. "I always have."

Chapter 29

In thy breast are the stars of thy fate.

—JOHANN CHRISTOPH FREIDRICH VON
SCHILLER, 1759–1805

The wedding of the year—that of Christopher George Ramsey, twenty-ninth English earl of Ramsey and the twelfth Irish earl of Kilgannon, to Miss Mariah Shaughnessy—took place at Telamor Castle in Inismorn, Ireland, at the conclusion of the London season.

Lord Templeston stood up with his son. Lady Templeston stood up with Mariah. Lord Ashford Everleigh and Mr. Dalton Mirrant served as groomsmen, while Lady Iris Templeston and Lady Kate Templeston served as bridesmaids.

Since Father Francis O'Meara had baptized the groom and served as priest and confessor to the bride, he claimed the right to perform the wedding ceremony and the mass that followed.

The groom's solicitor, Mr. Martin Bell, represented the bride's father by giving her away in marriage and negotiating her dowry and settlement.

Five hundred guests, including the sisters of St. Agnes's Sacred Heart Convent, attended the ceremony and the wedding breakfast.

The bride and four assistants spent nearly a month creating the wedding cake decorated with hundreds of tiny pink rosebuds. It was, the residents of Inismorn decided, her finest creation.

And the bite she shared with her husband at the wedding breakfast was the first taste of cake she or Kit had had in fourteen years.

❧

Hours after the wedding, Kit shared a glass of whisky and conversation with his father.

"He hurt her," Kit said. "He abused her parents' trust by molesting Mariah, by taking her virginity before she was six years old."

"Then let's hope the bastard is roasting in hell for all eternity." Drew's condemnation was swift and unforgiving.

"What do I do?" Kit asked. "How do I—"

"Remember Zeus," Drew advised. "Follow Mariah's lead. I know you're eager, but you have the rest of your married life to satisfy your needs. Put her needs above your own. Make tonight special for her and you'll build the foundation for a long and satisfying marriage."

Kit took his father's advice.

Their honeymoon began where their romance began. In the room at the top of the tower ruins.

Kit knocked on the door to her bedchamber. "Mariah?"

"Yes?" She opened the door, and Kit saw that she was wearing a silk nightgown that was so thin as to be transparent.

"May I join you?"

She nodded.

Kit walked into the room, and Mariah walked into his arms. Desire sparked, igniting them like the strike of a Lucifer match against a rough surface. There was friction. Lots of it. But it was tempered with love. She leaned forward and closed her eyes as Kit sought her mouth with his own. He bent at the knees and swept her up into his arms.

"Where are you taking me?" she murmured. "There's a perfectly good bed over there."

"There's a better one in the place where I first met you. At the place where it all began."

"You're taking me to the tower?"

"Yes."

She grabbed the matching silk wrapper lying on the foot of the bed and held it close as Kit carried her out of her bedchamber, down the stairs, and through the front doors where he set her on her feet.

Mariah slipped her silk robe on over her nightgown as Kit reached for her hand.

"Aren't you going to carry me the entire way?" she teased.

Kit shook his head. "I value my neck and yours," he told her with a grin. "And I'll not be negotiating that path in the dark with you in my arms. Besides, I would rather save my strength for something much more important. . . ."

Mariah gasped when she saw the interior of the tower room illuminated by the light of the single brass lantern and the light from the stars.

Kit had transformed the tower into a bridal bower with a magnificent view of the stars. And as he placed his bride on the velvet-covered mattress, he promised to take her there.

"Did you bring the book?" she asked.

"Are we going to need it?"

"Unless you have it memorized we are," she teased. "For I want to try everything."

"Then why don't we start with *Coaxing the Nectar*?"

"Why don't we?" She reached up, wrapped her arms around his neck, and kissed him.

She deserved gentleness, Kit reminded himself in an effort to go slow. She deserved tenderness. And he devoted himself to giving Mariah everything she deserved. He nibbled at her lips, then traced the texture of them with a light brush of his own. Kit touched the seam between her lips with the tip of his tongue, showering Mariah with pleasure as he tasted the softness of her lips and absorbed the feel of her mouth; poring over every detail, every nuance of her lips and mouth and teeth and tongue, with a single-minded determination to give and receive pleasure.

He leaned into her, pressing the lower part of his body against the cradle of hers, and Mariah opened her mouth and parted her legs to grant him access. Acknowledging her generous offering, Kit reached up, tangled one hand in her hair, and sent her hairpins scattering in all directions as he pulled her closer to deepen his kiss and his tongue delved deep into the lush sweetness of her mouth. Her tongue mated with his, mirrored his as he plundered the depths, then retreated into politeness, before plundering again.

Mariah sank against him, shivering in delicious response as Kit left her lips and kissed a path over her eyelids, her cheeks, her nose; brushing his lips lightly over hers once again before he continued on his path to the pulse that beat at the base of her throat. Mariah had always prided herself on her independent spirit and her education, but she found she was sadly, shamelessly, lacking in both those attributes and she lay in Kit's arms.

He had much to teach and she had a lot to learn. And she was a little surprised to discover she was more than willing to relinquish her independence and become a willing slave to her desires.

Kit rubbed his nose into the hollow below her ear, inhaling the scent of her. She smelled of baking bread and cake frosting, and Kit laved the spot where her pulse throbbed with his tongue. He nibbled and teased and coaxed his way from her mouth to her throat, to the dainty pink shell of her ear and back again with a finesse he hadn't known he possessed.

A fierce longing flowed through him, making him shudder with the need to touch all of her, to taste all of her. He remembered the way her breasts had looked reflected in the mirror through the transparent fabric of the dressmaker's chemise, the way their pink tips puckered like ripe lips awaiting a lover's kiss. His kiss. And, ever the gentleman, Kit vowed not to disappoint them.

She melted back on the blankets and cushions of the bed he had made and gazed up at the twinkling stars through the hole in the roof as Kit cupped her breast with his hand, pushing it up and out of the confines of her nightgown and robe so that nothing separated her breasts from him. Mariah started as he rubbed the pad of his thumb over the tip of her breast until it hardened and then kissed his way down the front of her robe, stopping only long enough to untie the sash at her waist and lay the garment open before he pressed his lips around the hard little nub.

Fire, like the fire of a glass of brandy on an empty stomach, shot through her, only this fire was a thousand times better than anything alcohol induced. Mariah gasped as the warmth of his breath against her breast made her nipple swell and harden even more until she ached in the dark secret recesses of her body—all the places proper ladies didn't admit to having. Mariah arched her back, filling the night air with little incoherent sounds she made in her throat. She wiggled in his arms, moving steadily closer until she finally reached up, clamped her fingers into his thick dark hair, and held him pressed against her. She whimpered hoarsely as Kit gently tucked her bare breasts back inside the bodice of her nightgown, then dampened the thin silk with his tongue and forced his warm breath through the fabric, igniting spontaneous little shooting stars of desire that flared throughout her body.

Kit chuckled deep in his throat, thrilled with Mariah's impatience and heady with the powerful sensations swirling around them and with the incredible realization that she enjoyed his touch as much as he enjoyed touching her.

He turned his head so that he might breathe once again, then slowly worked his way over the silk fabric, and past the little silk roses embroidered on the bodice to her other breast. He wanted to bite off the roses and tear the silk with his teeth, but he fought to control that urge, until, unable to prolong the teasing, he freed her breasts from her bodice once more by cupping his hand beneath them and pushing them up and over the top of the nightdress. Once his mission was accomplished, Kit lavished her nipple with a rush of hot, moist air. God, but he wanted to touch her, all of her. He wanted to suckle at her breast and taste the sweet hot essence of her. He wanted to bury his length inside her warmth and to feel the heat of her surrounding him as he throbbed and pulsed within, and he wanted to capture her lips and swallow her cries as they careened toward the heavens on an intimate journey where two became one, where desire and passion were forged like iron and carbon melded into steel, to form an exquisite blend of love and faith and trust.

Kit worked his way from her breasts back to her lips. His warm rough tongue plundered her mouth. Kit slipped his hand beneath her nightdress and traced a path up her thigh and down into the valley between her legs. He gently eased his fingers into the nest of silken curls and the damp swollen flesh hidden beneath them.

"Kit, please," Mariah moaned his name and begged prettily as she thrust her hips against his incredibly talented fingers while Kit traced the contours of her flesh and teased the tight little bud hidden within the folds. There were no words to describe the myriad delicious and forbidden sensations she felt as Kit slid his skilled fingers into her petal-soft folds.

She felt the impact of those sensations deep inside her womb as longings she had felt only once before on the swing shot to the surface and raged in an unladylike dance of passion. Mariah knew she should be scandalized by Kit's familiarity with all the secret places on her body; knew she should be alarmed at the way he played her like a violin, coaxing sweet music from an instrument that had once been invaded and abused. But Kit stroked and probed with such infinite tenderness and such agonizing care that she couldn't be outraged. How could she be shocked and angry when all he gave was bliss? Incredible bliss?

"Please," she murmured in such a heartfelt tone of voice that Kit couldn't tell if she was inviting him to continue or begging him to stop. He deepened his caress and wiggled his fingers. Mariah immediately pressed her legs together in reaction, before opening them again to give him access. And Kit had his answer.

Mariah squirmed as pleasure—hot and thick and dangerous—surged through her body filling her with urgent longings she couldn't name and a starburst of vibrant emotions—all of them emanating from the place Kit graced with his magnificent attention. She thrust her hips upward as she moaned her pleasure and gasped out his name in short frantic little breaths.

Kit continued to kiss her, gently at first, and then harder, consciously matching the action of his fingers to that of his tongue as he feverishly worked his magic on her. He knew she was desperately close to finding wondrous satisfaction, even if she still didn't quite know what to expect or what was happening to her. His body chafed beneath his self-imposed restraint. He ached to join her in blissful release, but Kit had to take his time. He pressed his thumb against her soothing her aching core with the sweet honey she lavished on his fingers.

Mariah sighed against his lips, and then shuddered deeply as her fragile control shattered, and she came apart in his arms. She opened her eyes and looked up at him with such an expression of sheer wonderment and joy that Kit's breath caught in his throat. He was humbled by the look in her eyes and rewarded tenfold for his remarkable restraint.

Mariah blushed. "I did it again," she whispered in an awe-filled tone of voice.

"Yes, you did," he told her. "Quite beautifully. And now our little exploration has yielded the discovery that you can do it on a bed under the stars and well as on a swing in a secret garden under the noonday sun."

"What do you call it?" she asked.

"I call it *Reaching the Stars*. I hope you succeeded," Kit said tenderly.

"I not only reached them"—she smiled at him—"but I caught hold of Draco's tail and held on for the ride." Her eyes shimmered with emotion as she reached up and placed her palms on both sides of his face.

"Thank you," she said simply, pulling his face down to meet her lips.

"It was an honor," he whispered seconds before he captured her mouth with his own.

Kit kissed her again—this time with all the pent-up passion and frustration and longing he'd been holding in check so long. He kissed her until her breasts heaved with exertion, until her bones seemed to turn to jelly, until all she could do was cling to him while she fervently returned his kisses measure for measure. Kit's mind reeled from the flood of sensations she evoked as her tongue mated with his.

Shaking with need, Kit finally pulled his mouth away.

"What's wrong?" she asked.

"Nothing's wrong," he answered.

"Then, why did you stop kissing me?"

"Because I want you." Kit leaned his forehead against hers and drew a shaky breath. "All of you."

"You have all of me," she told him.

Kit shook his head. "I'm not entirely sure you understand what I mean, Mariah."

The smile Mariah gave him was angelic. "Then, why don't you show me?"

Kit's leer was positively lustful as he placed a knee on the bed and leaned over her. "I was hoping you'd say that." He lifted her limp and relaxed body and struggled to work her damp nightgown and robe over her head.

Mariah should have cringed at his vivid curse, but she giggled instead. Kit's honest frustration with her feminine accoutrements was proving to be a powerful aphrodisiac.

He sighed with relief as he finally managed to pull her

nightgown and robe up and over her head, leaving her gloriously naked.

Completely nude and suddenly shy, Mariah squeezed her eyes shut and tried to roll to the side of the makeshift bed to extinguish the lantern he'd left burning, but Kit wrapped his arm around her waist and stopped her. "Leave it," he said. "I want to look at you."

"Please," she began, "I'm . . ."

"So lovely you take my breath away," he whispered, genuinely awestruck.

Mariah opened her eyes to see if the expression on his face matched his tone of voice and was instantly gratified to see that it did. She blushed. "What comes next?"

Kit raised an eyebrow at her and grinned. "You do. Again. Lie there and enjoy while I see if you taste as good as you look. This, my lady, is called *Sipping the Nectar.*"

Mariah met his unerring gaze, trusting that Kit meant to continue his intimate exploration with his talented fingers. She was startled when he stretched out between her legs and, resting his head on her thigh, turned and pulled her toward him. The feel of his hot breath brushing her secret curls came as a complete surprise. Mariah clamped her legs together. Kit raised his head and looked at her. "Trust me, Mariah. I'm not going to hurt you. I'm only going to love you. If you'll let me."

When he looked at her like that, Mariah found she couldn't deny him anything—didn't want to deny him anything. He was the teacher and she, the student. He was the baker and she was the pastry dough. As long as he kept his promise to love her, her body was his to do with as he pleased. "Please do," she begged politely.

"My pleasure."

Mariah thought she'd reached the stars while his fingers caressed her, but when Kit stretched out between her thighs, pulled her to him, and began to taste the places his fingers had explored, she captured the stars and held them inside her.

He drove her to the brink of rapture and beyond. Kit

moved up her body and cradled her beside him, capturing her cries with his mouth as she shuddered back to the earth in his arms. He brushed her damp hair off her flushed face, wiped the tears from her eyes, and murmured love words of praise and encouragement in her ear.

She opened her eyes to find Kit staring down at her.

"Hmm," she murmured, snuggling beside him and stretching languidly, like a cat.

"How were the stars?" he asked kissing the tip of her nose.

Mariah gazed at him. "Beautiful," she answered. "But I wanted you there beside me."

"Really?"

She nodded. "I'm quite certain that exploring the stars is much nicer when you have a companion on the journey."

"Just a companion?" He sounded disappointed.

"Well"—she wet her lips with the tip of her tongue as she pretended to ponder his question—"a husband would be better."

Kit sucked in a breath as his body tightened and the bulge beneath his silk robe grew so insistent it began to tent the fabric, staining it with the pearls of moisture that appeared each time he looked at her. "Are you in the market for a husband, Miss Shaughnessy?"

"I'd like to think I just found one, Lord Kilgannon. And I'll have you know I no longer answer to that name. It's a spinster's name," she teased. "I'm Lady Kilgannon when we're in Ireland and Lady Ramsey when we're in England."

"Who are you when we're in bed?"

"Your wife and your lover." She pulled his head down and kissed him. "Unless you'd like me to be someone else."

"I'm not complaining," Kit assured her.

"I am," Mariah admitted. A wicked little smile played about the corners of her mouth and her eyes sparkled with merriment. She reached up and pulled him down to kiss her. "Because only one of us is naked."

Kit kissed her quickly, then untied the sash of his robe.

"May I?" Mariah brushed his hands away.

"How can I refuse when you ask so nicely?" He held out his arms, giving himself up to the pleasure of her touch.

She slid his silk robe off his shoulders, down his arms, and over his hands, exposing the hard muscles of his chest and stomach. Mariah rubbed her hands over the mat of hair on his chest; then leaned over and indulged herself by allowing the tips of her breasts to rub against the soft hair.

Kit's blood rushed downward. The hard male part of him throbbed with each beat of his heart. He ached to sheathe himself in Mariah's warmth. He ached to end his exquisite torment. Wrapping his arms around her waist, Kit gently rolled her onto her back. Mariah followed the line of his spine, sliding her hands down his back and over his tight buttocks. Kit groaned aloud as she brushed her fingers against him and the hard jutting length of him spilled into her waiting hands.

She caressed him, marveling at the velvety soft feel. And she would have continued her exploration if Kit hadn't gently lifted her hands from around him, then guided her legs up over his hips, and pressed himself against her; gently probing her entrance.

Lost in a frenzy of need, Mariah locked her legs around his waist and pulled him to her.

"Now we *Share the Nectar*." Kit pushed inside her. He closed his eyes, threw back his head, and bit his bottom lip as he sheathed himself fully inside her warmth. His entire body shook with the effort as he fought to maintain his control.

Mariah tensed as he entered her, but did not cry out.

Kit waited as long as he could, allowing her body to mold itself to his length, but when she moved experimentally, Kit lost his battle to maintain control as she urged him deeper inside her. He began to move his hips in a rhythm as old as time.

Mariah followed, matching his movements thrust for thrust. She clung to him, reveling in the weight and feel of him as he filled her again and again, gifting her with himself in a way she'd never dreamed possible. She squeezed her eyes shut. Tears of joy trickled from the corners, ran down her cheeks, and disappeared into the silk of her hair. And as she felt the first tremors flow through her, Mariah surrendered to the emotions swirling inside her; gave voice to the passion with small incoherent cries that escaped her lips as Kit rocked her to him and exploded inside her.

He brushed his lips against her cheek as he buried his face in her hair. He tasted the saltiness of her tears, then lifted his head and looked down at her face. God, but she was beautiful. Kit shuddered as a rush of emotions raced through him. He should have spoken words of love instead of words of passion. He should have cherished her and treated her more tenderly instead of using her to slake his raging desire. She deserved a better wedding night. And he'd give her one. In a moment. When he recovered. He'd love her again and again until he proved that she was loved above all others. He kissed her forehead.

"I love you, Mariah."

"That's a very good trait in a husband." She smiled up at him. "Thank goodness you meant it when you proposed all those years ago. Because I loved you when you were eight and I'll love you even more when you're eighty."

Her eyes were shimmering with emotion as Kit leaned down and touched his mouth to hers in a kiss so gentle, so loving, so precious, it brought fresh tears to her eyes.

"I think we waltzed among the stars," he breathed at last. "And we returned with tiny bits of stardust. See?" He leaned down and kissed her tears from the corner of her eyes.

"Tiny bits of stardust born of the most incredible love and pleasure any girl could ask for." Mariah touched his face with her palm of her hand. "I was afraid, Kit. But you didn't hurt me at all. You made me feel so wonderful. It wasn't at all like the times he touched me. Thank you, my darling."

"For sharing paradise with you?" Kit murmured as he held her in his arms. "I'll be honored to do that for the rest of my life and beyond."

"Then, do it again, Kit." She rolled to her side and propped herself on her elbow and looked down at him. "Now. Find a page in that wondrous book of yours and take me to the stars for as long as you can."

"I don't need the book." Kit reached up to touch the lock of black hair curling just above the tip of her breast. "For that page is called *Pleasing My Lady*."

"How?" she asked.

"By giving her my heart."

This time the bits of stardust they brought home were tears of profound joy. And this time they sparkled in his eyes.

Mariah awoke at daybreak to find Kit reading a letter in the pool of light that filtered through the crenellations. The lantern still burned beside him, and Mariah knew instinctively that he been sitting there for some time. "Kit?"

"Good morning." He turned to her and the smile he gave her was so full of love and lust and satisfaction that Mariah blushed.

"Have you been awake long?" She stretched languidly and rubbed her eyes.

"For a bit," he answered. "I've been carrying this around for over a year now. I was afraid to open it because I was afraid of what it might say and of what I might learn. I kept thinking that it might be some sort of Pandora's box and that once I broke the seal, I'd never be able to get everything back inside the way it was."

"What is it?" she asked, sitting up.

"A note from George Ramsey telling me that the enclosed envelope contains a letter from my mother."

"Lady Templeston?" Mariah looked perplexed.

"No." He shook his head. "My other mother. The one who died. Today is the beginning of my new life. Of our new life together as man and wife, and I decided that it was the right time for me to lay all the ghosts of my past to rest."

"Oh."

Kit patted the seat next to him. "Come sit beside me. I'll read it to you, and when I've shared this part of my heritage with you, I want to begin the day *Sharing the Nectar* with my wife—for as long as I live."

Mariah sat down beside him, wrapped her arms around his waist, pressing her bare breasts against him as she leaned her head against his shoulder, and listened to the words that laid the past to rest. . . .

Epilogue

A woman's whole life is a history of the affections.

—WASHINGTON IRVING, 1783–1859

My darling child,

Today is your birthday. My birthing pains began early this morning and have continued throughout the day, and I know before the sun rises on another day, I shall hold you in my arms.

I am filled with mixed emotions as I write these words. Elated, yet fearful. Proud, but humble. And terribly, terribly grateful for the man who is your father, for he brought me out of a world of grief and taught me how to love again.

I have loved two very different men in my life. The youthful one I married and the older one I clung to when I believed myself to be a widow. God willing, you will grow up to know and love the one who has claimed you as his own. You will grow up believing he is your papa and you will be secure in his love. But, my darling child, you should also know that there is another man who loves you even more than your papa—for he is the one who gave you life. He will never be able to claim you as his own—except to those closest to him—but he will be there should you ever need him. All you need ever do is call upon him and present the locket he gave me.

Both of the men in my life have proven themselves

to be extraordinary. But my love for them pales in comparison to the love I feel for you. Always know that you are loved and wanted and needed and welcomed into this world as no other child could be. You are the product of the love I felt for a wonderful man and of the love he felt for me.

Never forget that, my child. Always know that I intended my son to be Christopher George Ramsey or my daughter to be Marina Estella Ramsey.

Enclosed you will find an ancient deed to the ruined tower. It has no legal value, only sentimental value, for the land all belongs to my father, your grandfather, the earl of Kilgannon, but one day it will belong to you, for I am my father's heir. Because he had no son, he petitioned the Crown to amend the ancient letters patent to make me a peeress in my own right and to allow my firstborn child—son or daughter—to inherit. If I should predecease my father, my firstborn child shall be named as his heir, and all that would have come to me will belong to you.

So I am giving you a piece of your inheritance today.

The tower ruins. Where I sat long ago and dreamed of finding love, of marrying, and of being a wife and mother.

I have been a wife to a wonderful man, and I am about to become a mother to you, my child. And I have been greatly loved by two men who were greatly loved in return.

I have fulfilled my life's ambition. And I wish the same for you. My dreams were born in that old crumbling tower, and my tower of dreams is my gift to you. My beloved child.

From

Your loving Mother,

Lady Alanna Farrington, née Kilgannon.

Turn the page for a preview of

BARELY A BRIDE

The first novel in Rebecca Hagan Lee's
Free Fellows League trilogy

THE KNIGHTSGUILD SCHOOL FOR GENTLEMEN
Derbyshire, England, 1793

They slipped away in the dead of night.

The three young men moved quickly, quietly weaving their way through the rows of identical iron cots in the dormitory of the Knightsguild School for Gentlemen. Three young gentlemen enrolled in the school—scions of the oldest and most prestigious families of England and Scotland—carried with them paper, pens and ink, sealing wax, leftover stubs of candles, a paring knife, and a yellowed bit of newspaper printed with the seditious writings of the colonial rebel Thomas Jefferson for inspiration.

Wrapping themselves in blankets to ward off the bitter January chill, the boys headed toward the storeroom behind the kitchen. They moved with great stealth and cunning, tiptoeing out of the dormitory, down the stairs, past the schoolrooms, and the refectory toward the vast kitchens and the little used storeroom behind it.

The candle stubs they carried barely illuminated the way, but perhaps that was just as well, for the work they were about had to remain a secret. Even from the other boys.

"Damn!" Griffin Abernathy, the seventeenth Viscount Abernathy, swore as his candle stub guttered and hot wax dripped onto the back of his hand.

"What happened?" Colin McElreath, the twenty-seventh Viscount Grantham asked in a loud whisper that bespoke his Scottish heritage.

"My light's gone," Griff answered. "You'll have to lead the way."

"Quiet! Both of you!" Jarrod Shepherdston, the twenty-second earl of Westmore, warned. "You're making enough noise to wake the dead. And if we get caught, there will be canings all around."

"We've suffered canings for lesser crimes," Colin answered, cupping his palm around the candle flame, shielding it from the draft as he changed places with Griff. "Without complaint."

Griff nodded at Jarrod. "You've never minded canings before."

"And I don't mind them now," Jarrod said. "What I mind is missing the puddings." He stared at his friends. "It's bad enough that they practically starve us to death in the name of discipline, but you know that in addition to caning us, the headmaster will take away our puddings—for at least a fortnight."

Jarrod's companions nodded. They didn't object to suffering through the painful canings the headmaster inflicted nearly as much as the other punishment he inflicted. The meals served at Knightsguild were served on a strict regimen of two full meals a day—at breakfast and at the nooning—and a light afternoon tea. The students did not receive an evening meal, for that meant paying a staff to work extra hours, and even if Knightsguild had provided another meal, none of them could begin to compare with the meals the boys enjoyed at home.

Breakfast at Knightsguild consisted of porridge, tea, and toast, and the nooning meal consisted of boiled meat and vegetables. Pudding, as the dessert was called, was served only at afternoon tea and only because the headmaster had a voracious sweet tooth. Afternoon tea was the one meal the boys all looked forward to. The pastries, cakes, biscuits, and puddings served in place of a meal

were the highlight of their existence at Knightsguild, and
forfeiture of the puddings was the most effective punishment the headmaster had yet devised.

He had learned long ago that growing young men never
willingly gave up dessert.

Griffin grinned at Colin, then at Jarrod. "Then we'd
better not get caught." He nudged Colin in the shoulder
and urged him forward in his best imitation of a Scottish
burr. "Lead on, MacDuff."

"McElreath," Colin growled. "My name's McElreath,
not MacDuff."

"I was quoting Shakespeare's *MacBeth*," Griff told him.

"Shakespeare?" Colin smirked. "I suppose you think he
was an expert on Scottish kings?"

"Not all of them." Griff grinned once again. "Just the
mad ones."

"Quiet!" Jarrod pushed past both of them. "Follow me,"
he ordered. "I'll lead the way."

"Go ahead." Colin shrugged his shoulders. "You always do anyway."

Jarrod led the way through the kitchens to the storeroom. He set his candle on the brick window ledge, took
out the paring knife, and carefully sliced through the
leather cord holding the wooden latch. Once he gained
entry, Jarrod pushed the door open and stepped inside.

Griffin and Colin followed.

The heat from the kitchen ovens on the other side of
the brick wall kept the storeroom warm enough for the
boys to shed their blankets. They folded the blankets into
neat, woolen squares to use as floor cushions before pulling a battered wooden crate they had hidden in the storeroom into place to use as a table. When the crate was
situated to everyone's satisfaction, the three companions
placed their collective offerings of pens and ink, paper,
candles, knife, and sealing wax on it and set down to work.

By the time they emerged from the storeroom, an hour
or so before the breakfast bells rang, the three boys had
formed a secret society that bound them together and fash-

ioned a charter to govern it. And their composition was worthy of Thomas Jefferson's best efforts.

They called it the Official Charter of the Free Fellows League, and as they pricked their thumbs with the paring knife and signed their names to the paper in blood, Griffin, Colin, and Jarrod swore to honor the agreement as long as they lived.

Official Charter of the Free Fellows League

On this, the seventh day of January in the year of Our Lord 1793, we, the sons and heirs to the oldest and most esteemed titles and finest families of England and Scotland, do found and charter our own Free Fellows League.

The Free Fellows League is dedicated to the proposition that sons and heirs to great titles and fortunes, who are duty bound to marry in order to beget future sons and heirs, should be allowed to avoid the inevitable leg-shackling to a female for as long as possible.

As charter members of the Free Fellows League, we agree that:

1.) We shall only agree to marry when we've no other choice or when we're old. (No sooner than our thirtieth year.)

2.) We shall agree to pay each of our fellow Free Fellows the sum of five hundred pounds sterling should any of us marry before we reach our thirtieth year.

3.) We shall never consort with unmarried females (other than our female relations) or darken the doors of any establishments that cater to "Marriage Mart" mamas or their desperate daughters. Nor shall we frequent the homes of any relatives, friends, or acquaintances that seek to match us up with prospective brides.

4.) When compelled to marry, we agree that we shall only marry suitable ladies from suitable families with fortunes equal to or greater than our own.

5.) We shall never be encumbered by sentiment known as love or succumb to female wiles or tears.

6.) We shall sacrifice ourselves on the altar of duty in order to beget our heirs, but we shall take no pleasure in the task. We shall look upon the act in the same manner as medicine that must be swallowed.

7.) We shall install our wives in our country houses and resume our bachelor lives in London.

8.) We shall drink and ride and hunt, and frequent gaming dens with our friends and boon companions whenever we are pleased to do so.

9.) We shall not allow the females who share our names to dictate to us in any manner. We shall put our feet upon tables and sofas and the seats of chairs if we so choose, and we shall allow our hounds to sit upon the furnishings and roam our houses and grounds at will.

10.) We shall give our first loyalty and our undying friendship to our brothers and fellow members of the Free Fellows League.

Signed (in blood) and sealed by:

The Right Honorable Griffin Abernathy, 17th Viscount Abernathy, aged nine years and two months, eldest son of and heir apparent to the 16th earl of Weymouth.

The Right Honorable Colin McElreath, 27th Viscount Grantham, aged nine years and five months, eldest son of and heir apparent to the 9th earl of McElreath.

The Right Honorable Jarrod Shepherdston, 22nd earl of Westmore, aged ten years and three months, eldest son of and heir apparent to the 4th marquess of Shepherdston.